With Good Behavior

a novel by
Jennifer Lane

OMNIFIC PUBLISHING
DALLAS

Omnific Publishing
P.O. Box 793871, Dallas, TX 75379
www.omnificpublishing.com

First Omnific ebook edition, July 2010
First Omnific trade paperback edition, July 2010

Library of Congress Cataloguing-in-Publication Data

Lane, Jennifer
    With Good Behavior / Jennifer Lane – 1st ed.
    ISBN 978-1-936305-26-1
    1. Young Women—Fiction. 2. Romance—Fiction. 3. Crime—Fiction.
    4. Chicago—Fiction. I. Title

10 9 8 7 6 5 4 3 2 1

Book Cover Design by Micha Stone and Amy Brokaw
Book Interior Design by Barbara Hallworth

Printed in the United States of America

With Good Behavior

a novel by
Jennifer Lane

OMNIFIC PUBLISHING

DALLAS

Omnific Publishing
P.O. Box 793871, Dallas, TX 75379
www.omnificpublishing.com

First Omnific ebook edition, July 2010
First Omnific trade paperback edition, July 2010

The characters and events in this book are fictitious.
Any similarity to real persons, living or dead,
Is coincidental and not intended by the author.

Library of Congress Cataloguing-in-Publication Data

Lane, Jennifer
   With Good Behavior / Jennifer Lane – 1st ed.
   ISBN 978-1-936305-26-1
   1. Young Women—Fiction. 2. Romance—Fiction. 3. Crime—Fiction.
   4. Chicago—Fiction. I. Title

10 9 8 7 6 5 4 3 2 1

Book Cover Design by Micha Stone and Amy Brokaw
Book Interior Design by Barbara Hallworth

Printed in the United States of America

1. Reconvictation

Jerry Stone sighed wearily as he reviewed the list of parolees on his schedule. Tossing the printout onto his metal desk, he leaned back in his squeaky chair and rubbed the bridge of his nose.

It was Wednesday, and the Department of Corrections always stuck it to him on Wednesdays. Two newbies in a row, right off the bat. Two inmates freshly released, about to give him the old song and dance about how they would never return to prison, they were now on the straight and narrow, they were *rehabilitated*. What a joke. If they weren't cons by the time they entered the Illinois corrections system, they surely were cons by the time they left. They should call it *reconvictation*.

A knock brought him out of his reverie, and the fifty-four-year-old parole officer gruffly called out, "Enter!"

The door creaked open, and his first parolee of the day tentatively entered the office. Jerry arched his eyebrows. She was not the typical bottom-dweller inmate, reeking of unwashed clothes, hostility, and despair. She was tall and thin, with strawberry-blond hair, and she carried herself with an almost regal air as she floated into his office. He bet they had eaten her up at Downer's Grove Women's Penitentiary.

She swallowed hard, accentuating a defined jaw line. "Mr. Stone?"

"Yeah, who are you?"

"Sophie Taylor, sir."

"Back number?"

She announced the digits robotically. She had used them daily for the last year. "72634."

"Take a seat," he gestured toward the metal chair facing his desk as he opened her file. There must be one hell of an intriguing back story leading this gorgeous chick into criminal activity, and his curiosity got the best of him.

Sophie dutifully folded her lean body into the chair and looked around her, taking in the dirty cornflower-blue walls, the steel desk piled with uneven, wobbly stacks of papers, and the moldy white blinds covering the only window in the grungy office.

She was to report here weekly for an entire year, and the décor of this government office was uncomfortably similar to that of the administrator's office at Downer's Grove Women's Prison. She crossed her legs and hugged her shabby handbag in her lap, studying the parole officer's salt-and-pepper hair and stern face as he read her paperwork.

After a few moments, Jerry looked up from the file with surprise. "You were a psychologist?"

She managed a tight smile. "Yes, sir."

"Should I call you Dr. Taylor, then?"

Hearing her former title caused a squeezing sensation in Sophie's chest, and she looked down, embarrassed. It had been over a year since anyone addressed her that way. She thought back to her last therapy client to use those words, *Dr. Taylor*. His smooth, deep voice reverberated in her mind. She had been enthralled by his rich, slowly enunciated baritone as it caressed and possessed her name with loving care. Well, with what she thought was loving care, but turned out to be something else entirely.

Jerry noticed her blush as she lifted her head and responded, "No, I'm not a psychologist anymore. The Illinois Board of Psychology revoked my license once I entered prison."

"I see." He continued to scan her file. "I'm not finding any reports in here from your sessions with a prison psychologist."

Sophie cleared her throat nervously. "That's because I never met with one."

He raised his bushy gray eyebrows again. "You didn't attend therapy in prison? I thought with your prior vocation you'd be all over that."

"I, uh, I didn't want to be anywhere *near* a psychologist after what happened. Frankly, I don't think I believe in therapy anymore."

Jerry sat back in his chair, studying her carefully. "You went to prison because of a massive lapse of judgment, right, Ms. Taylor?"

She nodded.

"And now after one year in prison, you're trying to get your life back, right?" When she nodded automatically, he ordered, "And don't just tell me what I want to hear, young lady."

"No, sir. I really do want to start my life over. I have to."

"So if you were still a psychologist, and you knew of a woman in these circumstances—needing to figure out what led to a huge mistake in order to prevent it from happening again, reeling from a year in prison despite a perfectly clean record before that mistake, hoping to move forward—in your professional opinion, would you say this woman made a good candidate for therapy?"

Sophie realized where he was going and tried to head him off at the pass. "There are lots of ways to get one's life back on track," she said. "Therapy doesn't always lead to rehabilitation. Not everyone believes in therapy."

"You spent, what, six or seven years after college training to become a psychologist? And now you don't believe in it?"

Sophie crossed her arms and pursed her lips, remaining silent.

"Because *I* think you're a perfect candidate for therapy. And I'm making that a condition of your parole: weekly counseling."

"Court-ordered counseling doesn't work!" Sophie's chestnut-brown eyes flared with anger.

Jerry felt the tension in the room rising. "What are you afraid of?"

"I'm—I'm not *afraid*," she lied. Therapy was about reliving the past, uncovering hidden motivations, discussing family. She was not about to delve into those painful memories. She searched for an excuse. "How am I supposed to afford therapy? I don't have a job yet."

"The DOC will pay for it," he assured her.

He had thwarted her every objection. "What if I refuse?"

Jerry had heard enough stalling. "Do you *want* to return to prison?" he thundered.

Sophie closed her eyes. "No, sir."

Jerry rose from his chair, incensed, and marched around the desk. "You don't get it, do you? You're out of prison, with good behavior, but you have an entire year left of your sentence. I could throw your ass back inside so easily your head would spin."

Her eyes widened as he towered over her, and she glanced at the handcuffs dangling from his belt. One wrong move and they would be coldly clasped around her delicate wrists once again.

"I'm sorry, Mr. Stone." She watched his anger begin to dissipate. "I don't want to go back. I—I'll do whatever you say."

He peered at her, wondering how genuinely contrite she felt and how willing she was to do whatever it took to stay out of prison. *Newbies.* He hated his first session with parolees, having to sniff out their true intentions after knowing them for mere minutes. He hated the little cat-and-mouse game: the lies, the deception, the empty promises.

With thirty years in the DOC under his belt, Jerry had become a sharply accurate observer of human intention. He could sort through all kinds of bullshit to discern the truth. But this one made him nervous: a woman with a doctorate, a *shrink* nonetheless. She could fool and manipulate. She could play people like cards if she so desired. Jerry hated to be played.

Returning to his chair behind his desk, he stared at her for a moment, then advised, "Doing whatever I tell you to do—that is precisely the attitude you need to stay out of prison."

"Yes, sir. I—I don't want to start off on the wrong foot with you, Mr. Stone. I know you must have all kinds of cons giving you a hard time, and I don't want to be one of them."

"I'm glad to hear that, but we'll see if your word means anything." He reached into his filing cabinet and handed a typed sheet to Sophie. "Here's a list of therapists who work with the correctional system. You are to schedule an appointment with one of them before we meet again. Understood?"

"Yes, sir." She nodded, glancing at the list of names and exhaling when she did not recognize any colleagues.

While she folded the paper and placed it in her handbag, Jerry continued. "I expect you to report here every Wednesday at nine a.m. If you miss one meeting, you will return to prison. There will be random drug tests, and if you fail even one, you will return to prison. I expect you to secure employment in the next two weeks. If you do not find a job, you will return to prison. Are the terms of your parole clear, Ms. Taylor?"

She gulped, thinking this parole thing didn't sound all that much *better* than prison. "Yes, sir."

He clicked a pen and prepared to write notes in her file. "Where are you living?"

"With a friend."

"I need an address."

"Um, 900 North Lake Shore Drive, Unit 10."

Recognizing the downtown Chicago address, he asked, "Zip code?"

"It's 60611."

"What is your friend's name?"

"Kirsten Holland."

"What does Ms. Holland do for a living?"

"She's a therapist." When he continued staring at her expectantly, Sophie added, "We went to grad school together."

"But she's not a psychologist?"

"Um, no, she's ABD, um, All But Dissertation? She hasn't finished her degree, so she can't call herself a psychologist yet."

"Does Ms. Holland have any criminal background?"

Sophie chuckled. Kirsten was as straight-laced as they came. "No, sir. She offered to have me live with her as long as I kick her butt to get her dissertation done."

Jerry stifled a smile. This *had* to be the first time he'd discussed doctorates and dissertations with a parolee. "Very well. Do you have any questions for me, Ms. Taylor?"

Sophie thought for a moment, wondering if her question would be all right to ask. "How long have you been a parole officer?"

"Thirty years," he responded, shaking his head slowly. "And I think that's the first time I've been asked a personal question like that."

"Sorry." She winced. "I don't mean to pry. I just wondered, Mr. Stone, in those thirty years... what percentage of people violated their parole and had to return to prison?"

He looked up to his right. "I'd say, ballpark, about sixty percent."

"Wow."

"It's serious business, Ms. Taylor. We're not messing around here."

"I get that. Well, I want you to know that I will definitely be in that *other* forty percent. I'm *not* going back to prison."

"I hope that's the case." There was something about the twenty-nine-year-old woman that made him like her immediately. A keen warmth and intelligence shone through, despite the circumstances of their meeting. He stuffed down those fond feelings quickly, however, knowing never to trust the convicts walking through his door.

Jerry glanced at his watch. "It's time for my next appointment," he said brusquely. "See you next Wednesday at nine, Ms. Taylor."

"Thank you, Officer Stone." She rose from her chair, extending her arm. He grasped her slender hand in his and they shook their goodbyes.

Exiting his office, Sophie exhaled deeply, feeling the stress of her first parole meeting dissolve. That relief was short-lived, however, once she opened the door and found herself eye to eye with a man whose black, buzzed hair and golden-brown skin highlighted eyes that held crystal-blue, bottomless depths. The next parolee on the docket? His nose was slightly crooked and his lips were full. His penetrating gaze bore a hole in her. She stood frozen, staring for several moments before regaining her bearings and muttering, "Excuse me."

She ducked out the door and strode down the hallway, daring to glance behind her to see the man watching her leave. A faint smile crossed his lips, and her cheeks burned.

Scurrying away from the building, the stranger's intriguing eyes seared into her memory, Sophie decided maybe being on parole wasn't all that bad. At the moment, parole definitely seemed better than women's prison.

2. Dishonorable Disappointment

Grant Madsen stood outside the closed door of the parole office, gaping at the departing figure of the stunning woman. Who *was* she? Her long legs, accentuated by tapered black jeans and high-heeled boots, carried her quickly away from him. Her luxurious blond hair swayed across her shoulders with each click of her heels down the tiled hallway.

Fighting the urge to follow her, he was rewarded for his restraint when she stole a coy glance behind her. Their eyes locked once again, and he felt his lips curl into a grin before she immediately flitted away, seemingly embarrassed by their unexpected encounter. Would he ever see her again?

Before Grant could even knock, the door abruptly swung open, and with cat-like reflexes he avoided the metal slab careening toward his body. He looked up to see a frowning older man giving him the once-over.

"Are you here for a nine-fifteen with Officer Stone?" the man questioned in a gravelly voice.

"That's me," he confirmed.

Wondering what was so interesting in the hallway, Jerry ordered, "Well, get in here then, and don't keep me waiting."

Grant stood a little taller upon receiving the admonishment and nodded, adding "Yes, sir" before following the slightly shorter man into his office.

They sat on their respective sides of the desk, and the parole officer pulled out a file. For the second time that day, Jerry was struck by the atypical attractiveness of the parolee sitting across from him. "Name and number."

"Madsen, Grant, 92115."

"Mr. Madsen, I'm Parole Officer Stone. It says here you were just released from Gurnee State Penitentiary yesterday?"

"That is correct, sir."

Jerry noticed how the parolee stared directly forward when responding, his body aligned rigidly on the uncomfortable metal chair. Although his navy-blue oxford shirt and khaki pants did not look expensive, they were neatly pressed and perfectly fitted over his lean frame. Jerry knew a military man when he saw one.

"What were you in for?"

Grant sighed internally. He hated these questions. "Aggravated robbery, sir."

"And that got you sentenced to three years?" Jerry asked, glancing down at the file.

"Yes, sir."

Jerry's forehead wrinkled, and he began thinking out loud while reading the report. "Hmm, you served twenty-six months of that . . . if you followed the rules you would have gotten out sooner . . . I don't see—ah," he nodded, turning the page. "You got sixty days in solitary on your first day inside."

He glanced up to find Madsen's clear blue eyes darkening with an unreadable emotion. Grant's chest tightened as his parole officer inquired, "Why were you thrown in solitary?"

An image flashed through Grant's mind: cold, black eyes staring at him, forcing him to submit to their will; eyes Grant had known for years . . . intense, intelligent, frightening charcoal eyes. He swallowed, trying to shake off the past.

"I was sent to solitary for assaulting another prisoner. The warden wasn't too pleased with me getting in a fight on my first day."

"I would think not," Jerry replied, resuming his reading.

Grant closed his eyes, dreading what might come next. *Please, please, don't be in the report. Please.*

"Huh, it says here you didn't stay in the hole for the entire sixty days."

Shit. It was there. Grant opened his eyes to find the officer staring at him, and then he continued to read.

"You, uh, had a breakdown of some sort, and had to be transferred to the psych ward after three days in solitary." He watched a blush form on Madsen's neck and creep upward, blooming across his cheeks. Grant found himself gazing down at his hands.

Jerry observed him twisting his hands nervously in his lap. They were an artist's hands, with long, elegant fingers, not a convict's hands. They were not the hands of a man who assaulted a fellow prisoner. They were not the hands of a man who attempted to burglarize a club, waving around a stolen gun in the process.

Jerry sighed. He could tell Madsen was intensely uncomfortable, but he had to know what he was dealing with. "What happened in solitary?"

Continuing to look down, Grant waited a few moments before responding, "I had a psychotic break, I guess. That's what they told me anyway. They put me in the psych ward and made me take medication, and I had to stay there until my sixty days were up."

"Are you still taking the meds?"

Grant looked up sharply. "No, sir. I was fine once I got out of solitary."

Studying the man across from him, Jerry had to admit he didn't *seem* crazy. But he would have to pay extra attention to this one, as violence and mental illness were not a palatable combination.

Perhaps Madsen could benefit from the psychological services of the woman who had just left his office, Jerry thought. He smirked, thinking of a million reasons *that* would be a bad idea—particularly because Taylor no longer had a license, and it was never a good idea for cons to commingle.

Sometimes Jerry and his fellow parole officers joked about starting their own dating service, matching up the hapless cons who crossed their doorsteps. When they were in particularly contemptuous moods, they would brainstorm potential names for the company. Instead of *Perfect Match*, Jerry suggested *Perfect CONnection*. Al came up with a substitute for *It's Just Lunch*, offering *It's Just Cuffs* as an alternative. And Sheila perverted *match.com* to *myspouseleftmewheniwenttoprison.com*.

Jerry cleared his throat and tried to get back on task. "I need an address for you, Mr. Madsen."

"I don't have one yet," Grant admitted.

"Don't you have any family?"

Grant grimaced. *Not the type of family I want to see.* "No, sir. I stayed at the *Y* last night using a voucher from Gurnee, but I'm going to look for something today."

"And I suppose it would be presumptuous of me to assume you already have a job?"

Grant bit his lip. "No job yet, sir. But I'll get one. I promise."

The officer and parolee looked at each other awkwardly after that comment, both knowing a con's promise was worth exactly zilch.

"You were twenty-eight when you began your sentence two years ago," Jerry calculated. "What was your former occupation?"

Grant exhaled in frustration. More questions he'd rather not answer. More questions eliciting his shameful past. "I was in the Navy, sir."

Bingo. Jerry smiled inwardly, pleased that his intuition about Madsen was correct. "You were in the Navy when you were arrested?"

"Yes, sir…but I'm not anymore." Grant averted his eyes. "They discharged me when I was convicted of a felony."

Jerry kept staring at the parolee, wondering how the hell this young man had made such a mess of his life. Grant glanced at the peeling paint on the walls, the window, the grimy linoleum floor—anything to avoid meeting the disappointed gaze of yet another authority figure. Despite his best intentions, all Grant did was let down his superiors. He felt the familiar pangs of guilt when he thought about the man he had disappointed most: Joe, his mother's brother, who had become a father to him and who now wanted nothing to do with him.

"Your life is kind of fucked up, Madsen," Jerry observed wryly.

Grant half-chuckled. "Kind of, sir." He supposed he should feel offended by the comment, but actually the parole officer was right on. Grant was one fat disappointment to all those around him. And Officer Stone didn't even know anything about his family. How would the grizzled PO describe his life if he knew how destructive his family truly was? A hopeless failure?

Grant certainly felt hopeless much of the time, and his intense curiosity about the woman he had seen before this appointment surprised him. *Any* intense feeling surprised him at this point. Despite his conversation with Officer Stone, he felt a little lightness when thinking about her sultry eyes and shiny hair. A woman had not had an effect on him like that in quite some time.

When Jerry began speaking, Grant snapped his gaze back to his PO. "Let me explain how things will work, Madsen. We're going to meet weekly, same time, same place. You screw up just this much," he held his thumb and forefinger centimeters apart, "and your ass is going back to prison. Make your appointments, get a place to live, and get a job ASAP. Are we clear, sailor?"

"Aye, sir."

Jerry considered the abrupt changes in Madsen's life, including the Navy discharge, the violence, and the psychosis. Then he made an executive decision. "Our last order of business today is a drug test. When we're done here, you are to report to Room 212 down the hall and pee in a cup."

Watching Grant nod, Jerry added, "Should I expect a positive drug test? It would be better to tell me now."

"No, sir. I don't take drugs."

"Good. Keep it that way and you'll serve the last ten months of your sentence outside the walls of Gurnee. Our time's just about up. Do you have any questions?"

Eager to get out of there, Grant replied, "No, sir."

"See you at nine-fifteen next week, and don't be late, Madsen."

"Yes, sir." Grant unfolded his lean body, stood, and gracefully exited the office.

He went to the room where urine screens were conducted and endured the arduous process of registering, completing scads of paperwork. Then a parole officer observed as he performed his business at the urinal.

Although he'd tolerated far more demeaning experiences at Gurnee, he was still bothered by the invasive drug test. He'd hoped the humiliation of another man watching him take a piss was a thing of the past. Apparently, the DOC still wanted control over his mind, body, and soul.

Grant descended the courthouse stairs, squinting into the bright sun of the late-May morning in Chicago. He had absolutely no idea what to do next. Suddenly a man in a khaki U.S. Navy uniform caught his eye, and he looked to his left, doing a double take.

It was *him*. Uncle Joe! Grant inhaled sharply. Joe gazed at him expectantly, his hands pressed into the pockets of his uniform. Paralyzed, Grant wondered what his uncle might do. Hug him? Hit him? Yell?

"Come here, Grant," Joe demanded sternly.

Always obedient, Grant took tentative steps toward his uncle, whose graying blond hair stood in sharp contrast to his nephew's dark features. Once Grant was close enough, Joe enveloped him a rough hug.

"I've been looking all over Chicago for you," Joe said, squeezing his nephew tightly.

Grant felt tears spring to his eyes—tears of regret, tears of relief. An audible sob almost escaped his lips, and he held onto his uncle with a sense of desperation. He was with his Uncle Joe again after more than two years. He was home.

3. "If Yes, Please Explain"

Glancing around nervously, Sophie tucked a strand of blond hair behind her ear and refocused her attention on the clipboard in her lap. She had completed most of the job application in her neat handwriting, but one section remained blank. Clearing her throat, she returned to the dreaded unanswered question, her pen hovering inches above the paper:

> *Have you been convicted of or pleaded "No Contest" to a felony within the last five years?*

She sighed while tapping her pen against the clipboard, barely aware of the announcements pouring from the intercom over her head. Judging by the smooth female voice directing doctors to various operating rooms, Human Resources was located on a surgical floor at Northwestern Memorial Hospital.

Because Sophie had completed her pre-doctoral psychology internship in a Veterans Administration hospital, she figured she would start her job search in the familiar environment of a hospital setting. She obviously could no longer apply for psychologist positions, but she was hopeful about securing a post as a patient care assistant, orderly, receptionist—no job seemed beneath her at the moment.

The mocking words of the question danced before her eyes. Should she be truthful? If she admitted her felony conviction, she would likely forfeit any chances of securing a job. If she lied, she didn't know how she could live with herself.

Sophie was an honest person, although in prison she'd learned how to be secretive and dishonest by necessity. She also realized the hospital might find out the truth anyway. Her father had kept her arrest and conviction on the down-low, but if potential employers were to dig deep enough, they could certainly find the public records of her ignominious crime.

With a resolute frown, she hastily scribbled *Yes.*

The subsequent question then stared her in the face:

If yes, please explain:

Explain? Explain how she crossed every boundary to fall in love with a psychotherapy client? Explain how she let him and his influence seep further and further into her life, only to find out he was a Mafia thug who had used her for his own purposes? Explain how she'd ruined her career and her dignity in the process? How the intense shame of her actions had destroyed her family?

Exhaling in frustration, she scrawled:

Convicted of accessory to armed robbery and possession of illegal weapons. Sentenced to two years of prison.

It still felt surreal to write those words, though it had been more than a year since she'd heard the court's judgment against her. No matter how she tried to deny it or hide behind her illustrious academic career, her well-bred family, her good intentions, the truth was she was a felon. She felt trapped in a nightmare created by one client. Listening to herself rationalize and deflect, she felt a flash of anger. *Stop externalizing blame.* This nightmare was her own creation.

Sophie scooped up her handbag in one hand and held the clipboard in the other. "You can kiss *this* job goodbye," she muttered.

As she left the hospital, she felt despondency overtake her. She'd planned to apply for several jobs before returning to Kirsten's apartment, but after just the first application, she barely had the energy to keep trudging down Huron Street. Perhaps it was time to regroup.

Upon entering the small one-bedroom apartment, Sophie heard the tapping of a computer keyboard before she saw her roommate. Stealing a look into the bedroom, she noticed Kirsten sporting a bright smile while typing away happily. The twenty-eight-year-old woman's sleek brown hair was fastened in a ponytail, and her blue eyes danced with amusement.

"Looks like you're making great progress, Kir," Sophie observed, stepping into the room and collapsing on the bed.

Kirsten looked up, her smile fading quickly. "Oh, hey, Sophie. I didn't hear you come in." She tilted the laptop away from Sophie's line of vision.

"Kirsten …" Sophie's voice rose. "Are you chatting online again? You're supposed to be working on your dissertation!"

"I know," she replied. "But I just got home from work, and I had a crappy day, so the last thing I want to do is write my crappy dissertation."

Sophie could definitely relate to having a bad day. She kicked off her boots and scooted up to rest her back against the wall, hugging her knees to her chest. "What happened at work?"

Kirsten held up her finger and explained, "Just give me a sec to tell everyone goodbye, okay? Then I'll fill you in."

Sophie shook her head slowly, amazed at how addicted her roommate had become to the internet forum for her favorite TV show. While Kirsten typed a message, Sophie waited patiently to hear about the trials of her job as a counselor at a substance abuse treatment center.

Closing her laptop, Kirsten turned to Sophie. "My day sucked because I had three no-shows in a row this morning. I decided to give up and come home."

Sophie nodded. There was nothing more frustrating than clients failing to show up for their appointments. "Is your supervisor going to be upset?"

"I'm more worried about the lost income. I only make like thirty-five percent of each session fee since I'm not licensed yet, and when I get no-shows I have no idea how I'll make rent."

Sophie fidgeted with her hands in her lap. "I'm sorry," she said quietly. "I'll try to find a job soon."

Kirsten looked startled and immediately began apologizing. "Oh, no, Sophie. I'm not trying to pressure you to give me money for the rent. I …" She stumbled over her words. "Listen to me, going on and on about myself, complaining about the lousy pay of being a therapist …" She was about to complete her sentence with, *when you're not even allowed to be a therapist anymore,* but thought better of it. Instead, she tried to redirect the conversation. "Um, how was *your* day? How was your meeting with your parole officer?"

Still wringing her hands, Sophie replied, "It was awful. I hated it … I just want to be done with all of this, and I have a whole year of parole left. He told me I had to get a job in the next two weeks or I'm going back inside."

"That sounds scary. Did you put in some applications today?"

Sophie nodded absentmindedly. "Yeah, at the hospital."

After waiting expectantly a few moments, Kirsten prodded, "And? Where else?"

"That's it. Just the hospital."

"Sophie! You have to apply to more places than one if you want to find a job."

"I know, but...but what's the point? They're not going to hire a felon, anyway."

Kirsten waited a few moments before quietly offering, "If you don't find anything, you could always call your dad. He's loaded—maybe you could work for him."

Sophie snapped her gaze upward. "No, I cannot! I don't want anything to do with his construction business, and he doesn't want anything to do with me, especially after what happened, um, what happened," she gulped, her next words barely above a whisper, "...what happened to my mom."

Kirsten's eyes widened. "That is ludicrous! Your dad can't possibly blame you for your mother's death!"

"He can, and he does. You saw him. You saw how he was at the funeral. He wouldn't even look me in the eye."

Sophie could not prevent her consciousness from flooding with the memory of her mother's grave on a cold, rainy day last December. Icy winds and pelting raindrops had buffeted the group surrounding the gravesite of Laura Taylor. Sophie's mother had succumbed quickly following a heart attack, and despite the inclement weather, the gravesite had been packed with her father's work colleagues. After one brief, accusatory glance toward his daughter, Will Taylor had avoided all eye contact.

The overwhelming grief of losing her mother, the disdainful brush-off by her father, and the sheets of rain pouring over her as tears trailed down her face had seemed too much to bear in that moment. But the fact that she'd been handcuffed, dressed in her thin prison uniform while shivering in the wind, had only made it worse.

Fellow prisoners told her she was lucky the DOC had allowed her to attend her mother's funeral. She certainly had not felt lucky. She would never forget the shame of that day.

Kirsten's blue eyes filled with concern as she watched her friend withdraw into a cocoon of despair. Seeing Sophie handcuffed like a common criminal, flanked by two police officers as if she were some danger to society, had been one of the most bizarre experiences of Kirsten's life. At the reception after the funeral, there had been whispers that Laura's heart attack was brought on by the stress of watching her only child go to prison. This had horrified Kirsten.

Clearing her throat nervously, Kirsten attempted a smile. "Hey, roomie, I'll make you a deal. For every job you apply for, I promise to spend one hour on my dissertation."

Sophie glanced up, grateful for Kirsten's transparent attempt to cheer her up. She took a deep breath and felt a slight dissipation of her crushing guilt. "Two hours," she countered, a small grin spreading across her face.

"One job application for two hours of dissertation time? Hmm…" Kirsten stroked her chin, considering the negotiation. "You drive a tough bargain. Okay, it's a deal."

They reached forward to shake hands, smirking.

Eyeing her friend's lean frame, Kirsten asked, "Did you eat any breakfast today?"

"Yes, Mom."

"Sorry, I just worry about you. You're so skinny now."

"The prison diet works wonders. Nobody wants to eat that swill."

"Well, now that you're residing *chez* Kirsten, there's no excuse not to eat. C'mon, let's make some lunch."

Kirsten hopped up and headed into the small kitchen with Sophie following. They began cooking some noodles and making a salad. In the midst of chopping tomatoes, Kirsten glanced at her roommate.

"So, your parole officer's a guy. Is he cute?"

Sophie scoffed, "He's like sixty years old, Kir!"

Laughing, she wiped her hands on a towel and set a couple of plates on the table. "Okay, okay. We do need to find you a man, though. You've had a long drought since *him*."

With a far-off look, Sophie drifted back to the deep-blue eyes that had once stared into her own, eyes that had been at one moment wounded and vulnerable, then suddenly suspicious and angry. She'd thought those eyes communicated love and devotion, but in reality they'd simply been playing her.

Expecting the familiar ache of betrayal, Sophie was surprised to find this recurring vision abruptly interrupted by a new image instead. Flashes of clear, innocent eyes flooded her brain, their color a lighter, warmer blue. These eyes had stolen her breath and left her wanting more. These were the eyes she'd seen outside Officer Stone's door.

She felt a steadying hand on her wrist, bringing her back to the present. "Sophie, I'm sorry. I shouldn't bring him up like that."

Sophie gazed at her apologetic roommate and swallowed guiltily. Kirsten would be thoroughly disappointed to learn Sophie was already obsessing over yet another criminal. The two men actually looked somewhat alike, now that she thought about it. Maybe she really did need help!

"So, listen to this. My damn PO is forcing me to attend therapy as a condition of my parole."

Kirsten quietly continued lunch preparations, refusing to empathize with the indignant anger in Sophie's voice. What had happened to Sophie was every psychologist's nightmare, and it scared Kirsten immensely. She desperately wanted her friend to move on and heal.

"And why is therapy such a bad idea?"

"It's not … it's …" Sophie sighed in frustration. "I know I need to talk about it. I just don't want to, you know?"

"Absolutely." Kirsten often felt that way about her dissertation.

"Officer Stone gave me a list of therapists. Will you maybe, um, help me find a good one?"

Kirsten smiled encouragingly. "Of course. If you want, I can ask my supervisor what she thinks of the people on the list. She knows a lot of therapists in Chicago."

"Okay." Sophie joined Kirsten at the little round table in the nook next to the kitchen. She began twirling pasta on her fork.

Ready or not, Sophie was going to start building her life back, trying to make sense of the mess it had become. *If yes, please explain.* With the help of a supportive friend and hopefully a good psychologist, she was going to explain how she'd gotten here.

And as those beguiling turquoise eyes flashed through her mind once again, she hoped maybe she could explain why she was immediately attracted to another criminal.

Or maybe the explanation was that the man was fucking hot.

4. Solitary

Joe Madsen thought he'd heard a sob, and when he realized his shoulder was damp from accumulated tears, he knew for sure the strong man he held in his arms was crying. He also knew Grant would be embarrassed as hell to be weeping in public.

Gently he pulled out of the hug, looking away while Grant stared at the sidewalk outside the courthouse and furtively wiped his cheeks. His nephew nervously kicked at the concrete with the toe of his shoe, reminding Joe of when eight-year-old Grant and his mother had come to live with him. It was a full minute before Grant slowly looked up, meeting the worried gaze of his uncle.

"You've lost some weight," Joe observed.

Grant sniffed and nodded.

They stared awkwardly for a few moments until Grant finally found his voice. "I didn't think I'd see you again."

"Well, you sure didn't make it easy to find you. I figured you'd have to meet with your parole officer at some point, so I've been camped out here for a while."

"Sorry."

Joe had waited long enough to ask the question that had gnawed at him for two years. "Why the hell wouldn't you let me visit you at Gurnee?"

Shooting a culpable glance at his Uncle Joe, Grant sighed. How could he explain his failure to stand up to his own father?

Miffed, Joe continued. "I couldn't believe it when they said you took me off your visitor list. I thought there had to be some mistake. I begged for leave time, and then I couldn't even use it."

"Did your captain approve your leave this time?"

"I'm due back in Virginia tomorrow. But don't change the subject, Grant. Why wouldn't you allow me to visit you? Did I do something wrong?"

Grant snapped his head up, startled. "No! No, sir, it was nothing you did. It was…" He sighed, knowing he would never escape his destructive family, no matter how hard he tried. "It was my father."

"Enzo? Oh, shit. I should've known. Of all the bad luck, to be thrown into the same prison as that gangster. What did he do to you?"

Grant stared into the distance, eventually mentioning with a slight smile, "He doesn't like you very much."

"Yeah, well, the feeling is mutual," Joe said. "I hate Enzo for what he's done to your brother Logan. And for what he did to your mother as well, God bless her soul."

An unspoken sadness crossed Joe's face as he remembered his beautiful sister, Karita, who'd been left alone to care for two boys after her husband was sentenced to life in prison. Enzo had summarily abandoned his wife and sons, and Joe had tried to assemble a new family for his sister. But when Logan had run away and Karita fell ill with cancer, the patched-together family was destroyed. Yet Joe was determined to help Grant get his life back together.

"She deserved a better husband," Grant said softly.

Joe's eyes narrowed. "I never wanted her to marry that bastard. Did Enzo hurt you?"

"It was my first day at Gurnee," Grant explained, thinking back to the abject fear he'd felt at being caged in a state penitentiary for three whole years. It was day one of a 1,095-day sentence, and he'd been scared out of his mind.

It was a chilly March day out on the yard, and cons mingled in their dark-gray jackets. Grant stood alone, leaning on the fence, nervously scanning for any sign of trouble. That was when he noticed the charcoal eyes staring him down from across the way. His father's jet-black hair had grayed, and he'd lost perhaps an inch in height as he aged, but his eyes had not changed one bit—deep, black, Italian eyes that seared into his son as he strode toward him.

As the group of men approached him, Grant stepped forward. Naturally his father had an entourage with him—men who protected and deferred to their leader. Grant recognized a couple of the Mafia thugs from his childhood. Maybe the big guy had babysat his brother Logan and him once or twice?

"I heard you were coming," Enzo Barberi said evenly. "What's it been, Grant, twenty years since we've seen each other?"

Grant remained silent, feeling the suspicious stares of his father's men coat him like olive oil in a skillet.

"You got three years?"

Grant gave a slight nod, wishing his throat had not constricted with fear in his father's presence.

"Three years is a long time to be alone in here," Enzo said coolly.

"I don't want anything to do with you." Fierce determination flared in Grant's eyes.

"That is a very unwise approach, Grant." Enzo glanced around in the yard. "There are lots of cons licking their chops, eager to get to you. There's a buzz about a handsome young fish arriving at Gurnee. The talk of the block is about a new, fresh, *pretty* con."

His father's emphasis made Grant's throat run dry. His eyes drifted in the direction his father had just nodded, and he noticed several men edging closer, leering at him.

"Join us, son. Let me protect you in here."

"Why do you care?"

"Hey." Enzo's eyes narrowed with steely rage. "Even though you abandoned me in here—even though you didn't visit me *once* in twenty years—I can forgive and forget. I can be the bigger man and offer my hand to you now that you need it."

Grant knew there would be strings attached. His father was a businessman at heart, and it did not take long for the terms of the deal to be revealed. Grant tensed as his father warned, "But if you so much as say one word to Joe Madsen while you're in here, all bets are off. If you want my protection, you choose to be with *me* now, not him. You can't have us both. That fucking man has led you astray, and you need me to set you straight. But I'll only do that if you cut all ties with your uncle."

Grant knew his father was jealous of Joe's influence over him, but he had not expected an immediate standoff on the issue. His nostrils flared, and he seethed, "Joe is a better dad to me than you'll ever be."

"No wonder you got caught in that two-bit robbery. I see you're as dumb and naive as ever." Enzo glanced at his men. "Let's go," he ordered. He then looked back at his son, shaking his head. "Have it your way, Grant."

Enzo and his posse skulked off, clearing a path for a new predatory group to approach. The leader was tall and solidly built, blond with icy blue eyes. His two equally blond companions, who appeared quite young, walked a deferential step behind him.

The leader's calculating stare roamed over Grant's fine physique. "Fresh meat, boys," he crowed. One of the underlings smiled lasciviously.

Grant took a slight step back.

"Aw, nothing to be scared of, sweetheart," the leader assured him. "We just want to get to know you." One of the accompanying youngsters began to hum "Getting to Know You" from *The King and I*, eliciting a grin from the leader. "What're you in for?"

Grant remained silent.

The man pursed his lips and took a step closer, and one of his followers sidled up to Grant, hissing, "Answer the question, boy, if you don't want to leave Gurnee on a gurney."

The other youngster cackled like a hyena, and Grant had a feeling this group had used that joke many times before. When the blond leader reached out to stroke Grant's face, he'd had enough and instantly unleashed a vicious punch, nailing the predator right in his gut. The tall man doubled over, gasping for air.

"Fuck you!" one of his minions cried, swiftly landing on Grant and delivering a sharp blow to his midsection. Despite his groan of pain, Grant gracefully broke free from his attacker's grasp and sent a glancing blow across someone's jaw. He couldn't tell which lackey was which in the melee.

Apparently the leader recovered, because suddenly there were three men raining strikes and punches on Grant's defenseless body, forcing him onto the ground where they continued the assault. Grant raised his arms to shield his head, feeling his torso on fire from punishing punches to his ribcage. Excited shouting rose up across the yard as the inmates noticed the altercation. Waves of testosterone pulsated as the basest of male instincts played out in the battle.

Then came the staccato of warning shots from the snipers in the guard towers. Blessedly the assault on his body ceased, but Grant soon found himself roughly hauled to his feet by two corrections officers. They quickly cuffed his hands behind his back and led him to the administration building, where a CO dumped him into a chair in the warden's office.

"This one just got in a fight, sir," the CO informed his boss. "Inmate Grant Madsen."

"Wait outside," the warden instructed, and the officer dutifully left the room. The warden opened a file drawer and extracted a manila folder.

Grant shifted uncomfortably in his chair, trying to release the pressure from the handcuffs. Noting the absence of other inmates, Grant determined that apparently he would be the only one punished for the fight. His father probably had worked out an arrangement with the COs in Gurnee, some sort of *quid pro quo* in which Enzo paid them to leave him and his business alone. Some things never changed.

He studied the older gentleman across the desk as he read the file. Warden Raymond Arthur appeared to be in his late fifties, with receding black hair, ruddy cheeks, and a belly protruding beneath the vest of his three-piece suit. Large glasses magnified his shrewd eyes, which now gazed at the prisoner.

"You're a college graduate and a former naval officer, Mr. Madsen." Raymond's voice was weathered from years of smoking cigars. "I wouldn't expect you to be disturbing the peace on your very first day."

Grant felt a sharp pain in his ribs with each breath, but he managed to say, "Yes, sir."

"What was the fight about?"

Swallowing, Grant said, "I had a, um, disagreement with another inmate, sir."

"Which inmate?"

Grant's stared straight ahead and remained silent. Evidently nobody at Gurnee knew he was the son of Vicenzo Barberi, the head of a Mafia organization, and Grant intended to keep it that way.

Frustrated by the prisoner's silence, Raymond coldly ordered, "This is your first day at Gurnee, Madsen, and it seems you're unable to play nice with the others. Sixty days in solitary. And when you get out, I don't want to see your face in here again."

Grant's heart pounded and sweat trickled down his back at the thought of being locked in a tiny, dark cell for that length of time, but he showed only a resolute coolness as he met the warden's stare. "Yes, sir."

"Guard!" Raymond's voice boomed authoritatively.

"Jesus," Joe exhaled, bringing Grant out of solitary's claustrophobic walls and back to the open-aired brightness of the courthouse steps in downtown Chicago. "No wonder you took your father's protection when you got out of solitary."

Grant looked down.

Joe chewed the inside of his cheek. "Did they, uh, those guys ever, uh ...?"

Grant quickly shook his head. "My dad's a powerful man."

Squinting, Joe's expression became stormy. "He is." He sighed heavily. "So, how was solitary?"

Grant found his hands balled into fists. It became difficult to breathe as dark walls closed in on him.

"Grant?"

Shaking his head to stop the disturbing images, Grant jammed his hands into the pockets of his khaki pants. "I'm sorry. You deserve better after taking care of me all those years, after helping to get me into the Navy, after saving my life, really."

Joe peered at him strangely. "What *happened* in the hole?"

"Please, sir, please don't make me tell you what happened." Grant's eyes begged right along with his voice. "I understand if you never want anything to do with me ever again. Just please, please don't ask me to explain."

Joe was pained as he watched his nephew trembling before him, seemingly on the verge of tears once again. What the hell had transpired in prison?

"It's okay, Grant. You don't have to tell me. Of course I want to be part of your life. I..." He looked away, clearing his throat. "I love you."

"Th-th-thank you." Grant couldn't get out the words *I love you too*, although they were certainly true. Love for his uncle was what landed him in prison in the first place.

"Just don't cut me out of your life again, okay?" Joe was the one pleading now.

Grant took a deep breath. He would not have to abide by his father's rules now that he was out of prison. He no longer needed his father's protection. "Okay."

"You're the only family I've got."

His nephew silently agreed. Joe was the only family who mattered to him, the only family with his best interests at heart. His father, brother, uncle, and cousin only looked out for themselves, desperately craving more and more power and dragging down anyone who stood in their way. Grant could not get away from them fast enough.

"So." Joe smiled faintly, trying to lighten the mood. "I don't suppose you've found a place to live yet?"

"No, sir."

"Or a job?"

Grant shrugged. "Haven't found that either."

"C'mon, I know a guy who maybe can help with both."

Joe stepped to the curb and hailed a taxi. As they passed the Wrigley Building, Grant remembered the excitement of his first cab ride to Michigan Avenue for a shopping trip with his mother and brother. He must have been only five or so, and he'd clutched his mother's hand while gawking at the tall, elegant buildings. It felt wrong to be back in the city without his mother by his side.

When they arrived at the docks of the Chicago River near Navy Pier, Grant curiously stepped out of the cab, shielding his eyes from the glare of the sunlight off the water.

Joe headed for one of the ships docked by the pier, and Grant read the clapboard sign sitting on shore:

Book Your Architectural Cruise Here!
Cruises Depart Daily at 1:00, 3:00, 5:00, and 7:00

"Roger!" Joe called out, tentatively stepping onto the gunwale of the ship and looking naturally at home in his khaki Navy uniform. "Yo, Rog!" he bellowed again, this time producing a short, rotund man from the ship's interior.

"Son of a bitch!" the bald man cried, breaking into a huge grin. Joe hopped down onto the deck and they grabbed each other in a bear hug, slapping each other's backs fondly.

"Christ, Rog," Joe laughed, glancing at the man's sizable belly. "You been eating deep dish pizza every day or what?"

"I'm missing your goddamn PT every morning, you asshole. You're a commander now, huh? A fucking XO? The big cheese is here! So, what in the hell you doing in Chicago, sir?"

Still chuckling, Joe glanced up to find Grant carefully watching them from the pier. "I'm here to visit my nephew. Hey, Grant, come down here. I want to introduce you to a friend."

Grant hopped onto the deck with one smooth motion, clearly at ease on the watercraft as well.

Joe nodded toward the shorter man. "This is Roger Eaton, former ensign serving with me at Great Lakes." He then draped his arm protectively across Grant's shoulders. "And this is my nephew Grant, former lieutenant at Great Lakes."

"Oh fuck, you both outrank me then." Roger grinned, his hazel eyes twinkling. "At least you were smart enough to get out of the Navy, unlike the commander here," he added, looking up at Grant.

Grant gave a plastic smile. His exit from the Navy had hardly been voluntary.

"So," Joe began, feeling his nephew bristle beside him. "Grant needs a job. I was wondering if you could use a capable assistant on board?"

"Hmm…" Roger scratched his chin. "Well, I just hired a few guys, but I'm sure I'll need more help with the season about to start. Anything for you, Joe."

Joe removed his arm from his nephew's shoulders and reached out to shake Roger's hand, pumping vigorously. "I knew I could count on you. I have to return to Norfolk tomorrow. Is there any way Grant could sack out at your place until he finds an apartment of his own?"

Grant watched the interaction with amazement. His uncle was shamelessly persuading this stranger to take care of him.

"No problem, sir. We Navy boys got to stay together." Roger turned to Grant. "How long you been out, kid?"

Grant blushed. "Just a day."

"You got out of the Navy yesterday?" Roger asked incredulously.

"Oh, no, um, I, um, left the Navy over two years ago."

Watching his nephew squirm, Joe stepped in. "Rog? I should probably tell you that Grant was just released from prison. He's had a rough go of it, but he won't cause you any problems, I promise. He just needs to stay away from his family and he'll be fine."

Roger squinted warily at Grant, while Grant peered at the spotless white deck of the ship. "Prison, huh? Convenient you told me that *after* I agreed to hire him, Joe."

"Sorry about that. That was wrong of me. But Grant is a good man, and he'll be your best employee. Just wait and you'll see."

Scowling, Roger reluctantly nodded. When Grant slowly raised his head to meet his gaze, his new boss told him, "You pull any of that prison shit on me and getting fired will be the least of your problems, you got it?"

"Yes, sir."

Roger's glower abruptly turned into a grin. "I got a lieutenant calling me 'sir.' I love it. Okay, kid, you go up there," he pointed to the door of the administration building nearby, "fill out some paperwork, and you can start work tomorrow. Eleven hundred hours, sharp."

"Thank you, sir."

Joe broke in, "Hey, Rog, when are you done tonight? Let's go out and get a drink."

"If you want to meet me here around twenty-thirty, I'll take you to the place with the best pizza in the city."

Joe grinned. "You look like you've tried a few pizza joints in your day."

"Can you believe this guy?" Roger asked Grant. "He insults me at the same time he asks me for a favor. Unbelievable."

Grant began to feel a sliver of relief wash over him. Maybe he wouldn't have to be so solitary anymore. He returned Roger's smile. "Yep, that's my Uncle Joe."

"Ah, you guys love me, you know it," Joe said. "Let's get that paperwork started, Grant."

Grant nodded. "See you tomorrow, Mr. Eaton."

"See you then, kid."

Roger disappeared below deck, muttering grumpily. His business wasn't no halfway house, damn it. Joe's nephew had better perform like the fucking Employee of the Month or there would be hell to pay.

5. The Jacket

Sophie leaned back in the metal chair outside her PO's office, nervously glancing at her watch. It was five past nine, and although she didn't know Officer Stone all that well, he didn't seem the type to run late. Should she knock again? She didn't want to be a pest, but she also didn't want to get in trouble for being late if he was somehow in his office yet hadn't heard her first knock.

Glancing down at her form-fitting white sleeveless tank, layered with a flowing white silk blouse and navy-blue walking shorts, she hoped she was dressed all right. What exactly was the protocol for parolee fashion?

Anxiously twisting the silver ring on her right forefinger, she weighed her options and was just standing to rap on the door again when Jerry rounded the corner, flustered as he swiftly made his way down the hallway. Sliding the key into the doorknob lock without looking at Sophie, he muttered, "Sorry I'm late. C'mon in."

Despite keeping his head down as Sophie followed him inside the office, she detected redness around his eyes and a sad, defeated body posture. She also heard a heavy sigh as they both sat down. She did not even need her keen powers of observation to detect that something was wrong.

"Is everything all right, Mr. Stone?"

He glanced up at her and held her concerned gaze for a moment before peering down at her file again. She noticed a white nametag on his shirt, and immediately recognized the Northwestern Hospital logo.

Biting her lower lip she inquired, "You were just visiting someone in the hospital, sir?"

He looked up again, startled. Scrunching his forehead, he asked, "How did you…" He then gazed down at his shirt and ripped the nametag off, angrily crumpling it in his hands before tossing the sticky wad into the garbage can.

"So, Ms. Taylor, how is your roommate's dissertation coming along?"

Sophie was disappointed that he'd evaded her questions, but touched that he remembered this tidbit from their first meeting. "I made her write five pages!" she beamed.

"I see," he gruffly replied. "And do you have a job yet?"

Her smile faded. "Um, no sir."

"Time is running out, Taylor. How many jobs have you applied for?"

Sophie looked up and to the right, visibly performing mental calculations. "About twenty-four jobs, I think?"

Jerry raised his eyebrows and leaned in. "Twenty-four?"

"Yes, sir."

"How many interviews have you had?"

Sophie began twisting her ring again. "None."

"That doesn't sound right. Where have you applied?"

"Um, about five hospitals, um, one of them being Northwestern," she added pointedly. "Three doctors' offices, ten or so boarding schools, a couple of counseling centers…" She sighed. "I don't think they want to hire a felon."

Jerry sat back in his chair and studied the parolee across from him. She looked classy, fresh, and young—a sharp contrast to the bleak institutional setting of the hospital he'd just left.

His tone softened. "I think you're aiming a bit high."

Sophie frowned. "But I have my PhD. What do you want me to do—sell hot dogs on the street or something?"

"There's no shame in that, Taylor. Hell, I was just at a Cubs game the other day, and they were hiring vendors to push hot dogs and beer. Why don't you go apply at Wrigley?"

She shot him a hostile glance, offended by his preposterous suggestion, but then she noticed a slight smirk on his face. So, he was joking with her. Smiling a mischievous smile, she retorted indignantly, "*Cubs* games? The only way I'd take a job like that is for White Sox games."

"Don't tell me you're a White Sox fan," he groaned. "They should *never* have allowed you out of your sentence early. In fact, I should send you right back to Downer's Grove now that I know this about you. A Sox fan. Ugh."

She giggled, and he felt drawn into her engaging smile. She seemed bright, caring, and warm. Jerry was a confirmed bachelor who had devoted his life to his career, but if he ever had a daughter, he'd want her to be something like Sophie Taylor. Well, minus the criminal history.

"Seriously, though," he continued, "I want you to expand your job search. Get something temporary and look for a position more suited to your tastes while you're working. You know what they say: It's easier to get a job when you already have a job."

Sophie nodded. "I'll keep looking, Mr. Stone. But if you see me walking up and down the aisles at *Cubs* games, you'll know I've sunk to a new low." That wasn't true, actually. Having to crawl to her father and ask *him* for a job would be the lowest of lows.

Getting back to business, Jerry asked, "Have you attended therapy yet?"

"My first appointment is at ten this morning, sir." Sophie said solemnly.

"And which shrink did you choose?"

"Dr. Hunter Hayes."

Jerry arched one eyebrow. "You chose one of the only men on the list?"

"Well, I thought I'd relate better to a psychologist, and there weren't that many listed. I hear he's very good."

The PO continued to shoot her a dubious stare, and suddenly she understood his consternation. "Oh! You're worried about me seeing a male psychologist. You're thinking that, um, maybe, um, something will happen again?"

"Exactly, Taylor," he curtly replied.

"Uh, that is not going to happen, sir."

"And how do you know that for sure?"

How could she answer without outing a colleague? Kirsten's supervisor had let it slip that Dr. Hayes was gay, but Sophie wasn't sure this was common knowledge, and she was determined not to cross professional boundaries again. "Well, uh, he, um, is, well, let's just say I'm not his type. I seriously doubt Dr. Hayes is going to fall in love with me."

Jerry stared blankly at her for a moment, then seemed to come to an understanding. "Dr. Hayes is gay?"

Sophie cleared her throat. "That's what I hear, yes."

He moved on. "You say your appointment is at ten today?"

She nodded.

Opening a file drawer, Jerry extracted a paper and scanned it quickly before dialing the phone. Sophie observed curiously and had no idea who Jerry was referring to when he said, "I got his voice mail."

She felt sick when she heard Officer Stone begin leaving a message.

"Hello, Dr. Hayes. This is Parole Officer Jerry Stone with the Illinois Department of Corrections. I am calling to confirm your appointment with a parolee in my charge, Sophie Taylor. I will also need weekly updates regarding her attendance and progress in therapy. Please contact me at this number…"

Sophie dropped her head in shame. They'd had such a nice conversation, but this reminder that she was an untrustworthy con smacked her in the face. At times in the past week she'd felt almost normal, very nearly worthy, but something always took her back down to her status as a lowly, lying criminal.

Jerry hung up and was surprised to see Sophie looking so crestfallen. "What's wrong, Taylor?"

Her tone was wounded. "You don't believe me? About the therapy appointment?"

He sighed. "Trust has to be earned. I learned that the hard way too many times to count. You simply haven't earned my trust yet."

Nodding slowly, Sophie still felt hurt, although she knew his words were wise. She had given her trust too easily once, and now she was paying the price. She vowed to be more careful in the future.

"Taylor, we're out of time," Jerry informed her.

Sophie rose to leave, but after a moment's hesitation, he added, "It's my mother."

"Excuse me?"

"I was visiting my mother in the hospital," he said, shocked he was telling a parolee. "She's dying of cancer." What was this psychologist doing to him?

"Oh, I'm so sorry. You, um, had to come straight from the hospital to deal with a bunch of us convicts?"

Jerry did not respond. He looked as if he was about to cry.

"I'd better go. I don't want to make you late," she murmured, hastily exiting the office to help him save face.

Once Sophie opened the door, she found herself almost colliding again with the gorgeous man from last week. He had his right hand suspended in midair, his fist curled to knock, when she came busting through the door. He seemed as unsure about knocking as she had.

"Um, h-h-hi," she stammered, closing the door behind her. Meeting her gaze were crystal eyes like blue shards of glass.

Grant appreciatively took in her bright, beautiful appearance and tilted his head in the direction of the office. "So, what kind of mood is he in today?"

Feeling her heart pound, Sophie managed, "Not so good today. His mother is dying. He just visited her in the hospital." She cringed, realizing she was inappropriately sharing personal information.

The man showed a look of such utter sorrow that Sophie fought the urge to wrap him in a hug. She wondered what the hell she was thinking. He was a total stranger! And a criminal too.

"That's awful," he said, shaking his head. He took a deep breath and squared his shoulders. "Well, I better get in there."

As he opened the door, Sophie caught sight of the logo on his shiny black athletic jacket. "Wait!" she whispered.

Grant turned to her, bewildered. "What?" he whispered back.

"Your White Sox jacket!" she hissed. "He's a die-hard Cubs fan!"

"So what?" he retorted. "I would hope we've advanced to a world where Cubs fans and White Sox fans can peacefully coexist."

"Maybe. But he almost had a conniption when he found out I cheer for the Sox. This is the man who could put you back in prison in a second. Do you *really* want to get on his bad side?"

"Good point." He began shrugging out of the jacket.

"Madsen, is that you?" Jerry growled from inside the office. "Get your ass in here!"

Grant's eyes widened in alarm. "I gotta hurry!" He now held the jacket crumpled in his hands, and Sophie admired the length of lean brown arms extending from a heather-gray short-sleeved T-shirt. The shirt's brown piping accentuated his sinewy triceps.

"I can't leave the jacket out here or somebody might take it. Here!" He thrust it into her unsuspecting grasp. "You hold it for me."

Sophie was about to protest when he opened the door wide and dashed inside, leaving her alone in the hallway. She glanced down at the jacket. *But I can't wait outside for you. I have an appointment.*

She sighed, stuck in a moment of indecision. Why hadn't he just taken it with him, hiding the logo? She walked toward the exit, carrying the stranger's jacket. Would there be any way to return it to him before next week? She drew up the collar of the jacket to see if his name or phone number was written inside.

Unfortunately there were no identifying marks, but as she held the jacket so close to her face, a subtle scent of aftershave wafted toward her nose.

Sophie stopped walking and inhaled deeply, mesmerized by the masculine scent of bergamot and sandalwood. She closed her eyes and breathed in the tantalizing scent.

Suddenly she glanced up, her eyes darting guiltily to discern whether anyone had caught her, lost in a horny trance. She shook her head slowly. Apparently Officer Stone was a wise man in mandating therapy for her. She needed some serious help! She scurried away to hail a cab, hoping Dr. Hayes could set her straight.

⌒

"What was the holdup, Madsen?" Jerry demanded.

"Uh," Grant stalled as took his seat. "I thought I saw a guy I knew in the hall—a guy I ran into at the Cubs game on Sunday." He was surprised how easily he spun a lie, thinking on his feet. Dishonesty must run in his genes. "But it was a false alarm. It wasn't him."

Jerry brightened considerably at the mention of the Cubs. "*I* was at that game. Where were your seats?"

Grant squirmed. "Uh, behind third base?"

"No wonder you're so tan," Jerry observed. "Those seats are right in the sun."

Or the glare off the water after working on a ship the past week, Grant thought, but he went along with it. "Yeah, it gets pretty hot in the sun."

"Who'd you go to the game with?"

Grant paused. "My uncle?"

"I thought you said you didn't have any family in town."

"No, sir, I have lots of family. They're just, um, not the kind of people I want to associate with. Except for my uncle. He's a commander in the Navy, and he's always been there for me."

"A commander in the Navy? He must have been pretty pissed off about you getting kicked out after your conviction, huh?"

"That's putting it mildly, sir." Grant had never felt more ashamed than when he had to tell his uncle he'd been arrested for aggravated robbery.

"Is your uncle on your dad's side of the family?"

"No, he's my mom's brother."

"So, where's your mother? Is she one of the family members you don't associate with?"

Grant felt the familiar ache in his heart, and he broke the parole officer's gaze, looking down. "No, sir. She's, uh, dead."

"Oh."

"She died when I was twelve, from pancreatic cancer."

"Pancreatic cancer?" Jerry repeated. "How long was she sick?"

"Not long—a couple of months? The doctors said it was one of the deadliest cancers. Back then, anyway."

Jerry frowned, feeling a kinship with the man across from him. So, his own mother probably had only weeks left. Almost twenty years after Madsen's mother's death, pancreatic cancer was still one of the deadliest.

During the awkward silence that ensued, Jerry glanced down at the parolee's file, trying to move on. "Lucky for you, your drug test from last week was negative. What do you have to report to me today?"

Also eager to venture into happier territory, Grant proudly announced, "I got a job!"

"Well, la-dee-dah, Madsen!" Jerry grumbled, mocking the parolee's exuberance. "Aren't you happy with yourself. What kind of job?"

His enthusiasm taken down a notch, Grant reported stoically, "It's with Eaton Tours. They run Chicago architectural cruises."

"And what do you do for them?"

"I hope to work my way up to chief navigator, but right now it seems I am chief toilet cleaner."

Jerry chuckled. "I need some evidence that you are gainfully employed, for your file." He reached into his desk drawer and extracted his business card. "Give this to your boss and have him fax me a letter verifying your employment."

"Yes, sir." Grant pocketed the card. "His name is Roger Eaton."

"And where are you living?"

"I'm staying at Mr. Eaton's apartment for now, sir."

"You're living with your boss?"

"Yes, sir. Mr. Eaton is my uncle's old Navy buddy."

"Ah, that makes sense."

"But he snores like an outboard motor, so I'm hoping to get my own place when I can afford it."

Jerry noted Eaton's address in Madsen's file. "All right. Good job, Madsen. See you here next week."

Rising from his chair, Grant nodded. "Thank you, sir."

Back in the hallway, the woman Grant had met was nowhere to be found. How would he get his jacket back? Joe had bought him that jacket as a reminder of their days of attending White Sox games together. Rubbing his hand across his shorn hair, Grant found himself desperately hoping to see the blond beauty next week. He needed to retrieve his jacket! Or not. Who was he kidding? He simply wanted to see her again.

6. In Treatment

Sophie glanced nervously around her, eyeing the homey furniture and magazines strewn across the end tables in the small room. Another woman sat in the chair across from her—another client awaiting her therapist. Sophie felt her cheeks flush with embarrassment. She did everything she could to avoid eye contact with the woman.

So, this is what it's like to sit in a psychologist's waiting room. No wonder her clients had appeared so apprehensive when she retrieved them from her own waiting room for the first time. The ignominy of needing professional psychological help was enough to make anyone want to hide. She stared at the gray speckled carpet, anxiously rehearsing her answers to questions she might face.

"Sophie?" She looked up to see a clean-cut man with tanned skin and short blond hair looking her way.

"That's me." She grabbed her handbag and the black athletic jacket from the chair next to her. Clutching the jacket calmed her, and she stood, facing the man with whom she was supposed to share all her secrets.

His warm hazel eyes crinkled as he smiled, and he shook her hand firmly. "I'm Dr. Hunter Hayes."

"Hi, Hunter."

He paused. "Feel free to call me Hunter, by the way."

Sophie winced.

Grinning, he said, "Please follow me to my office."

As he turned to walk down the hall, Sophie noticed they were roughly the same height. She wondered how old he was. He looked about thirty-five, but he also appeared to take good care of himself. His broad shoulders tapered into a lean waist, indicating he was likely a frequent flyer at the gym. His casual black shirt and jeans helped Sophie feel slightly more at ease.

Hunter led her into his office, and Sophie was immediately drawn to the huge aquarium set into one of the walls. She placed a slender hand on the glass, mesmerized by the colorful fish peacefully swimming in lazy patterns. "This aquarium is beautiful."

"Do you like it?" He stood by a chair, waiting for his client to step over to the sofa. "My partners in the group practice were a little dubious, but I'd like to think it works."

Sophie nodded, and noticing him still standing, politely waiting for her, she gracefully took a seat on the sofa.

"The fish seem to provide a soothing presence for my clients," Hunter noted as he took his seat.

"What a great idea. Oh, look, a Nemo fish!"

He chuckled. "Ah yes, my percula clownfish. Let me go over a few things with you before we get into it, Sophie. Looking over your paperwork..." She feigned interest while he launched into a description of confidentiality, as if she didn't know the laws governing privacy and duty to warn for psychologists. But her focus sharpened when he added, "Apparently I'm supposed to report your attendance and progress to your parole officer?"

"Yes," Sophie confirmed, adding uncomfortably, "Officer Jerry Stone."

"Okay, then, I'll need you to sign this release of information form, giving me permission to speak to Officer Stone."

"What exactly do you have to share with him?" she inquired warily, taking the form and pen he offered to her.

"The POs never want the details," Hunter responded. "They're too busy. I just need to tell him whether or not you attended and provide an overall sense of how we are progressing toward therapy goals."

Sophie reluctantly scrawled her signature, barely managing to avoid adding a "PhD" at the end of her name. She still had her doctorate, but the degree was useless for practicing psychology without her license.

"So," Hunter began, settling back into his chair and preparing to take notes as they chatted. "Have you ever been in therapy before?"

"No." Her graduate program had encouraged students to obtain their own therapy as they learned to become therapists, but Sophie never had the time or the inclination. Perhaps she should have taken her professors' advice. Perhaps she could have avoided this whole mess if she'd done some work on herself before delving into the problems of others.

"You must be nervous, then, not knowing what to expect." He smiled warmly.

You don't know the half of it.

"Therapy is basically a conversation. I'll be asking lots of questions today, and you answer them to the best of your ability. It's okay to 'pass,' and it's okay to ask *me* questions. Were you mandated to attend therapy as part of your parole?"

"Mm-hmm." She nodded, tight-lipped.

"Well, that Officer Stone must be some kind of jerk to force you into therapy, huh?"

Sophie looked up, startled. "He's not really a jerk. He's just doing his job. The truth is I probably need therapy. I made a colossal mistake, and I need to figure out why so I can prevent making another…" Her voice trailed off, and she eyed her psychologist suspiciously, gleaning sudden insight into his techniques.

Oh, he was good. He'd just made her argue that she needed and wanted to be here, despite the mandate.

"You made a mistake?" he repeated curiously, his pen poised above the file in his lap.

Sophie raked both hands through her strawberry-blond hair and sighed. "Thank you for explaining what therapy will be like," she began. "But I'm actually a psychologist myself. Well, I *was* a psychologist…before I went to prison and my license was revoked."

He cocked his head to one side, intrigued. "Really? You were a psychologist? Where did you go to school?"

"Undergrad at Northwestern and grad school at DePaul."

His interest was further piqued. "And your pre-doctoral internship, where did you complete that?"

"At a VA hospital in Virginia." She studied the clownfish, darting in and out of the coral in the tank.

"Huh, I went to U of I. I wonder if we know some people in common. What year did you get your PhD?"

Sophie wasn't quite in the mood to schmooze about her past life. "In 2004."

Hunter rubbed his cheek pensively. "Do you know Chris Dowd? He went to DePaul."

She shook her head.

He glanced at her smooth, alabaster skin and long, toned legs clad in youthful navy shorts. "Oh, he was probably before your time. I'd already been practicing ten years by the time you graduated."

Her mental calculations put his age near forty. At least she was getting an experienced psychologist.

"So, you were a psychologist, but you were never in therapy yourself?"

"I never had time. I was trying to hold down another job in addition to classes, research, and practicum. Even with the extra job I still came out with some hefty student loans."

"You're in a lot of debt?"

"Yeah, about sixty thousand dollars' worth. Officer Stone told me I need to get a job soon, but I have to find something that pays well enough, or I won't be able to make my loan payments."

"Can't your parents help you out?" Hunter asked casually.

Sophie froze, shame clenching in her chest. She recalled her father's cold stare at her mother's funeral, his frosty blue eyes laying blame that sliced through her like an icicle. Then an earlier memory emerged of those same eyes filled with fury when she was only nineteen years old. Her father had screamed incessantly upon discovering her plans to study psychology instead of joining him in the family construction business. He had groomed her for years to be his protégé, but she wanted nothing to do with his world. *You ungrateful girl! You want to be some namby-pamby shrink? You're on your own, then!* Shocked by his words, she had fled their house, vowing never to return.

Hunter carefully studied the beautiful young woman, whose sorrow was evident. She eventually returned his gaze and feebly requested, "Can I pass on that question?"

"Of course," he nodded. She seemed relieved to be given a reprieve.

Glancing down at his notes, Hunter cleared his throat. "Let's see…I got us off track a bit. You were saying you made a huge mistake?"

She worried what might happen if she continued to evade his questions. How many passes would he allow? She had to share the reason she went to prison or she would never begin to heal. Hunter seemed trustworthy enough.

"It was about two years ago. I had just passed my licensing exam, and I was thrilled that I no longer had to report to a supervisor. Well, thrilled and a little nervous, I guess. Anyway, I was renting office space over on State Street, trying to start a practice. But insurance companies were giving me a hard time, and it was tough to get clients."

"Insurance companies giving you a hard time?" he asked, a twinkle in his eye. "Say it ain't so."

Sophie gave a wry smile. "Going to battle with managed care is one thing I do *not* miss about being a psychologist, that's for sure." She swallowed hard before she continued. "You can imagine my relief when I picked up a client who said it was no problem to self-pay. He said he didn't have health insurance anyway. He was in a similar situation as I find myself now—mandated by the court to attend therapy. He had a gambling addiction that got him into trouble." Sophie recalled the flutter in her heart upon meeting him.

He had strode confidently into her office, wearing a tight royal-blue T-shirt that showcased the musculature of his arms and chest. On the tall side of six feet, he was a formidable presence. Sophie could not help but allow her eyes to drift down the length of him, taking in his dark jeans and black boots.

"Dr. Taylor?" his deep baritone rang out in the room. She glanced up at his cavernous cerulean eyes, hardened and mysterious. His jet-black hair bled into the stubble of a five o'clock shadow lining his chiseled jaw. The man exuded sex.

"Yes, it's Sophie," she corrected, offering her hand.

He grasped it and shook robustly, causing the muscles of his forearm to contract and ripple. He looked her in the eyes as he introduced himself.

"Logan Barberi."

"Barberi?" Hunter repeated. Sophie flinched, reorienting herself to the present. "The Barberi? As in the Barberi crime family?"

She smiled sadly. "That's the one. He's the son of Vicenzo Barberi. If only I had known."

Hunter appeared puzzled. "You didn't know his family was Mafia?"

"I didn't know! In my defense, Vicenzo was sentenced to life in prison when I was only seven years old."

"Oh, that makes sense." Hunter nodded. "But didn't you follow Angelo Barberi's trial? It was the talk of the town when he got off on a technicality."

Sophie shrugged. "That happened when I had just started grad school. Back then I didn't have time to sleep, much less follow the news."

Hunter continued writing, and he waited patiently for her to resume the story. She crossed her long legs and exhaled deeply, maintaining an elegant posture on the sofa. Her mind drifted back to her first meeting with Logan, as it had done so many times while sitting in her cell.

He had just told her his name, and she was drowning in the magnetism of those deep blue eyes. The timbre of her voice was tremulous. "Um, welcome… Please have a seat."

He eyed her appreciatively as he crossed to the sofa. "Damn, if I knew shrinks could be so pretty, I would have started this therapy thing long ago."

Backing unsteadily into her own chair, Sophie felt her cheeks redden, and she emitted a nervous giggle. Oh Lord, the physical attraction appeared to be mutual. It definitely seemed like the time to refer this client to another psychologist before they even started this charade of therapy. Instead, she found herself asking, "What brings you in today, Mr. Barberi?"

"It's Logan. None of that formal stuff. A judge, uh, ordered me to see you. I had a little, uh, incident, and they think I have a gambling problem."

Her mind, overwhelmed by his ferocious intensity, drew a blank. What would her supervisor tell her to say in this moment? *When in doubt, make an empathic statement. Reflect the client's feelings.* Sophie racked her brain for an appropriate response. "And you're angry about that, Logan? You don't think you have a gambling problem?"

He exhaled derisively. "A problem implies lack of control. I'm always in control of my bets. I know what I'm doing."

"Fair enough," she responded, wanting to establish rapport before challenging him too much. "So, what was this 'little incident'?"

He looked around the small office, sizing it up. Taking in the bare walls and sparse furniture, he observed, "You haven't been in this office long."

"That's right, less than one month."

His leg jiggled nervously as he continued his visual scan. Abruptly popping off the sofa, he strode to the lone object on the wall: a framed document. Peering at the date on her psychologist's license, Logan turned to her and arched one eyebrow. "2006? You've been in this office about the same amount of time you've been a full-fledged shrink, huh? Only one month?"

Sophie nodded her head, and her throat felt dry. So she was green. A freshly licensed psychologist. So what?

He returned to his seat and shot her a disinterested smirk. "What the hell are we supposed to do in here?"

"Well, I'd like to get to know you better, Logan. Why don't you tell me a little about your family?"

"Oh, you know, they're … family. Nothing to talk about there."

Watching his eyes dart around the room, Sophie decided to try another tactic. "How about gambling then? What's your favorite game?"

He brightened immediately. He turned his deep-blue gaze back on her, and on her it stayed. "Blackjack," he responded. "It's got the best odds of any game at the casino, and I'm crazy good at it. Just yesterday I made seven thousand dollars."

Sophie raised her eyebrows. "That's a lot of money."

"Yep," he agreed. Of course, he neglected to mention that he had lost nine thousand dollars the day before. Logan winked and gave her a dazzling smile. "Maybe we could go gambling together some time."

Hunter did not allow his client to remain in her trance for long. "That was your mistake?" he asked. "Keeping Logan Barberi as your client?"

Sophie blinked and shook her head sadly. "No. My mistake was not keeping Logan Barberi as my client. My mistake was falling in love with him."

7. Man Overboard

Grant yanked the pillow from underneath his head and stuffed it over his face, unsure if he was just attempting to drown out the noise or actually suffocating himself. His feet dangled over the low armrest of the sofa in Roger's studio apartment, and he tossed and turned with every thunderous snore emanating from the man in the bed across the room.

Skaeeeeennnnng … hhuuuuuuhhhhh … skaeeeeennnnng … hhuuuuuuhhh …

How the hell could a human being make that sound? It seemed like a machine or some type of snuffling, feral animal. Grant groaned as he glanced at the alarm clock on the end table. Great. It was the freaking middle of the night.

"Rog!" he stage-whispered, and was rewarded with even louder snores. Grant upped the volume, hissing, "Rog!" The clatter continued unabated. Next, he tried clearing his throat loudly, his raspy coughs filling the space between snores. However, nothing could stop the Roger Roaring Rumble.

Finally, Grant sat straight up and grabbed a heavy naval navigational manual from the bookshelf. He held the thick book high above the hardwood floor and bit his lower lip. Should he be so cruel? Then the *skaeennnnggg* noise resumed. Grant shot his boss a hostile glare and determinedly let the book fall. The hardback manual seemed to drop in slow motion and caused a deafening *thwap* when it finally hit the floor.

Blessedly, the snoring stopped, but Grant froze when Roger seemed to awaken for a moment, clearing his throat and sighing. The rotund man then rolled over to his side, and Grant closed his eyes with hope for at least a temporary reprieve.

Falling back on his pillow and drawing the blanket over him, Grant settled in contentedly until he heard his boss growl, "Madsen, did you just make a loud noise?"

Grant paused a second before admitting, "Yeah."

"Was I snoring?"

"Uh-huh."

"Well, just tell me to roll over, you fucker! Don't scare the bejesus out of me like that!"

"Yes, sir."

"And quit calling me 'sir' when we're on land! You're driving me crazy with that shit!"

"Okay, um, Rog."

Repositioning himself on the sofa, Grant tried to relax and get some shut-eye before Roger began again. Grant mentally challenged him to a race. Who could fall asleep first? He was determined to win and enter dreamland before Señor Snore resumed conducting his mariachi band.

❧

The next morning a sleepy Grant somehow found the energy for his daily run, which he'd begun taking along Lake Michigan. He loped along easily, watching the city wake up around him, the rising sun accompanying the rising hum of traffic along Lake Shore Drive. He crossed paths with mothers guiding baby joggers, elderly men out for a stroll, and serious marathoners pounding out the miles in a fast, steady cadence. Grant felt exhilarated to be part of this bustling city scene. He sloughed off his fatigue and managed four miles before heading back to Roger's place.

The smell of sausage sizzling on the stovetop greeted him as he entered. Roger was kicking back his last sip of coffee while using a fork to turn over a link, and he looked up to find Grant watching him cook.

"S'okay if I take a shower?" Grant asked, sweat dripping off his nose.

"Sure, I'm all done in there." Then Roger added, "I made us some breakfast. I'm heading to the ship early, but I'll leave some out for you."

Touched by the gesture—a peace offering, perhaps?—Grant suppressed a grin. "I thought you said, 'This ain't no fucking bed and breakfast'?"

"Yeah, well, don't get used to it, kid," Roger replied, returning his attention to the frying pan.

A few minutes later, Grant reveled in the steaming shower. He closed his eyes and inhaled deeply, feeling rivulets of hot water cascade down the length of him, loosening and relaxing his tired muscles. It was sheer heaven to linger in a private shower. After twenty-six months of brief community showers that were never safe—whether the threats came from predatory cons or the Mafia thugs supposedly protecting him from said cons—he would never take showering as a free man for granted again.

Grant stepped out and was greeted by silence. He wrapped his lower body in a towel, tucking in the white terrycloth rectangle at his hip, and stood at the sink to shave. As he scraped the razor down his chin and then rinsed the blade under the spigot, he studied his reflection.

Although he was only thirty years old (and was often told he could pass for twenty-five), to his own eyes he looked old. He had aged considerably during those two years in prison. He could identify traces of weariness, cynicism, and regret in his face, and he did not like what he saw.

He missed his days in the Navy, when life was orderly and neat, when things made sense. Right now he was a man thrown overboard, thrashing and desperately striving to stay afloat in the unfamiliar and stormy sea.

After smoothing on some aftershave, Grant dressed in the navy-blue jumpsuit that was his uniform for the ship. Wearing a uniform was one thing that had not changed in about twelve years, ever since he started in the Navy Reserve Officer Training Corps in college.

Making his way to the elevated counter at the end of the small kitchen, Grant pulled up a barstool and grinned at the plate of eggs, sausage, and toast, covered with plastic wrap. Roger acted all tough, but these little acts of kindness confirmed his softer side.

Grant sat still for less than two seconds before popping off the stool and heading for the bookshelf, carefully sliding out a hardcover book: *Chicago Architecture and Design*.

He carried the book back to the bar and sat down as he thumbed through the pages to find his place. Resuming his reading, he happily stuffed a forkful of eggs into his mouth and continued learning about Millennium Park.

While cleaning during the cruises, Grant listened intently to Roger's description of each architectural marvel for the enraptured audience. After only two weeks on the job, he had already memorized most of his boss' spiel, and he enjoyed finding factoids in the book that Roger failed to mention. He was particularly fascinated by the newly constructed park in downtown Chicago—

perhaps because he was consumed with constructing and repairing his own internal structures, trying to build a new life.

∴

It was 10:45 when Grant made it to the ship. He was fifteen minutes early for his shift, but according to Navy standards, he was right on time. Clouds had begun to obscure the sun, and it was chilly by the water on this early-June day. A swift breeze kicked up off of the river, causing Grant to shiver as he stepped onto the deck. The Windy City was earning its name.

Failing to locate his boss, Grant descended the stairs and went to the supply closet for the bucket and mop. Quietly wheeling the yellow bucket toward the pump room, steering with the long handle of the mop, he halted as Roger exited the head and almost ran into him.

"Madsen!" he boomed. "I was just thinking about you."

"Yeah?" Grant asked nervously.

"I just thought of something. Your mom was Joe's sister?"

"Yeah, what about it?"

"Joe Madsen is your uncle? Your mom's brother?"

"Uh-huh."

"Then why is your last name Madsen? Shouldn't you have your dad's last name?"

Grant froze. His name, of course, had been Barberi before Joe had legally adopted him upon his mother's death.

Attempting to cover his consternation, Grant drummed up a look of incredulity. "I've been working for you more than two weeks, Rog, and you're just realizing this now? No wonder you never advanced past ensign. You're not too bright, are you?"

Roger's jaw dropped, and a twinkle gleamed in his hazel eyes. "You little prick," he said fondly.

Grant smirked. At first he'd been upset that Joe changed his name. But later, when he came to understand the horrific acts perpetrated by his family, Grant realized it was one of the kindest things Joe had done for him. If only a legal name change could also disentangle him from the emotional ties to his family.

Grant met Roger's gaze and his slight smile faded. "Joe adopted me after my mom died. And it was fine with me. My dad, well, he's not a good man." He looked down and sniffed.

"I'm glad you have your Uncle Joe, then," Roger said, his heart going out to Grant.

"Me too… Well, I better get to the head, now that you just trashed my clean bathroom. Is it going to smell like a bomb went off in there?"

Roger chuckled. "Actually, Madsen, I've got another job for you in mind. Put that stuff away. Tommy is going to be cleaning the shitters today."

Arching his eyebrows, but not about to refuse, Grant did an about-face and began wheeling the bucket back to its home, while his boss fell in step with him and explained. "That faggy young kid, Blaine, I got working as server—what the fuck kind of name is that? Anyway, he can't work anymore because his family is going to Paris or something for the summer. That lucky rich shithead just up and quit on me, so I want you to take over for him up top."

"Yes, sir," Grant nodded, closing the door to the supply closet.

"You know how to play waiter?"

"I think I can figure it out, Rog."

"Good. That grungy jumpsuit has gotta go, though. Hightail it to the office and get yourself a waiter's uniform."

"Okay." Grant followed Roger's order and emerged from the office ten minutes later looking dapper in black pants and a white shirt. Hopefully this was the next step up the ladder to chief navigator. And in the meantime, serving drinks simply had to be better than cleaning toilets.

"May I take your drink order, ma'am?" Grant asked, peering down at a middle-aged woman in a low-cut blouse sitting on one of the benches on deck. An eight-year-old boy, likely her son, jumped up and down at the nearby railing in a hyperkinetic frenzy.

She glanced up at Grant with a harried expression, planning to dismiss him, but paused once she saw his aquamarine eyes and tall, lean body. A brilliant smile bloomed on her bright-red lips. "Well, yes. Yes you can," she replied coyly. "My *ex*-husband tried to tell me never to drink alcohol before five p.m., but screw him. I'll take a chardonnay."

"One chardonnay," he repeated, scribbling the order on his notepad. The woman had scooted her body closer to his and was batting her eyelashes. Grant blushed uncomfortably.

"Would your son like a drink too, ma'am?"

Her smile faded, and she turned to the boy in a Chicago Cubs baseball hat. "Henry! Do you want a Coke?"

The freckly boy remained perched on the second rung of the white railing, but nodded his head distractedly.

"Uh, he's not allowed to climb on that railing, ma'am," Grant warned.

"Henry!" the woman scolded. "Get down from there right now."

The boy reluctantly climbed back onto the deck, whining, "This cruise is bore-ring, Mom!"

"Shh," she admonished. "People are trying to listen to the man on the speaker!"

Grant took advantage of the distraction to slink away, relieved when his exit went undetected. He then relayed the order to the bartender, Dan, who filled it all too quickly. Grant barely slowed down when he returned to serve the drinks, swiftly moving on to take the next order. This was only the first cruise of the day, but after filling drink orders for more than thirty passengers, his new job was already getting old. However, he reminded himself, it was still vastly better than prison.

A short time later, the cruise was headed back to the dock. The last drink order had been filled, and Grant had finally earned a little respite from his duties. He stood by the stern, gazing out into the blue-green water. The ship's engines left a churning trail behind them, and the steady hum and splashing lulled his mind into a peaceful state. The temperature on deck was at least ten degrees cooler than on land, and he shivered slightly. This would be a good day for his White Sox jacket.

His jacket. As he had so many times in the past few days, he remembered those gorgeous mahogany eyes gazing at him, warning him to take off his Sox gear before meeting with Officer Stone.

Her full, pink lips—inherently kissable lips. Her tall, lithe body with legs that stretched for miles—an irresistibly huggable body. Would he ever have the opportunity to get beyond their brief snatches of conversation in the courthouse hallway? He knew one activity she might enjoy: a baseball game. She was a Sox fan too.

The affectionate glow in Grant's eyes darkened as he thought of the first White Sox game he'd ever attended. He'd been eight years old—just him and his Uncle Joe, sitting up high, far above the field.

His uncle's invitation came only two weeks after his father began serving a life sentence at Gurnee, leaving Karita, Logan, and Grant Barberi to fend for themselves. Determined not to have her sons follow in their father's criminal footsteps, Karita had promptly moved them north of Chicago to her brother Joe's apartment at the Great Lakes Naval Base. Unfortunately, Logan refused to get on board with the change, challenging Joe's authority at every turn.

Between innings, young Grant had inquired, "Why can't Lo come to the game with us? Is he in trouble for running away?"

Joe peered down at the dark-haired, blue-eyed boy, kicking his skinny legs up and down in the black metal stadium chair.

"Logan is not going to stay with us for now," Joe explained.

"What?" Grant's voice trembled, and he blinked rapidly.

"He's going to live with his godfather, your Uncle Angelo."

"That's where he went last night?"

"Yes. Your mom tracked him down at Angelo's house this morning." Joe sighed. "Logan decided he'd rather live there. But your mom and I want you to live on the base, with us. You'll be safe on base."

The crowd roared as the White Sox pitcher struck out the third batter in a row. Grant was silent for several moments before he asked, "Doesn't Lo like me?"

"Oh, Grant, it's not your fault," Joe reassured him. "Your brother loves you. If there's anyone he doesn't like, it's probably me. I was pretty hard on him."

Joe glanced down lovingly at his younger nephew. Grant seemed awestruck by the sights and sounds of a major league baseball game. "We'll have to make it without Logan, all right? That means you and I can go to lots of Sox games, just the two of us."

Grant appeared pensive. "I'm sorry. I shoulda heard Lo leave our room last night."

"It's okay. Your mom didn't hear him either."

"Is Mom mad at me?" the little boy asked.

"Not at all." They sat in amiable silence, watching the game, before Joe added sternly, "Just don't ever let me catch *you* smoking, Grant."

He looked at his uncle with fear, nodding slowly. Joe reached out to hug him but pulled back with surprise when Grant visibly flinched at his approaching arm.

"I just wanted to give you a hug!"

"Oh – oh—okay." Grant nodded and allowed himself to be drawn into his uncle's arms. Joe was overcome by sadness as he held Grant, rocking him a bit.

Thirty-year-old Grant still remembered the feel of his uncle's strong arms that day—a sense of safety he'd never felt before. Far off in the distance he heard the cries of a young boy, echoing in his mind like his own helpless, abandoned whimpers. The fearful sounds became louder, and Grant snapped out of his trance to see the alarmed faces of ship passengers all around him at the railing.

"Somebody get him!" a man yelled.

"Henry!" a woman screamed. Grant followed the sound of abject panic and saw the chardonnay lady wildly waving her arms, staring at the river below. Grant trained his eyes on the water and was horrified to see the boy thrashing in the river, his small head bobbing precipitously, about to go under.

"Man overboard!" Grant roared, and without thinking, he climbed the railing and launched himself into the river.

The icy water sliced through him, but instinct and Navy training took over as he calmly swam toward the boy. The ship engines kicked off, and he inched closer to his rescue target in what felt like dead silence. The boy was sputtering and his eyes flashed with terror each time he was able to kick to the surface.

Almost there, Grant told himself as he took swift, sure strokes. His sopping clothing weighed down his arms, and he mentally kicked himself for failing to remove his shoes before he jumped into the water. He was a little rusty in Navy rescue techniques after two years in prison.

Finally he reached the boy, and he extended his strong arm, trying to rein him into a safe embrace.

"It's okay," he shouted. "Just relax. I got ya."

The boy frantically kicked and clawed before finally going limp in Grant's arms. He still appeared conscious, so Grant guessed he must be in shock. He treaded water with some difficulty, but kept them both afloat until Roger restarted the engines and navigated the ship closer to them. Tommy (who apparently used the commotion to take a break from Grant's former toilet-cleaning duties) tossed out a life buoy, which Grant retrieved, lifting the donut-shaped raft over the boy's head and encircling him in the floating device. Grant kicked and pulled them both toward the rope ladder that had been extended over the hull of the ship, and he carefully helped the young boy up before climbing the ladder himself.

Pulling himself over the gunwale, he heard the mother screech at her son, "Why in the hell did you jump off the boat?"

"My Cubs hat flew off my head!" he whined, his body shaking from the cold. "It went into the river, and I wanted it!"

His mother snatched the towel offered by a staff member. Wrapping her trembling son in the fluffy fabric, she placed her face within inches of his. "You ever try something like that again and I will *kill* you!"

Roger arrived on the scene, studying the soaking-wet white shirt clinging to his employee's chest. His eyes trailed down to the water dripping off Grant's black pants onto the deck below.

"You kept your shoes on, you idiot."

"Sorry." Grant grimaced, shaking water out of his ear.

Roger leaned in closer and whispered, "You just saved my ass, Madsen. Well done."

"Yes, sir."

"Looks like you're more valuable up here on deck. You'll never have to clean toilets again." Roger nodded, then turned on his heel and headed back to the bridge to guide the ship to the docks.

Grant grinned as Tommy handed him a towel. Maybe the man overboard had just swum closer to shore.

8. Forty Percent

Was she having a heart attack?

Sophie had trouble getting air as she paused outside Officer Stone's door. Her throat constricted with fear, and the dull pain in her chest sent waves of alarm coursing through her body. Had her mother felt this way prior to her heart attack? Would Sophie soon be seeing her mother again? She grasped the blurry frame of the metal door in front of her, maintaining a white-knuckled death grip as black spots danced before her eyes.

Wait a minute. Tightness in her chest? Racing heart? Fear of dying? This was no heart attack. This was an attack of another kind: a *panic* attack.

She'd come close to experiencing this heart-pounding panic in prison several times, but now she knew what a full-blown attack felt like. She suddenly felt complete empathy for her past panic disorder clients, who had tried to describe how terrified they felt, sensing impending death as their bodies broke down before their very eyes. Now she felt for herself their subsequent embarrassment upon realizing their bodies were quite fine. They had simply conjured up the physical symptoms in their minds.

What was the intervention for a panic attack? Oh, right—deep breaths. Sophie forced herself to inhale slow, strong gulps of oxygen, trying to reverse the quick and shallow breathing of her state of panic. Feeling her shoulders sag as she began to relax, she tried to clear her mind. *It's okay. It's only panic. Nobody has ever died from panic. Just breathe and talk yourself through it.*

She had no more time. She had to face her PO. She wasn't ready, but she had to do it.

Sophie forced her trembling hand upward and knocked on the door. Regrettably, she heard Officer Stone's immediate response, hollering for her to come in. Fighting the urge to flee, she swallowed hard and entered the shabby room.

"What's wrong?" Jerry asked as soon as she walked in.

She gave a tight smile and sat down gracefully, tucking one long leg behind the other.

Observing her trembling in the chair, Jerry repeated, "I asked what's wrong with you, Taylor. Spill it."

Sophie couldn't look him in the eye and instead kept her gaze glued to her hands. She finally mumbled, "I don't have a job."

"What? I couldn't hear you."

She lifted her gaze and locked her eyes on his, a trace of defiance mixed with her hopelessness. "I haven't found a job."

Jerry's jaw jutted out and his face hardened. "This is our third meeting," he growled. "I told you to get a job in two weeks or you would return to prison."

She nodded. "Yes, sir."

A palpable tension hung in the air. Suddenly Jerry popped up. The scraping of his chair against the cracked linoleum startled her even more than his menacing approach.

"Stand up, Taylor."

Her heart resumed its frantic thumping as she rose, stuffing her large handbag onto the chair behind her. He was right beside her now, the shiny handcuffs that swung against his belt reflecting the fluorescent lighting of the office. She felt the PO's thick hand grasp her lean bicep, and he roughly guided her to the wall.

"Spread 'em," he ordered, and she immediately placed her hands up and out against the wall, moving her legs apart as much as her beige skirt would allow. She tried to appear calm and composed, but her continued trembling revealed her fright. At least this time she knew what to expect, unlike the first surprise arrest in her therapy office. Sophie Taylor was returning to prison.

Jerry frisked her in a methodical and business-like manner, his stone face hiding his disappointment. He had thought this one might actually make it. But he had to follow through on the consequence for her parole violation. It was his job. He had no choice.

Unclasping the handcuffs from his belt, he drew one wrist from above her head down to the small of her back, feeling the tremor of fear in her body.

Encircling this wrist, then the other, with a cold steel manacle, he joined the two in a shameful binding. Unlike the large, burly men he typically had the pleasure of cuffing, Sophie's thin, delicate arms fit neatly behind her. She had dipped her head, and he wondered if she was crying.

"Have a seat," he commanded.

Sophie kept her head down, and they both sat on their respective sides of the desk. Jerry glanced at the panic button on the wall near his desk, for use if a parolee physically threatened him. It had been a few months since he'd pressed it, as the metal detectors at the courthouse entrance had greatly reduced attacks on parole officers. He still had a scar on his belly from a knife wound he sustained twelve years ago, though, and he could not allow himself to become complacent.

Suspiciously eyeing the docile woman across from him, he decided to use a less emergent means of communicating that he had a prisoner ready for transfer. He picked up the phone.

"Yeah, I've got a prisoner that needs to go back to Downer's Grove," he told whoever was on the other end of the line. Through a surreal fog, Sophie listened to him bark, "Well, don't make us wait too long. My next con is due in ten minutes."

He hung up the phone and gave her a stern glance. "Forty percent, Taylor."

She looked up at him with surprisingly dry eyes. Dry, hollow eyes. "Excuse me?"

"You told me you weren't returning to prison. You seemed determined to be in the forty percent who don't violate their parole. And I believed you."

"I'm sorry." She sensed his disappointment, and it made her feel even sicker. Kirsten was going to kill her. Sophie had not told her this was a possibility when she left for work this morning. She hadn't wanted to worry her, and there was nothing Kir could do anyway.

"What the hell were you thinking showing up today without a job? Did you think I would look the other way? Did you think you would just walk out of here?"

"No, sir." She felt his expectant gaze upon her, but what was the use of explaining? It wasn't like he cared. It was hopeless.

"I asked you a question," he prompted. "We have a few minutes before the officers arrive, and I want to find out how I was so wrong about you."

Reluctantly she began to speak. "Nothing was panning out, but I—I was waiting to hear from a hospital yesterday. I thought for sure I was going to get the job. They promised they would call. And then suddenly it was five, and they hadn't called, and human resources was closed. Yet another rejection. I didn't know what to do." Her expression turned sheepish. "I considered not showing up for our appointment."

He shook his head. "That would only have delayed the inevitable, Taylor. I would have been a hell of a lot more pissed off at you if you didn't show up."

"Yes, sir."

"I told you to apply for more jobs! Demeaning jobs, stupid jobs, scum of the earth jobs... anything to keep you out of prison."

"I did!" she insisted. "At least some jobs—I can't work for minimum wage because I have student loans to pay off, but I did apply for some! And they all told me I was overqualified."

"You're telling me that in this massive city, there was not one job you could find?"

"Yes, sir."

"Bullshit." She glared at him, and he added, "I think you *want* to go back to prison."

"No, I don't!" she shouted, then looked around, embarrassed by her display of anger. In a softer voice, she continued, "I don't want to go back. I just couldn't..."

"You couldn't what?"

She sighed. "I couldn't crawl back to my father and beg for a job."

"You could've gotten a job with your father this whole time? Why the hell didn't you?"

"Let's just say I don't want to work in construction."

Jerry sat thinking for a moment. "*That's* your father? Taylor? As in Taylor Construction?"

She smirked. "The very one. Will Taylor. Owner of the largest construction company in Chicago—in all of Illinois, probably."

"Are you sure you have a PhD? Because you might be the dumbest parolee ever to cross my doorstep! You're returning to prison instead of working for your father?"

Her eyes flashed with anger. "You don't know my father."

She couldn't hold in the tears in any longer. Why was Officer Stone arguing with her? She had acted unethically and unlawfully. She had selfishly brought on the death of her own mother. She was a horrible person. She should go back to prison. It was where bad people belonged. Where she belonged.

Tears slid down her cheeks, and frustratingly, she could not brush them away with her hands cuffed behind her back. Jerry averted his eyes, unable to watch her looking so broken.

"Maybe you're right," she muttered darkly. "Maybe I do want to go back to prison. We both know I can't make it on the outside." She exhaled derisively. "I can't even find a job. I'm a fucking felon."

Jerry was taken aback. Still puzzled by the woman across from him, he gently asked, "What is so bad about your father that you would choose to go back inside instead of work for him?"

Sophie sniffed. "He hates me." *Sniff.* "He blames me for my mother's death. She died six months ago, when I was inside." *Sniff.* "She died because of the stress caused by her only child going to prison."

His chest ached upon hearing her explanation. He couldn't bear the death of yet another mother, not when his own mother was hanging onto life by the thinnest of threads. As Sophie continued to sniffle helplessly, Jerry plucked a tissue out of the box and walked around his desk, kneeling next to Sophie and raising the tissue to her face.

"Go ahead, blow your nose."

Her eyes registered surprise, and she felt simultaneously touched and mortified by his paternal gesture. Not knowing what else to do, she gave a dainty blow into the tissue, and he wiped her nose for her. "Well, I couldn't have you getting snot all over my officers," he gruffly explained, rising and tossing the tissue in the garbage.

Jerry folded his arms across his chest and sat on the edge of his desk. His tone softened. "How did your mom die?"

"Heart attack." Sophie looked down. "I almost had a heart attack myself coming to your office today. I knew I was going back to prison."

He gave her a sympathetic look. "I'm sorry about your mom."

His unexpected kindness, minutes after handcuffing her, started her tears anew. "Thanks." She took a few breaths before asking, "How is your mom doing?"

"Not good."

There was silence between them. "It gets easier," she offered. Neither of them believed her words.

"Maybe you should try to make peace with your dad, Taylor. I bet he misses you."

"He doesn't," she corrected. "He's never approved of me, my whole life." Sophie took a shuddering breath. "Jeez, I'm crying more than a psychotherapy client." She flashed a wan smile. "You're a pretty good psychologist, you know? You've got me telling you my family history, bawling like a baby. Your tissue technique could use a little work, though. It would be easier for your clients to wipe their own noses if their hands weren't cuffed behind their backs."

With a twinkle in his eyes, he said, "Well, I sure don't want to wipe any more snot off of you, so you better stop the waterworks."

"Sorry, I'll try."

Jerry could not believe what he heard himself say. "Maybe I'll let you wipe your own nose. Maybe I'll un-cuff you. *If* you go get a job *today* from your father."

Sophie gasped. "But I can't—"

"Taylor, don't be an idiot! Tell him if you don't get a job, you return to prison. I'm sure he won't refuse you. No matter what's happened in the past, no father could send his daughter back to prison."

"You – you—you'll give me another chance?"

"Against my better judgment, yes. But if I don't get verification that you are employed by five o'clock today, I'm putting a warrant out for your arrest."

She gulped. Getting released from the damn handcuffs did sound pretty good. After considering her less-than-stellar options for several moments, she finally gave in. "Okay."

"Stand up." He extracted a set of keys from his pocket and expertly unlocked the cuffs. Once she felt the cool metal leave her skin, she sobbed with relief, weeping into her hands.

"Jesus, Taylor, you're crying harder now that I've let you go?" He shook his head disdainfully. "Women."

❧

Nervously jiggling his leg in a seat outside Jerry's office, Grant's eyes widened as two uniformed police officers brushed past him and entered the office. What was happening? Was that woman going back to prison? No, it couldn't be! He hadn't even had a chance to talk to her.

Grant heard raised voices in the office. Then the voices quieted, and the officers bustled out the door.

"Can you believe that shit?" one hissed to the other as they strode past him.

"As if we've got nothing better to do!"

Grant rose, wondering what the hell was going on as he watched the departing officers dash down the hallway. He turned back to the PO's office, and suddenly she was there. She had just come out the door, and she was crying.

Her blond hair was swept up high on her head, accenting the splotches of pink on her alabaster cheeks and nose. A few tendrils had loosened from her ponytail to softly frame her face.

A small whimper escaped her lips when she noticed his expression of pure sympathy. Sharing such an intimate moment of emotional vulnerability, despite being virtual strangers, neither knew what to do.

Instinctively Grant gathered her in his arms. Sophie gratefully folded herself into his strong frame. She rested her cheek on his shoulder, feeling the comforting cotton of his navy-blue hoodie on her skin. His body was warm and solid and—God, he smelled good. His strong arms soothed away her tension and gradually slowed her tears.

Only then did Grant realize how inappropriate it was to just scoop an unknown woman into an embrace. She seemed to lean into him, creating a cocoon of coziness, but he had a fleeting worry that she might think he was some kind of aggressive pervert for mauling her with a hug. He was suddenly aware of her breasts pushing into his chest, and he abruptly let go of her for fear that parts of his anatomy would also be pushing out.

He glanced at his watch and shook his head. "Wait for me?" he pleaded.

She stared and then seemed to come to her senses. "Oh! You must want your jacket back." She patted her bag, "I have it in here."

"My jacket? No, I don't care about my stupid jacket. You're crying. You're upset, and I want to talk to you. Wait for me?"

Sophie nodded. "I'll wait for you."

With one last glance in her direction, he disappeared into the office.

"You're late, Madsen!" Officer Stone yelled as the door closed. Sophie hoped he wasn't in too much trouble. It was no fun to be in trouble with their parole officer.

Wiping her eyes, Sophie sank into the metal chair in the hallway. She realized how tired she was after her emotional freakout. She unzipped her bag and peeked in on the White Sox jacket folded neatly inside.

She sighed. That had been a close one in there, but she was determined to stay in the prison-free forty percent. Her mouth tightened as she thought about going to see her father. But first she would speak to the crystal-eyed parolee, and she did not dread that at all.

She drew her shirt collar to her nose and inhaled deeply, drinking in the transferred smell of his aftershave. Sitting up a little straighter, Sophie eagerly anticipated a real conversation with the man. There seemed to be a mystery behind those gorgeous blue eyes, and she couldn't wait to learn more about him.

9. CONvocation

After what seemed like an eternity, Grant finally exited his PO's office and was relieved to find the woman still outside, just as she'd promised. Her tears had stopped, and her cap-sleeved white blouse and beige skirt seemed less disheveled than they had ten minutes ago.

His face lit up. "You waited."

"Of course. I didn't want to steal your jacket two weeks in a row, 'cause then you might have to report me for a parole violation." Hearing the man chuckle, she added, "I hope I didn't get you in any trouble with Jerry."

Grant raised his eyebrows. "Oh, so you two are on a first-name basis now?"

Sophie smiled. "We ought to be after what we went through today."

"I was worried when I saw two bulls go in there."

"That was a close call. Fortunately, Jerry let me go after I started bawling like a baby." Shrugging sheepishly, she continued. "Sorry for subjecting you to that cry-fest. I must look like a mess."

He did not believe this strawberry-blond beauty was calling herself that. She could never look a mess. "Not at all," he reassured her. Clearing his throat nervously, he added, "Speaking of *Jerry*, of, um, first names … I'm—I'm Grant."

She was about to introduce herself when a scruffy-looking man approached the door. He gave them a suspicious glance before knocking and entering the office, and the couple suddenly felt awkward conversing right outside their PO's door.

"Want to take a walk?" Grant suggested, extending his arm toward the exit.

She nodded gratefully, and they strolled in amicable silence, emerging into the bright sunlight outside the courthouse.

Perching on one concrete stair, she extended her hand to him, and his long fingers enveloped her skin warmly. He glanced down at the silver rings on her delicate fingers, particularly attracted to the band on her forefinger. The unusual placement of the ring made her seem both tough and sophisticated.

She smiled pleasantly. "I'm Sophie."

"Nice to finally know your name, Sophie." He reluctantly released her hand. "I probably should have introduced myself before I attacked you with that hug earlier."

Gazing into his eyes, shining in the sunlight, she confidently informed him, "It was exactly what I needed. You, um, you give great hugs." More demurely, she whispered, "Thank you."

"Well, I owed you one after you warned me about our PO being a Cubs fan. If I'd worn that Sox jacket in there that day, who knows what would have happened … maybe those cops would have been coming for *me*."

Sophie grinned and reached into her bag to extract the jacket. "I think it's about time I give this back to you."

He took it from her gratefully. "M-maybe—" he stuttered, then ducked his head nervously before starting again. "Maybe we could go to a White Sox game together some time?"

He looked absolutely adorable when he was all anxious like that. Sophie shot him a bright grin. "I'd love that."

Grant beamed. Enraptured by her beauty, he barely registered what she told him next. But when she sat on the steps, smoothing her skirt beneath her, he finally understood that she had asked him to sit with her. He eagerly folded his long, lean body next to hers.

They basked in the warm morning sun for a few moments before Grant inquired, "Why did those cops come for you today, if you don't mind me asking?" Watching her react to his question with reddening cheeks and a dip of her head, he added, "You don't have to tell me if you don't want to. I just wanted to know if there was something in particular I needed to avoid so I don't return to prison myself." He stared off into the distance. "I can't go back there."

"It's okay," Sophie said with a sigh. "The truth is I haven't found a job yet. Jerry told me I would return to prison if I didn't get a job in two weeks, and stupidly I decided to test him on his word." Grant watched her rub her wrists absentmindedly.

"He handcuffed you?" Grant asked quietly, wrapped up in his own memories of cops and cuffs.

"Yes. I thought I was going back inside, for a whole year … I'm not sure I would have made it this time. But then I let it slip that my dad would probably hire me, and Jerry pounced on that. He told me if I got a job today from my father, he wouldn't arrest me."

Observing her face, Grant ventured, "I'm guessing you and your dad don't get along so well?"

Sophie snapped her head toward him, meeting his concerned gaze. "How did you know?"

"I know it would have to be quite bad for you to risk going back to prison."

"Really bad," she said. "My dad pretty much hates me, and he hasn't exactly been father of the year."

Grant sighed. It seemed that they had something in common besides rooting for the Sox. "My dad and I don't get along so great either."

Sophie nodded sadly and then mused, "I bet most convicts come from awful family backgrounds. Long family histories of dysfunction … It's like we never learned how to 'get along' in society, you know?"

Grant took in her comment and looked at her, as if he were seeing her for the first time. Not only was she attractive, but also intelligent and insightful. "Never really thought about it," he admitted. "But 'awful' describes my family perfectly."

Thinking about family dysfunction, Sophie's thoughts drifted to her mother. Laura Taylor had been a high-maintenance, emotionally needy woman who could drive Sophie crazy with her controlling personality, but she still missed her deeply. At least her mother acted lovingly once in a while, in contrast to her father's stern, cold demeanor. Feeling tears threaten once again, Sophie said, "Let's not talk about our families. Let's talk about something else."

"Okay."

Tentatively she asked a question that had been troubling her since she first encountered Grant. "Um, why did you go to prison?"

Grant was quiet for a few moments. "Well, if we're not talking about families, then I can't really answer that."

His gemstone eyes scorched her with an earnest intensity.

"Tell you what. Let's make a pact, okay? No talking about family, about prison, about why we were inside, about how long our sentences were. No questions that cons might ask each other. No talking about the past. I don't know about you, but I'd rather never think of the past again."

Sophie nodded vigorously.

Grant continued to outline his plan. "We're both trying to move forward, to rebuild our lives. Let's focus only on the future."

She continued to nod, secretly hoping this handsome man might somehow be part of her future.

"We'll concentrate on the future—starting today with getting you a job."

"Getting me a job?"

"Yep. C'mon, let's go."

Grant bounded down the stairs of the courthouse. Sophie stared after him. Should she follow? She didn't even know him. A nagging voice in the back of her head urged her not to trust this con, this criminal, this delinquent.

But she was a criminal too. Would she want others to refuse to give her a chance because of one mistake? Would she want others never to trust her again? Taking a deep breath, she jogged down the steps and into the taxi Grant had hailed.

℘

Grant paid the cabbie, and they stepped out at the Chicago River docks. Rays of sun bounced off the blue-green water in a dazzling array.

"You ever been on a Chicago architectural cruise?" Grant inquired.

"I always wanted to," Sophie said. "But like most Chicago natives, I never got around to it."

He grinned. "Here's your chance then." Grant stepped onto the deck gracefully and turned around, extending his hand and beckoning to her. She cautiously grasped his hand, and he guided her over the gunwale.

"Rog?" Grant called out. "Rog?"

"Well, hello," Roger boomed as he emerged from the bridge, eyeing the blonde who had just walked onto his ship. He stood up a little taller and tried to suck in his gut as Grant brought her over.

"Roger Eaton, I'd like to introduce you to Sophie, um …"

"Taylor," she supplied. "Sophie Taylor."

Obviously smitten as he shook her hand, Roger said, "You must be the prettiest passenger we've ever had on one of our cruises."

Sophie shot Grant a nervous glance and he interrupted. "Um, Rog? Sophie is not a passenger. She … well actually, she's looking for a job on the ship. We, um, met outside our PO's office, and I thought there might be an opening for a server on your cruise now that I'm doing navigation?"

"Madsen, what did I tell you about my business? About this ship?"

Grant cleared his throat. "Err, 'It ain't no fucking halfway house'?"

Sophie tried not to laugh as Roger confirmed, "Damn straight. You think just because you saved that kid's life you're now my goddamn human resources department?"

What was this about Grant saving a kid's life? Sophie wanted details, but before she could open her mouth, Grant responded.

"No, sir. I thought it might be good for business to have a beautiful woman serving drinks on your cruises, that's all."

Oh God, the Adonis had just called her beautiful! Sophie couldn't hide her pleasure, and there was a satisfied twinkle in Grant's eye as he watched her react to his comment.

Roger caught their subtle flirting and gazed at Grant with a newfound respect. She was one hot chick, and the fact that she'd served time made her even more mysterious. He glanced back and forth from one parolee to another, considering whether or not to hire the broad.

"You ever worked as a server before?" he asked.

She paused. "Sort of. I used to serve meals at a homeless shelter."

Roger raised his eyebrows. "Madsen, you brought me Mother Fucking Teresa?"

"Hardly," Sophie scoffed. "I doubt Mother Teresa was a convicted felon."

"True that," Roger agreed. "So, what other work experience do you have?"

"Um, not the kind that will be much help on a boat, I'm afraid." She wondered if she should be truthful. After Grant gave her an encouraging nod, she confessed, "I don't have much job experience because I was in school for a long time, um, studying to become a psychologist."

Rog's eyes bugged out. "A psychologist?" A huge grin erupted on his face. "You got yourself one smart chick here, Madsen. She's waaaay out of your league, sailor boy."

Grant was too absorbed in Sophie's apparent discomfort to take umbrage at his boss' insult. He held his breath, eagerly anticipating the conclusion of this job interview/interrogation.

Still grinning, Roger mused, "Hmm, a psychologist. Can you hook Madsen up with some sleep medication then? The boy doesn't sleep real well."

This last jab did not sit well with Grant, and his mouth dropped open in protest. "I can't sleep because of your snoring! It would wake a man from a *coma*!"

"Oh, it's not that bad!" Roger argued.

"I was a psychologist, not a psychiatrist," Sophie jumped in. "I did not prescribe meds. I did therapy." She blushed as she concluded, "It doesn't matter now, anyway. I lost my license when I went to prison."

Grant watched shame and disappointment color her cheeks. She had experienced many recent losses too, just like him: career, family, and dignity, to name a few. Attempting to lighten the mood, Roger countered dubiously, "I don't know about having a shrink around all the time. Are you analyzing me right now?"

Sophie rolled her eyes. She had despised telling people her profession because they would invariably make some inane comment about their own mental health, or in Roger's case, their apparent mental illness.

"How original," Sophie snidely remarked. "No, I'm not analyzing you. It would take a whole team of shrinks to figure out your crazy ass, and I simply don't have the time or energy."

Taken aback, Roger scrutinized her carefully.

"Wow, that's the first time I've seen him speechless," Grant observed. "Nice work, Sophie."

He turned to his boss. "You've made her suffer long enough, sir. Are you giving her the job or what?"

Roger exhaled slowly, rubbing his hand across his bald head. After a few agonizing moments in which Grant and Sophie exchanged anxious glances, the boss finally relented. "Shift starts in thirty minutes. Eleven to eight."

"Oh!" Sophie replied worriedly. "Thank you so much, Roger, but is it okay if I start tomorrow? I have an appointment I have to attend today at noon."

"What kind of appointment?" he asked suspiciously.

Finding Grant staring curiously at her as well, Sophie gulped. "Therapy. My PO is forcing me to see a psychologist once a week."

"A shrink gotta go see another shrink, huh?" Roger scratched his chin. "Are you gonna be late to work every Wednesday then?"

"Oh, no, sir, I can ask for an earlier appointment in the future. It's just too late to reschedule it now, and I have to make my session or I'm going back to prison."

Roger turned to Grant. "Did your PO force you to go to therapy too? You never mentioned that before."

Grant looked down and jammed his hands into his jean pockets, murmuring, "No, no therapy for me."

Sophie considered that Jerry must think she was a total nut job to single her out for treatment. "You're lucky then," she said.

Turning to Roger, Sophie uneasily inquired, "Could you please contact Officer Jerry Stone by five today and tell him you hired me?" She rummaged around in her handbag until she located Jerry's business card. Roger took it grumpily.

"Be here at ten-thirty tomorrow so you can complete some paperwork," he ordered. Roger narrowed his eyes. "If she screws up one smidgen, Madsen, I'm blaming you." With this warning, he abruptly turned and left the couple standing on the deck.

They stared at each other awkwardly until Sophie leaned back on the railing, taking in the spotless deck and gleaming metal of the ship. "So, um, what's the pay like for this job?"

"For somebody who used to be a doctor, it's not great," Grant admitted, stepping closer to her. "But it can be temporary to keep Officer Stone off your back while you look for something better. And I figure you can get lots of tips as a server."

"Oh? And why do you think I'd get lots of tips?"

Her question had its desired effect, and once again he looked nervous, stammering, "Uh, well, you know, um, you're quite attractive…"

She grinned. "I'm just giving you a hard time." Waves of relief coursed through Sophie, knowing she would not have to beg her father for a job. She leaned closer to Grant, catching a whiff of his bergamot scent, and her eyes flashed with mischief. "I bet the ladies tipped *you* very well when you were a server. They probably were all clamoring for the hot waiter."

A crimson blush crept up his neck. Grant swallowed and inched toward Sophie, feeling the urge to gather her in his arms once again.

Staring into his blue-green eyes, which reflected the same hue as the river at the moment, Sophie felt a deep sense of intrigue. Yet the reality of obligations and cautions also filled her mind, and she broke their gaze. "I better go," she said. "I have my stupid therapy appointment."

Then, looking back up, she added, "I cannot thank you enough for what you did for me today. Somehow you knew how hard it would be for me to crawl back to my father, and I am so grateful for your help with this job. I promise, I'll work hard, and I won't let you down."

"You don't have to promise me anything," he replied. "I'm just glad you're not going back inside. I would miss seeing you every Wednesday."

"Well, now we get to see each other more often than that. Like tomorrow, for example. I'll be here," she smiled. As she turned to go, she caught a glimpse of the black White Sox jacket hanging over the railing where he had left it. "Don't forget your jacket. You have a tendency to leave it places."

With that last piece of advice, she climbed onto the dock, and Grant watched her long, limber legs carry her away. He smiled as he headed toward the bridge. She said she would go to a baseball game with him! Even better, she would be working with him every day. He was quite proud of himself.

10. The Slippery Slope

What's been on your mind, Sophie?" Hunter began their second therapy session.

"Not much," Sophie replied breezily, pasting a smile on her face. She was resolute not to reveal too much, determined to tread carefully this time around. In addition, she felt a bit distracted. Her mind kept floating back to the man she'd just left behind on the ship. Grant's kindness had been astonishing, and she could not get over the compassion he'd shown to a stranger.

Hunter sat back in his chair. An awkward silence descended upon them. She averted her eyes from his hazel gaze and stared instead at the fish tank, observing Nemo swimming lazy circles around the fake coral of his enclosed aquatic home. Sophie felt similarly trapped at the moment.

Her gaze then traveled to the set of framed documents over Hunter's desk. She stood to get a closer look at his credentials, but then realized she was behaving exactly like Logan Barberi had during his first session with her—cagey and evasive, attempting to deflect the focus from client to therapist. She knew she must be frustrating the hell out of Hunter with her silence.

"Ten percent," she finally said, sitting back down.

"Ten percent?"

Numbers had always come easily to her. Whereas most psychology doctoral students barely survived the rigors of graduate statistics, Sophie had thrived in the class, impressing her professor so thoroughly with her math skills that he had asked her to tutor the following year's crop of students. Numbers were nice, neat, and tidy, unlike the messy ambiguity of people. Perhaps she should have taken her father's advice and become an accountant for his construction business. Surely she would find herself in a better life situation now.

"I was just thinking about something I learned in my Professional Issues class," she explained. "Ten percent of male therapists admit to having sex with their clients. Only one percent of female therapists report doing that."

There was a slight lift to Hunter's eyebrows. Of all the possible topics his client could begin with, this is what she selected. Was she coming on to him? "Were the male therapists heterosexual or homosexual?" he quietly asked.

"I don't think this study reported the therapists' sexual orientation," she said. Did he realize she knew he was gay? Sophie wasn't sure how to handle the situation.

Hunter began to speak and then faltered. Thank God he was out as a gay man in his personal life. He'd been out for fifteen years now, and it made life so much easier. Secrets could be quite destructive. However, he was not out to everyone professionally. He treated each client individually, only revealing his sexual orientation to particular clients, and only if it seemed clinically relevant to do so.

Was Sophie's comment a subtle way to test him about therapeutic boundaries? If she was a psychologist, had she perhaps heard about him being gay from a colleague? Deciding this situation warranted a disclosure, Hunter said, "Well, I definitely won't be in that ten percent when it comes to you then. I'm gay."

She met his eyes for one of the first times in the session and swallowed anxiously. "I know. It was the deciding factor in me choosing you off that list. Well, that, and I heard that you are very good at what you do."

"Thank you," Hunter responded. "Though I have certainly made my share of mistakes over the years."

"Haven't we all," Sophie said.

"I want to be a good therapist to you, Sophie," he said. "I sense that it's quite difficult for you to talk openly in here. Is there anything I can do to make you more comfortable?"

"You've been fine. I just … I … I'm just so mortified about what has gotten me here. I don't know if I can talk about it. I never imagined myself in this position … on parole after a year in prison, my career in ruins, on the other side of the couch …"

Ah, he thought. She had mentioned the study as a way to talk about herself. "You feel embarrassed to be in that one percent of female therapists?"

She sighed. "Precisely. Why couldn't I be like the other ninety-nine percent? I committed the cardinal sin of therapists. I exploited my power. I exploited my client."

"It sounds like he may have exploited you as well. Not many therapists spend time in prison as a result of falling in love with their client."

"Not many therapists fall in love with a Mafia kingpin," she countered. They sat quietly before Hunter broke the silence.

"Has he been bothering you since you got out of prison?"

A disgusted look crossed her face. "Apparently he's nowhere to be found. Logan conveniently disappeared right when I was arrested, and no one has heard from him since."

"Whoa. So, the man you loved betrayed you, and then left you alone to deal with the fallout?"

"Yes." She felt bile in her throat, a rage that crept up her body with advancing tendrils of hostility and helplessness.

"You must feel so angry and bitter, and totally paralyzed when you try to move forward—like there's no way to get closure with him disappearing like that."

"Exactly!" she replied. "I haven't had the chance to say one word to Logan since this all went down. He just … he just … *left* me. He screwed me over and then left me hanging."

Watching her breathing quicken and her jaw clench, Hunter asked, "What would you like to tell him, if he was right here in this room with you?"

Her face contorted with anger. "I'd say, 'How could you do this to me? You said that you loved …'" Abruptly she stopped. "What is this, the empty chair technique?"

"No techniques, Sophie. Just two people talking. Just two people trying to make sense of the past so that they can move on to the future."

She folded her arms across her chest defensively, and Hunter sighed.

"I know how hard this is, for a shrink to talk to a shrink. Therapy felt stupid and artificial at first for me too. I tried to 'out-therapize' my psychologist—attempting to identify his theoretical orientation and the techniques he was using—but I didn't get anything out of it until I let go and started to tell him my story without censoring myself every second. You were doing so well. Can you try to get out of your head a little bit?"

Sophie exhaled with frustration.

"You seem like a sharp, caring woman," he continued. "How did all of this happen to you? When you're ready, will you share it with me?"

Taking a deep breath, Sophie uncrossed her arms and fidgeted with her hands in her lap. One of the blue devil fishes darted up to the surface of the saltwater tank, then dived down to the rocks, appearing agitated for some unknown reason. Sophie wondered if the fish had signed contracts promising to maintain confidentiality. They must have heard quite a few shocking tales in their day.

Whenever she thought about Logan while wasting away in prison, it was always the same. In reverse chronology, she would feel the intense fury and sickening betrayal of that last phone conversation before the police barged into her office. Then her hot rage would morph into a fire of passion when the scorching stimulation of their initial sexual encounter flooded her body. But the pull of swirling emotions from their tentative first kiss was what stayed with her the most—the tenderness of his vulnerability revealed at last, the ache of empathy she felt for his wounds, the relief of turning to each other, comforting each other with their sensual touch.

It was that last memory that Sophie decided to share first.

"I'd been seeing Logan for about five months," she began, looking down at her lap. Hunter settled into his chair and waited for her to continue. "We were making zero progress in therapy, and the judge was expecting an update from me soon. I told Logan I'd have to be honest in my letter to the court—he wasn't attending Gamblers Anonymous meetings or participating in therapy—but he didn't seem concerned."

"Sounds tough to feel like you were pulling teeth every session, trying to help a client who didn't want to be helped."

"Yes. He was tough."

"Were you in love with him then?"

"No. I barely knew him." She pondered Hunter's question for a moment and then added guiltily, "But I was thinking about him a lot. I was having dreams about him—frustrating dreams where I was chasing him or something stupid like that, and I …" She blushed as she admitted, "I found myself wearing shorter and shorter skirts on the days of our appointments." She threw her arms in the air and then brought her palms on the side of her head. "God, I'm an awful person!"

Hunter watched her berate herself, mentally filing away that observation. "So, if your client wasn't talking, how did you spend the sessions?"

"There was awkward silence at the beginning, and it was painful. Time would drag by. I'd try every trick in the book to get him to talk, but nothing seemed to work. He kept asking me questions about myself that I would try to deflect, but a couple of times he wore me down and I told him a few things.

Then he would open up more, so I thought I'd found a way to get him to talk: reveal a little about myself, and get rewarded when he disclosed some personal information as well."

"What kind of information did you reveal?"

"Um, benign stuff at first, you know, my age, that I was an only child, that I was from Chicago as well…We got into some good discussions about White Sox players, and I thought I was finally building rapport with him.

"Then I somehow let it slip that I was trying to schedule lots of clients, and when he asked me why, I told him I had substantial debt from school loans. He seemed interested in that information. We ended up scheduling an appointment for one evening, and he wondered why I was free then, why I didn't have a date that night. Stupidly I told him I was single."

She glanced nervously at Hunter, assuming he was thinking she was the most horrible therapist ever. "The truth is I have the absolute worst luck when it comes to dating." Smiling, she added, "But maybe I'll save that for another session."

"I look forward to it." Hunter winked. "So, it sounds like your situation with Logan was the slippery slope."

"The slippery slope?"

"There was a good paper written a few years ago on therapists' ethical violations. The authors described how therapists never start off by saying, 'I'm going to have sex with my client and ruin everything.' On the contrary, the boundary violations start subtly, innocently, then insidiously grow into something more dangerous and illicit. The psychologist might reveal that he had just gone through a divorce, for example, which inadvertently tells the client he is hurting and available. Then the psychologist gradually reveals more and more about himself, and with each disclosure, the boundary between therapist and client grows fuzzier and fuzzier until it is completely breached."

"That about sums it up," Sophie nodded. "I never intended for things to go so far, but at some point, I felt helpless to stop them. And when I finally realized what had happened and tried to put a stop to it all, it was too late. I was in too deep. And the only way to try to climb back up the slope was to pay the consequences by going to prison."

"You were starting to tell me about a session five months into treatment," Hunter prompted. "Was that the top of the slope?"

She sat pensively for a moment and then replied sadly, "I had already started slipping down the slope by that point, I guess." She closed her eyes and remembered that September day almost two years ago.

The clock ticked loudly as they stared at each other in her sparsely furnished office. Logan wore a white T-shirt and faded jeans that showcased his lower body nicely. Sophie could not help but stare at that hard, gorgeous ass when he had crossed in front of her to sit on the sofa. The muscles of his forearms rippled each time he fidgeted, rubbing his solid thigh or scratching his thick neck nervously.

He had been letting his hair grow out from his summer buzz-cut, and the short, black spikes framed his tanned face handsomely. His mouth worked on a piece of gum, drawing Sophie's attention to his perfectly shaped lips—full, luscious lips surrounded by the black stubble of five o'clock shadow lining his square jaw. Sophie was occasionally rewarded for her vigilant adoration of those lips when he would flick his tongue out to lick them slowly.

"How did you spend your Labor Day?" she inquired.

The thirty-three-year-old client chomped his gum. "You got any kids?" he shot back.

Sophie hesitated. "No."

"Well, I do. I spent the day with my son."

"You have a son?" she asked incredulously. "You never mentioned him before. How old is he?"

More chomping. "Thirteen. No, fourteen. He just had his birthday in July."

"What's his name?"

"You and all your questions," he replied derisively. "Why do you need to know that?"

"What's the big deal, Logan?" She was becoming frustrated. "I just asked you your son's name, not the secret formula for cold fusion. Have you neglected to tell me that you're married too?"

He frowned. "No, I'm not married. Just incredibly stupid. This chick I was dating back when I was nineteen told me she was on the pill. What a damn lie."

Sophie was beginning to understand his difficulty with trust. "So, what did you do with your son on Labor Day?"

"You know, just hung out. Went to a barbecue. At my Uncle Ange's."

"That sounds nice."

He grunted in response.

Sophie bit her lip. "What kind of parent are you, Logan?"

"Dunno. Don't get to see my kid much. He's usually with his mom. I know I'm better than my parents at least."

"Oh? You think you had bad parents?"

He exhaled with disgust. "Do you think I'd be here if the answer to that question was no?"

"Probably not," she conceded. "How do you try to treat your son differently from the way your parents treated you?"

His jaw muscles flexed as he worked furiously on the gum, and he avoided her gaze. Apparently he was clamming up once again. Sophie sighed and re-crossed her legs, pulling self-consciously on her short skirt. The black skirt had seemed long enough when she put it on that morning, but the material kept riding up when she was seated.

They again sat in discomfited silence. Eventually Sophie offered, "Lots of people disagree with how they were raised. I hated how my parents fought all the time when I grew up. My mother is overbearing, and my father can be a complete jerk."

He took the bait. "No father is more of a jerk than mine."

Sophie tried to stay quiet, silently willing him to continue speaking.

After a beat, his deep voice added, "He's a prick of the highest order."

When he was not more forthcoming, Sophie prodded, "You want to be a better father to your son, then?"

His face clouded over with an unreadable emotion. "I know this much: I'm never going to rule by fear, like that prick did."

It was a curious phrase. Ruled what? "Your father 'ruled by fear'?"

Sophie tilted her head to one side, watching the alpha male across from her change his body posture right before her eyes. He seemed to shrink, his commanding presence shifting into a more submissive stance, the deep blue of his eyes growing stormy, a glint of fear floating in their deep-blue pools.

Suspecting she knew what was happening, Sophie took some calming breaths. She had worked with many trauma survivors at the VA hospital during her internship—men who had endured gruesome, life-threatening experiences while serving their country. When they began to tell their combat stories, some of them had displayed the same body language as Logan now did. Her voice was soft and gentle as she questioned, "Your father hurt you?"

The troubled eyes bore into her, stealing her breath away with their vulnerability.

"He tried to hurt me," Logan responded with feigned bravado, enraged by the tremor in his voice. "But I didn't let him."

She swallowed slowly, attempting to figure out a nonthreatening way to question him. "How old were you?"

"I was a kid, like nine or ten. He came home all pissed off about something. The littlest thing could set him off. Who knows what the hell had happened." Logan gave an involuntary shudder, then started muttering, "Fuck."

"It's okay, Logan. You can tell me."

"Why?" he challenged angrily. "Why talk about this shit?"

"Because talking about the past makes it have less of a hold over you."

She thought he had closed himself off again, and was surprised when he said quietly, "He started hitting my mother … slapping and punching her."

Sophie closed her eyes. "Did he do that a lot?"

"Yeah. Like I said, he was a fucking asshole." He breathed out disgustedly. "The kicker of it was that I hated my mother more than him. Hated her for being too weak to stand up to him, hated her for …"

"For failing to protect you?" Sophie asked.

Logan's eyes narrowed. "Well, I sure didn't protect her. I got my brother the hell out of there and we went and hid like total chickenshits."

"You were nine! Of course you hid."

She watched him tremble as he stared off into space, numbly reporting, "But my dad found us anyway. He, uh, he … he dragged us down the hallway … and he threw us in the closet. For all we knew our mom was lying dead in the family room. It didn't sound good."

He took a ragged breath, and Sophie kept quiet. "That's when he came at us with his belt. He was just whaling on us in the closet, and it stung like a bitch … it was so dark, and my brother was crying … and when I tried to cover my brother so he wouldn't get hit, my dad started screaming at me."

Logan clenched both fists and continued. "He yanked me off and threw me into my room. He kept coming after me with the belt until finally he got tired or something, and then he left me alone."

Logan held his head in his hands and rocked back and forth on the sofa.

"Your brother?" Sophie asked tremulously. "How old was he?"

"Four."

"Where was he that whole time?"

Logan stopped rocking and sat completely still, frozen in the past. She watched his body start to shake while he kept his head down.

"Logan?" she questioned gently. Then she noticed a tear fall to the floor, followed by another and another. Sophie almost gasped. It was so bizarre to see this pillar of strength break down into sobs. He tried valiantly to hide his crying. Not knowing what to do, she stood up, hesitated, fidgeted with her hands worriedly, then finally crossed the room and sat next to him on the sofa.

"It's okay," she encouraged, wringing her hands in her lap.

"Fuck," he said in a strained, tear-filled voice. He radiated intensity in the small office.

"Where was your brother?"

Logan cried quietly, his head bowed. When he finally spoke, his voice was hitched and raspy. "He was in that closet the whole damn night. My dad wouldn't let my mom get him out. He was in the dark, all alone, scared shitless. He was only four!"

Logan's fists clenched tightly once again. "The next morning my dad finally hauled him out of there. When he found out that my brother, uh, that h-he had peed in his pants … he started … he … fuck! Uh, he started beating the shit out of him."

Sophie realized she was holding her breath. Not only was a four year old treated like an animal, but a nine year old was forced to witness that treatment and experience brutality himself. Involuntarily she reached out and rested her hand on his forearm, steadying and stilling him beneath her warm, caring touch.

Suddenly Logan was kissing her. It happened so fast, so uncontrollably, so head-spinningly fervently, that she didn't have time to think. Those perfect lips were caressing her own, and she felt she had no choice but to accept his desperate, passionate advance. He had flayed himself open in front of her, he had prostrated himself, and now he needed comfort—comfort she was more than willing to provide. His kiss comforted her, too. She closed her eyes and melted into him, his strong arms grasping her and his tear-stained cheeks transferring wetness to the smooth skin of her face.

"And things were never the same between you," Hunter surmised, bringing her back to the present.

"What?" Sophie continued to feel disoriented by the wounded, haunted blue eyes burned into her memory.

"That was the first major boundary-crossing. There was no going back after you let him kiss you like that."

She tried to remember to breathe. "I guess not."

"Did you think about telling someone? Consulting with a colleague?"

"I thought about it. I thought about consulting. I thought about referring him." She averted her eyes. "I could have done any number of things, but I think I didn't want it to end. But it did finally end. With me in prison."

Hunter listened to her guilty confession and gave silent thanks that he'd never fallen in love with a client.

"I almost went back to prison today," Sophie informed him ruefully.

"What happened?"

"You know how I was supposed to get a job by today? Well, I didn't find one. My PO had me cuffed and ready to go. We were waiting for the police officers when he decided to give me another chance, as long as I, um, begged my father for a job. But then I lucked out and a man I met, another parolee, got a job for me on an architectural cruise. He was incredibly kind."

Hunter frowned slightly. "We are out of time, Sophie, but it sounds like we have a lot to discuss in our next session."

"You probably want to know about my father," she said.

"Yes. And this man that you met—it doesn't seem like such a good idea to be fraternizing with another parolee. I want to talk about this further."

She rose, silently disagreeing with his warning about Grant. Of course it was a good idea to "fraternize" with a man as handsome and kind as Grant Madsen. Her psychologist didn't realize that yet, but he would.

As she left the office, she mulled over the session in her mind. Boundary violations, self-disclosure, hot kisses, Logan, Grant. If Hunter ever had Logan or Grant as a client, perhaps he would be heading down the slippery slope as well. Those particular men just seemed irresistible.

11. Taking a Gamble

From the ship's bridge, Grant gazed at the pitter-pattering raindrops splashing into the river as the architectural cruise made its way through increasingly choppy waters. He loved the suspended hush at the start of a storm, the skies emitting tiny drops of condensation before unleashing a torrent of water.

It was the five o'clock Wednesday cruise, and the sunshine of the morning had morphed into a cloudy afternoon. Grant hoped the storm would pass through completely before Sophie's first day at work tomorrow. Storms meant sparse crowds and meager drink tips.

"Straight ahead is the Trump International Hotel and Tower," Roger's gruff voice explained to the few passengers huddled amidships on the lower deck, seeking cover from the impending weather. The captain sat just a couple of feet from where Grant stood, and his ridiculous microphone headset continually made Grant chuckle. He looked like Madonna in concert, and Grant kept waiting for Rog to Vogue.

"Construction of the tower began in 2005, and they're making the finishing touches as we speak. The hotel portion opened in January.

"Initial designs for the building were not well received, but they finally agreed on the stacked boxes concept, which evokes an image of a commerce ship steaming through the city. The various tiers were designed to match the height of neighboring buildings, helping the new building fit in nicely with the skyline."

As expected, the rain began falling harder, partially obscuring visibility from the bridge. Grant powered down the engines to a safer speed in the storm.

Sensing the change in knots, Roger, ever the adept performer, stretched out his commentary. "As I was saying, the level of each tier in the Trump Tower matches the height of neighboring structures. That's probably one of the first times in his life that the shark, Donald Trump, has tried to get along with his neighbors."

It was a lame joke, and Grant was glad he was unable to hear the groans from the passengers. Some of Rog's jokes hit the mark, but others fell flat with a resounding thud.

They continued their journey on the Chicago River, and Grant was mesmerized by the sound of steady drizzle and water lapping on the ship's hull. Entering a melancholy trance, the sound drew him back to a summer day when the rain had similarly cascaded down on Chicago.

He had knelt beside her grave numbly, barely aware of the pelting raindrops on his shoulders and back. His khaki Navy uniform had become drenched, but the military forbade the use of umbrellas. Not that he cared anyway. It seemed fitting to match his emotional misery with the physical discomfort of getting soaked to the bone.

Grant placed a bouquet on the wet grass—jasmine, a flower that signified grace and elegance. There was no better way to describe Karita Ann Madsen. His mother had a noble air about her, carrying herself with poise and refinement.

Karita's parents had immigrated to the States from Denmark, and they had been thrilled when their children immersed themselves in American life—their son joining the Navy and their daughter attending an American university. Karita's bachelor's degree in education parlayed nicely into a job teaching history in a Chicago high school, where she met her dashing future husband.

She had surrendered many of her dreams upon discovering the brutality and manipulation inherent in Enzo's character, but one thing she had insisted upon was the naming rights for her sons. Instead of Italian monikers, Karita had demanded they celebrate Illinois history by naming their sons after two influential Civil War generals from the prairie state: John A. Logan and Ulysses S. Grant.

Karita's fair Scandinavian coloring stood in sharp contrast to the dark Italian features of Grant's father's side of the family. Grant recalled watching her brush her long, silky blond hair with fascination. He also remembered that same hair matted with blood after his father came at her one night. Soon tears mixed with the raindrops sliding down his face as he knelt by her tombstone in the cemetery north of Chicago.

Grant wasn't sure how long he'd been there, quietly mourning, before he heard a rustling behind him. Glancing over his shoulder, he gasped. Standing in the pouring rain was a tall, chiseled man with cropped black hair and a scowl.

Logan.

Grant rose and turned to face his brother, whom he had not seen since he was twelve, at their mother's funeral. That was fifteen years ago.

"How did you know I was here?" Grant asked.

Logan grimaced. "We had some guys staking out the airport, looking for somebody, and they saw you come in. You're kind of hard to miss in that uniform."

Grant would rather not know who the Mafia henchmen were stalking…probably an informant they wanted to kill. His eyes narrowed as he glared at his older brother. "Have you been tailing me since yesterday, then?"

"Nope. Shit-for-brains Carlo lost you in the airport shuffle. But I figured you'd show up here at some point."

Grant nodded sadly, stealing a glance at the delicate white-and-pink flowers drooping and wilting in the rain. "You live in Chicago. Do you visit her grave much?"

Logan swallowed hard. "No."

The younger brother sighed. They'd always been very different people. Grant was quiet and thoughtful, whereas Logan was loud and ill-tempered. They had inevitably chosen sides, one going to their mother and one to their father. Grant hated himself for thinking Logan might actually care about their mom. Of course he wouldn't visit her grave. He hated himself for that need deep within him, the need for his brother's love—a need that would obviously never be fulfilled.

"Why are you back in town?" Logan asked.

"I have to do some fitness testing at Great Lakes," Grant said. If all went well, he would be promoted to lieutenant, though he was not about to share that with a brother who couldn't care less. Growing weary of their forced conversation, Grant asked, "What do you want?"

Logan looked taken aback. "Who says I want anything?"

Grant looked at Logan with disdain. "Let's drop the pretense, Lo. I know you don't care about Mom. And you certainly don't care about me. What do you want?"

Logan stuffed his hands in the pockets of his leather jacket. "I hate to ask you this. But I need some money."

Grant looked away. He hated being right all the time. "What for?"

"I had a bad break in a poker game. I'll get it back. I will. But it was one of Carlo's associates who ran the game, and now Carlo is all over my ass for the cash."

"He's bad news, Lo. Stay away from him."

Logan sighed, and Grant knew exactly what his brother was thinking: that Uncle Joe was once again filling Grant's head with all sorts of rubbish about their paternal uncle Angelo and his son Carlo. "Carlo is our cousin. I can't turn my back on him like you have. Do you even care about our family? Do you even care about Dad?"

Grant's voice rose with indignant anger and a hint of childish wounded hurt. "Do they even care about me?"

An uncomfortable silence floated between them, the only sound the steady stream of raindrops tapping the leaves of nearby trees. Grant slid his hands into his pant pockets. "How much do you need?"

Crap. Now Logan had to come clean with the embarrassing amount. "Thirty K," he mumbled.

Grant's eyes bugged. "Thirty thousand *dollars*? How much do you think Navy ensigns earn?"

"Any amount you can help with, I'll take. I'm in deep, man."

Grant sensed his brother's desperation and realized Logan had a problem: a gambling problem. Grant had maybe three thousand dollars socked away, but even if he cleaned out his savings, it wouldn't put a dent in the debt. And who's to say Logan wouldn't just gamble it all away?

Grant looked down, feeling pained. "I can't help you."

"Great," Logan spat. "Thanks a lot, bro."

Stunned, Grant watched his brother turn and stride away. They hadn't seen each other for fifteen years, and that was how they were going to leave it? Would it be another fifteen years before they spoke again?

Roger paused his commentary and muted his microphone, gesturing to the left. "Watch out for that idiot kayaker off to port," he warned.

"Aye, sir," Grant replied, having spotted the small watercraft seconds before, even though he'd been lost in the past.

"Dumbass, kayaking out in this weather," Roger growled. Turning to glance at Grant, he noticed his forlorn expression. "You okay?"

Grant cleared his throat. "Yeah."

Roger nodded, flipped the switch on the mic's battery pack attached to his belt, and resumed his architectural tour of the city. He continued embellishing to accommodate their slow speed.

"For those of you who enjoy gambling, the closest opportunity is the Horseshoe Casino in Hammond, Indiana, about twenty minutes from the city. You can try your hand at blackjack or Caribbean stud poker there."

After Grant had adroitly docked the ship at the conclusion of the cruise, Roger put away his microphone and asked, "You ever been to that Horseshoe Casino, Madsen?"

"Nope."

"We should go there sometime," Roger suggested. "Maybe meet us some chicks."

Grant paused. He'd already met a lovely "chick." "No thanks. I'm not much of a fan of gambling."

"So you don't drink, you can't do drugs, and you don't gamble either? You are entirely too healthy, Madsen."

"And you are entirely too unhealthy, Rog," Grant shot back. "How about we get you some green vegetables for dinner?"

Roger made a gagging motion. "I think my body would go into shock if I fed it veggies." He grinned. "C'mon, let's grab some pizza."

Grant shook his head. Roger was hopeless. "Okay, but I'm cutting you off at two slices, boss." He grabbed his White Sox jacket and trailed Roger off the ship into the cloudy mist. Only one more cruise left tonight, and then Sophie would be joining them tomorrow. He knew she would brighten his day. He'd be willing to bet on it.

12. InSPIREd

S ophie's mind was full to overflowing with various alcoholic drink ingredients
and menu choices.

Although she'd studied the menu for an hour before the first cruise began
at one, it was tough to keep it all straight. She felt quite overwhelmed by the
time the five o'clock cruise rolled around on her first day. And naturally Dan,
the bartender, was out sick, so Sophie not only had to take the drink orders,
but fill them too.

She could just picture her Substance Abuse Treatment professor's disapproving look. She'd spilled a piña colada on her black skirt and could currently
feel sticky tomato juice all over her hands after delivering Bloody Marys to two
passengers. She was literally doused in alcohol.

In contrast to all the sitting in prison, today's five hours of scurrying around
on her feet had left her with some tired, barking dogs. And they still had one
cruise to go.

She sighed with relief as the ship approached a construction site near Navy
Pier and Roger began describing the Chicago Spire. She'd picked up on the
routine of the cruise by the third time around, and she now knew the Spire
was the last architectural marvel on the list, so they'd be docking soon. Sophie
continued collecting empty cups and napkins.

Roger's voice sounded strained as he bid farewell to the passengers over the
intercom and invited them to return for another cruise at any time. While Grant
was expertly docking the ship, Sophie wiped her hands on a towel and headed

to the gangway to smile pleasantly at the departing passengers. She wished them a wonderful evening in downtown Chicago.

Sophie glanced up at the bridge as she'd done after the earlier cruises, but this time she did not see Grant winking down at her. The parolees-turned-sailors had not found the opportunity to talk much during the cruises, but their exchanged glances had kept her going. Grant's dazzling blue eyes provided inspiring energy for her weary body, sparking excitement all up and down her spine.

Typically Roger and Grant had joined her and Tommy by the gangway to see the passengers off, but this time the captain and navigational officer were nowhere to be found. Sophie waited for the last passenger to disembark before taking tentative steps up to the bridge. She arrived to find Grant leaning over Roger, whose bald head was glistening with sweat. Roger's meaty paw clutched at his chest as his red face screwed up in pain.

"What's wrong with him?"

"Rog just started having chest pains."

"I'll call an ambulance," Sophie offered.

"No, don't!" Roger feebly insisted.

Sophie appeared confused, and Grant clarified, "He's refusing to go to the ER."

Stepping into the small control room, Sophie knelt by her boss. "You're having chest pain? What about pain down your left arm?"

"A little," he grunted.

"Pain in your back?"

"Yeah, there too."

"Is it hard to catch your breath?"

He nodded, and they could both hear him gasping for air.

"Do you feel nauseated?"

Roger continued nodding.

She frowned. "Have you ever had panic attacks before?"

Roger shook his head.

"And it's not indigestion, either," Grant said. "I've seen him with whopper indigestion, and this is different." Studying Roger, he chided, "Although you did eat an entire foot-long sub for lunch."

"What are you, the fucking food police?" Roger managed.

Sophie pressed her lips together. "Rog, you definitely need to go to the hospital. You're experiencing just about every symptom in the book of a heart attack."

"How do you know so much about them?" Grant asked.

"I did my internship in a VA hospital," she replied. Looking away, she added, "And my mother died of a heart attack last December."

Grant's eyes clouded over with sympathy, showing the same mournful look as the day she'd told him Jerry Stone's mother was dying. He reached out and held Sophie's hand, stroking her smooth skin softly, as his eyes locked onto hers. It was the most genuine expression of sympathy she'd ever experienced—the most compassionate response of all the times she'd painfully informed another person of her mother's death. She felt instantly nurtured and supported.

Wanting to avoid the fatal heart attack of yet another person in her life, Sophie turned her attention back to Roger. She sternly asked him, "How can we get you to go the hospital right away?"

"It's sold out," he rasped with difficulty. "The seven o'clock is sold out, and I refuse to turn paying customers away. I can't leave."

"Rog, surely you can miss the revenue from one cruise," Grant said.

"No," he panted. "I gotta pay alimony next week. I need every penny."

"You were *married*?" Grant asked incredulously.

"Don't look so surprised," Roger growled.

"Okay, focus, people!" Sophie admonished. "Grant, you can be the docent, right? You can take Roger's place?"

Grant's eyes widened. "What? Me? I can't be on the mic!"

"How hard can it be?" Sophie reasoned. "There's got to be a written script or something, right, Rog?"

Roger tapped his temple. "It's all up here."

As much as the prospect of playing tour guide created sheer panic within Grant, the idea of Roger's heart giving out was even more disturbing. Joe would certainly want his nephew to do everything in his power to take care of his friend.

"Okay!" Grant blurted. "I'll do it. Just go to the hospital, okay, sir? We'll take care of everything. Just go."

Roger must have been frightened by the increasing pain in his chest because he finally agreed. Figuring a taxi would be faster than calling an ambulance at this point, Grant and Sophie carefully led Roger down the stairs and onto the dock. It was a good sign that he could still walk.

Tommy also joined them, running to the street to hail a cab, and Grant frowned as they slowly approached the waiting taxi. "This is not right. We should go with you, Rog."

"I ain't going to that damn hospital unless you run the cruise," he protested.

Grant sighed and glanced at his watch: already 6:15. "Tommy, go to the ER with him and then get back here by seven, okay? I need you in the bridge if we're going to have a chance in hell of pulling this off."

Tommy nodded and slid to the other side of the back seat while Grant and Sophie helped Roger into the cab. Their hearts were racing, and it didn't help that Roger looked worse and worse with every minute ticking by. Thankfully the cab soon sped off, leaving Grant with his hands on his hips.

He turned his gaze to Sophie and felt a nervous flutter in his stomach. His eyes narrowed into a glare. "What the hell did you just get me into? I can't do this!"

She grinned. He was even cuter all angst-ridden and irritated. "C'mon, I'll help you," she said, locking her arm into his and leading him toward the ship. She couldn't believe how forward she was being, and she breathed a sigh of relief when he went along with her easily, matching her stride for stride.

"How are you going to help me? You'll be serving drinks the whole time. By the way," he added, glancing at the stains on her shirt and skirt, "you're supposed to pour the drinks into the glasses, not on yourself."

"Ha ha. Pour the drinks into the glasses?" she repeated in a high-pitched voice, giving him her best dumb blonde routine. "Who needs drink glasses? I was actually doing body shots with the passengers … didn't you see that?"

Grant's mouth dropped open. "No wonder you're making so many tips! Damn it, I miss all the fun stuck up there in the bridge."

"Well, the *chief navigator* does need to stay up there on his throne. It wouldn't be right for him to associate with us commoners on the poop deck."

Grant grinned. "You're learning the ship terminology so fast, Sophie!"

"If only I could learn cocktail ingredients as quickly. I'm running around trying to fill drink orders like a chicken with its head cut off."

Back at the ship, his grin faded as he glanced up at the bridge, the reality of his impending duty hitting him squarely in the chest. "I'm sure you'll do a better job as bartender than I will as docent," he said. "This is going to be bad."

"Oh, come on. It will be fun, a night cruise with a full house …"

"And thank you for reminding me that the cruise is sold out," he said. "That really calmed my nerves."

"Uh, sorry." Watching him shake like a leaf, she advised, "How about you take a few deep breaths?"

"Deep breaths? That's all the psychologist has to offer me?"

With a small pout, she replied, "Deep breaths would help if you tried them. But I have a better idea for how to help you chill out. Let me clean up my area a bit and I'll meet you in the bridge."

"Okay. I gotta stay here and collect tickets before I head up. While I wait for passengers to show up maybe I'll try to remember what the hell Rog says in his spiel."

"Good idea!" she called over her shoulder.

Twenty minutes later, Tommy returned from the hospital and took over the ticket collecting. Unfortunately, he had no status report on Roger because he'd had to turn around and leave the moment they arrived at the ER. But he did assure Grant that he'd left Roger in good hands at Northwestern Memorial Hospital.

Grant headed to the bridge and was dismayed to find his anxiety increasing as his performance approached. He glanced down at the benches on the deck, filling ominously with passengers. "Just go away," he wished, glaring at the teeming tourists.

Having just waltzed into the control room, Sophie paused. "You want me to go away?"

"No, not you," Grant said. "Them." He pointed behind him to the scads of passengers. "If you knew how to navigate this watercraft, I'd love to have you up here with me."

Then he noticed the tray in her arms, which carried a bottle of tequila, two shot glasses, lime wedges, and salt. "This is how you're going to help me? By plying me with booze?"

"Well, I would refer you to a psychiatrist for a good benzodiazepine but that doesn't look like an option, given that the cruise is starting in ten minutes." She caught him glancing anxiously at the bottle. "Do you like tequila?"

He cleared his throat and bashfully admitted, "I don't really know. I've never had a drink." He'd never admitted that to anyone. Now she'd think he was a total loser.

She looked astonished. "Never? Not one?"

"People in my family have addictive personalities," he said. "Like my brother for one." He silently added, *And my father. He was drunk that night. The night he killed that kid.*

"That's impressive self-restraint," she said. "And I would never encourage you to do something against your will. But, Grant, one drink can't turn you into an alcoholic. It might take the edge off if you want to try one."

He hesitated, the wheels turning in his mind. He should be thinking about Millennium Park and Trump Tower and the old post office building and the Sears Tower and the Spire, but instead he was dreaming up ways to touch her gorgeous, intoxicating body once again.

"The body shot thing you mentioned did sound kind of interesting," he smirked. What was he doing? He was never this suggestive with women.

"Oh?" There was a playful lilt in her voice. "You want your first drink to be a body shot?"

"Hey, you've been doing them all day with the passengers. The least you could do is to share one with me."

"Hmm…" She flashed a teasing grin. "Oh, what the hell? I'm already wearing alcohol all over my body anyway. We'll do a version of a body shot." Sophie whipped out her notepad and pretended to scribble officiously. "May I recommend a shot of tequila, sir?"

"Sounds heavenly."

Mesmerized by his oceanic eyes and liquid-smooth voice, Sophie absent-mindedly stuffed her notepad into her pocket. Grant's heart pounded and he decided take her previous advice—a few deep breaths—as she poured golden liquid into the shot glasses. Sophie's hand trembled slightly as she scooped up the salt shaker. She could not believe they were doing this.

"Give me your arm," she ordered. She looked down at the lean, sinewy muscles in his left forearm and lightly grasped his long fingers, admiring their grace. His hand was warm and smooth as she gently turned his palm upward. Smiling mischievously, she leaned her head down over his arm.

Grant's breathing hitched when he felt her warm tongue lick the baby-soft skin along the inside of his wrist. The moist spot felt cool when she lifted her head, and he watched curiously as she shook some salt onto the wet patch of skin. She maintained her light hold on his left wrist while lining up her shot and lime wedge with the other hand.

"Watch and learn how this works, 'cause you're going next," she said.

She dipped her head and he felt the glorious sensation of her tongue once again. Then she knocked back the tequila and grabbed a lime wedge between her teeth. He was entranced by her pink lips massaging the lime skin, puckering from the tartness. She finished by flicking her tongue back and forth over the green slice and flashing him an alluring smile.

Grant had observed quite a few shots taken by his Navy buddies in bars all over the world, but never had he witnessed anything involving his own skin as a springboard for a beautiful woman's tequila shot. He eagerly anticipated his turn.

Surrendering her arm to him with a twinkle in her chestnut-brown eyes, Sophie invited him closer. Self-consciously Grant grasped her delicate wrist and bent over to take a languid lick of her skin, drinking in her sophisticated perfume. He lifted his head and dumped some salt on the moist spot inside her forearm.

"And here begins my corruption, Dr. Taylor," he said, drawing a nervous breath. She giggled as he leaned forward, closing his eyes while tasting her once again. The briny salt mixed with her sweet skin was intoxicating, and he had not even had any alcohol yet. He stood up, clutched the full shot glass in his hand, and reluctantly tipped it to his lips. The tequila burned his throat, but he was determined not to cough—he couldn't compromise his manly image any further—and he successfully made it to suck on a lime, flashing a bright-green smile.

As Grant felt the hot tequila slide into his empty stomach, he realized they had forgotten about dinner in the melee with Roger.

"How did you like it?" Sophie inquired, studying him intently.

Feeling the alcohol warm his insides, Grant slowly nodded. "Not bad. I'm still kind of nervous, but if I drink enough of this maybe I won't even care if I screw up."

Sophie was about to reply when Tommy rushed in. "Hey, guys, it's time to start! Everybody's on board, and they need their drinks, Sophie."

"Okay! Good luck, Captain." She squeezed Grant's hand, then rushed down the white steps to the passengers.

Grant took a deep breath, attempting to quell the butterflies that were now dive-bombing his stomach. Searching for Rog's headset while Tommy moved to the controls, Grant found himself staring at the tequila bottle. Figuring his anxiety warranted a double dose of tranquilizer, he swiftly poured himself another shot and knocked it back. This time he did allow himself to cough a few times as the fiery liquid scorched his throat. He strapped on the headset and nervously turned on the microphone.

"Ladies and gentleman, welcome to Eaton Tours. We have a stunning architectural cruise planned for you this evening." Grant was relieved to find his voice clear and strong, without a hint of trembling.

Tommy fired up the engines and began backing the ship away from the dock as Grant continued, "Sophie will be serving your drinks tonight. If there's anything at all you need to make your cruise more enjoyable, please ask Sophie. She will take care of you." He grinned, pleased with himself for retaliating just a bit. She'd gotten him into this mess, and he'd better not regret it later.

"Here you go," Sophie smiled, passing two cokes to a father and son sitting aft on the ship.

The man returned her smile as he passed the beverage to his wide-eyed son before digging into his pants pocket and handing her a ten-dollar bill.

"I'll be right back with your change, sir."

Appreciatively eyeing her shapely legs, he murmured, "Keep the change."

Sophie's smile widened as she pocketed the money, quickly calculating that he'd tipped her five dollars. At this rate, maybe she wouldn't need a higher-paying job. "Thank you!" She blushed with pleasure.

She returned to the bar to mix martinis, listening to Grant describe Chicago's architectural wonders as they slowly passed above their vantage point on the ship. Not only was he breathtakingly handsome, his magnetic voice was charming her with every word. Deep and throaty, with just a whisper of tremulousness, his voice was warm and silky smooth. It lowered with intensity when something piqued his interest, as if he were sharing a precious secret with the listener.

"Straight ahead is the Trump International Tower and Hotel," Grant informed the passengers. "Donald Trump initially planned a one-hundred-fifty story structure, but after the nine-eleven attacks, we all know why he changed his mind and created a wider, stair-step version of the tower. However, not all architects are shying away from super-tall skyscrapers, as we will discover near the end of this cruise when we visit the construction site for the Spire."

Sophie began mixing cosmopolitans for a group of women on the third bench, but she listened intently as Grant continued.

"You may be interested to know that Chicago native Bill Rancic, winner of the first season of the television show The Apprentice, oversaw the construction for Trump Tower. This was his reward for managing to escape hearing the Donald say, 'You're fired!'"

Sophie giggled softly as Grant nailed the Donald Trump impression. To her delight, she noticed some of the passengers chuckling too. Captain Madsen was apparently a hit.

"To your left is Millennium Park. From the river, you can just make out the pavilion, which stands one-hundred-twenty feet high. The outdoor amphitheater has brushed stainless steel ribbons arching over the stage, with steel pipes extending in a crisscross pattern over the grass."

She paused her martini-shaking, fascinated. Where was he getting this stuff? Roger mentioned none of these facts during the first three cruises of the day.

"Architect Frank Gehry designed the pavilion to draw the crowd into the stage, making them feel part of the experience. I hope *you* are feeling drawn into this cruise right now. Who here is visiting Chicago for the first time?"

Multiple hands shot up in the crowd. "Well, I bet this won't be your last visit," Grant said. "What a remarkable town, this City of the Big Shoulders," he said, then continued quoting from Carl Sandburg's poem, "Chicago":

Come and show me another city with lifted head singing
so proud to be alive and coarse and strong and cunning.

He quoted poetry too? Sophie's jaw dropped. This was quite possibly the perfect man.

"But my favorite part of Millennium Park has to be Cloud Gate, affectionately known as 'the Bean' to Chicago natives," Grant's melodious voice asserted. "British artist Arnish Kapoor conceived of this shiny steel structure, which reflects the images of visitors and clouds overhead. Cloud Gate inspires a vision of liquid mercury, like a giant drop of silver wine falling from Zeus' massive glass in the heavens above. It is truly a work of art."

Grant was thoroughly enjoying himself, feeling so high that he never wanted this cruise to end. He was amazed at how natural it felt to spout off tidbits about his favorite Chicago haunts, and he was also thrilled that the facts he had read in Roger's architecture book came back to him so easily. Guiding the tour was much better than driving the ship.

Sneaking a glance at Tommy, who had his hand on the wheel, nervously scanning the river for evening traffic, Grant poured himself another couple of shots. If he felt this good after two tequila shots, surely a few more would make him feel even better. The amber liquid did not even burn his throat anymore.

As they continued the hour-long cruise, Sophie found herself repeatedly lulled into a trance by his honey-smooth voice. Then, realizing she was inattentively staring into space, she would force herself back to the harrowing bustle of bartending for more than one hundred passengers.

How was it that she'd never heard these fascinating stories about the city before? She supposed her workaholic father had been too busy to teach her about their hometown. She now knew that skyscrapers were first constructed in Chicago following the Great Fire of 1871, and some were designed with an inner and outer core for stabilization in strong winds.

Sophie was so busy with the drinks that she didn't notice Grant's voice begin to change. It had become more warbling and less precise. His words blended into each other as he stretched out particular syllables languidly—turning from honey to molasses. His commentary also became a little goofy.

"And here is our last architectoooral wonder," he slurred. "The Chicago Spire." Grant leaned back on the railing of the bridge, suddenly feeling light-headed. The swaying of the ship was uncharacteristically unwelcome, and his legs felt tingly and warm. He closed his eyes to try to steady himself and gripped the railing tightly. Only five more minutes.

Several moments passed, and Sophie wondered what had happened to Grant, but suddenly his voice filled the speakers once again. "Construction on the Spire begannn one year ago, and right now the ssstructure is not yet above-ground, but, dude, I so wish you could see the completed product. It's gonna be one-hundred-fitty stories highhh—taller than the Ssssears Towerrr—and its design will make it look like a giant drill bit. It's freakin' one of the most phallic things you have everrr sssseen. It's like a huuuuge, throbbing penis piercing the skyyy."

Sophie dropped her tray with a deafening clatter.

Grant chuckled lightly over the speakers, a low sexy rumble that made her knees wobble. "Mmmm, the architect is Sssantiago Calatrava. I wonder how biggg that guy is? He seems kinda obsessed with sssize."

Sophie frantically gathered the plastic cups scattered on the deck near the man and his son she'd served earlier. She looked up to find the man covering his son's ears and shooting her an angry glance. She gulped.

Standing up and walking the tray to the bar, Sophie glanced around at the passengers, expecting a revolt to erupt. But instead she found most wearing bemused expressions, some sporting looks of disbelief, and some chuckling to themselves. The majority seemed to crave more commentary from the crazy man up on the bridge.

Teetering on the brink of exhaustion after a long first day on the job, worrying about Roger in the hospital, and working alongside the hottest man on earth, who now appeared to be drunk off his ass, Sophie felt a slap-happy giddiness overtake her. She tried desperately not to laugh.

What the hell was Tommy doing up there? How much had Grant had to drink? Should she go up to the bridge and find out? She still had several drink orders pending. Frozen in a moment of indecision, she looked back and forth between the bridge and the passengers, then heard Grant's voice once again.

This time he was singing.

> *Hey, now what can happen to me*
> *In an awesome city like thisss?*
> *I give a shout-out to Chicago, baby!*
> *And smooooch you with a big fat kissss…*

Sophie cupped her hand over her mouth. Grant was *really* losing it now.

"Join in, everyone!" he encouraged loudly. Considering his creative lyrics, it took the crowd a couple of lines to realize he was singing Sinatra's "My Kind of Town." It figured ol' crystal eyes was singing a tune by Ol' Blue Eyes. If his speaking voice was sexy, his singing voice was orgasmic—smooth, mellow, and melodic, with perfect pitch. But then his slurred serenade was replaced by static and the sound of harsh, unintelligible words.

Several of the passengers actually had joined the singing, and a raucous mood flowed throughout the ship as they pulled into the dock. Diners at a nearby restaurant, Dan's Dock, craned their necks to see what was causing such an uproar.

Sophie quickly scurried to settle up the last bills, then scampered down to the dock, plastering a fake smile on her lips and nodding pleasantly at the departing passengers. She did not even wait for the last stragglers to leave before she bolted up the steps to the bridge, finding Tommy wrestling the microphone headset from Grant's grasp.

"I want to sssing ssssome more!" he pleaded.

She glanced at the bottle of tequila and her eyes widened at the paltry amount left. That had been a full bottle of Cuervo Gold!

"Grant!" she shouted. "How many shots of tequila did you have?"

Startled into lucidity by her sharp tone, he gave her a puzzled, glassy-eyed stare. "Dunno … Maybe five? No, ten?"

Her jaw dropped. "Tommy! How could you let him drink that much? He's never had alcohol before!"

"I didn't know that!" he hissed back, finally gaining possession of the headset and hiding it behind his back. "I was busy navigating the damn ship, not babysitting Frank Sinatra over here!"

"I get a big kick from tequila," Grant began singing, a huge grin on his face as he continued to maul Sinatra songs. "Cuervo Gold, it makes me feel so damn bold…"

He moved unsteadily toward Sophie, and before she knew it, he had her in his arms, leading her in an impromptu waltz around the bridge. Despite her misgivings, Sophie let herself be drawn into his arms, surrendering to the spontaneous joy of the moment.

He spun her around, and Sophie squealed as she twirled in the small space. Apparently the motion was a little much for Grant, as he went careening into the controls for the ship, crashing into the panel and sliding to the floor like an accordion.

Sophie gasped and ran to his side. "Are you all right?"

Grant nodded with a serene, happy grin, closing his eyes and continuing to hum Frank Sinatra. Tommy rolled his eyes disgustedly.

"Awesome," he spat. "The substitute captain is wasted, and the real captain is in the hospital having a heart attack." He rubbed his temples. "What a day."

"What are we going to do?" Sophie asked.

"We gotta lock up. And one of us should probably go check on Rog."

Tommy peered down at Sophie, his sandy-blond buzz cut topping a frowning face. He seemed young, maybe in his early twenties, and Sophie felt guilty that at ages twenty-nine and thirty, respectively, she and Grant were the irresponsible ones.

"Well, I can try to take Ol' Blue Eyes home," she negotiated, "if you can check on Rog?"

Tommy nodded. "Here, let's get him in a cab." He knelt down. "Grant, you need to get up!"

Grant began laughing softly. "Donnn think ssso."

"Shit. Now that he's on the floor there ain't no way we're getting him up on his feet." Glaring at Sophie, he proclaimed, "This is all your fault, you know! You're the one who gave him booze."

Tommy tapped his foot pensively while Sophie bit her lip, trying to figure out how to help. Then Tommy leaned in near Grant's ear and barked, "Lieutenant Madsen! On your feet!"

Miraculously Grant scrambled up and snapped to attention.

Sophie marveled at this abrupt change. "Lieutenant?"

"He was in the Navy," Tommy explained. "So was I, and so was Rog. I figured that would get his attention."

"Huh," Sophie mused, lost in thought. Visions of Grant in a crisp white uniform that hugged his lean body swam in her head. The perfect man just became more perfect. She wondered what else she would learn before the night was over.

"Let's go, Lieutenant," Tommy ordered, firmly grasping Grant's elbow and leading him toward the stairs.

"Where we goin', bossss?" he asked.

"Boss?" Tommy asked. "Don't you mean 'sir,' you drunkard?"

A sad frown quietly crept over Sophie's delicate features. She knew exactly why he was using the word "boss." It was a term of respect for corrections officers, a word that made her shudder. Apparently Roger had not shared Grant's prison history with his coworkers.

They made it to the street in the fading daylight and thankfully didn't wait long for an available cab. A few minutes more and Grant might start singing again—or possibly start vomiting. He seemed more incoherent with each passing moment.

As Tommy helped her stuff Grant into the taxi, grunting with exertion, he asked, "So, you'll be okay, then?"

"I think so," she replied nervously, feeling Grant's warm body close to hers in the backseat. His head lolled against the headrest, and his eyes were closed.

"I'll lock up and go see about Rog," Tommy said. "Catch you tomorrow."

When Tommy closed the door, the cabbie looked at Sophie expectantly. She realized she had no idea where they were going. "Grant? What's your address?"

He laid there motionless. "Grant!" she repeated, poking his shoulder. "Where do you live?"

"Studio," he mumbled. "Eggs and sausage." She scrunched her forehead. His next utterance was not any more helpful: "Snoring. Really *loud* ssssnoring."

She gave up and told the cabdriver, "It's 900 North Lake Shore Drive." She hoped Kirsten wouldn't be upset about an unannounced houseguest.

During the ten-minute cab ride, Sophie wondered how she was going to get an unconscious, six-foot-one man up to Kirsten's apartment. However, about a minute into the drive, Grant came back to life. His long eyelashes fluttered open and he glanced around, his intense blue eyes coming to rest on the strawberry-blonde returning his gaze.

"Sophie." He smiled, reaching out to caress her face with his hand. She held her breath. "You're so beautiful," he murmured, stroking her cheek softly. "You're my angel. My elegant angel."

Her face burned with his touch, and the heat only intensified when he leaned in and brushed his lips across her cheek. She closed her eyes and reveled in the sensation of his full, luscious lips planting soft kisses, starting at her temple and then languorously descending to her jaw. She stroked the length of his thigh, urging him onward. His usual sandalwood scent had been replaced by the sweet, almost nutty smell of agave emanating from his pores. He was a walking tequila shot. Well, the walking part remained to be seen.

"We're at 900 North Lake Shore," the driver announced after the fastest cab ride ever. Sophie glanced at the meter and grimaced as she withdrew a ten-dollar bill from her pocket. Living in the city could sure cut down on her profits. As she started to hand over the cab fare, Grant, suddenly lucid, reached out and clutched her wrist.

"No, I got it," he insisted, energized by kissing her soft skin. He quickly whipped out his own money despite Sophie's protests. After he paid the driver they both managed to scoot out of the seat and stand at the curb.

"Where are we?" he asked.

She stared into his tired, half-lidded eyes. Grasping his hand in hers she told him, "We're home, Grant." He nodded gratefully. Indeed, when it came to Sophie, he definitely felt he had found his home.

13. Low Lo

The cries of seagulls could barely be heard over the pounding surf. A solitary man stood silhouetted against the setting sun's brilliant orange glow. Frothy ocean waves crashed at the shore and raced toward his cowboy boots before receding once again. Like the repeated screw-ups in his own life, the waves just kept coming.

He was a strong, strapping man, and he cut an imposing figure if anyone were to study him from the beach. His black leather jacket and worn jeans were out of place in Hilton Head, South Carolina. He faced the mysterious and powerful sea, his chiseled features drawn with lines of worry and regret as his deep-blue eyes stared, mesmerized, at a piece of driftwood bobbing in the ocean.

Logan Barberi had been hiding out on this island for a little over a year, feeling as adrift and cast aside as the piece of weathered wood now capturing his attention. He had disappeared the moment Sophie called him, her voice shaking with betrayal and disbelief. It had taken only a few heatedly exchanged words for her to arrive at icy resolve. When she'd coldly informed him it was over, he'd realized she was lost to him forever. *And* that he'd better get the hell out of Chicago if he didn't want to spend a long time locked away with his father.

"Sophie…" he whispered gruffly. The painful memories threatened to drown him.

As soon as Logan had entered her office, she asked, "Would you like some coffee? I can just go down the hall and get some from the break room."

Stuffing his hands into his pockets, he shook his head.

"I was hoping you'd come back."

"Do I have a choice?" Logan retorted.

"We always have choices, Logan. You just might not like the consequences of particular choices. If you choose not to return to counseling, the consequence will likely be prison. That's not such an appealing consequence, but you still have a choice."

He shot her an uncomfortable glance. He despised being tied to her, betrothed to her stamp of approval. Once she gave him the thumbs up, confirmed that he was cured of his gambling addiction, he could end this little dance they performed once a week: her asking questions and him evading her at every pass. Nevertheless, Logan had realized he would miss her once this was over. She was beautiful and kind, a real classy chick. Certainly out of his league.

"I was worried that last week's session might have been a bit rough for you," she explained, and they both silently recalled him bawling like a baby as he discussed a childhood beating by his father. Sophie had assumed his tears were about failing to protect his brother back then. But she was wrong. What really hit him in the gut, causing him to weep uncontrollably, was his guilt about something that happened to them as adults. What he had done to his brother was unforgiveable.

"It was fine," he lied.

Sophie gave a nervous smile. It was now time to address the kiss—the smoldering smooch Logan had planted on her as she tried to comfort him last week. The kiss she did not stop. The kiss that heated her to the core.

She cleared her throat. "Uh, I need to talk to you about something."

He watched her slide her hands beneath her lithe, long legs, tucking the sides of her unusually long skirt against them. Dismayed to find those gorgeous gams hidden, Logan eyed her blushing cheeks curiously.

"The, uh…" She cleared her throat again. "When I sat next to you, and tried to, um, provide support as you were reliving that painful memory, well…"

Logan was amused to watch her avert her gaze, not daring to meet his intense stare. After her countless comments about how he refused to maintain eye contact, he enjoyed this little role-reversal.

"I—I'm flattered that, um, you kissed me," she continued, her cheeks burning. "But that—that can't happen again, Logan. That was, um, inappropriate. That was not right for a therapist and client to kiss."

Although they were discussing a serious topic, Logan could not help but grin. She was absolutely precious all nervous and apologetic, and he felt warmth in his heart just looking at her.

Sophie glanced down and murmured, "I apologize for letting that happen. I exploited my power, and therefore I think it would be best to refer you to another psychologist."

Logan's grin vanished. "No way! I'm not seeing another shrink. If you try to refer me to someone else, I won't go. And then it'll be your fault when they send me to prison."

At first she'd looked sympathetic and guilty. Now she was angry. "That is ludicrous! I am not responsible for your choices." Looking away, she added, "I'm only responsible for my own. And my recent choices have not been looking out for your best interests. I don't think I can be objective when it comes to you."

He licked his bottom lip mischievously. "And why is that, Sophie?"

She glared at him. "My ethics code dictates that I am to avoid multiple relationships," she explained, feeling protected by the intellectual-sounding words she used. "I can't be your therapist and your ... well, someone you kiss. I can't be both."

He exuded pure charm. "Well, if you're drawing a line in the sand, I'm okay with just being the someone you kiss then."

Her intense, serious expression lightened considerably upon hearing his retort, but she soon grew pensive and sad. "The second you walked through my door as my client, the possibility of romance between us ended. That's just the way it is. That's what my professional ethics demand. I have no choice."

"You said we always have a choice, remember?"

She felt stymied to have her words thrown back at her. "I mean ..."

"Listen," Logan interrupted. "I get what you're saying about ethics, blah, blah. And I would say I'm sorry for kissing you, but really I'm not. It was an incredible kiss, babe. But I promise it won't happen again. Just give me another chance. Don't make me go to prison, Sophie."

He watched her falter. His false reassurances were starting to get to her. Driving forward, capitalizing on her compassion, he added, "Here I go to the trouble of bringing you a gift today, and then you want to kick me out of here? You want to abandon me?"

Sophie looked startled. "A gift?"

"Yeah." He smiled proudly, reaching into his jacket. Handing a thick envelope to her, he explained, "This should help you with your student loans."

Puzzled, Sophie reluctantly accepted the envelope and gasped when she looked inside, finding crisp one-hundred-dollar bills neatly stacked together. Her voice rose shrilly. "What the hell is this?"

"It's five grand. I wanted to thank you for trying to help my sorry ass."

"You already pay me one-fifty for each session. I can't accept this!"

"What's the big deal?" he asked defensively, his face falling. He'd expected her to be grateful. They'd just robbed a nightclub—effectively eliminating the biggest competitor to Angelo's club, as well as pulling in a boatload of cash—and he wanted her to share in his good fortune.

"The big deal?" she repeated incredulously. "It's exactly the same thing as you kissing me. It's a boundary violation." She stuffed the envelope back into his unsuspecting grasp. "I can't take this, Logan."

His prominent brow furrowed. This was not going as expected. People did not usually say no to him.

"Where did this money come from?" Sophie asked, not sure she really wanted to know.

"We got a consulting contract," Logan lied. A few sessions back he'd finally answered her repeated questions about what he, his uncle, and his cousin did for a living. His initial responses of "run the family business" had not satisfied her. He'd told her his family owned a consulting business, figuring nobody knew what the fuck consultants did anyway. "Consultant" was an excellent cover for organized crime. After all, he would often demand that drug dealers or other thugs on the payroll "consult" with his fist if they didn't stay in line.

Continuing to stare at him, her expression a mixture of anger, compassion, and uncertainty, Sophie had no idea what to say.

"Look, sorry I tried to do something nice for you, okay? I won't do it ever again. Can we just forget this and move on?" Returning the envelope to his jacket, he began massaging his temples. "Um, could I get that cup of coffee you offered me before?"

She gave him a look of sympathy. "Caffeine headache?"

"Yeah, something like that."

Sophie frowned. "I don't mean to be ungrateful," she said, her voice softening. "It was sweet of you to try to help me. It's just that this relationship has to have rules to make it work, okay? I can't be an effective therapist if I'm your friend or lover."

He stared at the floor, his rough hands moving from his temples to rub his scalp, appearing deep in thought.

"I'll go get us some coffee," she said.

Once she was gone, Logan took the envelope back out of his jacket and turned it over and over in his hands. He did not have a safe place to keep cash like this. He could hardly deposit the dirty money in a bank, and stashing it at his apartment was unwise as well since his cousin Carlo had a tendency to make unexpected visits. If he kept the cash on him, it would just be a matter of time before he gambled it away. Sophie believed he was making zero progress on his gambling addiction, but he really was trying to cut back. He didn't want to disappoint her.

Hearing her footsteps outside the door, Logan swiftly stuffed the envelope underneath the sofa. It was the best hiding place he could think of. When she entered the office, he suppressed a grin. She'd accepted his gift after all.

Logan's cell phone vibrated in his pocket, shaking him back to the warm beach. Seeing *Restricted* on the caller ID, he cautiously answered, "Yeah?"

"It's me," Angelo Barberi informed him.

Logan exhaled slowly. "Godfather."

"How ya doin'? You outside or somethin'?"

"Yeah, I'm at the beach. How you been?"

"Ah, same old, same old. Business hasn't been great."

Logan closed his eyes. For the past year, his uncle had been moaning about running the business without him, his right-hand man. The complaints and dropped hints had become louder of late, and Logan suspected he knew the nature of this call. Angelo wanted his godson to return to Chicago and resume his rightful place as heir to a Mafia throne.

"Sorry to hear that," Logan responded. "How's the heat in Chicago these days?"

"*Caldo.* Our police contact confirmed that you are still very much a wanted man."

Logan exhaled. He had nobody to blame but himself for the police heat. They'd discovered too late that the Chicago PD had tapped family bodyguard Anthony Tanketti's phone. Logan could still remember the conversation that had likely led the cops to Sophie:

"What do you want, Tank?" Logan growled into the phone.

Tank sounded offended. "Good to talk to you too, Logan. The, uh, 'profits' from our activities last week ... they safe?"

Logan hesitated. "Who wants to know?"

"Carlo. He told me to ask you about it."

"Carlo has nothing to worry about. I know how to take care of profits."

Tank blurted, "You know how to lose it all in a poker game, too."

"Fuck you, Tank." Logan's hands itched with the desire to punch him again. Apparently he hadn't learned his lesson the first time.

Tank backpedaled. "Hey, don't shoot the messenger. You know how Carlo can get. He was having a hissy-fit about the cashish—you know what he's like."

"Yeah, I know," Logan said, nodding. "Look, you can trust me. It's safe. I've got someone on the side, taking care of things."

"Who?" His voice was insistent.

"None of your fucking business. She's fine—she won't talk. And she's got a real nice office. Nobody will find the money."

Tank sounded impressed. "You getting yourself a little tail, Logan? Nice…very nice."

Logan said nothing.

"Just watch out," Tank warned. "Girls can weaken guys like us."

"Logan, you still there? When're you coming back?"

Angelo's voice in his ear returned Logan to the present.

"How can I come home? It's too soon, too dangerous."

"Maybe," Angelo acquiesced. "But I'm not calling about just business woes." He took a dramatic pause, and Logan's heart rate increased. "Your brother is out," he finally said.

"Grant?" Logan's voice rose. "He's out? I thought he had another nine months."

"According to Enzo, he got released with good behavior. Your brother was always a goody two-shoes, Logan."

"How long has he been out?"

"About two weeks."

"Why didn't you tell me earlier?"Logan practically shouted into the phone.

"Relax! It took me a while to secure a safe phone. The fucking feds have been riding our asses since Blackfoot."

Logan sighed, recalling the botched delivery of stolen goods to the Blackfoot casino in Gary, Indiana. Several of their men had been arrested in the melee, though none of them had turned on the Barberi family. Yet. Carlo had arranged the delivery, and Carlo had fucked up once again.

Biting his lip, Logan inquired, "Does Carlo know Grant's out?"

Angelo was silent, and Logan's heart sank. "Yeah, he just found out. I thought you'd want to know."

"Damn straight I want to know. Can't you do anything? Can't you contain Carlo?"

It was a familiar argument: Logan urging Angelo to cut loose the one man who seemed to destroy all their plans, and Angelo balking. "He's my son," Angelo said, his voice breaking.

Logan sighed. "Yes, Godfather."

"I'm trying to keep Carlo away from the books, Logan. But someday he's going to find out I've been bankrolling your little getaway to the tropics, and he's not going to like it. Someday you're going to have to start contributing more to the business. Wanted man or not."

"I know. Just leave Grant out of it. I've already involved him way too much as it is."

"I hear you, Godson. But as you know, Carlo disagrees. He talks nonstop about the money you lost, and if you don't pay it back soon, he's going to try to get it any way he can."

"Shit," Logan muttered. "Do you know where Grant is?"

"No, no one knows. We don't think he'd be stupid enough to return to Chicago."

"You're probably right," Logan lied, trying to sound convincing. He could just about guarantee his brother was somewhere in Chicago. That was where their mother was buried.

Suddenly rushed, Angelo whispered, "I gotta go. Take care of yourself. *Ciao.*"

Logan closed his phone, continuing to gaze at the sea. His regret regarding Sophie was a single drop of saltwater compared to the ocean of remorse he felt about Grant.

It was a little over two years ago, a couple of weeks before the court ordered Logan into therapy with Sophie. One week before his actions sent Grant to prison.

This time Grant saw Logan coming. This time Grant was not surprised by his brother approaching the grave. This time it was their mother's birthday, and Logan had known his brother would be here.

As Logan sidled up to his brother, Grant continued staring at the headstone. They stood wordlessly side by side, roughly the same height, with the same closely cropped midnight-black hair. Finally, Grant said, "Hey."

"Hey," Logan responded. After waiting a beat, he added, "I heard you were back in town."

"How the hell did you know?"

The muscles lining Logan's jaw flexed. "Carlo found out. I don't know how. He hears everything."

"I told you to stay away from him."

The corner of Logan's mouth twitched, amused by his little brother trying to tell him what to do. The half-smile quickly faded, however, when he remembered the recruitment task ahead of him. Staring sadly at the bare ground in the headstone's shadow, Logan asked, "What, no flowers this time?"

Grant sniffed. "I didn't have time. I have a flight to Norfolk in a couple of hours."

"To visit Joe?"

"Yeah."

They stood in silence once again, and Grant shivered slightly in the cool March breeze. His eyes did not move from the grave. "I wonder what she would think of me now," he murmured.

Logan's lips tightened. He knew their mother would be very proud of the man Grant had become, in contrast to her feelings for Logan. Her older son was now a no-good crook.

Wincing, Logan realized he was about to let down his dead mother yet again. But it had to be done. He had no choice.

"Your trip to see Joe might have to be delayed. I've got something for you to do before you leave," Logan told Grant.

"No," Grant responded immediately, vehemently.

Logan swallowed hard. "I'm afraid I can't take no for an answer."

Slowly turning to face his brother, Grant's crystal eyes clouded over. "What does that mean?"

Unable to hold his brother's intense gaze, Logan cleared his throat uncomfortably, hating himself. "It means that unless you help us, we're going to hurt Joe. You do a job for us, or Uncle Joe will die."

Grant gasped at the hideous threat. It was preposterous for Logan to threaten the life of their own mother's brother. Part of him wanted to laugh—a sick, harsh chuckle at the cruelty of his own family. But it was no laughing matter. Closing his eyes and scraping his hands across his buzzed hair, Grant knew the truth: This was a lethal and imminent threat. They had killed before, and they would kill again. They would take away the only remaining person he loved in this world, unless he did their bidding. He had no choice.

Grant heard a numb voice that had to be his own. "What do I have to do?"

"The bar near Great Lakes," Logan replied evenly. "We're going to take something back from there that belongs to us. And we need your help, Lieutenant Madsen."

He had joined the Navy to get away from his family, and now they were using his military status against him. Grant felt sick. "Let's get this over with."

"That's what I wanted to hear." Logan smiled encouragingly. Once they accomplished this robbery, Logan promised himself he would never involve Grant again. He would keep him safe from Carlo no matter what it took.

Suddenly, Logan realized it was almost pitch black at the beach around him. The sun had long ago descended below the horizon, and he could barely see his hand before his face.

Sighing heavily, he trudged through the sand toward the plantation hotel. Once he reached the sidewalk, he shook out his boots and brushed the sand off his jeans, wishing he could shake his memories of Sophie and Grant just as easily.

He had utterly failed at keeping Grant safe, and now that Grant had sacrificed his freedom by going to prison, Logan was determined not to fail again. Though he was still pursued by the police, he would have to return to Chicago and pay his debt. Logan would remain hidden no more.

14. Talking in Your Sleep

Continuing to serenade her softly with Frank Sinatra tunes, Grant leaned on Sophie's shoulder as they slowly made their way up two flights of stairs in the brownstone apartment building.

Then, just outside Kirsten's apartment door, Grant passed out. How could a man who appeared so lean be so heavy? Knowing muscle weighed more than fat, Sophie surmised that Grant must be pure muscle. He had been in the Navy after all.

Somehow managing to keep hold of him while simultaneously knocking and yelling for her roommate, Sophie was relieved when Kirsten finally threw open the door.

"Forgot your key, So—?"

She stopped her question midstream and gaped at Sophie struggling to hold up a dark-haired man who appeared to be melting into her.

"I need your help, Kir," Sophie groaned.

Kirsten immediately tucked her neck under the man's opposite shoulder, effectively sandwiching the hunk of meat between them.

"Thanks. Can you help me bring him inside?"

Bursting with curiosity about her unexpected guest, Kirsten replied, "Sure, let's get him to the sofa."

Sophie loved her roommate for jumping to help without one question asked. What a different reception she would have encountered on her father's doorstep.

Carefully they plodded into the apartment, half pushing, half dragging the unconscious Grant.

Kirsten scrunched her nose. "He reeks!"

"Yeah, he had one too many tequila shots."

Finally, they hauled him to the sofa and allowed him to plummet into the cushions with a thud. Sophie bent over to arrange him neatly on his side, huffing from the exertion of adjusting his dead weight. Once she stepped back, Kirsten admired his perfectly shaped head, tanned and flawless skin, long eyelashes, and plump lips.

"Who *is* he?" she demanded. Before Sophie could answer, Kirsten added, "Wait a minute. Did you finally take my advice and get yourself a boyfriend?"

"He's not my boyfriend!" Sophie countered, glancing down at Grant. "At least not yet. I barely know him."

"That's got potential!" Kirsten grinned. Peering more closely at Grant, Kirsten wondered, "Do we need to take him to the ER?"

"His color is pretty good," Sophie said, leaning down to grasp Grant's hand in hers. "His breathing is okay, and his skin is not cold or clammy. I think he'll be all right."

"As long as we keep him on his side," Kirsten finished. He appeared to be sleeping it off peacefully with a slight smile ghosting his striking features. "We should also keep an eye on him, which shouldn't be too difficult." Kirsten grinned. "He sure is easy on the eyes. How many drinks did he have?"

"I'm not sure," Sophie shrugged. "This is my fault. He'd never had alcohol before, and I encouraged him to drink some tequila to calm his nerves."

Kirsten gaped at her roommate. It was certainly out of character for Sophie to get a strange male teetotaler drunk. Had she changed in prison?

After they both stared wordlessly at the sleeping beauty for a few moments, Kirsten asked, "Okay, Taylor, are you going to tell me who this guy is, or do I have to beat it out of you?"

Sophie met her roommate's inquisitive eyes. "You know that guy who got me the job yesterday? On the ship?"

"That's *him?* Oh my God, you didn't tell me how gorgeous he was! Why can't I run into a yummy McSailor like him?"

Sophie chuckled. "McSailor is actually a great name for him. I just found out he used to be in the Navy. But don't get too excited, Kir. Do you remember what else I told you about him?"

After a beat, Kirsten frowned. "He was in prison."

Sophie nodded.

"What for?"

"I don't know. We made a pact not to discuss our pasts."

Kirsten absorbed this information, and her eyes narrowed suspiciously. "So, it's possible that you brought a murderer into my apartment?"

Sophie was startled. She hadn't considered this possibility. "He's—he's not a murderer," she insisted.

"How do you know?"

"I just know, that's all. He's very sweet. You can't see them now, but he's got the kindest blue eyes—the most soulful, expressive eyes you've ever seen. And our boss said something about him saving a kid's life. He can't be a murderer."

Kirsten remained skeptical, her arms folded across her chest.

"Don't you trust my judgment?" Sophie implored. "You know me! I have a good intuition about people."

"Uh-huh, and what exactly did your intuition tell you about Logan Barberi?"

The words escaped Kirsten's mouth before she had a chance to think, and once she saw Sophie's face crumple, she immediately regretted them. "Oh, Sophie, I'm sorry. I didn't mean it."

Sophie turned away and slowly sat on the futon. "You're absolutely right," she said, looking at her feet. "I shouldn't be trusted. My judgment is horrible. Now you've got two felons in your apartment. I'm probably going to drag you down with me."

Kirsten knelt beside Sophie. "Would you please ignore what I just said? I'm an idiot. Of course I trust you, and I have faith in your judgment. You're the smartest person I know. I would never have gotten through grad school without you. Who in the world finishes her dissertation in six months? You're amazing."

Sophie still looked heartbroken. Searching for the right words, Kirsten added, "You're also the most compassionate person I know. Who else would have tried to help that nut job Elena get through school?"

This time Sophie grinned faintly, remembering their fellow counseling student Elena Roja, who had appeared mentally unstable and completely over-whelmed from the start. She'd been dismissed from the program after only one semester.

"But, Sophie," Kirsten gently continued, "sometimes you're a little too kind. I think that's why that Barberi guy manipulated you so well, and I'm just scared you're going to get involved with the wrong person again by reaching out and trying to save them."

Sophie raised her head. "Thank you, Kir. But so far Grant is the one who's saving *me*. He helped me get a job when I desperately needed one, and he's been nothing but a gentleman." She paused for a moment, fondly recalling the warm kisses he'd planted on her face and neck in the cab. Perhaps that behavior wasn't so gentlemanly after only their first day of working together, but Sophie didn't mind. "If I don't trust him simply because he was in prison, then how can I expect anyone to give *me* a chance? I'm a felon too."

"Please don't use that word," Kirsten said.

"It's what I am, Kirsten. A felon. I'd better get accustomed to it." Sophie rested the back of her head on the futon and yawned.

"Looks like you had a long first day of work."

"You could say that." Sophie smiled weakly.

"Did you have any dinner?"

Sophie thought a moment. "Actually, no."

Popping up, Kirsten ordered, "You stay here and rest then, and I'm going to heat up some stir-fry leftovers."

"No," Sophie protested, trying to get up from the low futon, but Kirsten pressed firmly on her shoulder.

"Let me get you some food. Somebody needs to watch over drunken McSailor anyway," she smirked.

"Oh, I guess I'll make the sacrifice then." Sophie returned the smirk and added a wink.

Kirsten busied herself in the kitchen, and as she nuked the stir fry, she caught Sophie staring intently at the man on the couch. *Grant* was his name? Sophie gently rearranged his arm, trying to shift him to a more comfortable position. Then she sat back on the futon and sighed happily.

Kirsten froze. She knew that look. Sophie had exhibited that same blissful, contented stare every day in their Theories of Personality class. There she'd aimed that look at their dashing professor. Kirsten had attempted to discourage Sophie's pursuit of a man twenty years their senior to no avail. Sophie had been forced to learn the hard way—a mortifying, ego-shattering rejection of her earnest confession of love. Despite his flirtations, their professor had been happily married.

Kirsten did not want her friend to endure that kind of pain again. She brought in the steaming plate, but did not capture Sophie's attention until she was standing right over her. Sophie jumped a bit and smiled gratefully, reaching up to take the food.

Kirsten slowly shook her head, her mouth tightening with disapproval. Sophie warily inquired, "What's wrong?"

She pointed at Sophie. "That look on your face. I know that look. You like him. You like McSailor!"

"Kir—"

"This is not good at all. You are positively smitten with him."

"Kir—"

"I can't believe it. You are falling for another criminal!"

"Can I talk now, please?" Sophie interjected more aggressively than she intended. She took a deep breath, intending to protest, but found she couldn't refute Kirsten's suspicions. Sophie sheepishly admitted, "Yeah, I do like him."

"As if you could deny it!" Kirsten gave a satisfied nod and pulled a chair from the kitchen table into the small living room, plopping down across from Sophie and waiting expectantly for her to continue.

Her face glowing, Sophie bashfully confided, "He kissed me in the cab."

"Really? How was it?"

"Nice," she responded dreamily. She stole a glance at Grant and hoped he really *was* passed out. "We haven't kissed on the lips—yet—but it was still lovely." Frowning slightly, she added, "I hope it wasn't just beer goggles, or should I say, tequila goggles."

Snorting, Kirsten retorted, "I highly doubt that. You're a great catch, Sophie. You're gorgeous, but more importantly, you have a fantastic personality. Grant should be so lucky."

Sophie could not stop tears from springing to her eyes. After a lifetime of her father's criticism and a year of the judicial system throttling her self-confidence, she could scarcely believe such kind words. "Oh, I'm a real catch," she said, blushing. "A woman who went to prison, a woman on parole for being incredibly naïve and stupid. I can see my profile getting all kinds of hits."

Kirsten's eyes narrowed wickedly. "Ooh, I know what your screen name could be: Prisoner of Love!" She giggled.

Sophie simply shook her head and brought a forkful of rice and vegetables to her mouth.

"Ex-Con in Search of McSailor?" Kirsten asked hopefully.

Finishing her bite, Sophie countered, "I thought you were *against* me falling for a criminal."

"I am," Kirsten replied definitively, reminding herself of her prior position. "Although this is one of the first times I've seen you smile since you got out." Gazing at the long form of the sleeping man on her couch, she added, "And he is hopelessly cute."

"Hunter wasn't so thrilled about me fraternizing with a con either," Sophie admitted. "But if he met Grant, maybe he would change his mind. I can't wait for you to see what Grant is like. You're going to love him, Kir."

I could say the same for you, Kirsten thought. Sophie seemed like she was well on her way to loving Grant already.

❦

She awoke to a strange sound. Sophie blinked several times in the darkness, and pressing silence greeted her ears as she lay completely still on the futon. Then the sound occurred again—from the direction of the sofa. Listening intently, Sophie determined it was a whimpering noise, a soft, helpless cry. And the cry was coming from Grant.

Sophie sat up on the hard mattress, barely making out the contours of his lean body in the blackness. Once her pupils dilated further, she could see his eyes were closed. He must be dreaming.

His breaths came in quickened rasps, and he began talking in his sleep. At first his words were unintelligible, but then she heard "I promise." She waited, frozen, consumed by an uncomfortable feeling that she was invading his privacy.

"No, no," he pleaded urgently. "No. I promise I'll be good."

His voice cracked, and Sophie's heart almost broke. Who was he pleading with? Was he having a nightmare? Should she wake him?

His body trembled, and his breathing intensified. "Please. No. I promise." He gave a shuddering cry. "I'll be good. I'll be good."

Sophie's throat tightened as she listened to a grown man speak a child's words. But then he lapsed into stillness and his breathing gradually slowed. Tiredness overtook her as his steady breaths lulled her toward sleep, and she returned her head to her pillow. A short time later, she was startled awake again. This time his words were clear, sharp, angry. "Leave!" he snarled. "Get away from him!"

She held her breath.

"Leave Ben alone," he demanded. *Who was Ben?* "Leave him alone."

Several moments passed and then he murmured, "I'm his uncle. Don't you know what that means? I protect..." His words were hard to make out until he reiterated, "I'm his uncle!" Then he inhaled sharp breaths, gulping for air. "No!" he cried.

His breathing crescendoed before halting entirely for a few seconds, then his panting slowly decelerated as he shifted around on the sofa. Sophie knew he was now awake. He sat up with a start, then brought his hand to rest on the top of his head, emitting a slow groan of pain.

"Grant?" Sophie called to him, knowing he might be disoriented in the strange apartment.

Silence. Then his confused voice, "Sophie?"

"Yes, it's me. We're at my friend Kirsten's apartment."

His tongue felt like the Sahara desert, but he managed to get out, "Why do I feel like a CO just clubbed me on the head with a billy stick?"

"Because you had way too much tequila, Grant. Come on, let's get you some water."

She rose from the futon and groped through the dark, finding his hand and clasping it securely in her own. "The bathroom is this way."

He followed her obediently, and once they reached the small bathroom he haltingly requested, "Uh, Sophie, could you ...?"

"Sure." She retrieved a tall glass of water from the kitchen and waited in the hallway, hoping their late-night hijinks would not awaken her roommate. Sophie heard the toilet flush, then Grant sheepishly opened the door.

"Here you go." She offered him the glass. "I suggest a couple of aspirin, in the medicine cabinet, for your headache."

He immediately downed the cool liquid and refilled the glass at the tap before opening the cabinet and shaking out a couple of aspirin. After two full glasses of water, he looked at her expectantly.

"I'm surprised you didn't throw up from all that tequila," she whispered.

"I have a stomach of steel," he whispered back. "But how much did I have anyway?"

"You told me you had ten shots."

"Wow," he responded, clearly impressed with himself.

"Let's see how proud of yourself you are tomorrow." She grinned.

"What does that mean?" His whisper was demanding.

Sophie guessed he was probably still drunk. "Nothing. Let's talk about it tomorrow, okay? It's the middle of the night."

His eyelids already drooping, he followed her back to the living room where they each collapsed on their respective makeshift beds. He was still dressed in his cruise uniform, a light-blue collared shirt and navy pants, although she and Kirsten had removed his shoes.

For a moment, Sophie and Grant each considered how much they would enjoy cuddling up to the other, but both dismissed that idea quickly—for so many reasons.

"By the way, I called the hospital, and it sounds like Roger is doing okay," Sophie reported as she settled into the futon.

"Good," Grant whispered into the darkness. He was quiet for a few seconds. "Thank you for taking care of me, Sophie."

"Of course I'll take care of you, Grant. I was the one who stupidly gave you alcohol in the first place." After a moment she added, "Drunk Grant is a handful, though," which caused him to chuckle.

They were quiet once again, and Sophie thought about his gratitude. It felt good to care for him. Caring for others was in her blood, as natural to her as breathing. Grant seemed to possess a similar intrinsic consideration for others.

Sophie wondered if she would hear Grant talking in his sleep again. There was so much she didn't know about him, about what made him the man he was. Reliving his kisses from the cab ride—and hoping that there were more to come—Sophie floated off into sleep with a soft smile.

15. Sexy Vegetables

He awoke to a splitting headache and the return of cotton mouth.

"Evil," he whispered. "Tequila is pure evil."

With a groan, he lifted his sore neck from the sofa armrest and caught a glimpse of tousled strawberry hair splayed across the pillow on the futon. Slats of morning sunlight filtered through the blinds, surrounding Sophie with a warm yellow glow. She was lying on her side with her back to him, and she had kicked off the sheet and blanket, which afforded him a nice view of her curvy behind and revealed the thin T-shirt and shorts clothing her body. Her shirt had ridden up in her sleep, leaving the small of her back exposed. Her smooth, milky skin enticed him.

Though his temples throbbed to the beat of his pounding pulse, he felt no pain as his cool blue eyes traveled up and down her body, taking in every curve, every angle, every freckle. Those long legs, responsible for her five-foot-nine height, caught his attention most of all. His college girlfriend, Pamela, had been barely over five feet, forcing Grant to lean down awkwardly to kiss her. They'd always seemed like a mismatch. He felt certain kissing Sophie would be a much smoother and well-matched endeavor.

Drinking in Sophie's smooth, sexy legs, Grant imagined those endless limbs wrapped around him, entangling him, trapping him like their prey. He could almost feel the warmth of her skin, and he craved such intimacy with her.

She shifted in her sleep and slowly rolled over, causing Grant to tear his eyes away. Laying his head back on the armrest, he pretended to sleep.

"Grant?"

"Yeah?" He took the risk of opening his eyes and looked in her direction, only to find her staring back at him.

"Good morning." She grinned. "How do you feel, tequila boy?"

"Stop smiling. It's not funny."

She kept grinning. "Yeah, it kind of is, actually."

He narrowed his eyes in feigned anger before his expression turned more serious. "How is Rog?"

"You don't remember my midnight report?" she teased. "He seems to be fine, but I was thinking we could go to the hospital this morning to check on him."

"Good plan."

She studied his wrinkled shirt, which had partially unbuttoned in his sleep, rewarding her with a view of his strong, defined chest. Trailing her eyes upward to find his gaze boring into her, she nervously cleared her throat. "Would you like to shower first?"

A bemused expression danced in his eyes. "But I don't have any clean clothes."

Who cares about clothes? she almost said out loud. "Oh," she murmured instead. "I could try to find some baggy sweats that might fit." *It might take me awhile. And while I'm looking, it would be quite all right for you to stand there dripping in a towel.*

While he considered her offer she added, "And I could make us some breakfast."

Grant shook his head. "No food."

"What happened to your stomach of steel?"

"How do you know about that?"

"You told me last night. There's *lots* you don't seem to remember."

"Drunken boasting, I guess. Apparently tequila can burn a hole through steel, judging by how my stomach feels right now." He paused a moment and then confided, "I do have a strong stomach though. I had to have one in my former career."

"Yeah, wouldn't be too cool to get seasick on an aircraft carrier."

Once again he looked at her with disbelief. "How did you know I was in the Navy?"

"Tommy told me. I found out all kinds of fun facts about you last night, Lieutenant Madsen."

A tendril of fear crept up his spine. He wondered what else she now knew about him. He needed to be more careful. Grant swung his legs around the sofa and willed himself not to groan as he sat up. "Actually I better go get cleaned up at Roger's."

Sophie hid her disappointment and nodded. Kirsten would be bummed not to see the conscious McSailor before he left.

Once Grant determined Kirsten's apartment was not all that far from Roger's place, he went home to shower, but promised to return immediately so they could walk to the hospital together.

❧

An hour later, Grant and Sophie walked to the hospital: him freshly shaved with a splash of tantalizing aftershave, her smelling of soap and lavender.

"So, about last night," Grant began. "I don't remember everything, but…" His eyes widened with horror. "Oh my God, was I singing?"

She giggled. "Yes, you were!" She wondered if he remembered the best part of the evening—the cab ride home.

"Oh." He groaned in embarrassment.

"How did you know the lyrics to all those Frank Sinatra songs?"

"My mother was a huge fan of Frank."

"She *was* a fan? What—she doesn't like Ol' Blue Eyes anymore?"

Grant looked down awkwardly. "Actually, my mother is deceased."

Sophie wondered if her entire foot would fit in her huge mouth. "Oh, Grant, I'm sorry." They walked in silence until she quietly asked, "How old were you when she died?"

"Twelve."

Sophie suddenly understood his kind response to learning of her own mother's death. They had yet another thing in common. Affectionately she stroked his hand, and her touch made Grant feel instantly better.

"That must have been really hard, to lose her when you were so young," she ventured, drawing herself closer to him.

"It was horrible."

"You said your dad was a jerk. Did you have to live with him then?"

"No, my mom left him before she died. My uncle adopted me instead. Wait a minute." He paused midstride. "I thought we agreed not to discuss our pasts?"

"Whoops, there I go into psychologist mode again. I obnoxiously start interrogating everyone. No wonder my dates think I'm analyzing them."

"Your *dates?*" Grant cracked a smile. "Do you wish to elaborate on that?"

Sophie returned his smile. "No talking about the past, remember?"

"Oh, so that rule only applies when it's convenient?"

They continued walking until Sophie could no longer contain her curiosity. "So, anything else you remember about last night?"

"Hmm, let me think. It seemed like the cruise went pretty well, but I don't recall much after that. How did we get to Kirsten's place?"

"We took a cab," she reminded him.

"A cab? No, I don't remember that. Though there *is* a memory nagging at me. Seems like there was something I wanted to do last night, but I didn't get a chance. What was that?"

With his free hand he tapped his chin while Sophie studied him, almost bursting with anticipation.

"Ah, now I remember!" he cried victoriously. "I wanted to do *this*." He pulled her toward him and gathered her in his arms as his hand lovingly cradled the back of her neck. She stopped breathing as he leaned down—*ohmigod*, the Adonis was about to kiss her—and planted the softest, most sensual kiss on her lips.

Time stood still on the busy Chicago street.

She drew her hand to his face and gently stroked his cheek as their lips melted together. Their first kiss lasted far longer than a chaste peck, but not so long that Sophie lost the ability to stand. But the intensity and spine-tingling power of his exquisite lips caressing hers lingered long after he reluctantly ended their liplock.

Sophie glanced around and was relieved that nobody seemed to be staring. "You, uh…" She cleared her throat. "You remembered what you started in the cab."

He smiled, noticing the flush of her cheeks and the fire in her eyes. "Kissing you on the cheek was only the beginning, Sophie." He gave her hand a squeeze. "I may have been drunk, but I would *never* forget kissing your beautiful face."

Arriving at Roger's hospital room, Grant and Sophie heard an argument inside. Grant rapped lightly before sticking his head cautiously into the room. Roger glared at the nurse, who looked disapprovingly at her patient.

"How's it goin', Rog?" Grant inquired uneasily.

"Not good, Madsen. Not good at all. This *nurse*," he gestured emphatically toward the older woman standing at his bedside, "wants to 'accompany' me to the bathroom. Ain't no way a chick is gonna watch me take a piss."

"It's standard protocol, Mr. Eaton," she replied. "You're at a higher risk for falls following surgery."

"You had surgery?" Sophie asked.

Roger grunted. "It's no big deal. They went in and messed with my ticker, and now I'm good as new."

"Mr. Eaton had a procedure called an angioplasty," the nurse chimed in. "We inserted a stent into his artery to open up the blockage to his heart."

"That *does* sound like a big deal," Grant said.

Roger rolled his eyes.

Grant glanced at the nurse. "How about I take Mr. Eaton to the head? Would that be okay, Rog?"

Roger reluctantly nodded. This hospital thing *sucked*.

The nurse briefed Grant on preventing falls as he assisted Roger into the bathroom. "Tell Mr. Eaton I'll return to give him his sponge bath later," she said.

A few minutes later, Sophie was dismayed to see the color drained from Roger's face as Grant helped him back into bed. Walking across the room was clearly exhausting.

"Where did Nurse Ratched go?" Roger spat.

Sophie giggled. "She's coming back to give you your sponge bath later."

Grant arched his eyebrows. "I think she likes you, Rog. Maybe if you weren't such a pain in the ass, you two might get along better."

"Save it, Madsen," Roger growled. "Now, give me an update. Did you two sink my ship last night? Do I have a business to return to when I get the hell out of here?"

Grant and Sophie exchanged nervous glances, and he tentatively spoke first. "Yes, we had a sold-out cruise last night, sir."

"No shit. I'm asking how it went. You were almost pooping a brick about being the docent for the cruise. What happened? Did you pull it off, or royally fuck it up?"

"I think it went well," Grant said.

"You *think* it went well?" Roger studied Grant, wondering why he looked a bit ill. He turned to Sophie. "How did Madsen do?"

"He did great, Roger. *I* was the one who struggled, trying to get the drink orders right."

Sensing evasiveness, Roger folded his meaty arms across his chest but stopped when it turned out to be painful. Angrily he demanded answers. "Tell me how you described the Trump Tower to the passengers, Madsen."

"You know, I said the same stuff you say, but I added how Trump was planning a one-hundred-fifty story building before the World Trade Center thing, and I tied in the winner of *The Apprentice*—stuff like that."

Roger narrowed his eyes. "People don't want to hear about goddamn TV shows on an architectural cruise."

"Yes, sir," Grant replied dutifully.

"And the Spire?" Roger asked. "That's the end of the cruise. Were you still doing okay by then? What did you say about the Spire?"

Sophie suppressed a smile, but Grant squirmed nervously.

Grant's blush deepened in color. "I don't really remember, sir."

"What do you mean you don't remember?"

"I, um, had some tequila."

His eyes bugged out. "You were *drinking?* You were driving the ship *drunk?*"

"Tommy was driving the ship, sir."

"Well, thank God for Tommy, then! But you still broke all kinds of watercraft regulations. If the Chicago PD had boarded the ship, we'd all be in a shitload of trouble!"

"It was my fault, Rog," Sophie interjected. "I gave him the tequila to calm his nerves."

"Did they teach you that maneuver in shrink school?"

Sophie looked down. "No."

"It wasn't her fault," Grant said. "She gave me one shot of tequila because I was nervous about taking your place, but I was the one who kept drinking."

"How much did you have, you idiot?"

Grant continued to fidget, feeling helplessly guilty for all the trouble he had caused. "Around ten shots."

"*Ten?* And you don't drink! No wonder you look like shit," Roger grumbled under his breath as Sophie and Grant exchanged desperate glances. "I shoulda known better than to hire two parolees, goddamn it. You two are no good for each other, you hear? Madsen was doing just fine until you showed up, Taylor. I should fire both your asses."

Grant inhaled sharply. "Please, Rog, don't fire Sophie. I'm the one who screwed up." He felt panic rising in his chest at the thought of returning to prison.

Sophie watched Grant fall on the sword for her with a sense of wonder and gratitude.

"You sure as hell did screw up!" Roger hollered. "Here I am stuck in this fucking hospital, hoping you two could keep my business afloat—that's all I asked—and I come to find out you're drinking on the job? You think this cruise is some sort of joke or something? I worked my ass off to buy that ship! You're not going to tear it all down with one night of partying. Joe will not be pleased with you, Madsen, when he finds out you couldn't hold down this one simple job."

Sophie suddenly flashed with anger and words tumbled out of her mouth. "You're being so unfair, Rog! You left us both in the lurch when you had your heart attack. Granted, it's not like you asked for it, but we did you a *favor* by taking over your business, and now you're *yelling* at us? Now you're threatening to fire us? I'll have you know that Grant did an incredible job at the mic. The customers absolutely loved him, and his commentary… well, it was even better than yours!"

Grant's eyes widened, and he tried to gauge Rog's reaction. Sophie calmed down to realize she had just insulted her boss, the one man who could keep her out of prison. She swallowed hard.

But Roger began chuckling, slowly shaking his head. "You got balls, Taylor. Swear to God, you two make quite a pair. Who wears the pants in this relationship, Madsen? You got a live one here. She's going to be tough to handle."

Glancing at Sophie, Grant felt strengthened by the intensity flaring in her shiny chestnut eyes. She would fight for him, he now knew. And he wanted to fight for her in turn.

"I don't need to *handle* her, Rog," Grant informed him with a twinge of disgust. "She takes care of herself quite all right all on her own. But it looks like you're going to be stuck here for a while, and you have nobody to run your cruises today except for us. Sophie and I make a good team, and I promise I'll do a better job. I'm never going to drink again, I tell you. It's vile."

Roger remained silent, so Grant added, "Give us another chance, sir. We won't disappoint you."

Stroking his chin, Roger conceded, "If you run the ship today, you will return tonight to tell me how all four cruises went, in detail. None of this 'I can't remember' bullshit."

"You got it, Rog. Your business is in good hands."

"Let's not exaggerate, Madsen. You're on toilet duty when I finally get out of this fucking hospital."

"Mr. Eaton?" a voice called from the doorway, breaking the tension.

A young blond woman entered the room. She was thin and petite, with big blue eyes and rosy cheeks. "I'm Jodi Roman, your dietitian." She smiled as she wheeled her cart toward the bed.

Roger raised his eyebrows, gaping at the human Barbie now standing by his bedside. "Dietitian?"

"That's right. We're going to get you started on a healthy diet to prevent another myocardial infarction. Would you like to introduce me to your friends here? Are these your children?"

Roger's body shook with laughter for quite a while before he could respond. "Hardly! These are my employees." He shot a stern glance toward them both. "Well, they're my employees for now, anyway."

"Great!" Her reply was bubbly. "They can help you make smart food choices at work." She turned to the plastic cart and extracted a piece of plastic broccoli. "These are my food models."

"What the hell does that plastic crap have to do with my heart?" Roger growled.

"Let me explain," she said, pulling up a chair. "You had a blockage in your artery that caused a heart attack. Do you know what caused the blockage?"

"I'm the captain of a ship, not some fucking heart doctor," he rumbled.

"I see. You're a sailor, then," said Jodi, not missing a beat. "Let me ask you this, do you have any hoses on board your ship?"

"Yeah, we got a hose that pumps water out from the galley if necessary," he replied, trying to keep it simple for Barbie.

"And does that hose ever get clogged?"

"Sure," he replied. "Brine, barnacles, all kinds of shit can get in there and clog it up." Roger turned to Grant. "By the way, check on the filter system today, Madsen."

"Aye, sir."

"Well," Jodi resumed her analogy. "Your heart artery got clogged just like that hose. And what clogged it was fatty cells called plaque. A clogged artery is not good, Mr. Eaton. If you have another heart attack, you could die."

Roger sat quietly with a frown on his face. Grant was pleased to see him shut up and listen for once.

"Hardening of the arteries is partly due to genetics. Do you have any family history of heart disease?"

"I don't think so."

"The buildup of plaque is also related to your diet. Do you know which foods should be eaten only sparingly because they are not heart healthy?"

Roger had a good idea but he was too pissed off to answer.

"Deep dish pizza?" Grant offered, and Roger shot him the stare of death.

"Yes!" Jodi replied. "Cheese, red meat, fried foods, cream sauces…"

"All my favorites," Roger cried mournfully.

"I'm not saying you can never eat those foods again, Mr. Eaton. You just need to add in more heart-healthy foods, like this vegetable here." She held up the stalk of broccoli, and Roger eyed it with disdain. "I'd like you to meet my friend here, Ms. Broccoli." She placed the green blob on the top of the cart and began lining other plastic vegetables next to it.

"Rog and vegetables don't get along too well," Grant explained. "They have a hate-hate relationship."

"Aw," Jodi replied, petting the broccoli. "That hurts broccoli's feelings when you say mean things about her like that."

Roger gawked at the dietitian and began to suspect the three people around him were having fun at his expense.

"Yeah, she's really good for your body, Rog." Sophie jumped into the fray. "Ms. Broccoli *lurves* you."

"Aren't those vegetables sexy?" Grant cooed, trying to hold in laughter. "Sexy, sexy veggies. You two need to go on lots of dates together."

"That's it, you two. Get out!" Roger ordered.

"You want us to leave, sir?" Grant asked innocently.

"He and Ms. Broccoli need some time alone." Sophie winked, taking hold of Grant's arm.

As they headed out the door, Roger called, "Taylor! Get some cash from the ticket vendor by the docks, and stock up the bar before the one o'clock cruise!"

"Will do, Rog," Sophie nodded.

"I want receipts. And that tequila is coming out of both of your paychecks!"

"Understood, sir," Grant acknowledged.

The pair left the hospital and walked toward the ship, choosing to forego the city streets and head south along shimmering Lake Michigan instead. Both were quiet, lost in thought. Grant finally spoke. "One thing I like about you is that you don't talk all the time."

She looked at him, showing a hint of surprise as well as self-consciousness. "I guess that's just leftover from my former career. Psychologists tend to listen a lot."

They walked a little further and Sophie admitted, "I'm thinking about what happened back there. That was a close call, and I'm a little freaked out that I'm going to lose this job. I don't want to go back, Grant."

He sighed heavily, nodding in agreement. Returning to prison was his number one fear.

"Frankly I'm just trying to figure out how I got here. How in the world did I end up on parole after serving a year in prison? How did I end up playing waitress on a ship, with no home and no family? It's plain crazy." She sighed, but then glanced at Grant. "But I, um … I'm glad I'm not in this alone. I'm grateful you're here with me."

He looked genuinely touched, and his piercing eyes seared into her. "I'm trying to work out how I screwed up things so badly in my life too," he said. "But if not for prison and those awful meetings with Officer Stone, we never would have met. Maybe it was somehow all meant to be."

Sophie felt like she was floating, as high as a kite. How could one man make her feel so damn good?

They continued on, both with a bounce in their step, actually looking forward to running four cruises, *together*.

Grant could see the Spire construction site ahead of them, and he turned to Sophie. "How *did* I describe the Spire last night? That part I simply can't remember."

Sophie blushed. "Are you sure you really want to know?"

"Give me the hard truth, please."

"The hard truth, huh?" She bit her lip, but a few giggles still spilled out. "It's appropriate that you say that. As I recall, you said the Spire was the most phallic thing ever." Grant's eyes widened and Sophie forged ahead. "You told everyone it was a throbbing, um, *penis* thrusting upward into the sky."

His jaw dropped.

"You really don't remember?"

He shook his head and climbed over the railing onto the ship. Time to begin another long workday. "You're right," he said. "Drunk Grant *is* a handful."

16. Say Uncle

Sophie smiled as she bid farewell to the passengers from the seven o'clock cruise. Today's cruises had been far less eventful than the previous night's, and Sophie almost missed the entertainment of a drunken captain at the helm. But they both needed this job, so they'd performed their duties efficiently and with no shenanigans. However, Sophie continued to be impressed by Grant's narration of the architectural wonders. He seemed to add new information every cruise.

Two women, among the last departing passengers, approached Sophie. One had platinum-blond hair pulled back in a ponytail, with a button nose and big blue eyes. She was shorter and perhaps slightly older than Sophie was, and she nervously clasped Sophie's forearm. "The guy who was the tour guide—he said his name was Grant. Is he, um, Grant Madsen by any chance?"

Sophie stared at the woman curiously. "Yes, he is."

"I *thought* so!" she declared victoriously to her friend. "Could I, um, maybe talk to him?"

Suddenly feeling jealous and somewhat protective of the "guy who was the tour guide," Sophie squinted and suspiciously inquired, "Do you know him?"

"Yes." She nodded decisively with increasing confidence. "I'd like to see him. I need to talk to him. He's up there?" She gestured toward the bridge, beginning to walk in that direction.

"Hold on. I'll take you to him," Sophie said, desperately wanting to know how this cute blonde knew Grant.

"Wait a minute!" the blond woman's brown-haired friend cried, tapping Sophie's shoulder. "I have a question for you."

Sophie turned around and was dismayed to see the blonde ascending the stairs. "How can I help you?" Sophie asked politely through gritted teeth.

"I was told there would be singing on this cruise," the woman said.

"Singing?"

"Yes. My friend Maureen took one of these cruises last night, and she said she had a total blast. The tour guide was leading everybody in a Frank Sinatra song or something?"

A smile crept onto Sophie's face. Perhaps the drunken singing had been a good idea after all.

Up on the bridge, Grant was placing the microphone headset into a drawer when he noticed a shadow in the doorway. He glanced up. "Ashley?"

Hearing his deep, smooth voice, she grinned and took a step toward him before hesitating. Both stared awkwardly for a moment. Then Grant came to his senses and gave her a quick, chaste hug.

Ashley pulled back, admiring his tall frame and tanned face. "You're—you're all grown up. You're a man now," she said. "I mean, what has it been? Five years?"

"At least," he nodded. "How's Ben?"

"He's turning sixteen next month."

Grant's eyes widened, and he shook his head with wonder. "No, that's not possible. Sixteen? My nephew is sixteen? God, I feel old."

Ashley chuckled. "Yep, sixteen. He's going to be driving soon, so you best avoid the roads in the near future."

He smiled, but his eyes showed only sadness. Ashley's grin faded, and she wondered if visiting him had been such a good idea. "How long you been out?"

Grant looked down. "Almost a month now. Logan told you what happened?"

She bit her lip nervously. "Well, Angelo said you got sentenced to three years, but I don't know the details."

His eyes darkened, like an ominous gray cloud obscuring the bluest sky. "What are you doing with Angelo? Stay away from him, Ashley."

"That's actually why I needed to talk to you. I want to invite you to Ben's sixteenth birthday party." She pressed her lips together. "At the compound."

His voice trembled with anger. "Angelo is hosting Ben's birthday party? No. You and Ben should never go there! Keep away from them!"

"How am I supposed to do that, Grant? I can't ban him from his father's entire family!"

"When the family is as sick as ours, then you damn well better keep your son away from them. Letting Ben see his father is one thing, but you need to steer clear of Angelo and Carlo."

"I *can't* let Ben see his father," she hissed. "Logan has been missing for over a year."

"Missing?" Grant took a step back. "Why?"

"The cops wouldn't tell me, but they're looking for him. What a surprise. He's in trouble with the law." Her tone dripped with sarcasm. "Such a wonderful father *he's* turned out to be."

Grant rubbed the bridge of his nose, feeling the morning's headache beginning to return. "So Ben has been without a father for the past year?"

"Ben has been without a father his entire life," she corrected. "Without a good one, anyway."

"Still, you can't let Angelo host a birthday party for him. You can't let Angelo get his claws into him."

"I'm afraid it may be too late. Ben worships Angelo and Carlo. He thinks they're cool. They're tough. That's why you have to be there, Grant. You have to help Ben or he's going to turn into a mobster just like them. He'll end up in prison like his grandfather, and like his father too, once the police catch up to him."

"And like I'm such a positive influence? I just got out of prison myself. I'm a felon, Ashley. Ben would be better off without me."

"That's not true!" She was sad to find Grant viewing himself so negatively. "I was so shocked when Angelo told me you were going to prison that I begged Logan to fill me in on what happened. Lo did admit that he threatened to hurt your Uncle Joe unless you helped him commit a crime."

Grant's wounded eyes met her intense gaze, and he swallowed, feeling bile rise in his throat. "I can't believe he owned up to that."

"I think he almost needed to tell me, like he had to confess or something. He seemed to feel really guilty about the whole thing."

"Yeah," Grant scoffed. "He feels really bad. He's all torn up inside. In the meantime, I go to prison and he goes scot-free."

"Logan did get sentenced to court-ordered counseling."

Grant was too incensed to respond. His hands had curled into fists, and his breathing came in short, shallow rasps. All the tequila in the world could not numb the resentment washing over him.

"Grant?" she asked gently. "What happened that day? Will you tell me?"

He leaned against the console and rubbed his hand over his clipped black hair. He sighed, glancing out the window to see Sophie conversing with a female passenger on the deck below. He did not want her to learn the sordid details of his crimes, but he supposed he owed the story to the mother of his nephew. Maybe once Ashley heard the tale, she would cease recruiting him as a positive role model for her son. Ben certainly deserved better.

"It was two years ago, in March," he began.

The brothers continued to stand at their mother's grave, planning a robbery over her plot. Grant felt sick.

"We need the security code to the basement room in that bar near the base," Logan said.

"And why do you think I would know it?"

"Because you have Navy buddies who gamble there all the time."

"It's against regulations to go down there."

"You always had to follow the rules—Uncle Joe's good little boy," Logan sneered.

Grant's blood boiled. "You never gave Joe a chance!"

The older brother, stronger and burlier, held out his arm to restrain the younger one. "Do I have to remind you what's at stake here? The very man you're defending. Get that code or Joe is dead."

Grant had no choice. He got the needed information from his old bunkmate, Simkins, who was still stationed at Great Lakes. The next day he found himself in the driver's seat of an unfamiliar car, idling outside the bar near the naval base. Logan sat next to him, dismayed to see his little brother trembling with fear.

"It'll be okay," Logan promised. "You're a Barberi. You're Dad's son. This stuff runs in our blood."

"Dad got caught," Grant reminded him.

"We both know that wasn't his fault. He was only protecting his nephew. Family means everything to him."

"Whatever," Grant scoffed, turning off the ignition. "Let's get this over with."

"Wait," Logan insisted, extending his arm across his brother's chest. He reached into the waistband of his jeans. "You need some protection."

Grant gasped when his brother extracted the gleaming handgun from its hiding place. He thrust the weapon at Grant, who eyed the Glock 17 with trepidation. "I won't need that, Lo."

"I'm not gonna have my brother go in there holding only his dick."

"I'm not going to shoot somebody!"

"Take it. You never know what you're going to find. Just having a gun on me has gotten me out of some tight spots."

Grant's breathing quickened as his eyes locked on the weapon. He had trained with quite a few handguns and rifles in his Navy career, but those weapons were legally issued by his superior officers, who sanctioned and ordered their use. This was quite different. Grant was sure this gun was as illegal as the theft he was about to perpetrate.

"Take the damn gun! We're stealing money from a gambling establishment, Grant, not robbing Garrett's Gourmet Popcorn. If anybody catches you, this gun may be the only thing that saves your life." Logan added condescendingly, "Joe would be crushed if his cherished nephew died because he was unprepared."

Aiming a hostile glance at his brother, Grant yanked the weapon from his grasp and placed it in the rear of his waistband, tucked securely against the small of his back beneath his uniform. The cold metal felt odd against the sweat sliding down his spine. *Get it under control, Madsen*, he silently told himself. *You can do this.*

"What if I can't find the bag?" Grant asked for about the tenth time. Logan had lost a substantial amount of cash to a Navy lieutenant in a poker game at Angelo's club in downtown Chicago a few nights before, and afterward he'd tailed the lieutenant north to this bar. Logan had watched the lieutenant carry the bag of cash into the bar, then emerge empty-handed. There had been more than one hundred thousand dollars in that bag, and now it was stashed somewhere. Logan knew if he didn't get the money back, Carlo would be quite angry—the kind of anger that led men to kill.

"You'll find the bag. Get into the basement room your buddy described, and I'm sure it will be hidden there somewhere."

Grant, ever the planner, felt increasingly nervous as the robbery approached. "What if they've changed the code? Simkins hasn't been there for months."

Logan sighed. "Calm down. It will be fine, okay?"

"You're calm because you're fucking staying in the car! Why don't you do this?"

"Because I already have a record, unlike you, Mr. Über Patriot Boy. And because that Navy uniform will help you blend in."

Logan placed a large hand on Grant's forearm before he exited the car. "You're not going to run into anybody you know, are you?"

"I doubt it. I haven't lived on the base in ten years."

Reluctantly releasing his grasp, Logan added, "If anything bad goes down in there, you don't know who I am, got it? You don't want anything happening to Joe." Logan let his cruel words sink in before adding, "Be careful, bro."

Grant glared and felt a catch in his throat as he stared into the deep-blue eyes of the brother who once tried to protect him from their father. Their adult relationship could have been different. Grant could have loved his older brother, if only Logan had let him. And Logan could have encouraged his little brother, instead of threatening him and dragging him into criminal activity. But wishing it didn't make it so.

Hastily exiting the vehicle, Grant straightened his khaki uniform and strode into the bar, hoping nobody could detect the quivering throughout his body.

He gave a plastic smile to the bartender, then turned to the stairwell. Grant quickly descended, pausing for a moment at the base of the stairs. He glanced to his left, the direction he intended to go, and then to his right, where the restrooms were located. At just that moment, the door swung open and Grant froze as a man in a captain's uniform emerged. Grant spun on his heel and headed left when he heard a deep voice call out behind him.

"Grant?"

Shit. He *had* seen him. Closing his eyes, Grant turned and faced his uncle's former boss. They exchanged salutes. "Captain Lockhart! How are you, sir?"

"That *is* you!" Archibald Lockhart's booming voice rang out in the basement corridor as he gave a big smile, stepping closer.

Feeling his face flush, Grant tried to hide his palpable anxiety.

Archie's smile faded. "Is something wrong?"

"N-n-no, sir. I was just looking for the bathroom."

"Well, you know where it is, Grant. You used to come here all the time with Joe."

Grant nodded. "Yeah, I guess I got turned around or something."

A lieutenant came bustling down the stairs, and she stopped immediately upon noticing the captain. Archie tilted his head dismissively, and she scampered toward the women's restroom.

After an uncomfortable silence, Archie finally spoke. "So, you decided to visit your old stomping grounds?"

"Yes, sir, something like that."

"Why don't you come join me for a drink, Madsen? You can fill me in on how that fucker Joe is doing."

Grant laughed nervously. "Uh, thank you, sir. But I, um, I can't." He forced himself to relax. Nodding his head toward the bathroom, he said, "I gotta hit the head. Good to see you, sir."

Grant quickly ducked into the restroom, hoping the captain wouldn't follow him. The few moments he waited were beyond tense, but the door never opened.

Stealthily emerging from the restroom, Grant peeked out the door and swiftly made his way down the hall, his heart pounding furiously.

He arrived at a heavy steel door at the end of the hallway, just as his buddy Simkins had described it. Grant was suddenly thankful for Simkins' otherwise annoying motormouth. There was a keypad located on the wall to the right. Furtively glancing down the dimly lit hall, Grant held his breath and entered the code: POKE HER, 7-6-5-3-4-3-7. Though the code was incredibly sexist, Grant was relieved to have the reminder for his fear-addled brain.

Sighing with relief when the door clicked open, he slipped inside. He stood in the darkness for a few seconds, listening to the frantic beating of his heart. Groping along the wall, he located the light switch, and suddenly the room was bathed in buzzing fluorescent light.

Grant heard himself panting and willed himself to relax, knowing he would not find what he needed if he continued to be this jumpy. The framed painting was right where Simkins had told him it would be, hanging slightly askew on the left side of the far wall. It was, of course, a group of dogs playing poker, and Simkins was right. It stuck out in otherwise bare room, and its off-center placement looked suspicious.

Grasping the sides of the ugly brown frame, he lifted it off the wall and discovered a secret compartment behind. He set the framed picture on a wooden table and studied the thick padlock on the little handle to the compartment set into the wall. He had brainstormed several possible lock combinations involving famous Navy dates, and Grant swiftly took out a crumpled piece of paper before spinning the numbers on the lock.

To his surprise, his fourth try, 12-7-41, resulted in a beautiful clicking noise as the lock fell open in his hand. Grant froze, but there were no angry knocks at the door, no shouts about an intruder breaking in.

Gulping, Grant opened the compartment. To his immense relief, he found a blue gym bag stuffed inside. Carefully pulling out the bag, Grant unzipped it and peeked in, detecting bundles of cash. Joe would be okay.

Grant was then all action: in one motion closing and locking the compartment door, then replacing the hideous poker painting on the wall. Checking around him for any evidence left behind, he backed out of the room and slowly creaked closed the steel door.

The hallway was clear. Making his way down it, carrying the heavy gym bag over his left shoulder, he tasted freedom just ahead of him. He would get the money to Logan, and Logan would leave him and Uncle Joe alone.

His reprieve was short-lived, however, when he neared the base of the staircase and found Captain Lockhart descending the stairs quickly.

"Grant!" he boomed, seemingly out of breath. "I've been looking all over for you. I just talked to Joe and—"

Archie stopped midstream upon noticing Grant's panicked expression. "What's wrong?"

Grant bit his lip while dread pulsed throughout his bloodstream. What was he supposed to say?

Archie continued staring at him. "What's in the bag?"

"Nothing, sir. Please excuse me, I gotta go."

With wary brown eyes, Archie stood fast, blocking the stairwell. "What is wrong with you, Grant? I called Joe, and he's trying to get in touch with you. Why are you acting so weird, son?"

Grant's voice turned to ice. "I can't explain. Just please get out of the way."

Much to Grant's consternation, Archie didn't budge. The captain kept staring at him with disbelief.

Forcing a swallow did not help Grant's bone-dry mouth, and his skin tingled with terror. Why the hell didn't Captain Lockhart step aside? Would he ruin the robbery? The same man who had been so kind to Grant as a child? The same man who, along with Uncle Joe, had inspired him to join the Navy? Smart as a whip, firm, caring, and always knowing what to do—Joe and Archie were cut from the same cloth. Grant was about to betray them both.

With a trembling hand, Grant slowly removed the gun from his waistband and aimed it squarely at Archie's chest. "Move out of my way," he demanded, attempting to sound authoritative.

The older man did not even flinch. His only detectable reaction was a change in his eyes, where confusion steeled into suspicion.

Grant's own crystal-blue eyes flashed terror, his face was bathed in sweat, and his arm was visibly trembling. His portrayal of a toughened criminal was wholly unconvincing. He felt like a scared kid, forced into something that went against every fiber of his being.

"Step aside, sir," Grant ordered, feeling nauseated.

"Don't do this, Grant. This isn't you."

They were mere feet from each other, and Archie still looked cold and calculating.

"Please, sir," Grant begged. "Just get out of my way. I don't want to hurt you."

"I know you don't. And you won't. Give me the gun, Grant."

Both heard the footsteps on the stairs, and the second Grant glanced behind the captain, Archie lunged forward. He was on Grant immediately, and they tumbled backward as Archie wrestled the gun from Grant's grasp. The gym bag fell to the floor with a thud.

Grant desperately tried to hold onto the gun while Archie pinned him on the tile floor. But his resolve didn't hold for long. Once his former mentor had subdued him, his heart wasn't really in it anymore. He'd never wanted the gun in the first place.

Archie leapt off Grant's prone body to stand over him, panting. Now Archie aimed the gun at the man lying on his back.

Still breathing quickly, Archie seethed, "Unlike you, I will fire this weapon if necessary."

Grant closed his eyes with utter resignation. He had fucked it all up. It was over.

"Stay down, Grant," Archie ordered.

His voice was plaintive, sorrowful. "Yes, sir."

Glancing up at the warrant officer gaping at them, Archie commanded, "Call the cops!"

The officer nodded and flew back up the stairs.

Lying flat on his back, a gun pointed at him, Grant felt more at peace than he had in a week. It was over now. He had screwed up so completely that there would be no pretending anymore. He could no longer believe he was an honorable man who could escape his destructive family. They had swallowed him whole.

"What is in the bag?" Archie asked.

"Money," Grant answered quietly.

"You're stealing it?"

"Yes, sir."

"Why?"

Grant did not respond. The wait for the police seemed interminably long.

Archie relaxed his hold on the weapon. "What I was starting to tell you is that Joe's been worried sick about you since you didn't show up in Norfolk yesterday. He's been trying to contact you."

Closing his eyes again, Grant groaned, his feeling of peace quickly smashed to pieces. Once Joe discovered he'd been arrested, at a bar frequented by naval officers no less, he would surely disown him. And how would Logan and Carlo react to his botched robbery attempt? Grant's heart seized with fear.

"Why are you doing this?"

Grant remained silent.

Just then, two Great Lakes police officers hustled down the stairs. Grant listened numbly as Archie surrendered the Glock to them and explained how he'd caught Grant attempting to steal the bag of money. The officers clarified that they'd consult with military police, but they believed the location of the arrest and nature of the crime meant the military would likely defer to them, the civilian authorities.

The officers approached Grant and roughly flipped him over on his stomach, snapping handcuffs into place on his wrists behind his back. He offered no fight as they dragged him to his feet. The arrest began a two-year string of interrogations, harsh treatment, and confinement: the life that awaited a Barberi man.

Ashley's jaw had dropped open during Grant's tale. "What happened to Logan?" she asked, snapping Grant back to the present.

Grant shook his head disgustedly. "I think he tried to drive off, probably once he saw the police arriving, but they detained him. I guess he told some bullshit story about trying to meet up with his buddy—that lieutenant who'd won the money from him in the first place. Then they interrogated the lieutenant, who confirmed that he met Lo while gambling at Angelo's club. Since there was only circumstantial evidence tying him to the robbery, and he had the best lawyer money can buy, Lo pled guilty to some silly misdemeanor and got probation with court-ordered counseling."

Ashley's stared incredulously. "I'm so sorry, Grant."

He took a deep breath and glanced down at his hands. The look of betrayal on the faces of Captain Lockhart and Uncle Joe continued to haunt him. "Now do you understand why I don't want to be anywhere near Logan, Angelo, the lot of them?"

"I understand," she nodded. Then her maternal instincts kicked in. "But that awful story proves one thing. Ben needs you even more than ever. Don't let him go down the same path, Grant."

He closed his eyes and exhaled loudly, feeling the crushing responsibility of being an uncle in a dishonest, caustic family. When he opened his eyes again, he was startled to find Sophie standing in the doorway of the bridge.

She eyed him curiously, having never seen him so utterly exhausted and broken. "Is everything okay?" Sophie asked, stealing a glance at the blonde at his side.

Pushing himself off the console into a standing position, Grant cleared his throat. "Sophie, this is Ashley. Her son Ben is my nephew."

Sophie nodded slowly.

"We were just catching up," Grant explained. "I hadn't seen Ashley since I, um, since I got out."

Sophie continued nodding and said nothing.

"I'll think about what you asked me," Grant told Ashley. "I will."

Ashley smiled sadly. "Take care of yourself, Grant." Then she brushed past Sophie and rejoined her friend to disembark the ship.

"You look upset," Sophie finally said.

Grant appeared to close himself off before her very eyes. "C'mon, we better go report to Rog. Let's see if we still have jobs."

Without looking at her, he strode down the stairs. His own uncle could not save him from his family. How could he save his nephew?

17. Caretaker

"You look tired," Hunter commented.

Sophie nodded. "I'm beat. We've been working four days straight without our boss, and it's exhausting. I'm starting to understand why his body gave out on him."

Noticing Hunter's puzzled stare, she explained. "My boss, Roger, had a heart attack last Thursday." His eyes widened with concern. "He's doing fine now," she added. "I think they're letting him come home today."

"So, how did your duties change in his absence?"

"I'm still serving drinks." She smiled. "Not quite what I trained six years for, but at least the tips are good. But I've also been trying to help Grant fill in for Roger as docent."

"Grant?"

Sophie blushed. "Um, the man I told you about? The parolee I met outside of Jerry's office? The one who got me this job?"

Hunter cocked one eyebrow. "The one I warned you about letting into your life?"

"That's the one." Sophie laughed.

"How have you been helping him?" Hunter asked, deciding to be open-minded about the relationship.

"Well, I haven't gotten to the 'helping' part yet, I'm afraid. Before his first cruise I gave him some tequila to calm his nerves." She looked embarrassed. "Then Grant proceeded to drink half the bottle, and I had to take him home." A smile bloomed on her face. "God, he was a funny drunk. He was singing, then he grabbed me for an impromptu dance, and then on the cab ride home…" Her voice trailed off as she noticed her psychologist studying her with a bemused grin.

"The cab ride home?" he prompted.

"Let's just say he was really cute," she managed. "I haven't felt that close to a man since…" Her voice faded again, lost in memories. Then she frowned. "But it's not like that closeness with Grant materialized into anything. He's been pretty distant with me since that night."

"What do you make of that?'

Sophie sighed. "Typical. If I like a guy, then it's for sure that he doesn't like me. I am a *disaster* when it comes to relationships."

"That's kind of harsh, isn't it, Dr. Taylor? What would you tell a client who criticized herself that way?"

Another long sigh. "Ah, yes, the old cognitive approach. Challenge dysfunctional thoughts to improve your mood." Her tone became mocking. "Just because I've had some tough luck in past relationships, it doesn't mean *all* my relationships are doomed."

She paused, then continued. "In grad school, cognitive therapy always intrigued me. It makes so much sense. You know, if I say, 'I *should* be perfect, people *should* understand me, the world *should* be fair'—I just have to stop *should*-ing on myself. The thing is, I always enjoyed using cognitive techniques for my clients, but I don't really like that approach for myself."

Hunter let out a big guffaw. "Truer words have never been spoken, Sophie. I know cognitive therapy is all the rage—the insurance companies love it since it's easier to measure progress—but it doesn't work for all people, that's for sure."

"What *does* work, then? Can people really change?"

Her earnest question threw him off for a moment, and he paused before answering. "Therapy is all about change, and therapy is my career, so obviously I believe people can change. Change is really hard, though. One of my supervisors used to say, 'Change is good for all of us. You first.'" He smiled and continued. "In my opinion, a trusting therapeutic relationship is key to that change—a relationship in which the therapist and client can partner together to help the client cope with life better. I also find that it's important to understand how our family experiences affect our adult relationships with ourselves and others." Adding a classic shrink response, he asked, "What do *you* think?"

She crossed her legs. "I always believed I was doing my best therapy when my client was linking family experiences to current struggles and learning to do things differently, if the old childhood patterns were not working. I remember this one nurse I was seeing, Lauren."

Hunter nodded.

"Anyway, Lauren came in for therapy because she was depressed. Turns out Lauren was a total doormat for her family. She took care of everyone but herself, and they treated her horribly. Her mother was constantly on her case.

"I asked Lauren how she felt when her mother criticized her, and she could not answer me. She just told me a good daughter *should* help her parents. I eventually got out of her that she was a little upset, and she finally admitted she was damn angry."

"It sounds like you were very close with this client. She really trusted you."

"Yeah, I saw her for almost a year, until …" Sophie ducked her head. "Well, until I was arrested."

After a moment of silence, Sophie resumed her story. "Lauren's role in her family was to be the caretaker, to take responsibility for making her parents and sister happy. It worked for her as a child, but as an adult, she had no idea what *she* felt or needed. At the hospital, they gave her all kinds of unpleasant nursing assignments because she never stood up for herself. She often bought presents for her friends, but they rarely returned the favor. And her live-in boyfriend could also be a total mooch.

"Lauren started to realize she didn't have to knock herself out to make others happy, and she didn't have any control over others' emotions. She was totally subverting her own needs for her family, which made her feel resentful, and she was still failing to earn the approval she so desperately wanted. We worked on assertive communication strategies, and she actually set some limits with her family.

"Then it was like Lauren started emerging from her shell. She decided to quit nursing to pursue her real love, computers. She figured out her boyfriend was a jerk who treated her badly, and she kicked him out, only to find a better guy later. Lauren totally blossomed."

"Very insightful." Hunter nodded appreciatively.

Sophie blushed. "Well, my client did most of the work."

"I wasn't talking about your client," he said. "I was talking about *you*. That was deep insight about yourself."

"What do you mean?"

"Weren't you talking about yourself there? Your role in the family as the caretaker?"

"How do you know that? I've told you hardly anything about my family!"

"And why haven't you told me anything about your family?"

Sophie looked down, her cheeks blooming with shame. "Because they hate me."

"They hate you? They 'treat you horribly'?"

She glanced up, startled, then a sadness crept across her face. "But I deserve it."

"You deserve it? Lauren's family was unfairly mistreating her, but your family *should* treat you badly?"

"It's not really 'they.' It's 'he.' My dad. I'm an only child, and my mom died last year."

Hunter studied her mournful expression. "The pain of losing your mother is still quite fresh, huh?"

Sophie nodded.

"And your father *hates* you? What makes you think you deserve his hate?"

Her words were almost a whisper. "He blames me for my mother's death."

"Did you murder your mother, Sophie? Is that why you went to prison?"

She gasped. "No! I told you I went to prison because of Logan Barberi." Looking wounded, she inquired, "Do you think I'm actually capable of *murder*?"

"Of course not, Sophie. I said that to shake you up, to show how preposterous it is for your father to blame you for your mother's death."

"But she had a heart attack because she was so devastated that I went to prison!"

"I see. And how exactly was her devastation *your* responsibility? How were you supposed to control her emotional reactions? I'm still waiting to hear how you killed her."

Sophie gaped at Hunter with a bewildered expression. "But … but my mom wouldn't have had a heart attack if I hadn't totally screwed things up by going to prison."

"How do you know that? How do you know it wasn't some inevitable heart defect? Maybe her heart would have given out even sooner, but she stayed alive to help you through your sentencing."

Sophie felt utterly flummoxed. All those years, she'd just wanted her parents to be happy with her, to be proud of her. She was good at taking care of them, she thought. Her attempts to make them happy, to take care of them—had those efforts been misdirected? It had been so awful when her father screamed at her to leave home and never come back. She looked away as tears began to fall.

Hunter watched her and took a deep breath, wanting to give her some time. They were finally getting somewhere. He prompted gently, "You're feeling sad about your mother?"

Sniffing, Sophie replied softly, "I miss her."

"What was she like?"

She wiped tears from her cheeks. "She was pretty complex. She could be a lot of fun, but she could also be exhausting. My mom had a rough childhood, and she definitely had some Axis II thing going on," Sophie explained, referring to the diagnosis for personality disorder. "I couldn't pinpoint if she was avoidant or paranoid. At times she had major depression, and she met criteria for alcohol abuse."

Hunter sighed. "Instead of diagnosing her, how about you tell me what she was like as a mother?"

"Not very good," Sophie immediately responded, followed by a guilty grimace. "Oh, God. That's not a nice thing to say about someone who died!"

"It's okay to feel anger, Sophie. Naturally your mom wasn't perfect."

"She and my dad fought a lot. My mom would come to me and complain, and I hated it. But I tried to listen and help because my mom didn't have any other friends."

"So your mom, who was an adult responsible for taking care of herself, did not have any friends."

She looked at him blankly. "What's your point?" Hunter did not answer, but continued to gaze at her kindly. Sophie chewed her bottom lip and asked, "You're saying it's not my fault my mom didn't have friends? That I shouldn't have had to listen to her complain about my dad if I didn't want to?"

"Exactly!" He let that sink in and then inquired, "How did you feel inside when your mother criticized your father?"

"Anxious. My stomach would get this knotted-up feeling, all tight and tense."

"Did you ever tell her that? That you felt sick to your stomach when she complained about your dad?"

"No." Sophie glanced at the fish swimming in the aquarium. "I didn't want to hurt her feelings. She needed me."

"And what did *you* need?"

Getting no answer, Hunter continued. "You and your client Lauren are two peas in a pod, Sophie. Can't you see that? You take care of everybody except yourself. Lauren benefitted from learning how to put herself first. Do you think you can do that too?"

"I don't know," Sophie said. "I still feel so guilty about my mom dying. I don't think that's going to fade anytime soon."

"Change definitely takes time. Give yourself some time." They both sat contemplatively for a few moments. "Maybe it was a good thing you lost your psychologist license," Hunter said.

She stared as if he were crazy. "What?"

"Sophie, you cannot be an effective therapist until you work through your own issues. We hear awful stories all day long in our jobs, and we absorb a lot of our clients' pain. If we don't know how to take care of ourselves, then we become overwhelmed—anxiety, insomnia. I think you would have burned out quickly if you hadn't lost your license."

"We'll never get to know that now, will we?"

"You haven't fully answered your own question yet," Hunter said. "Do *you* believe people can change?"

"I used to think so. When Logan told me about his father beating him, about his failure at protecting his brother, I could almost see the hardened man become softer before my eyes, like he was healing from that childhood trauma. I thought he could escape his negative family influence. I thought I was helping him. I thought he really trusted me." She exhaled derisively. "But then he killed that trust in one fell swoop. He'd been trained to be a criminal by his family, and he couldn't change."

"Do you want to tell me about it?"

"Not really. I don't want to burden you with the sordid tale."

"After all this discussion about caretaking, are you trying to take care of *me*, Sophie?"

She dropped her mouth open to protest, but she realized he was right. She was incorrigible. She smiled. "Touché, Dr. Hayes. You'll get the whole damn story. Just remember, you asked for it."

She had been just zipping her skirt, her face flushed with a post-coital glow, when there was a soft rapping at her office door. Thinking Logan must have left something behind, Sophie grinned as she waltzed to the door, teasing in a sing-song voice while she twisted the doorknob, "What did you forget—"

She stopped immediately once she opened the door. Instead of looking up at the six-foot-one Logan, she found herself looking down at her five-foot-two colleague, Jacki Fernandez.

"Oh! Um, hi, Jacki. What's up?"

The dark-haired woman seemed to study Sophie curiously, and Sophie began feeling self-conscious about her untucked and wrinkled silk shirt, disheveled skirt, and bare feet. Jacki looked up at her friend and pouted, "What, no Jaquita Chaquita?"

Sophie laughed, hearing her refer to her nickname. "Sorry," she apologized, opening the door wider and gesturing for Jacki to enter. "Bienvenidos, Jaquita Chaquita."

Jacki tentatively entered, followed by Sophie, who crossed the room and slipped her feet into her black pumps, which made her tower over the diminutive Mexican. "What can I do for you, Jacki?"

"I won't stay long—I have a client coming in five minutes. I just wanted to give you the heads-up that some of us are having the cleaning company deep clean our offices this weekend."

"Deep clean?"

"Yeah, in addition to their normal trash collection and vacuuming, they wipe down everything, steam-clean the furniture, you know, make it spic and span. I paid extra for it in my office last spring, and they did a great job."

"Hmm." It had been almost a year since she began renting this office, and the space needed refreshing. She stole a guilty glance toward the sofa. That particular piece of furniture could definitely use some steam cleaning. A pulse of electricity sparked at the base of her spine as she remembered the feel of Logan's sure, strong hands massaging her inner thigh, his rough fingers creeping toward her wet, receptive center...

"...so they can move the furniture around."

"What?" Sophie shook her head rapidly, snapping out of her sexy daydream.

"I said, you have to get your belongings off the floor so the cleaners can vacuum underneath the furniture."

"Oh."

Jacki narrowed her eyes. "What's with you lately, Sophie? You haven't joined me for lunch in over a month."

"I'm s-s-sorry. I've been busy."

Frowning, Jacki touched Sophie's thin forearm. "You seem stressed. Anything you want to talk about?"

Talking to colleagues was the last thing she wanted to do. Her lips tightening, Sophie said, "Thank you, Jacki. You've been great helping me start my practice. I'm just, it's all rather overwhelming—fighting with insurance companies, collecting on unpaid bills—I'm trying to get to know all these new clients." She gulped as she realized she now knew one of those clients in the biblical sense. "And I'm feeling exhausted at the end of the day."

"I hear you," Jacki smiled. "My first year was rough too. It gets easier, though. So, are you in for the deep cleaning?"

"Sounds great. Thanks for letting me know. They'll just add it to my cleaning bill?"

Jacki nodded. "Yep. I gotta run. Catch you later, Sofita."

Sophie giggled. "Adios, chica."

When Jacki left, Sophie turned her attention to her office, suddenly noticing the accumulated dust and grime. Examining the offending sofa, she was relieved when she could not detect any stains on the cushions.

"I wonder if I can move this puppy myself?" she wondered out loud. Grasping the armrest, she wriggled the bulky sofa away from the wall.

Peering down into the shadowed space behind, Sophie tried to identify the uncovered objects. There appeared to be thick white envelopes littering the floor. Squatting down, she shoved the sofa out a few more inches, which allowed her to reach one of the envelopes.

A sick feeling kindled in her gut. She had seen this envelope before. Her uneasiness bloomed into full-blown nausea as she lifted the flap to find crisp one-hundred-dollar bills stacked neatly inside. Sophie staggered backward, landing in her chair with a thump. Her hand tightened around the envelope and she clutched it to her chest. Logan.

Sophie rose and wrenched the sofa completely away from the wall, almost toppling over the lamp on the nearby end table in the process. She frantically scooped up the envelopes, horrified by the sheer number of them, and threw her bundle on the sofa.

Despite her panic, she methodically opened each envelope and counted each and every bill. Once finished, she counted again. There were fifty one-hundred-dollar bills in each envelope, and twenty envelopes lying in a pile, staring back at her menacingly. She gasped, drawing her hand to her mouth. She had one hundred thousand dollars hidden in her office!

Why the hell had Logan left that much money here? What did he plan to do with it? Where had it come from? When had he hidden it?

Questions swirled through her brain, making her feel dizzy.

She pushed herself up to standing, swaying a bit, and went to sit at her desk. Intending to call Logan right away and demand that he explain, Sophie instead opened her computer. Swiftly clicking the internet icon, her fingers flew over the keys as she typed LOGAN BARBERI into the search engine.

The first hit was a newspaper photo: "Angelo Barberi Acquitted." Sophie frantically clicked the link and was stunned to see a photograph of a younger Logan sitting in what appeared to be a courthouse. The caption read: Logan Barberi attends the trial of his uncle, Angelo Barberi.

Sophie returned to the search engine and typed ANGELO BARBERI. Once she read the first paragraph of the story, she knew she was going to vomit.

> November 10, 2001—In a shocking end to the trial of alleged mobster Angelo Barberi, attorney Nick Gladden (known in some circles as "Slick Nick") was able to clear his client of all racketeering charges by discrediting several material witnesses. Gladden's skillful questioning of the government's linchpin, Steven Albeiro, owner of Albeiro Construction, revealed that Albeiro had failed to pay taxes in 1999 and 2000, calling into question the witness' integrity. Albeiro had brought forth allegations that his business went bankrupt due to being forced to pay protection to Barberi's consulting firm, Barberi Family Consulting. Angelo Barberi is the younger brother of Vicenzo Barberi, who has been serving a life sentence for first-degree murder since 1986.

Sophie tried to swallow, but her mouth was completely dry. With trembling hands, she typed VICENZO BARBERI into the search engine. Utterly horrified, she read that the Mafia godfather had been convicted of murdering a seven-year-old boy during a home invasion twenty-one years ago. The article made a point of mentioning that Vicenzo's wife and two sons, ages thirteen and eight, had not attended his trial. She did the math in her head, knowing Logan was now thirty-four. He was Barberi's older son.

Slumping back in her chair, Sophie stared dumbly at her computer screen. Logan's father and uncle were in the Mafia. Logan had to be a mobster too. Sophie knew it. She knew it was true. She had trusted him completely. She had given herself to him, and the whole time he had been a sleazy, deceitful criminal. He and his family were not fucking consultants! They were Mafia!

Why hadn't she searched his name on the internet before? Why? Because she was too damn trusting. She had listened to his every lie with rapt interest and deep concern. She'd tried to take care of him, while every session he was hiding dirty money underneath her sofa. Their entire relationship was dirty. Dirty and depraved. She now felt sick at the thought of his rough touch on her smooth skin, and she dissolved into tears.

Once she finally raised her head to gaze again at the stacks of money on her sofa, she knew she needed to confront him. She removed Logan's chart from her desk drawer to locate his cell phone number, finding it ironic that she didn't know his number by heart. They'd actually never seen each other outside their regularly scheduled appointments, maintaining the illusion that everything between them was prim and proper. Well, the illusion was now over. The illusion was smashed to a million little pieces.

He answered on the second ring. "Yeah?"

Sophie's heart shattered, hearing his deep baritone. "Logan?"

"Who the hell is this?"

"It's Sophie."

There was silence, and then, "Hey! You've never called me before. What's up, Doc?"

Her voice was cold. "I found the money."

Another silence. "What did you say, Sophie?"

"I found the money, you son of a bitch. Where did you get it? Drug deals? Roughing up business owners to pay for protection? I bet it's dirty as hell."

"I can explain—"

"Don't even try. I should hand it over to the police."

"What the fuck, Sophie? That's my money!"

"Your money? Why the hell did you keep it in my office? I'm not a goddamn bank!"

"Sophie, listen to me. I gotta get some things in place, then I'll be right over. I'll take everything away, okay? I'll take care of everything."

Her voice cracked. "I don't want to see you."

"Please, Sophie. Stay there, okay? You don't want to go to the cops, believe me. Don't get us in trouble like that. Stay there."

Overwhelmed, she hung up the phone with a shaking hand. Somehow she managed to call the next two clients on her schedule and cancel their appointments. She wanted to avoid bringing them anywhere near the thug who'd be visiting her soon.

She was frozen by indecision. *Should* she call the police? Although she disagreed with several aspects of the way her parents had raised her, they'd done a superb job of teaching her right and wrong. And keeping quiet about the money would definitely be wrong. But if she involved the authorities, she'd likely have to come clean about her ethical breach of sleeping with a client. She felt even sicker thinking about that.

Sophie wasn't sure how much time had elapsed when a sharp knock jarred her out of her overwrought trance. Logan had arrived, and she hadn't called the police yet. Evidently she'd be doing the wrong thing a bit longer.

She strode to the door, expecting to meet those troubled blue eyes, but she was surprised to find three men waiting for her instead.

"Dr. Sophie Taylor?" asked a man in a business suit, flanked by two uniformed officers. "I'm Detective Mike Kozlowski. We have a warrant to search your office."

Sophie's face froze. She gaped at the paper he held up. *So that's what a warrant looked like.*

"Step aside, ma'am," the detective added, pushing forward into the office.

Sophie glanced at the sofa, which was littered with cash-filled envelopes.

Detective Kozlowski followed her gaze, then gave a triumphant smile to the officers behind him. "Ah, the motherload."

"That's not my money!" Sophie sounded frantic. "A client brought that in here!"

The detective looked suspicious. "What's your client's name?"

She hesitated. "I …"

"Take her outta here, Holloway, while we finish the search."

Officer Holloway reached for her arm. "Let's go, Doc."

"My, my charts," she protested.

"We'll take good care of them," the detective responded condescendingly.

Sophie squirmed in the brawny officer's hold. "That's confidential information in there!" The officer ignored her protests and guided her toward the break room down the hall. Sophie blushed furiously as Jacki curiously peeked out her office door.

After about fifteen minutes, the other officer entered the break room. "Both of you need to come with me," he said.

Sophie walked to her office with one officer in front of her and one behind her. She gasped when she entered the room. Lying on her desk were five handguns.

Her eyes as wide as saucers, her trembling voice inquired, "W-w-where did you get those?"

Detective Kozlowski eyed her skeptically. "I found them behind your desk."

"What?" she asked shrilly, taking a step toward the desk. Officer Holloway forcibly pulled her back, and she began to realize the gravity of the situation.

"Those are loaded weapons," Kozlowski growled. "Where did they come from?"

"I've never seen them in my life. I promise." Sophie's stomach dropped as she realized Logan had hidden more than money in her office.

"You're still not talking, Doctor? What's the name of this supposed client?" Detective Koslowski's tone was snide.

Sophie inhaled sharply. "You're not suggesting the guns and money are mine, are you?"

"We don't know what's going on yet," Koslowski said. "One thing I do know is you're under arrest. We'll sort this out at the station."

She stood between the officers with a glassy stare. She barely heard her Miranda rights as Officer Holloway frisked and cuffed her. It was all a blur, a sickening haze. She was led out of her office and paraded down the hallway, past her esteemed colleagues' offices and the disapproving stares of clients in the waiting room.

"Whoa" was all Hunter could say once she finished. "I guess you came forward with Logan's name after you were arrested?"

Sophie cleared her throat. "Yes. My attorney told me confidentiality didn't apply because it was probably a Tarasoff situation, so I finally caved. Giving them Logan's name made it possible for me to plead the charges down to accessory. If they'd proven aiding and abetting, I'd have gone away for a long stretch. Turns out one of the guns was used in a murder." She shuddered.

"But how could they prove those charges?" Hunter asked. "Wasn't it obvious the money and guns weren't yours? That you just got mixed up with the wrong man?"

"It was the *way* I got mixed up with the wrong man. Once they found out I'd slept with Logan, they really started going after me."

"How did they find that out?"

Sophie pressed her lips together, looking off to the side. "I told them."

Hunter stared at her for a few moments.

"I wanted to do the right thing after I'd so royally screwed up everything," she said. "My attorney was livid. He said I'd have no credibility in front of a jury once they found out I'd behaved so unethically."

"Jesus," Hunter said. "I'm taking notes on all of this, you know, to prevent something like this from happening to me."

She smiled grimly. "I'm glad somebody can learn from my mistakes."

He glanced at his watch. "Sophie, I'm sorry to end our session abruptly, but we are out of time."

"That's okay. It wasn't as bad as I thought it would be."

"I'm glad, but I know it must be rough all the same. Next week we'll talk about your father."

"We will?"

"Yes. We're working to connect your family experiences to your current struggles."

Sophie recognized her own words repeated by her psychologist, and he winked. "I want to do my best work with you, Sophie. We're going to make sense of why you did what you did, okay?"

She nodded and rose to leave, feeling a bit drained. She had a long day of cruises ahead of her, and she needed some energy to make it through. A warm smile from Grant would help immensely, if only he were not so distant these days.

As she left the office building, she ruminated on Hunter's belief that she was a caretaker to the extreme. She was determined to try to do better.

Caretaker, she mused. Logan had certainly taken care of her. He'd taken care of her career, her ethics, her self-respect, her *dignity*. With an acrid bitterness in her heart, she headed toward the docks.

18. Fucking Carrots

Sophie hopped from the dock to the deck and glanced around the empty ship, sighing. Despite her morning therapy appointment, she'd arrived at work ahead of Grant. She wanted to confront him about his standoffish demeanor and hoped she'd have enough courage.

Heading toward the bar to check on her inventory for the day, she stopped short when Grant emerged right in front of her from the stairs leading to the machine room. He wiped black engine oil off his hands with a towel, looking rugged and manly in a dark-blue jumpsuit.

Once he caught sight of her sad, tired eyes, lacking their typical coppery glow, he asked, "Are you all right?"

"I'm fine," she immediately replied, hearing the edge to her voice.

He looked at her uncertainly for a moment, then began to walk away. Sophie called out, "Actually—"

As he turned back to face her, Sophie heard Hunter's words, *Take care of* your *needs*, in her head. "Actually, I'm not fine. I had a rough therapy session this morning."

He nodded sympathetically. "You look like you've been crying."

"No, I…" Her voice trailed off as she gazed into his eyes: so earnest, so caring, so entrancing. "Yeah," she finally admitted. "We were talking about some family stuff."

He nodded again and continued wiping his hands with the old rag he clutched nervously.

Sophie couldn't turn off the nagging internal voice that encouraged her, implored her, to tell Grant how she felt. *Use assertive communication!* Her heart pounding in her chest, she took a deep breath. "Grant, I, um ..." She found his intense gaze searing into her, making her feel unsteady and unmoored. But she continued. "I—I feel kind of hurt, um, hurt and puzzled that you've been so aloof lately."

There. She said it. Oh God, was he going to be mad at her? Was he going to think she was a clingy psycho woman?

His eyes registered surprise. "I have? I've been aloof?"

"I think so. You haven't really said much at all to anyone since, um, Ashley was here." Sophie watched him listen and tried to explain further. "I just, you know, I've missed you. I've missed your smiles." Her cheeks flushed pink.

"I'm sorry. I didn't realize I was being such a jerk."

"No, no—you weren't a jerk."

He took a deep breath and averted his eyes. "Not that it's much of an excuse, but I've had a lot on my mind since I talked to Ashley. I told you how my Uncle Joe got me this job, right?"

He glanced at her and she nodded, feeling grateful for Joe's indirect employment help for her as well.

"Well, Joe did more than that. He pretty much saved my life. He's been like a father to me since I was eight years old. And now *I* have a nephew—Ben—who's almost *sixteen*." Grant's voice warbled with emotion. "And he needs me, like I needed Joe. He needs his uncle to save him, if it's not too late."

Grant was surprised at how much he shared with Sophie, but he didn't want her thinking she was to blame for his recent introversion. He looked down.

"The problem is, I'm not as strong as Joe. I'm too chickenshit to stand up to my family like Joe did." He clenched his fists. "I don't know why I'm not stepping forward—it's not like I have anything to lose. They've already destroyed my life. But I'm just standing back watching it all happen, watching them take down Ben with their sinking ship ... I'm not even willing to throw him a damn life-raft."

It hurt her to see the self-hatred in his scowl. She knew she was violating their pact not to discuss the past—hell, they'd both already broken that rule this morning—but her inner therapist could not help but ask, "How did your family destroy your life?"

Drinking in her beautiful brown eyes, her high cheekbones, and her perfectly sculpted lips, he sighed. He wanted to keep this classy, elegant woman away from his destructive family, but apparently that wasn't possible.

"Sometimes I like to pretend it's my family's fault that I was busted for aggravated robbery," he said. "But the truth is it's all my fault. I'm the one who screwed up my life."

Aggravated robbery? At least now she could confirm for Kirsten that Grant was not a murderer. She felt deep gratitude that he'd opened up to her.

"I feel sad that your family has made things hard for you." She grasped his wrists with her delicate fingers. "I went to prison because of guns and money too."

"You did? Guns and money?"

He looked shocked. Then his widened eyes crinkled as he choked down laughter.

"What is so funny?" Sophie asked indignantly.

"You are like the most vanilla girl ever. Guns? *You?*" He let out a hearty laugh. "Yes, you are quite the thug, Sophie Taylor."

"Hey, I could be a bad girl. You'd never know."

"Yeah, you could be Bonnie to my Clyde." He winked suggestively.

She smiled, and he dropped the rag to the deck below, needing his hands free to fix another type of engine. "Come here, you little lawbreaker," he demanded with a grin.

Sophie stepped forward and he lovingly circled his arms around her waist. He leaned into her, his bemused eyes inches from hers.

Peering up at him, she reminded herself to keep breathing.

His sultry voice quietly apologized, "I'm sorry for acting so distant. But no matter how messed up I get about my family, you know how I feel about *you,* right?"

She swallowed hard. "This is kind of new…Sometimes I'm not sure." Her voice trembling, she confessed, "Sometimes I'm afraid you don't want to be with me."

He frowned and a determined look set in his eyes. His hand snaked up her spine and gently cradled the back of her head, her soft hair running through his fingers as he drew her face to his. Their lips barely brushed for a few tantalizing seconds. Sophie cupped the smooth skin of his jaw with her hand. Her peripheral vision blurred completely, and she was conscious only of his hypnotic gaze, enraptured by the flecks of emerald green in a sea of sapphire blue.

Finally, his full lips crashed onto hers. He stole all her oxygen in his absorbing liplock, and his tongue playfully flickered into her mouth, exploring and grazing her own. Her hand angled down from his hip and tentatively landed on his rear end, feeling the solid, sculpted muscles beneath her fingertips and causing them both to come up for air.

Their noses nuzzling as they paused, he whispered, "I hope that answered your question. I hope you're no longer afraid."

Sophie smiled seductively. "Maybe just a little afraid. I might need more convincing." She leaned in to resume when a gruff voice loudly interrupted them.

"Un*freaking*believable. No wonder you two wanted to work together."

They scrambled out of their embrace to find none other than Jerry Stone glowering at them from a few feet away. How had they not heard their parole officer approach?

"Officer Stone," Grant acknowledged anxiously. He stood perfectly straight. "I didn't see you there, sir."

Sophie blushed as she stared at their surprise visitor. "I guess you got the news that I'm working for Eaton Tours?"

Jerry raised his eyebrows. "You call *that* working?" Smirking, he added, "If that's working, then I obviously chose the wrong career."

Grant coughed nervously. "Sir, you're here to check up on us?"

"Yes, Madsen. It's standard procedure to visit you at home and work to make sure you're not getting into any trouble. I tend to avoid informing you in advance because I enjoy keeping my parolees on their toes. I like the element of surprise."

"Well, you sure surprised us, sir," Sophie confirmed uncomfortably.

Jerry chuckled. "Thirty years and that was definitely a first: parolees sucking face right in front of me." He shuddered. "Jesus, I could have done without that!"

Grant forced himself to recover. "I apologize for the unusual welcome, sir," he said as he firmly shook Jerry's hand. "May I show you around the ship?"

Looking at the parolees skeptically, Jerry relented. "That would be fine. Is that your uniform?"

Glancing down at his navy-blue jumpsuit, Grant grinned. "I wore this when I was chief toilet cleaner. But since then I've been promoted. I was just doing some maintenance in the engine room down below."

"You made it up to chief navigator, Madsen?"

"Yes, sir. And I've also been filling in as docent on occasion. Would you like to see the bridge?"

Nodding, Jerry appeared impressed. He followed Grant up the stairs to the top deck.

Sophie bit her lip, unsure if she should follow. She looked up at the bridge and found Grant engrossed in explaining the various controls for the ship, with Jerry listening attentively. She sighed and headed toward the bar, her original destination before running into Grant, who was truly a good man, she thought. And who had given her quite a good kiss.

She knelt down, reaching deep into the cabinet for a wayward bottle of rum, and heard Grant's voice patiently explain, "We run four cruises daily."

"When are your days off?" Jerry inquired, trailing Grant into the passenger seating area.

"Uh, so far we don't get any days off," Grant responded.

Sophie rose and nervously eyed her parole officer from behind the bar.

Noticing her appear over the counter, Jerry asked, "And what are your duties on board, Taylor?"

She blushed. "I, um, serve the drinks, sir?"

Jerry looked disgusted. What kind of boss put a parolee in charge of booze? "And you don't get any days off? Where is this Roger Eaton?"

Grant and Sophie exchanged nervous glances.

"Who the fuck wants to know?" a familiar male voice grumbled from behind them. Turning around, Grant and Sophie both inhaled sharply to find their boss strolling slowly and unsteadily toward them, working to get his sea legs back.

Grant quickly approached Roger. "Do you need any help, sir?"

Roger waved him off, continuing to stare at the salt-and-pepper-haired invader on his ship. Clearing his throat, Grant introduced them, "Mr. Eaton, this is Officer Stone from the DOC—our parole officer."

Finally shuffling over to Jerry, Roger breathed heavily as he extended his hand, and the two men shared a vigorous handshake. "The PO is checking up on his cons, huh?" He took a sideways glance at his employees, smirking, "No wonder these two look like they're about to crap their pants."

Jerry wasn't quite sure what to make of this greeting, so he got down to business. "You're Madsen and Taylor's employer?"

"That I am," Roger confirmed. "Though what possessed me to hire *two* parolees is beyond me."

"Are they causing you any trouble, sir?"

Roger decided joking around might not be the best idea at this juncture. "They've been doing fine," he said. "They told you they've been running the cruises the past four days?"

Jerry shook his head.

"Yeah, I had a goddamn heart attack and just got released from the hospital," Roger said. "I had to let these two take over, and from what I can tell so far, they didn't fuck it up."

Grant felt his shoulders drop an inch, and he realized how anxiously he'd been awaiting his boss's assessment of their performance. He had the sense that "not fucking it up" was high praise.

"I'm a little concerned about Taylor working the bar, Mr. Eaton. Has she had proper bartending training?"

Roger shifted uncomfortably. "She's just a server. We have a bartender who has trained her on spotting fake IDs."

Sophie stopped breathing at Roger's lies. They did indeed have a bartender, Dan, who was another of Rog's old Navy buddies, but he was constantly hung over, which made his attendance at work spotty.

"Have you had any problems with tardiness, insubordination, or association with criminal activity from either parolee?" Jerry asked, still a bit suspicious.

"Nah, none of that," Roger replied.

Mentally checking off his list of questions for employers, Jerry added, "Any use of alcohol or other substances at work that you know about?"

Now Grant held his breath. He could imagine how fast he would return to Gurnee with an allegation of drunk boating.

Roger maintained his poker face. "Look, I'm just returning from the hospital, so I have to do some investigating to see how these two truly performed in my absence. But I got nothing to report to you indicating that they should go back inside. They were royal pains in the ass, making me go to the hospital when I had chest pain, but they probably saved my life in the process. And they both work very hard."

Sophie wanted to kiss Roger right then and there, but she restrained herself, anxiously twirling a tendril of blond hair in her fingers instead. She glanced surreptitiously at Grant, who broke his military gaze forward to shoot her a nervous look.

Suddenly, Roger barked, "Speaking of working hard, what the fuck are you two doing just twiddling your thumbs? Get this ship ready for the first cruise!"

"Aye, sir," Grant replied, immediately striding toward the storeroom.

"You got it, Rog," Sophie added, taking a wet rag and beginning to wipe down the benches.

Five minutes later, Sophie and Grant's cleaning duties brought them together again, and they gazed apprehensively up at the bridge, where their parole officer and boss remained deep in conversation.

Sophie grimaced. "Why do I feel like our parents are up there discussing our punishment or something?"

"I don't know, but I feel the same way," Grand said with a chuckle. "Hopefully that punishment won't involve a return to prison." His expression turned serious. "We both owe Rog big time."

"Yep. And thank God Jerry didn't quiz me on spotting a fake ID."

"I can't believe Rog failed to mention my little tequila bender," Grant said. "Though those body shots may have made going back inside worth it."

She scooped his hand into hers, and their fingers intertwined. The warm touch calmed their nerves, and Grant softly stroked the back of her hand with his thumb, causing a chill of excitement to journey up Sophie's arm into her chest.

They heard a loud guffaw as Roger emerged from the bridge with Jerry trailing behind him. The parolees immediately scattered, finding random tasks to busy themselves as the two men headed down the stairs and strolled toward them.

"Quit pretending you're actually working and come say goodbye to your PO," Roger called out.

Coming together from the port and starboard sides of the ship, Sophie and Grant stood at a respectful distance from each other. "It appears you two passed this little inspection," their PO informed them. They nodded with relief.

"Can I tell my roommate, Kirsten, when we should expect your home visit, Officer Stone?" Sophie ventured.

Jerry raised one eyebrow. "Now that wouldn't be any fun, would it? See you both tomorrow morning in my office. Be on time."

"Yes, sir," they replied in unison.

After the long arm of the law had departed, all three breathed a sigh of relief.

"You should have warned me the po-po would visit!" Roger grumbled.

"But we didn't know," Grant countered. "We were just as surprised."

"How are you feeling, Rog?" Sophie asked.

"Like shit," he wheezed. "But I've been gone too long, and I had to check things out as soon as Nurse Ratched discharged me. Where the hell are Tommy and Dan?"

"They'll be here soon," Grant promised, hoping Tommy was not too late and Dan actually showed up for once. Apparently Roger's absence had not exactly inspired hard work in the two men. But Grant and Sophie had been operating the business quite adeptly on their own.

"Well, we got one hour to show time," Rog growled. "I'm going to meet with the ticketing company to find out how much money you two lost me. And when I come back, I'll be observing you sorry parolees at work. I want to watch you play docent, Madsen, and you better knock my socks off if you want to keep this job."

Roger turned and Grant stared after him fretfully.

"You gotta do it, Grant," Sophie encouraged.

"What? I can't do it with him watching me!"

"You have to. There's a reason we're selling out all the time now. You know it."

Grant brought his hands to his hips and exhaled loudly. "You're going to get us both fired, Bonnie."

She was grateful to find a twinkle of amusement dancing in his eyes. "C'mon, Clyde," she urged. "I'll help you clean the bathrooms."

❧

"That is, of course, Lake Michigan ahead of us," Grant said into the headset microphone, "the only Great Lake entirely within the boundary of the United States. The lake is the fifth largest in the world, slightly larger than the country of Croatia. Do we have anyone from Croatia on the cruise today?"

Grant glanced at Rog, who sat at the controls, watching him intently.

"Just pretend I'm not here," Roger had instructed. *Yeah, right.*

Roger was eating baby carrots—with a vengeance, taking his anger out on the hapless vegetables with ferocious chomping and gnashing. Grant took a deep breath and continued his narration.

"Perhaps there are no Croatians onboard today, but we've had folks from all over the world on this cruise. This is not surprising given that tourism is one of Chicago's top industries. I've been asked if there are any shipwrecks in Lake Michigan, and there are many. There are also plane wrecks in the lake, as Navy Pier was used to train pilots on aircraft carrier takeoffs and landings during World War II."

Roger raised his eyebrows as he began turning the ship to starboard, heading inland on the Chicago River. Grant was providing far greater detail than Roger typically shared, and a quick glance at the passengers told the older man that the rich commentary was well received. Roger grumpily bit into another carrot.

"What you're seeing all around you was formerly swampland, folks," Grant explained. "In fact, the name Chicago comes from the Native American word *chicagoo*, meaning a wretched and smelly swamp."

Sophie served two sodas and listened happily to Grant's confident narrative, feeling a bounce in her step after their morning kiss. With a light breeze swaying her ponytail, the bright sun beating on the back of her neck, and all hope restored in her relationship with Grant, she could work one hundred cruises without tiring.

Grant finally forgot about Roger sitting next to him and simply connected with his love for the amazing city he described. "This land around you is named Ogden Slip, which refers to William Ogden, the first mayor of Chicago. He was responsible for much of the construction and restoration that took place here. And straight ahead of us is the Trump International Hotel and Tower. Trump's beautiful hotel lobby features the enticing aroma of vanilla candles."

Grant went into his Donald Trump impression, and they continued their hour-long journey down the river. Roger sat silently, but felt amazed to learn quite a few facts about the city, despite having owned the business for almost ten years.

As they headed back to the dock, Grant delivered a *tasteful* tale about the construction of the Spire, then grew suddenly quiet. He stole a nervous glance at Roger, who was preoccupied with the navigation of the ship, then walked to the rear of the bridge to glance down at the passenger section.

As if she sensed him staring at her, Sophie looked up from her tray of empty cups and their eyes locked. She smiled her support that he follow through on their unspoken agreement. She nodded at him, and he reluctantly nodded back.

Grant returned to the mic and—closing his eyes for courage—announced, "Ladies and gentlemen, thank you for your attention this afternoon. We will be docking soon, and I'd like to leave you with a song."

Grant saw Roger's eyes dart toward him, narrowing warily.

His voice as smooth as silk, Grant started into his standard crowd-pleaser, Sinatra's "My Kind of Town." Sophie silently mouthed the words along with him, hoping that when Grant sang about what could "only happen in Chicago," he was referring to meeting her.

"Everyone, join in!" Grant cajoled, and once the passengers heard the familiar refrain, quite a few sang along. Chicago was their kind of town too.

Roger docked the ship, and the jovial passengers began to disembark. Tommy and Sophie stood by the exit, thanking them for their patronage.

Grant took off the headset, feeling an oppressive silence between him and his boss. Roger's face was completely unreadable, and Grant had no idea how to interpret his current lack of cursing.

After a few moments, Roger ordered, "Get Taylor up here. I want to talk to you both."

Nodding, Grant replied, "Yes, sir," and descended the steps to collect his partner in crime. Soon they both stood before their boss, putting on their best brave faces.

Roger slowly shook his head. "I've been running this business ten years," he told them. "Ten long-ass years." He looked out at the water on his left, mesmerized by the green hue of the rollicking waves. "Fucking carrots," he muttered, taking another bite of his healthy snack.

"And in ten years, I have to say, that was the best damn cruise I've ever seen." He broke into a wide grin, and Sophie's mouth dropped open. Grant felt immensely relieved.

"You two have sold out almost every cruise since I've been gone!" Rog exclaimed. "I wondered how you pulled it off, how you were so successful, and I'm still not sure, but I think it has something to do with your fucking singing, Madsen. How the hell did you come up with that idea?"

"Sophie encouraged me to do it, Rog."

"Grant sang one night, and the passengers kept asking for him to do it again," Sophie added. "Doesn't he have a gorgeous voice?"

"I wouldn't go that far, Taylor," Rog retorted. "But it does seem to put the passengers in a good mood, and happy customers are returning customers. Look, it's clear to me that you two have done a kickass job running my business. I'm going to rip Tommy and Dan a new one in a second, but I want to reward you for your hard work. After tonight's cruise, you have two days off."

Sophie almost squealed, but Grant said, "Are you sure you don't need us on Wednesday and Thursday?"

Roger chuckled. "Christ, Madsen, take some time off and don't complain! Now go tell your two coworkers to get their lazy asses up here."

As Sophie and Grant made their way down the stairs, Grant reached out his arm to stop her. "Do you know where we're going after meeting with Jerry tomorrow?"

She shook her head.

"The White Sox versus the Cubs, baby. An afternoon game!"

Her face lit up with pleasure. "It's a date."

19. The Womanly Touch

She came out of Jerry's office and immediately noticed him sitting on the chair. His head was tilted back against the wall and his eyes were closed, revealing eyelashes that seemed much too long to occur naturally on such a masculine face. Female runway models would kill for those luscious lashes. His position showcased his long tanned neck and the slight protrusion of his Adam's apple.

As Sophie approached his quiet form, she smiled fondly, realizing he had fallen asleep awaiting his turn with Jerry. Softly she sat down next to him and gently nuzzled the crown of her head into the crook of his neck.

His first conscious awareness was the clean lavender scent of her hair. What an exquisite way to wake up. He was touched by her intimate snuggle, and with eyes still closed asked, "Did I conk out?"

"Yes, sleepyhead. Why are you so tired?"

Sophie sat up and Grant slowly followed suit. Both nightmares and Roger's snoring had limited his sleep. He decided on a half-truth. "The snoremeister is back."

"Oh, that's right. Rog is home from the hospital! You poor thing."

The door swung open and Jerry gave Grant the evil eye. "Do you need a goddamn engraved invitation, Madsen?"

Grant jumped out of his seat and swiftly entered the office.

"At least I didn't catch you two kissing this time—yack!" Jerry growled.

Ten minutes later the two parolees strolled outside. Grant wore a coral-colored plaid madras shirt over jeans, and Sophie a baby-blue camisole and white pants with light blue stripes: cool clothing for a hot late-June day.

Grant was in a hurry. Rushing to keep up, Sophie asked, "How was your meeting with Jerry?"

"Fine," he replied, tight-lipped.

They hustled down the steps, and Sophie felt an irritated tightness in her chest. Mr. Aloof had returned.

"Hey," she cried, causing him to pause on the concrete sidewalk. "The Sox game doesn't start for a few hours, right?" Grumpily he nodded. "Well, where are you going then, in such a rush?"

He didn't have an answer for her. He just had to keep moving, had to keep running from his past. Unfortunately, she insisted on following him.

"How about we use the time to find you an apartment?"

"An apartment?"

"Yes. You told me staying with Rog was temporary, and with the fat paycheck we just got, you should be able to afford the deposit on a place now."

Lost in thought, he bit his lip. "But I don't have any furniture."

She smiled. "Me neither. I think that's why there's something called a *furnished* apartment."

Her teasing did not go unnoticed, and he would have smiled if not for all his nervous fidgeting. "You've already thought this all out, huh? Are you also, um, planning on getting a place of your own?"

"I can't afford it right now. I have school loans to consider. Besides, I like living with Kirsten."

"Well, what if I like living with Rog?"

Sophie snickered. "Yeah, you love living in that little studio with Señor Snore—our boss nonetheless—listening to him complain all day long about eating vegetables."

This time he did manage a smile. "Aw, c'mon, Rog and Ms. Broccoli are getting along much better these days."

"Well, I don't want to be the one they turn to for couples counseling," Sophie said. "Can you imagine being married to that man?"

"I *still* can't believe Rog was married," Grant replied.

He scraped his hand through his cropped black hair, eventually admitting, "I need to move out. I need to find my own place. It's just … I don't know, for some reason it's hard to go through with it."

Sophie sighed. She knew exactly what he meant. "Maybe because getting your own place would signify starting a new life after prison? Maybe that's why it's hard to bite the bullet?"

He seemed jarred by her comment. Her profound psychological insight always caught him off guard. He also kept forgetting she had a first-hand understanding of re-entering life after prison. She was probably scared as well, wondering if she could make it on the outside. Prison had ripped away their fledgling twenty-something sense of self-confidence.

"Maybe. Maybe I don't feel ready to start over," he finally replied. "Maybe I don't know if I can. That, and I've never really lived alone. I always had roommates in college, and I bunked with my buddy Simkins in the Navy. And then," he ducked his head, "I lived with a cellmate for two years."

She instinctively clasped both his hands in hers, her soft skin cradling and comforting his fidgeting hands. "It's okay, Grant. There will be no more cellies for either of us. We're not going back. And after the total lack of privacy in prison, you deserve your own place."

He glanced at their enjoined hands and then into her piercing gaze. "We both have lots of memories we'd like to forget." After a pause, he continued. "I want to move forward. I do. I want to start over, whatever the hell that might bring." He swallowed hard. "I, um, I wouldn't mind, um…"

His voice was halting, trembling, before he muttered, "Damn!" He dropped her hands and angrily jammed his into his pockets.

"Grant?" she ventured tentatively.

After a long exhalation, he reluctantly returned her gaze.

"You know you can talk to me, right?"

He immediately nodded but still had trouble getting words out, feeling flooded with anxious energy. "I was going to tell you…I was going to tell you, um, that I wouldn't mind…if you…well, if you moved in with me someday." He looked terrified to have uttered this, and quickly backtracked. "You must think I'm pathetic—"

She inhaled sharply, interrupting him. "Oh, I'm so glad you said that! I was thinking that too, but I didn't know if it was appropriate to say something, and it was kind of tense between us when we were talking about getting you an apartment. I've only known you really for one week, and it probably wouldn't be a good idea to suddenly move in together since I'm trying to be less impulsive—"

His laughter stopped her nervous jabber midstream. With reddening cheeks and a bright smile that matched his, she calmly amended, "Yes, I would love to live with you someday, Grant. But right now my psychologist would *kill* me if I moved in with you after only knowing you for such a short time."

He nodded. He wasn't ready either, but the possibility of cohabitating in the future made him ebullient. Then his grin quickly faded. "Your psychologist wouldn't be the only one upset. Officer Stone would go ballistic too."

"Probably," she agreed.

He abruptly appeared withdrawn again as Sophie studied him curiously. "Grant, it was so sweet of you to think about living together. Why did you hesitate in asking me that? What made you stop?"

Looking down, he sighed. "It was something Officer Stone said."

"Jerry? What did he say?"

"He told me I better not hurt you."

"What? Why would you hurt me?"

"I would never hurt you, Sophie, I promise. It's just … I've been mixed up with some bad people in my life, and I would never want you to be anywhere near them. They're dangerous."

He looked into her warm brown eyes as she tried to understand his vague warnings. Feeling exposed, as if she could read his mind, Grant clenched his teeth. "You're an angel, Sophie, and they're—well, they're not angels."

"I'm not an angel, Grant," she insisted. "I'm a felon. I was in prison, just like you. And I'm trying to figure out why Jerry didn't tell *me* I better not hurt *you*. Because we're in the same boat, sailor."

Her response was a salve to his guilty conscience, and as he exhaled, he felt tension drain from his muscles. Then he felt a shred of indignation. "Wait a minute. Jerry found out we're together, but he only yelled at *me* about it? He didn't warn you not to hurt me? What's up with that?"

She shrugged innocently and then smirked. "I guess Jerry likes me better than you. He thinks I'm more trustworthy."

Sophie began sauntering away.

"That is so unfair!" Grant called after her. "You have him wrapped around your finger—what, because you're a woman? Because you *cried* in his office?"

"The womanly touch can be magical."

"Whatever," he scoffed, matching her stride for stride as they continued down the street.

"You'll see," she promised. "When we find you some god-awful bachelor pad, I'll make it look presentable by adding my womanly touch."

His eyes danced. "No flowery crap in my bachelor pad, Taylor."

"Well, we're not going with a cheesy nautical theme, I can tell you that much. You spend enough time as it is on the water."

"Fair enough. All right, let's check out some apartments."

As they continued walking, he suggestively inquired, "What were you saying about your womanly touch?"

"You mean this?" she coyly asked, wrapping her arm around his back and drawing his body close to hers. As he lifted his long arm and draped it across her shoulders, she leaned her head into his chest, inhaling the fresh scent of sandalwood.

∞

They tentatively entered enemy territory: Wrigley Field, the Chicago Cubs' home park. En route, Grant had purchased them both White Sox ball caps to celebrate their miraculous find of an immediately available furnished apartment, as well as show their allegiance to the 2006 World Champion White Sox. It was too hot for Grant to wear his fated jacket.

"Do you think we'll run into our PO?" Sophie asked.

"I doubt it. I bet he's working this afternoon, probably embarrassing poor parolees by surprising them at their job."

Sophie grinned.

Grant adeptly navigated them to their section, and they took in the beauty of the park's ivy-covered brick walls as they stepped down the concrete aisle, making their way to their seats.

"How did you get these tickets?" she marveled, gaping at their prime location behind the third-base dugout.

"One of Uncle Joe's buddies," he replied. "Inter-divisional play is the *only* time it's good to be friends with a Cubs fan."

Settling into her blue metal seat, she asked, "So, is your Uncle Joe the one who got you into the Sox?"

"Yep."

"Joe seems like he's really important to you."

"He is," Grant confirmed. "He's been the best father I could ask for. He taught me a lot—he's been a wonderful mentor."

Grant noticed the Cubs jogging to their positions on the field. The game would begin soon. Deflecting the attention from himself, he asked, "Who is *your* mentor?"

His question caught her off guard, and she thought about her response carefully. "I'd have to say my graduate advisor, Anita Green."

"What's she like?"

"She's this totally smart psychology professor at DePaul. She began teaching there right when I started as a grad student. I was trying to find an advisor to do research with since the professor who recruited me had left for another school, and she agreed to take me on. We made a great team."

"What kind of research did you do?"

Sophie eyed him suspiciously. "Do you really want to hear about this?"

"Of course! Why wouldn't I?"

"I don't know. This egghead research stuff could be boring." Noticing his rapt attention, she continued. "You're not going to believe this, but my dissertation was actually on prisoner rehabilitation—whether or not counseling in prison helped female prisoners adjust to life when they got out."

"Whoa! What a coincidence, huh?"

"You're telling me. I had actually been to Downer's Grove Women's Prison in grad school to interview inmates and prison psychologists. When I rolled in there last year as an inmate myself, I recognized some of the people I had interviewed three years ago." She looked straight ahead, the bill of her baseball cap partially hiding her face. "It was mortifying."

Grant sighed. "So, what did you find? Did counseling help?"

"Well, the research is part of a longitudinal study that's still going on—Anita is running it—so all the results aren't in yet. But we found the most common counseling issue discussed by female prisoners was men." She smiled wryly, thinking of the man implicated in her own imprisonment. "Which makes sense because most of these women went to prison for assault against husbands, boyfriends, fathers—trying to fight back against the men who abused them."

"Wait a minute—most female prisoners go to prison because they're trying to defend themselves?"

"A lot of them, yes." He looked disgusted, and she added, "But these women are not saints. Some are in there for hurting or killing their own children. Women are locked away for all kinds of crimes—drunk driving, drugs, prostitution, murder, robbery—but many of them have histories of physical, emotional, and sexual abuse. And a lot of those histories involve men."

Grant absorbed her words. "And the depression? Did counseling help the prisoners decrease their depression?"

Sophie shrugged. "Statistically, yes, but clinically it didn't mean much. The women started the study with such intense depression that even though their scores decreased over six months, they were still quite depressed."

The announcer's voice boomed over the sound system, and the first White Sox batter stepped up to the plate. His announcement was met with mostly boos in the Cubs-dominated crowd.

Sophie frowned. "Sorry to take us to such a dark place."

"I'm the one who asked," Grant said with a smile. "You tried to warn me."

She smiled as well as they turned their attention to the game.

Seeking a lighter topic, he asked, "Who made *you* a Sox fan?"

"My dad."

Her soft, terse reply told him he had not succeeded in lightening the mood. "Oh."

"I think he wanted a son," she said sadly. "My mom had four miscarriages before me. Anyway, my dad would drag me to Sox games when I was little, but eventually I learned to love the game. Pretty soon I wanted to go more than he did, but then he started his company and got too busy for baseball."

"Well, I'm never too busy for baseball," Grant said, stretching out his lanky body comfortably. "Except when I have to work for weeks on end. Thank God for Rog giving us some days off."

A hot dog vendor meandered down the aisle, already sweating in the hot sun. She was a petite little thing carrying a deep metal tray, and both Grant and Sophie were surprised by her volume when she belted out, "Hot dogs! Five dollars!"

As the ponytailed vendor paused at the row across from them, Sophie leaned into Grant and whispered, "That could be me. When I couldn't find a job, Jerry told me to sell hot dogs at Cubs games."

Grant raised his eyebrows in shock and muttered, "The horror."

Sophie giggled, scoffing, "As if I'd work at Wrigley Field, the enemy's lair!"

The vendor continued down the aisle and Grant proudly said, "Working on an architectural cruise is far superior to hawking hot dogs. Although I bet you'd get great tips here too."

Still grinning, Sophie mused, "I wonder if guys ask her if her buns are warm?"

Grant snickered.

"How would you like your sausage, sir?"

His mouth dropped open. "You're right—you are *certainly* no angel. And I *like* it, you felon." His mind desperately whirred. "I wonder if she has some ketchup. *Put a squirt of that here!*"

Sophie laughed.

The hot dog vendor now headed back up the aisle. Suddenly Grant turned to Sophie in mock surprise. "You fit that *whole thing* in your mouth?"

She looked stunned for a moment, then cackled with delight. "Grant Madsen! You are a naughty boy!" She punched him in the arm and was rewarded with a mischievous shrug of his shoulders.

Three hours later, the game was over and Grant and Sophie were hoarse from cheering. Their Sox had narrowly defeated the Cubs, six to five.

As they headed up the aisle, Sophie commented, "It looks like Carlos Quentin is headed for an All-Star berth."

Grant could not help but smile proudly at Sophie's baseball knowledge.

"And what about my little All-Star?" he grinned, wrapping his arm around her sexy bare shoulders. "Would she like some dinner?"

"Wow. A new apartment, a baseball hat, a game, and dinner, all in one day? Aren't you Mr. Big Spender?"

"Well, a womanly touch is priceless," he countered, squeezing her shoulder. "C'mon. I'll take you to my favorite restaurant."

20. Mideast Feast

Their stomachs growling, Grant and Sophie were grateful to be seated immediately at The Chic Sheik. They'd removed their baseball caps, but Sophie still wondered aloud if they were dressed too casually for a restaurant with the word *chic* in its name. Grant assured her they were fine for the early evening hour.

"Have you ever had Mediterranean food before?" he asked, guiding Sophie to the table with a hand on the small of her back.

"I don't think so."

"Marat will be your server this evening," their host announced as he handed them menus. He smiled and left the table.

"Are you up for trying something new, then?" Grant asked.

"Of course, Grant. As long as you give me some suggestions on what to order."

He nodded. "I can order for you, if you like?"

Sophie considered his offer, her fiercely independent and mistrustful streak battling the swooning part of her that wanted to dive into those bottomless blue eyes, allowing him to take care of her completely. Then a sense of calm overtook her.

"That would be lovely."

"Are you a vegetarian, or do you have any food allergies?"

Astounded again by his considerate nature, she shook her head.

"Um, I'm not going to order a drink, but would you like one?"

"No tequila shooters?" she grinned, noticing that his face turned slightly green at the mention. "I'm still a little warm from the game. It was pretty hot out there, so a drink doesn't sound very good to me right now either."

Grant nodded gratefully, and his smooth velvet voice adeptly gave their orders to Marat when he sidled up to the table.

"Very good, sir." The Turkish waiter nodded his approval. "I'll be right out with your tea and appetizer."

Once they were alone again, Sophie inquired, "How did you come to like this type of cuisine, Grant?"

"I was stationed on an aircraft carrier in the Persian Gulf. Whenever we visited ports, the food was amazing."

"Oh, right. So how long were you in the Navy?"

"I was in ROTC for four years in college, and then on active duty, um, for six years." He chewed his bottom lip. "Until I was twenty-eight."

"What did you like about the military?"

Grant paused. "Initially I wanted to be in the Navy because of my Uncle Joe. I idolized him and wanted to be just like him." With a pang of guilt he considered his admiration for Captain Lockhart as well, but kept those thoughts private. "Luckily, once I was in, I loved it—the order, the precision, the bonding with my fellow sailors, but most of all, I liked fighting for the good guys. I believed in what we were doing, fighting the good fight."

He looked up to find her mahogany eyes riveted on him. Sounding embarrassed, he continued, "And I was moving up the ranks. I guess I do well at following orders or something—my superiors liked me." *But not anymore,* Grant thought. He had screwed up their trust in him big time.

Watching him avert his eyes, seemingly barricaded in a prison of remorse, Sophie ventured, "You really miss being in the Navy?"

He looked down. "Yeah."

Realizing what she was doing, Sophie quickly apologized. "I'm sorry. Here I am interrogating you about your past again." She shook her finger at herself. "Bad psychologist!"

"Our pact never to discuss the past is kind of hard to follow, huh?"

She smiled. "When I told my psychologist, Hunter, about our pact, he thought it was the dumbest idea ever."

"He's probably right," Grant said, chuckling. "We were foolish to think we could be with each other while hiding our pasts. The truth is the Navy is a part of me, and I can't pretend otherwise." *Just like my Mafia family is a part of me.*

Sophie grimaced, considering how her shameful ethical breach with Logan was interwoven into *her* very being, though she had no desire to unravel that truth just now.

"Here we are!" Marat swooped in, placing a plate of hummus and vegetables between them, along with a basket of warm pita. "And chai iced tea," he offered, setting down sweating glasses of the dark liquid. "The perfect refreshment for such a hot day." Glancing at their discarded Sox hats, he inquired, "You took in the baseball game today, yes?"

When they nodded, Marat gave them a disapproving stare. "But you cheered for the wrong team, no?"

"We cheered for the *winning* team," Grant corrected playfully.

"Ah, the Sox got lucky today," said Marat. "The Cubs will persevere tomorrow, I'm sure."

"Are we going to have to sit in another section?" Grant bantered back. "I'm a little worried about a bitter Cubs fan poisoning our food."

Marat laughed. "Lucky for you I do not believe in sour grapes. Or sour grape leaves, for that matter." He gestured to the appetizer. "Please enjoy."

As Marat departed, Sophie glanced uncertainly back and forth from the appetizer to her fork.

"No utensils required," Grant said as he scooped hummus onto a cucumber and presented it to her.

"I've had hummus before, you know," she said. "Just not this flavor. What is it?"

"Roasted red pepper," he answered, popping a loaded pita into his mouth. "It's good, though nothing compares to Riem's garlic hummus."

"Who's Riem?" Sophie asked.

Grant looked suddenly uncomfortable as Sophie studied him quizzically. "Riem is a Jordanian woman," he finally said, causing Sophie to wonder if she was about to hear sordid details of his relationship history.

"She was Simkins' girl."

"Simkins? He's your Navy buddy, right?"

He nodded. "My bunkmate." He exhaled loudly, frustrated that he'd opened his big mouth. Eating Middle Eastern food for the first time in more than two years had unleashed a flood of memories, and now Sophie was staring at him expectantly.

"Simkins, Riem, the Mideast … um, well, they take me back to a happier time, a time before I lost it all when I got arrested, before I ruined my life."

"Oh," she replied, not knowing what else to say. "If you don't want to talk about it, that's okay. I mean, we don't know each other very well, and it does take time to build trust."

He reached across the table and gently clasped her hand with his long fingers. "But I do trust you, Sophie."

Sophie smiled warmly. "It might help to talk about it. As much as I fought Jerry about seeing a psychologist, I have to admit I'm starting to feel a little better."

Breaking off a piece of pita and dragging it across the red hummus, Grant took a deep breath before placing it in his mouth. Chewing, he realized they were breaking bread together, a sign of trust in Middle Eastern culture. There was no better time to share himself.

"I—I was trying to steal some money from a club when I got caught. I didn't want to do it, but I had to." His cheeks flushed with shame.

"Why did you have to do it?"

He sighed. "I thought I was protecting somebody. But there had to be a better way. I shouldn't have agreed to do what I did. I ended up betraying—"

"All finished?" Marat interrupted, gesturing to the almost empty plate of hummus.

Grant seemed far away, ensconced in the past, so Sophie answered, "Yes, thank you."

"Excellent." He disappeared with the plate and basket from the table, only to swoop back moments later with their entrees. "Let's see, we have Chicken Shwarma Salad for the lady," he announced, setting down a crisp green mélange. "And the Mujudara Plate for the gentleman. Is there anything else I can get for you right now?"

"This looks wonderful," Grant responded, attempting to smile. "The chef must be a Sox fan. Thank you, Marat."

"No, the chef knows what he's doing. He's a Cubs fan, of course." With an impish wink, the waiter left them alone again in his largely empty section.

Sophie took a bite of the chargrilled chicken drenched in a lemony olive-oil dressing. "Yum. Grant, this is delicious."

He smiled. "Would you like to try some of mine?"

"If it's half as good as this salad, I'd love to."

He shoveled some lentils, onions, and grilled beef onto his fork and slowly raised it to her mouth.

"Interesting," she murmured. "I like it, but I like my salad even better."

"Yeah, this lentil dish may be an acquired taste," he replied. "The Doha version of this dish was incredible. It's hard to replicate in America."

They ate a few bites before Sophie asked, "You were saying something about betrayal?"

Grant swallowed and nodded, drowning in the fury he felt toward his brother. That betrayal was too raw to discuss. If he let even a smidgen of that rage seep out, he didn't know what would happen. Instead, he focused on another betrayal: the one he had caused himself.

"I betrayed the only father I've ever had. I betrayed Uncle Joe … He didn't understand why I pulled the robbery, and I couldn't tell him."

Grant looked nervously toward Sophie. Her fork paused midair, and she returned his gaze, waiting for him to resume the story.

"Why, Grant? Why?"

He met his uncle's pleading blue eyes through the visitation glass at the courthouse, his heart thumping in his chest. Logan had told him to keep quiet or Joe would pay, but he didn't know if he could continue the silence. He was hurting Joe deeply.

"I'm sorry, sir" was all he could repeat.

Joe continued to question to no avail. Finally, resigned, he slumped in his chair, rumpling his khaki uniform. "You know what they do when you get a felony conviction, don't you?"

Grant glanced down at his yellow jumpsuit, a different kind of uniform than he was used to. Softly he replied, "A discharge from the Navy."

"More tea?" Marat asked.

Grant glanced confusedly at the waiter and his pitcher of iced tea. He then looked at Sophie, whose warm brown eyes were filling with tears. She averted her gaze.

"Uh, maybe later?" Grant told the waiter.

Noticing their distress, Marat nodded. "Of course, sir."

As the waiter left, Grant gently asked, "Are you all right?"

She sniffed and nodded. "So then they discharged you?"

Grant sighed, smiling grimly. "Yeah. I'm not fit to serve anymore, I guess. I sure have messed up my life."

Sophie could not stop herself from weeping and used her napkin to dab at her eyes.

Grant clasped her hand in his. "Why are you crying?"

"It's just awful," she choked out. "I know how much you loved the Navy. I just have to watch you on Rog's ship to know how much you loved it."

A lump formed in Grant's throat as she continued.

"I bet you were a great sailor." She didn't know if she was crying for his losses or for hers.

Grant quickly withdrew his hand, angrily jamming it in his lap. He looked away and squared his jaw with resolve, determined not to cry. He had never allowed himself to cry about the damn discharge, and he wasn't about to start now.

They sat in silence. Watching Grant valiantly fight off tears reminded Sophie of something—another time, another situation—but she couldn't place it. She tried to pull herself together.

"Let's pay the check and get the hell out of here. I've lost my appetite," Grant said.

Unfortunately, Marat was suddenly nowhere to be found. Grant miserably returned his gaze to Sophie. "Well, now I've made you cry. Great, just great. This is probably the worst date you've ever been on."

She'd never felt as close to a man as she did right now. "No—"

"And I definitely do *not* feel better after talking about the past. In fact, I feel worse. Is this what therapy is supposed to be like?"

She shrugged crossly. "What the hell do I know? They took away my psychologist license, remember? Thanks for reminding me about that, by the way."

They glared at each other, but within moments softened into smiles.

"If you think you've got the corner on the market on messing up your life, well, you ain't seen nothin' yet, Madsen. I am the queen of self-destruction."

Grant stifled a laugh. "Yeah, you were popped for guns and cash, yo. You're a real gangsta badass."

Sophie began giggling. Her laugh was infectious, and Grant found himself chuckling too. Ah, life. If you don't laugh, you cry. And sometimes, if you're with the right person, you laugh *while* you cry.

Marat finally showed up, tentatively handing Grant the bill and temporarily halting their laughter.

"You have impeccable timing, Marat, just like a batter for the Cubs."

The waiter just gave Grant a curious stare. "I thank you for visiting us tonight. Enjoy your evening."

While Grant was mentally calculating the tip, Sophie lovingly feasted her eyes on her man, parolee McSailor. He'd said he didn't feel any better after describing his crime, but perhaps he would soon. The more she learned about him, the more Sophie trusted Grant. Their burgeoning emotional intimacy only increased her physical desire for him, and she definitely knew a way to make him feel better.

She felt her face flush, thinking about the queen-size bed in his new apartment, just waiting to be christened. As Grant stuck some cash in with the bill, Sophie suggested, "How about we buy a few things for your apartment?"

He looked up at her. "What, like towels and soap?"

She nodded. "And sheets."

Their eyes locked, and Grant felt a stirring down below. Maybe he was feeling better after all.

21. Fit

Sophie snapped the flat sheet out in front of her, making it billow over the queen-sized mattress before Grant caught it in his sure grasp on the opposite side of the bed. They gently let it float down, then smoothed it over the fitted sheet. That task complete, they stared awkwardly across the bed, and an edgy vibe filled the room.

"They're perfect." Grant nodded toward the sage-green, leaf-patterned sheets. "Thank you so much for buying them."

"You've already thanked me about ten times." Sophie grinned. "I was happy to buy them. It's my little housewarming gift to you."

She thought back to the department store they'd visited after dinner. It was obvious Grant liked the sheets and towels she picked out for him, but he seemed to hesitate. Nervously murmuring that he needed to find an ATM, he'd scurried away, leaving her standing alone with the bedding near the cash register.

He'd returned to find her beaming as she proudly presented the items, already purchased and bagged.

"You didn't have to get me a gift, you know."

"Well, I couldn't find a congratulations-on-your-first-apartment-after-prison card," she said with a smile.

His hearty laugh dispelled the tension. Grant felt full of gratitude. All he wanted to do was to be with her—hold her in his arms and ply her with kisses.

He set one knee on the bed and swiftly crawled across the mattress. Kneeling on the bed with bare feet, he met her eye-level.

His presence mere inches from her, the strength of his body next to hers, the warmth in his eyes, the curve of his lips, his laugh—it all flooded her senses. Placing her hands on his shoulders to ground herself, Sophie leaned into him.

Clutching her slender hips, he drew her into in a yearning, sensuous kiss. Her knees pressed against the bed and her hands slid down his back, massaging and kneading his taut muscles. As their kiss deepened, they intuitively moved together: Grant pulling her forward and Sophie following his lead up onto the bed, both kneeling on the mattress now while their hands groped each other hungrily.

Grant pried his lips from hers only to nuzzle his mouth near her ear, planting feathery kisses down the curve of her neck until his moist lips landed on her bare shoulder, rosy and freckled from the afternoon sun. His mouth continued its journey, languishing along her collarbone and sliding up along her neck, causing her to tilt her chin and revel in the sensation of him devouring her. Sophie closed her eyes and sighed with pleasure as his mouth grazed over her skin, heating her with his warm breath.

When he slid the spaghetti strap of her light-blue camisole down her shoulder, Sophie began to unbutton his lightweight madras shirt. She simply *had* to get it off of his body. Their undressing had a driving, frantic quality, and each eventually realized it was faster to remove their own shirt. Sophie crossed her arms over her waist and lifted her top over her head while Grant shrugged out of his now unbuttoned short-sleeve shirt.

Only when they faced each other, their shirts carelessly tossed to the beige carpet beside the bed, did they pause. Eyeing Sophie's lacy strapless bra, Grant cleared his throat.

"You're so beautiful, Sophie…" His voice trailed off, but he forced himself to begin again. "It's, um, it's been a dry spell for me. I've been locked away in a men's prison for more than two years."

Sophie nodded. She was a little rusty herself. She brushed her fingertips across his solid pectoral muscles, which she'd been craving to do ever since the night drunken McSailor had crashed at Kirsten's apartment. Playfully stroking his chest, she asked, "So, your sentence was four years?"

Grant inhaled deeply, distracted by her soft caress, before he refocused and shook his head. "Three."

She gazed up at him, puzzled. "But with good behavior, you'd be out in about half of your sentence, wouldn't you? Eighteen months?"

"With good behavior?" he repeated distractedly, buying himself some time. Unconsciously curling his fingers, his right hand tingled with the memory of careening into another prisoner's jaw. The ensuing image of a small, dark solitary cell jammed itself into his consciousness, and he found himself having trouble getting air. He panicked, thinking she would intuitively know about his psychotic breakdown in the hole.

Misreading his anxious expression, a coquettish smirk played on Sophie's pink lips. "Maybe your behavior wasn't so good? Maybe you were…" She dropped her voice huskily. "Very bad?"

All images of Gurnee were gone in a flash. "Bad?" Grant asked. He brazenly lifted one hand to cup her breast, his smooth voice matching the silky softness of her bra. "I feel *very* bad behavior coming on. What do you think about that?"

"I think I can handle it." She sat back on her heels and locked eyes with him as she unclasped her bra. Allowing the lingerie to fall softly from her small breasts, she tossed the bra to the floor, where it joined the outer garments in a heap.

Suddenly seized by nervousness, one hand unconsciously flitted up to cover herself. "I'm, um, I'm kind of flat. Sorry."

He looked almost wounded. "You're exquisite," he countered, drawing her back up to kneeling. Her nipples grazed his chest, driving him crazy with anticipation. He smoothed one hand over her hair, and she released the band holding her ponytail. Thick reddish-golden hair brushed over her shoulders and curled near her breasts. Her coppery eyes scorched him.

Grant plunged forward to ravage her mouth with kisses while his hands explored her firm breasts—cupping, caressing, and stimulating her hardening flesh. "You see, they fit in my hands perfectly." Gasping for air at the touch of his long, supple fingers, she skimmed her fingertips down his ribcage and along the hard lines of his hips.

"I like Bad Grant," she murmured between kisses. Her slender fingers skated on his waistband and began unbuttoning and unzipping his jeans.

"Ladies first," he urgently whispered back, dropping his hands and racing to remove her white pants. Grant whipped them down her lean thighs before she'd even pulled his jeans over his rear end. Although to be fair, he cheated by gyrating his hips and preventing her from getting a firm grasp on his jeans. His evasive maneuvers made her giggle.

Next, Grant problem-solved by playfully pushing her backward on the bed to finish removing her pants. Sophie's head landed on a pillow as she willingly fell onto the sheets, circling her calves around to extend in front of her. Soon her creamy, lithe legs were fully exposed.

Grant paused at the vision of her smooth, milky skin adorned only with silky white panties. Her long, lean body lay before him in all its glory, beckoning. She grinned at the sight of his jeans hanging jauntily off his hips, the waistband of his navy-blue boxers easily visible. "Take off those jeans, McSailor," she ordered.

He raised one eyebrow. "McSailor?"

"Oh!" she erupted in giggles once again. "Didn't I mention the nickname Kirsten gave you?"

Narrowing his eyes, his voice sounded suspicious as he asked, "Exactly what happened the night I passed out in her apartment?"

"Maybe I'll tell you about it after you take off those pants."

He considered her offer and quickly peeled off his jeans. Crawling up the bed, he sidled in next to her and leaned on his elbow as they lay side by side. His right hand grazed the skin inside her right knee, then his fingertips brushed up the length of her thigh. With each advancing inch, she breathed in a little more, her chest rising and expanding with each inhalation until she was almost hyperventilating.

Her skin tingling, Sophie's mood turned serious. Grant could read the want and need in her brown eyes. Both felt a catch in their throats as the air became thin. Grant's hand rested lightly on her stomach, his tantalizing fingertips teasing her with a promised advancement and breach into her territory. His military training would not go to waste tonight.

Both knew exactly what they wanted, but taking this opportunity to practice *direct* communication once again, Sophie planted a warm kiss on Grant's awaiting lips before sliding off her panties in one fluid motion.

Grant's grateful face hovered over hers, and he whispered, "Let's christen these sheets, shall we?"

She nodded and his lips crashed onto hers again, his hand moving to cradle her face as they kissed passionately. His hand stroked her long, silky hair, then slowly traveled south, pausing at her breasts to caress and massage her nipples, then snaking down the center groove of her flat abdomen.

Enraptured by his kisses, Sophie felt weightless and floating, utterly aroused and craving his attention to her body. But when his nimble fingers finally made their way to her receptive core, she entered a new level of ecstasy. Those long, artistic fingers that seemed so out of place on his muscular, military body; those fingers that were nonetheless perfect for Grant since they fit his gentle, intelligent nature; those fingers that adeptly repaired any piece of equipment on the ship; those fingers that fidgeted when he was nervous—those fingers now fired up a heat inside her so intense and so deep that she let out a guttural moan.

He expertly rubbed and circled her clitoris, and Sophie could not stifle her explicit sounds of pleasure with each rapid exhalation. Was he going to bring her to orgasm *already?* She closed her eyes and tilted her head back, providing Grant with a burst of satisfaction and confidence as he read her look of pleasure and arousal at his hand.

As her pelvic muscles contracted around his fingers, Sophie felt heat spread into her abdomen and radiate throughout her body. She shuddered and a look somewhere between bliss and alarm crossed her flushed face as she realized he was undoing her, leaving her with little self-control. She simultaneously wanted to beg him to continue and plead with him to stop, lest she cry out like an animal from his astonishing touch.

McSailor's fingers were miraculous and marvelous! Suddenly an image appeared in her mind, like a marquee flashing in her eyes:

FOR A LIMITED TIME ONLY... MCSAILOR'S MAGIC FINGERS!

A bright smile formed on her lips, and she somehow regained enough focus to gaze into those crystal-blue eyes.

"Something funny?" he asked, resting his hand on her inner thigh.

Her response was breathy and low. "You're very skilled, McSailor."

With a sudden move, she rolled onto her side and maintained eye contact while she entangled her legs with his, something *he* had desired since the morning he woke up in Kirsten's apartment and watched her beautiful body at rest. He sensed her weight leaning into him, causing a pressure to well forcefully inside his boxer shorts. As her delicate lips met his, he gave in and was soon lying on his back, defenseless.

Unlocking their lips, her hands traced the contours of his abdominal muscles. She glanced at the growing bulge in his boxer shorts and grinned, pleased that she was arousing him too. Sliding her finger beneath his waistband, she peered up at him with a wicked smile. "What do we have here?" she inquired, lifting the waistband as if she were planning to peek inside his shorts.

Instead, she yanked down his boxers, exposing his erection to the light, to breathe and grow. "Oh my," she cooed appreciatively, tossing the boxers toward the expanding heap of clothing on the floor. "Looks like we have our very own Spire right here!"

He gave a low, sexy laugh, slowly shaking his head. "You are crazy, Soph—"

A gasp prevented him from finishing his sentence. Her soft hands firmly stroked and stimulated him as he became harder and harder. Her expert touch slid down the length of his shaft and caressed the tip, which made him clutch at the fitted sheet and nearly buck off of the bed. Where had she learned how to incite such arousal in a man, leaving him vulnerable and helpless? Grant didn't know and he didn't care. He just wanted her to keep going.

Feeling a rising force below his belly, he panted for air and instructed, "My jeans…the pocket…Sophie!"

She pushed off him and contorted her body across the bed, stretching for his jeans and rummaging through his back pockets until her hand discovered the desired item. Crawling back toward him, she held the packaged condom up for his inspection, eyes questioning.

Grant swallowed. "There was a drugstore next to the ATM."

"Wishful thinking, Madsen?"

He shrugged. "Hey, *you're* the one who bought the sheets."

Tracing the condom across his thigh, she inquired suspiciously, "So, you don't carry these around with you for a quickie with a cruise passenger?"

He smiled and reached for her, drawing her body on top of his. "I much prefer the cruise staff," he informed her. "Particularly the hot waitress."

They resumed their kissing, and Sophie felt his erection pushing against her lower abdomen. Drenched in excitement and desire, and sensing it was time, she helped him slide the condom onto his throbbing penis. They could not move fast enough. Grasping his wiry biceps, Sophie gazed down at him with yearning.

Craving to be inside her, to be joined with this amazing woman, Grant eased himself into her wetness, and they both exhaled to finally be as one.

Sophie inhaled sharply as he cupped her bottom with both hands and pressed her toward him. With each thrust deep inside her, she felt a shuddering sensation that intensified and spread throughout her body. Her sighs and moans were swallowed by Grant as they continued their sweet kisses. He provided the perfect mix of ravishing and respect during their lovemaking, and a rhythmic tightening overtook her as the Grant tsunami crashed over her, wave after wave, making her call out in rapture.

He too felt rapid contractions below and an upsurge building while his fingers raked up and down her slender back. Trembling, he experienced a crescendo of pressure, thrusting and plunging into her, rising and building, mounting, peaking, soaring, until finally he reached a sky-scraping climax and his body sank back into the mattress, spent. Utter euphoria enveloped them as they clung together, their breathing gradually slowing to match each other breath for breath.

They lay with a sheen of sweat covering their reddened skin. As Grant had imagined earlier, their bodies fit together perfectly. Her cheek rested just below his chin, and her luxurious hair tousled across his chest. Her long legs encircled his, ensnaring her prey. They melded together like lock and key. Only they were no longer locked away—they were free.

As he gently stroked his hand through her strawberry locks, he murmured, "Can you spend the night?"

"Sure," she said, and he felt her smile against his chest. "I hope Kirsten won't worry. I can't call her since you don't have a phone hooked up yet."

Continuing to pet her soft hair, he observed, "I bet we are the only two people on earth who don't own cell phones."

"Maybe one day, Parolee Madsen," she teased. "Soon we'll both be grown-up enough to own phones." Lifting her head and staring into his half-lidded eyes, she asked, "Will you text me? When we get phones?"

"Of course," he responded. "As long as you'll text me back."

"Deal," she nodded. "Um, Grant, if I'm going to stay tonight, do you mind if I take a shower?"

"Jeez," he muttered with feigned disgust. "You buy me sheets and towels and now you think you own the place."

She chuckled and bit her lip. "Are you saying that as the owner of this apart-ment, the only way you'll let me use your shower is if you take one with me?"

His eyes widened and he thought for a moment. "Yesss," he said, nodding, a grin lighting up his face. "That's exactly what I'm saying."

"I thought so." Her smile matching his, she propped herself up and stepped out of bed, extending her hand to him.

Taking her hand in his, he allowed himself to be led into the bathroom.

She kept her eyes glued on his lower body. He cleared his throat. "Do you see something you like, Taylor? Feeling in*spire*d?"

Expecting a nervous laugh since he'd caught her staring, he was surprised when she confidently held his gaze.

"I was thinking about our earlier conversation at the ballpark," she said in a sultry voice. "I wonder, do you think I can fit that *whole thing* into my mouth?"

He had never moved so quickly toward a shower in his life.

22. Naked

Naked, they snuggled together front to back, wrapped between the sheets, clean and content. Grant's cheek nestled over Sophie's left shoulder and brushed against her long hair, still damp from the shower. He had curved himself around her body with his knees tucked in behind hers and his left arm folded over her. It was not possible to get much closer. They had no need for a blanket as their colliding skin and the summer evening provided more than enough heat. With a satiated sigh, Grant felt his eyelids droop.

Sophie did not feel so at ease. Although spooning with McSailor was precisely the blissful experience she had imagined, her mind would not stop processing an image that had caught her eye in the bathroom. In the act of soaping each other's bodies under the pulsating shower, Sophie had seen an angry scar on Grant's lower back. Slightly below his waist on his right side—a line of raised skin, pink and jagged. She figured he would tell her about the scar one day. She really wanted to respect his privacy by letting it go. But her analytical, inquisitive brain would not allow it.

Her faltering voice sliced through the darkness. "Grant?"

"Hmm?"

He sounded so tired. She bit her lower lip, wondering if she should proceed. "It's nothing."

There was silence, but then his piqued curiosity got the best of him. "What is it, Sophie?"

She took a deep breath, deciding to go for it. "I don't want to be nosey, but... um, how did you get that scar on your back?"

She felt his body bristle immediately and just as quickly regretted her question. "Forget it," she backpedaled. "I—I, um ... I shouldn't have asked you."

He felt his face redden as he remembered the sting of the belt on his four-year-old body, snapping and cutting into him frighteningly. But the sting was nothing compared to the words spat out by the drunk, black-haired man. *You peed in your pants, you fucking baby! Do you need a diaper?* Sarcasm had dripped from the towering tormentor's mouth. *Karita, get the boy a diaper!*

Grant blinked several times as he refocused on the bedroom, dimly illuminated by city lights, and realized he had been holding his breath. The scar was where his father's belt had always found his backside, and though the other welts had faded, that mark stayed. His father had branded him.

Sophie felt Grant exhale slowly, and she waited for him to speak. His voice warbled with emotion when he told her, "It's okay. You can ask me anything. Our stupid pact is shot to hell by now, anyway."

Sophie smiled in the darkness.

He attempted to sound nonchalant as he explained. "It happened during military exercises. We, ah, we were doing maneuvers in the Atlantic, and I was, uh, running to deliver coordinates to the radio operator, when I—I slipped and crashed into a pump handle. It had a sharp edge that cut me." Producing a fake little chuckle, he added, "The lieutenant sure was pissed off at me for getting blood everywhere in the passageway."

It could not have been more obvious that he was lying. Why he lied was beyond her comprehension, and it instantly frightened her. She was painstakingly crawling back toward dignity after losing it all to the biggest liar and deceiver there ever was, and she did *not* want to repeat her mistakes.

Her mouth tightened. "Maybe I should go home."

"No!" he insisted, all signs of fatigue vanishing as he gave her arm a gentle squeeze. Could she tell he was lying? Did she know the shameful truth behind the scar? More quietly, he implored, "I don't want you to go."

She lay in his arms quietly, pensively, tensely for several moments. She didn't really want to go, to leave the cocoon of his warm embrace, but she could *not* get hurt again. She was terribly frightened of being deceived, of being manipulated, and something about this situation felt oh-so-familiar.

"After the incredible day we've had—finding this apartment, the game, dinner, shopping for sheets, um, well, making the bed—"

She couldn't help but grin at that.

"—taking a shower, you're going to leave *now*? You can't do that. It would be crazy."

She considered his entreaty. After that mind-blowing sex, how in the world could she think of leaving? It had been magical, the most romantic evening she'd ever experienced. She would probably never find a man like him again.

Bravely taking a deep breath, she confessed, "I guess I'm scared."

"Scared?"

She swallowed hard. "Scared of…" She hesitated, the words *scared of falling in love* popping up in her mind. "Scared of getting hurt," she finished instead.

Grant squeezed her a little tighter in his arms. "I'm scared too," he said solemnly. "I don't want to be alone in this new apartment. I'm scared…" He paused dramatically. "Scared of the dark."

She burst out laughing when she realized he was joking, and it was joyous to feel her body shake with giggles in his arms. He nudged his mouth closer to her ear and whispered, "You can't leave, Sophie. The monsters under the bed might get me unless you're here."

"Well, I'm staying then," she said. "I can't leave you all alone in the dark, your first night in an unfamiliar home, forced to fend off the monsters all by yourself."

He brushed his fingertips lovingly across her cheek. "Thank you, Bonnie."

"You're welcome, Clyde."

Feathering a kiss below her ear, he explained, "It was either Bonnie or McShrink, and I figured you'd like Bonnie better."

"Mmm, good choice, McSailor."

His soft touch and melodic voice made her sigh deeply, nestling into him a little tighter, a little deeper. It was okay to let go. It was okay to trust him—he had promised not to hurt her. She felt a drowsy wave roll over her, and her eyes fluttered shut.

Now *his* eyes were wide open in the dark. Feeling her smooth skin pressed against him, Grant wondered if he would be able to sleep. Disjointed phrases swam in his mind: *How did you get that scar?… I'm scared of the dark… Monsters under the bed.*

Closing his eyes, he tried to stem the tide of painful memories. With an ache in his chest, he recalled pleading with someone else not to leave him alone in the blackness of his bedroom, lest the monsters emerge. It had not been a joke that time. It had been an earnest plea, and the someone he had begged had been his brother.

A short time later, Grant was dreaming.

They paused outside a thick steel door with peeling dirty paint, and he felt the CO release his arm as the guard whipped out a set of keys. Taking a step toward the rusty lock on the door, the CO instructed, "Don't move, Madsen."

"Yes, boss."

Once the CO unlocked the door and pushed it forward, the hinges groaning, Grant could see the consequence of standing up to his father: a dank, dark hole in the wall. So, this was solitary. The pitch-black space made Grant's heart thump with terror, and suddenly there seemed to be not enough oxygen in the hallway.

The CO grabbed Grant's handcuffed wrists and roughly unclasped the metal bindings. "Get in there," he growled.

Grant's feet felt glued to the floor as panic coursed through his bloodstream.

"I said—" The CO's upper lip twitched with anger as he gripped the back of the prisoner's light-blue button-down shirt, "—get in there!" Grant was shoved forward, and he yelped in pain as his bruised ribs made contact with the doorframe before he stumbled into the darkness.

Regaining his balance, Grant turned to find the CO's beefy figure silhouetted at the door. "Enjoy the next two months in here, con!"

Grant rushed back toward the light just as the guard slammed the door with a deafening thud. The jangle of the key sliding and turning in the lock would be the punished prisoner's last contact with anyone for days.

Blindly turning around and stepping backward until he made connection with something solid, Grant's back slid down the wall and he slumped forward. He could see nothing, and all he could hear were his panting breaths and the pounding of his heart in his eardrums.

You can do this, he told himself, nausea building in his gut and a heavy tightness constricting his throat. The walls seemed to close in, though he had been in solitary for mere seconds. His bruised, beaten body ached, and the cold, hard floor provided little comfort. Drawing his knees up, he hugged them to his chest and rocked himself in a huddled ball of misery.

Dead silence greeted his ears in the soundproofed cell. He was alone with his thoughts. He mentally replayed the fight in the yard. It had taken every ounce of strength Grant possessed to stand up to his father, only to be rewarded by Enzo allowing rapists to beat the shit out of him. His brain flashed back and forth between the blows from the prisoners and the lashings delivered by his father when he was a child. Grant could not distinguish past from present anymore.

Sixty days? He didn't know how to get through sixty minutes. He should have just obeyed his father, accepted his protection by renouncing Joe. An image of Enzo's cold charcoal eyes seared into him. The man who had whipped him and tossed him into a closet some twenty years ago had done it again. He would never escape his father.

Prisoners got sent to solitary all the time. Why the hell was he freaking out so badly? He must be weak, pathetic, cowardly—a basket case. "You fucking baby," he heard himself cry out. His voice dissolved into raspy whispers. "You fucking baby. Do you need a diaper, baby?"

Like the fucking baby he was, Grant began sobbing.

Time passed in the dark hole as Grant lost his grip on reality. He had no idea how long he'd been in there.

Then a blinding light pierced his retinas, and his hands flew to cover his eyes. His heart and mind raced. His body felt wet. Where in the hell was he? What day was it? Gruff male voices began to crash through his consciousness.

"Christ, what's that smell?"

"… don't know what's wrong—he wouldn't eat anything for days."

"Get a doctor down here."

"Fuck, he's gone j-cat."

"… whack shack population just increased by one."

There were disdainful laughs.

Then there was a hand on his forearm, shaking him gently, nudging him awake. Grant opened his eyes and gradually focused on a man sitting next to him with a gray-bearded face. Grant's eyes widened and with a start he sat up on the bed, scrambling back toward the wall as best he could with his hands cuffed in front of him.

"It's okay, Mr. Madsen. You're safe." The man attempted to assure him, though no assurance was to be found in this strange, unfamiliar room.

Grant glanced down at his pristine white jumpsuit, nervously darting his eyes around the sterile environment, then daring to look once again at the older man staring back at him kindly.

"I'm Dr. McIntyre. You're in the psych ward, and it's March 27, 2006. You came here yesterday after spending three days in solitary. Do you remember any of that?"

Grant slowly shook his head. His voice sounded strange and groggy as he inquired, "Why was I taken here?"

Dr. McIntyre hesitated. "You were not doing so well in the hole, son. You had not been eating, and you were, um, unresponsive. Now, I need to perform a mental status exam on you. I'm going to ask you some questions, and I want you to do your best to answer them, okay?"

Still disoriented and upset, Grant tried to be obedient. "Yes, sir."

The psychiatrist asked several simple questions. Grant guessed he aced the exam because Dr. McIntyre gave him a reassuring smile.

"The medication seems to be working," he said.

Grant's voice rose with alarm. "What medication?"

"You're on olanzapine, an antipsychotic, Mr. Madsen."

"No! I don't want any medication!"

"I'm afraid it's not your choice. You had a psychotic break in there."

"No, I'm fine. I don't need any drugs."

"You were catatonic, Mr. Madsen. And you, um, well, you had urinated all over yourself in the cell."

Once the words left the doctor's mouth, Grant knew they were true. True and devastatingly shameful. He quickly averted his eyes, turning his body toward the wall, away from the prying gaze of the shrink. Helplessly he felt hot tears rolling down his cheeks.

"I'm sorry," Grant murmured, ducking his head low as his restrained hands came up to cradle his face. He felt naked and exposed as tears of disgrace flowed. He just wanted to disappear. "I'm sorry, I'm sorry, I'm sorry."

A river of regret and humiliation streamed down his face.

"Grant, wake up!"

He felt a warm hand cradle his face, tapping him gently. "Grant, honey, it's okay, wake up."

With a startled flinch, he opened his eyes and stared into Sophie's worried gaze, the contours of her face visible in the dim light. He lifted his hands, surprised when they were not handcuffed together.

"You were having a nightmare, Grant."

Bringing his hands to his face, he was shocked to find his cheeks wet with tears. Clambering into a sitting position, he frantically passed his palms across the sheets, praying he would not find those wet too.

Baffled by his actions, Sophie stared. "What are you looking for?"

Feeling dry sheets beneath him, Grant exhaled, but then noticed her bewildered expression. Oh, God! She was seeing him cry like a little baby! And he could have wet the bed, with her in it next to him. He thought he had peed his pants—a fucking thirty-year-old man wetting the bed! Mortified, he quickly turned away from her. He prepared to flee, run and hide somewhere, when he felt her delicate hand on his shoulder.

"Grant?" Her voice was gentle, so caring. "What's wrong?"

He angrily shook his head, keeping his back to her. He could never tell her or surely she would leave him. She could never know.

"Why did you keep saying 'I'm sorry'?"

Fear gripped his heart. How much had he said aloud? He lay back down, keeping his back to her.

Thinking she could help him, Sophie doggedly pursued her line of questioning. "Who were you apologizing to? Who were you telling 'I'm sorry'?"

You, he thought. *I'm sorry you ever met me outside the parole office. I'm sorry I ever dragged your beautiful spirit into my wretched, worthless life. I'm sorry you've become such an essential part of my world, when obviously I should let you go.*

Without realizing what he was doing, Grant rolled onto his stomach, folded his arms underneath his chest, and clenched his hands tightly over his face. He once again repeated "I'm sorry," the words muffled by his hands. He felt humiliated that he could not stop crying.

Utterly confused, Sophie peered at his prone naked body—his smooth, muscular back and buttocks exposed defenselessly, revealing the jagged scar, and his entire body trembling as if he were awaiting punishment, a physical beating.

Gasping, she suddenly snapped the puzzle pieces together in her mind: his nightmare at Kirsten's when he'd pleaded with an unknown tormentor, promising to "be good"; his words about not getting along with his father, contrasted with the adoration he felt for the uncle who saved him; his warning that she stay away from the "bad people" in his life. Was he an abuse survivor? Had his father abused him?

Immediately she reached for him, gently rubbing her hand over his cropped black hair as she scooted closer to his body. Softly stroking his hair, she murmured soothing words. "You're okay, Grant. It was just a dream. You're safe here with me. It's all right to cry, honey. It's all right to feel scared."

The tension in his shoulders slowly released with each calming word and soft stroke of her hand. His breathing steadied and his sobs gradually subsided. Tentatively she lifted her naked body off the sheets and straddled his back. She stroked the well-defined muscles of his back with her fingertips, feeling his skin respond to her warm touch. She kneaded his taut shoulder blades with the heels of her hands, delivering a relaxing massage. He allowed her to pull each arm from under his chest, resting them by his side.

After a few minutes of her hands working magic, he let out a shuddering sigh, and Sophie lay next to him once again. He finally rolled over to face her.

She gently wiped the wet trail on his cheeks, then planted soft kisses as he closed his eyes. Eventually she returned her head to the pillow and gazed lovingly toward him. He fondly caressed her face.

Grant's words were shaky. "Thank you for making me feel better. How did you know what to do?"

"I'm not sure, but I sensed you were really hurting." Sophie nervously cleared her throat, then added, "Grant, I think I know how you got that scar."

His breathing hitched, and he could not look her in the eye. "And you're still here?"

Her eyes flashed sorrow. Like most abuse survivors, he apparently blamed himself. He thought his inherent badness caused the abuse and believed nobody would love him once they learned of it.

"Of course I'm still here. I could never leave my McSailor."

Slowly raising his gaze to meet hers, their eyes locked with a deep connection and shared understanding. He clasped her hand in his and softly stroked it.

She took a deep breath. "I'll stand by you as long as you tell me the truth. But if you lie to me again, Grant, I'll have to leave. I went to prison because a man lied to me, and I won't let it happen again."

He nodded. "I understand. But, Sophie, sometimes the truth is painful. I don't want to make you feel that pain."

"We'll get through it together, okay?" She blushed slightly. "I think we make a good team." She grinned, adding, "Bonnie and Clyde."

For the first time in hours, he smiled, and it was a lovely sight to behold. He lifted her hand to his full lips and affectionately kissed it.

"I think we need more sleep before our crime spree begins, Clyde. It *is* the middle of the night, you know."

Nodding, he drew her body to his, and she snuggled her head into the crook of his neck, feeling safe and loved in his strong arms. They drifted into a dreamless sleep.

When Grant awoke the next morning, sun streaming in the curtain-free windows, he was alarmed to find the space next to him empty. Hopping up, he glanced around the small apartment before spying a note on the kitchen counter. She had scrawled in her flowing handwriting on the back of a flyer advertising the pizza place next door.

> *McSailor,*
> *I had to go home so Kirsten doesn't worry. But we have another day*
> *off work (yee-hah!), and I definitely want to spend it with YOU!*
> *Here are my coordinates:*
> *900 North Lake Shore Drive, Unit 10*
> *(312) 555-4043*
> *See if you can navigate your way (sober this time) over to my ship.*
> *XOXO, Bonnie*

A bright grin filled his face. Then he realized he was standing buck-naked in the middle of his living room, so he dashed back to the bedroom to get dressed. He had to get to his Bonnie. He just had to bring her back.

23. Cugino Carlo

Chomping his gum, Logan looked down at his big hands and sighed. It was sticky hot in the car, and he was bored out of his mind. Where the hell was his brother? He'd been staking out their mother's gravesite for days now.

Given that Chicago had a population of nine million, Logan had no idea how to locate Grant. Perhaps he should have shown more interest in his brother, should have gotten to know him better—his likes, his dislikes, his hobbies. Maybe then he would have a fucking clue about where to find him. But he didn't know the adult version of Grant at all, so his only lead was this cemetery, where he'd hunted him down twice before.

It was unlike Grant to go so long without visiting her grave. He treated his visits to the desolate headstone like a damn duty or something. Logan hated being here, hated sensing her disapproval, even from six feet under.

Perhaps Grant had chosen another city to call home once released from prison. Nah, Logan just *knew* he was in Chicago somewhere. Just then, the glare of the sun on an approaching windshield momentarily blinded him. When the car pulled up next to his, he thought maybe he'd lucked out after all. The driver had short black hair, just like Grant, but when Logan squinted his eyes, he detected not the lean grace of his brother but the ferocious energy of someone else entirely, and his excitement morphed into a sick dread.

It was his cousin Carlo.

The shiny, sand-colored Lexus glistened in the summer sun. Carlo shut off the ignition and glanced in the rearview mirror, appreciatively admiring his immaculate appearance while briskly running two fingers through his hair. Then he turned his gaze to Logan. His steely black eyes rested on him disdainfully, and Carlo's smug acknowledgement made Logan's stomach clench with resentment.

A black cowboy boot emerged from the vehicle, followed by a solid leg clad in black pants. Carlo set both boots firmly on the concrete of the small parking area facing the grassy graveyard and stood, three inches shy of six feet.

His jet-black, spiky hair was paired with thick eyebrows. His white button-down shirt was open at the chest, but tucked neatly into expensive slacks with nary a wrinkle. Despite the humidity, Carlo appeared calm, cool, and professional. But Logan knew appearances could be deceiving. Beneath Carlo's frosty exterior was a fiery rage that could ignite instantly. He retaliated for any perceived slight with fierce ruthlessness and torturous cruelty.

As Logan also exited his car, he thought back to the storied death of Vince, one of Angelo's men. Vince had been stupid enough to criticize Carlo's mismanagement of the Blackfoot heist after botched plans resulted in the arrest of several wise guys. Two days later, Vince had been found in his apartment, stabbed to death, with charred, black feet. The rumor was Vince's feet had been singed while he was still alive, though nobody knew for sure, and the murderer had never been found. No one had openly questioned Carlo since.

The cousins approached each other guardedly. Carlo should have deferred to Logan, Don Enzo's firstborn. Instead, Carlo acted like *he* was in charge, which made Logan's blood boil. Logan had little ground to stand on right now, though, and he had nobody to blame but himself. Losing hundreds of thousands of family dollars and being on the run from the law had placed him in quite a vulnerable position—one he despised.

A sneer formed on Carlo's face. "Still grieving *la madre*, Lo? When are you going to let her go?"

Logan felt his throat constrict, and his knuckles whitened as he curled his fists tightly, though he said nothing.

Carlo shook his head. "It was *so* easy to find you, *cugino*. You're getting careless. You don't think the cops will track you down here too?"

Logan's jaw clenched. "What do you want, Carlo?" Hearing himself ask the same question Grant had asked *him* at their mother's grave, Logan felt ashamed. Did Grant view him the way he viewed Carlo? An evil, no-good, slithering snake, so damaged he was beyond redemption?

Carlo narrowed his black eyes. "You know what I want. You know what the family wants—what the family *needs*. Two hundred Gs."

Logan averted his eyes, and Carlo moved in closer, his forehead somehow dry while Logan's beaded with sweat.

"We all know where the first hundred thou went, don't we, Lo?" Carlo seethed. "You enlisted your little brother—the saint—and he can't even steal back your own money." Carlo laughed snidely. "But what about the second hundred thousand? Where did that go, cuz?" He sidled even closer to the larger man. "You holding out on us, golden child? You take that money for yourself?"

"I don't have the money!"

"Then you get it," Carlo snarled. "You and I got history—we're family. And out of respect for that, I'll give you some time to refill the coffers. But it better happen fast, cuz. If you don't produce for the family, I'll find someone who will."

"Leave Grant out of this," Logan warned.

Carlo laughed again, a maddening laugh. "That's cute, *cugino*. You're suddenly all protective of your brother—the same one you sent to prison for a three-year stretch." He stared menacingly into Logan's deep-blue eyes. "Which I hear ain't quite a full three years now, is it?" The wheels turned in his head and Carlo smiled. "That's what you're doing here, isn't it? Searching for a saint. To what—warn him about me? Let him know I'm looking for him?"

Logan's heart thumped though he showed nothing. He was much better at keeping his cards close to his chest than Grant. He was a much better liar.

"But *you* don't know where he is, either. Turns out Karita's baby boy is more resourceful than either of us predicted, *sì*?"

Swallowing hard, Logan remained silent. He remembered Carlo at eight years old. He'd been a spoiled boy, the only son of Angelo and Anna Maria Barberi, and the only cousin to Logan and Grant since Joe remained childless. When Carlo was eight, Logan was eleven and Grant six. Times had been different then.

The eight year old's laughter echoed in the basement playroom. Looking at the frightened expression on his little cousin's cherubic face, he taunted, "Why are you so scared, Grant Pants?"

Grant grimaced, furious that Carlo had somehow learned of his peeing his pants two years ago. Grant's wary crystal eyes darted back and forth from his cousin to his older brother standing nearby. His voice trembled. "Aren't you gonna get in trouble?"

"Trouble?" Carlo scoffed. "For telling my dad to shut up?" He exhaled derisively, "Hardly."

Grant and Logan exchanged knowing glances. They wouldn't dare talk back to their father. They knew what would happen if they tried.

"My dad told me his dad used to beat the crap out of him and Uncle Enzo when they were kids," Carlo explained. "He promised himself that when he became a dad, he wasn't gonna hit his kid, like ever." Shrugging, he added, "So I can do whatever the hell I want."

Grant's eyes lit up with terror at hearing his cousin use a bad word like *h-e-double hockey sticks*, and he nervously glanced up the stairs to make sure his dad and uncle were still up there, unable to hear the conversation.

Logan felt his chest tighten. He wished Angelo could be *his* father instead. It wasn't fair.

Carlo's honey voice belied the menace in his words, bringing Logan back to the present. "Maybe Grant isn't sufficient motivation for you, cuz. You threw him under the bus a little too easily. Maybe there's somebody else you *truly* care about—somebody with great potential to become a real businessman, somebody who can contribute his share to the family, somebody who's your own flesh and blood."

Logan lunged for Carlo, gripping the smaller man's arms. They were inches apart as Logan shouted, "Don't you dare touch Ben!"

Carlo flinched as his cousin grasped the scarred flesh of his upper right arm. But he recovered quickly. "Get the *fuck* off of me, you Neanderthal."

Realizing he was threatening Angelo's son, the second in command, Logan reluctantly released his cousin.

Brushing off and straightening his shirt, Carlo glared. "Swear to God, you are as stupid as your father."

Logan was at his limit. If this asshole didn't shut up soon, he was going to receive the beating of his life—regardless of his position in the Mafia hierarchy. Shaking his head incredulously, Logan fumed, "My father saved your sorry ass, *cuz*. And, yes, turns out saving you *was* a very stupid move."

Carlo couldn't help but flash back to when he was ten years old, his body thrumming with excitement. The smell of booze and the palpable fury emanating off his Uncle Enzo, the thrill of secretly tagging along on an adventure, finally feeling like somebody important, hiding in the back of his uncle's car, the hum of the tires on the highway…

He *despised* this memory. He wished he could banish the experience from his brain, but the images were there, and they would not go away. Carlo was forever haunted by his childhood mistake.

"That fucking pussy piece of shit!" Enzo raged, pacing the great room with a glass of scotch in his hand.

"Easy, brother," Angelo advised from his place at the wet bar. The two men, both in their thirties, both with midnight-black hair and deep charcoal eyes, traded intense stares.

Ten-year-old Carlo took it all in from his hiding spot behind the sofa. He had never seen his uncle so angry before and was delighted to hear such bad words spewing like venom from his mouth.

"Fanocelli thinks he's going to inform on me?" Enzo demanded incredulously. "Son of a bitch. When is the fucking indictment coming down?"

Angelo sighed. "From what I heard, about four days."

"I'll fucking rip his heart out. I'm not going to prison."

"I know you're not," Angelo replied. "And that's because we just found out his location."

"Whose location?"

"Fanocelli."

Enzo's eyes widened. "The cocksucker's not in protective custody yet?"

Angelo grinned. "Nope. He's all by himself in a house on the south side."

A wondrous smile erupted on the don's face. "You are a fucking genius, Ange. We're obviously paying off the right government pricks. Give me the address."

"Now wait, Enz, we gotta plan this out, send a team in there—"

"Bullshit! We wait, he goes into custody before we have a shot. I'm going there now."

"No, it's too dangerous." Angelo gestured to the empty glass in his older brother's hand. "Hell, you're two sheets to the wind by now, anyway. I got some guys on their way here and we're gonna—"

"Do you know who you're talking to? You give me that goddamn address this instant." Enzo's voice took on a menacing growl, and Carlo felt the hairs on the back of his neck stand on end. Maybe he should return to his bed, where he was supposed to be at the moment. This situation was becoming serious.

"This ain't right, Enz. If something happens to you, what are Logan and Grant going to do?"

"I'll take care of things and be back home before they know the difference," Enzo said.

Carlo grinned. He knew something Logan didn't! He finally had a leg up on his cousin, the boy his father constantly fawned over—it was so unfair. Carlo was finally part of the club. He was playing with the big boys now.

"Quit dicking around, bro," Enzo ranted. "If Fanocelli gets away and I go inside, I'll never forgive you as long as I live." His voice dropped as he stepped closer to Angelo. "Tell me the address, and I'm driving over there right now."

Hearing those words, Carlo slunk off to find a new hiding place: the back of his uncle's car. He wasn't going to miss the *real* adventure.

Tucked away on the floor of the backseat, the diminutive ten year old prayed he wouldn't be detected by his uncle. Luckily, Enzo didn't even bother to check the darkened interior before getting into the driver's seat and slamming the door.

His excitement building with each passing mile, Carlo shook with anticipation when the car finally stopped. He held his breath as his uncle rustled around in the front seat for a few moments before quietly leaving the vehicle. Peeking out the side window, Carlo watched him stealthily move toward a darkened house. His uncle wore black gloves, and he'd stuffed a handgun into his waistband.

Carlo gasped when he saw the gun gleaming in the streetlight. What was Uncle Enzo doing with a gun? Was he like a police officer or something? Was he going to arrest a bad man? This he had to see.

Crawling out of the car, Carlo watched from the bushes as Enzo glanced around, then leaned down and fiddled with the knob on the back door of the house. The ten year old was even more intrigued when somehow his uncle got the door open and disappeared inside.

Should he follow? Carlo stopped and started several times before telling himself to quit being such a pussy. He crept toward the same door that had swallowed his uncle. He winced as the hinges gave a small creak, and then suddenly he was inside the strange, dark house. Trying to adjust his eyes to the blackness, Carlo carefully stepped forward. His heart thumped and he wondered if this was such a good idea, but it was too late to turn back.

Just as Carlo made it to the base of the stairs, he froze. His uncle was descending, coming straight for him. Enzo inhaled sharply when he caught sight of the boy. He surreptitiously pocketed his gun. Swiftly making his way down the last few steps, Enzo seized Carlo by the scruff of the neck and growled in a seething whisper, "What the hell are you doing here?"

Wincing and squirming in his uncle's painful hold, Carlo whispered, "I was following you! T-t-t-to see why you had a gun."

"Jesus." Enzo narrowed his eyes. "I was looking for somebody, but he wasn't where I thought he'd be. Let's get out of here."

There was a noise to their left, and Enzo clutched his nephew's neck even tighter. He held his index finger to his mouth to signal Carlo to be silent. Carlo whimpered in pain—his uncle was really hurting him now.

"Shut up!" Enzo hissed, and suddenly a shot blasted through the darkness, causing Carlo to slump into his uncle's arms. His arm was on fire.

"Shit!" Enzo yelled, dragging Carlo to the floor of the hallway. Carlo felt his uncle claw at his pajama shirt, seeming desperate to find the source of the blood.

From the darkness came a small voice. "Dad?"

In his haze, Carlo tried to make sense of what was happening. There was another kid there?

Then a gruff adult voice admonished, "Get down, Tony!"

"Richie Fanocelli," Enzo angrily whispered, halting his search. "He fucking shot my nephew?"

Carlo moaned, which refocused his uncle's attention, and rough hands frisked his body. When his uncle's hands grazed the bullet wound on his right arm, Carlo gasped. Enzo's eyes lit up with fury.

Shaking with rage, Enzo whipped out his weapon and fired into the darkness. He gave a satisfied grin when he heard the other man holler, "Nooo!" But Carlo watched Enzo's grin vanish when the man started wailing. "Tony, nooo! My Tony. You're only seven—oh, God!"

Carlo sat up a little, panting with fear in his uncle's arms. Enzo frantically looked back and forth from his injured nephew to the place in the darkness where a grown man was whimpering. Carlo felt drawn to the darkness, wondering what had happened.

Enzo rose and attempted to pull Carlo to a standing position. Carlo cried out in pain, and Enzo flinched and backed away. In that moment, Carlo rushed forward into the room. "Carlo!" his uncle shouted after him.

Gingerly holding his right elbow, Carlo stopped short. There, lying on the floor next to a discarded handgun, was a young boy. Carlo felt his uncle come up behind him, but he couldn't look away.

A sticky, dark-red substance poured from a hole in the boy's throat as he clutched at his neck, wheezing and gasping for air. A heavyset gray-haired man crouched over him, cradling his small head in his hands and sobbing. Both man and boy wore pajamas.

The man turned his weeping eyes to Carlo and his uncle, standing in the dim light.

Carlo felt frozen, entranced by the blood oozing from the boy's throat. He heard himself say, "It's like Buckingham Fountain."

Enzo turned to him. "What?"

Feeling the wet stain on the sleeve of his pajamas growing by the second, Carlo nodded toward the other boy's throat with a zombie-like stare. "Blood. Gushing like that fountain in Grant Park."

Suddenly Enzo yanked Carlo into his arms, despite his cries of pain. Carlo looked up to see his uncle take one last look at Fanocelli and the stray gun on the floor before running out of the house, jostling Carlo's wound with every step.

Enzo huffed from the effort of carrying him across the lawn, but they finally reached the car.

"Stay with me, Carlo," he ordered.

Carlo felt his eyelids droop, and he moaned as Enzo buckled him into the front seat.

Enzo floored the accelerator, headed to an unknown destination.

Despite his wooziness, Carlo was thrilled to be in the car, speeding down the deserted road—on an adventure with his uncle. "Uncle Enzo, tell Lo about this, 'kay? Tell him I helped you and Dad." Carlo's voice faded, but he added, "He'll be so jealous."

"Stay with me!" Enzo shouted. Carlo felt his uncle's hand trying to prop him up in the seat, but all he wanted to do was sleep.

The tires screeched to a halt and Carlo squinted at the bright lights. Abruptly he found himself cradled in the arms of his uncle, who was sprinting toward some sliding glass doors.

"Help us!" Enzo shouted, bursting through the entrance.

A startled nurse instructed, "In here!" and guided them into a curtained room where Enzo laid Carlo on a gurney. "What happened?" she demanded.

"He's been shot."

The nurse began cutting off Carlo's pajama top, now sopping wet with blood. "How old is he?"

Enzo's voice sounded weird, sort of strangled. "Ten."

Two doctors bustled into the room and went to work.

Amidst the chaos of people darting around his bed, barking orders at each other, Carlo's head lolled to the side. The last thing he noticed before he lost consciousness was his uncle ducking behind the curtain and stealing away. Uncle Enzo had left him.

Weeks later, when Carlo asked where Uncle Enzo had gone, his father filled in the rest of the story:

Once out of the building, Enzo had broken into a run. He was almost to his car when a commanding voice ordered, "Freeze!" Enzo looked to find a uniformed police officer aiming his weapon straight at him. The officer's partner jogged up to join him, and Enzo had no choice but to halt, glaring at the two cops.

"Vicenzo Barberi, hands up!" the first officer shouted. The Mafia don did as he was told, noticing the gun weighing down one of his jacket pockets. The murder weapon. He was screwed.

The officers were on him in a second, forcing him to the ground, finding the weapon, and roughly cuffing his hands behind his back. One officer radioed headquarters, informing them of the arrest. They'd suspected Enzo might hit the hospital after a 911 call.

Fanocelli had called the police. The informant had fulfilled his duty.

"What's wrong with you, man?" Logan's deep voice broke through the memories.

"What?"

Logan squinted at his cousin, whose black eyes were even wilder than usual. Carefully he took a subtle step back.

A car engine rumbled in the distance, and Carlo demanded, "Stop looking at me like that!"

The noise increased, and Logan caught a glimpse of a car approaching. He inhaled sharply. Was that a cop? Quickly he jogged back toward his car.

"Ah, life on the lam for a wanted man." Carlo delighted in Logan's fear of capture.

As Logan hustled, Carlo called after him, "Don't be a stranger, *cugino*!"

As he started the car, Logan exhaled slowly, grateful for an excuse to get the hell away from his cousin. Carlo was bad news. He had to keep Grant away from him. He had to find Grant.

24. Nemo and Nema

Y ou got a new clownfish," Sophie observed.

"Yes, I did." Hunter smiled as they began their fourth therapy session.

"Nemo Junior?" she suggested.

"More like Nema, I think. She's a female, thank goodness, just like the shop promised. They warned me that if I got two males in there they might behave aggressively, trying to establish a hierarchy."

Sophie nodded. Percula clownfish didn't sound all that different from humans. "Their markings are so vivid, so vibrant," she said. "You'd think their predators would find them too easily."

"Ah, but clownfish know how to hide in an anemone," Hunter said. "Though no one has figured out how they avoid getting stung."

The two clownfish swam closely together, darting in and out of the plants in the aquarium. Although they'd met only recently, Nemo and Nema seemed quite happy together.

Hunter studied his client before clearing his throat. "Speaking of hiding out, managing to avoid getting stung—have you contacted your father yet?"

Her gaze left the serene water and lowered to the floor. "No."

"Is he even aware that you're out of prison?"

"I don't know."

After a moment she asked, "Why do you think I should call my father?"

"I'm not sure you should," he responded, surprising her. "That's a decision for you to make, and only you understand the consequences of doing so. I don't really know your father or the intricacies of your relationship with him—you haven't told me much. But I can imagine how lonely it would feel to be on your own with no family support after all you've been through—after going to prison and losing your mother."

Sophie sighed, not wanting to acknowledge her loneliness. "But I have Grant and Kirsten."

"I know they're important to you. I also know our parents have quite a hold over us, whether we want them to or not. And I don't think you can avoid your father forever."

"It's not like he's reaching out to *me*," she said bitterly.

"But he has no way of contacting you."

"He should have thought of that when he decided not to visit me *once* in prison." She felt a deep hurt pressing down on her chest. She gave him a hard stare. "Do you get along with your parents?"

"Now I do," Hunter said. "But there was a time when my dad didn't talk to me for almost a year." He leveled his gaze. "After I came out."

Sophie winced. "I'm sorry. Here I am whining about my father when people around me are dealing with *real* problems, like homophobia or child abuse."

"Child abuse?"

The image of Grant lying on his stomach, his arms tucked under his chest and tears tumbling from his tightly shut eyelids, filled her mind. The angry scar. She shuddered.

"Grant," she managed to get out, her throat tight with imminent tears. "I'm pretty sure his father physically abused him."

Hunter nodded, feeling a twinge in his heart as he watched her eyes pool with tears. She clearly cared deeply for Grant, and he tried to push aside his concerns about her rapidly developing intimacy with another convict.

"Has Grant ever been physically abusive to you?" he asked.

Sophie drew in a shocked breath. "No! He would *never* hurt me."

"Okay, okay," Hunter backtracked. "You and I both know sometimes the abused becomes the abuser. I was just making sure."

Taking a deep breath, she reminded herself that Hunter was only doing his job. He didn't know Grant. He didn't know that Grant seemed sad and wounded from the abuse, not outraged and vengeful like some abuse survivors. Like Logan Barberi.

"Every family is different, Sophie. We each have our own albatross to bear. You weren't 'whining' about your problems, and they're not insignificant. You have every right to feel hurt, angry, and abandoned by your father. It sounds like you and he both have made some mistakes." He looked at her kindly. "Would you like to talk about it?"

She twisted her hands in her lap. "I just wanted my dad to …" She glanced at the aquarium. "To be proud of me. I know he was disappointed he didn't have a son. All the miscarriages really took it out of my parents, I guess."

"How many times did your mother miscarry?"

"Four."

"Wow."

"Yeah, I was her fifth pregnancy. The doctors told her it was her last."

"They must have been thrilled when you were born. How do you think those miscarriages affected their parenting?"

"I think it made my mom super overprotective. She was always scared something bad might happen to me. And when it did…" Sophie trailed off, remembering her mother's devastation at her sentencing hearing. "I suppose it was too much for her."

Instead of chastising her once again for blaming herself for her mother's death, Hunter asked, "And your father? How did the miscarriages affect him?"

"He seemed happy that he finally had a kid, though I wasn't the boy he always wanted. I tried to play with the construction toys he bought me, I tried to learn all the White Sox players' names when he took me to games, but it never seemed like enough. He's just kind of a cold man."

"He disapproved of you?"

Sophie nodded.

"Did you argue a lot?"

"Not really—I was a good kid. Well, until my senior year of high school, that is. I started dating one of Dad's employees, Derek Bowden."

Hunter noticed her smirk.

"I met him when I visited my dad's office one afternoon. My dad had suspended Derek from the job site, forcing him to work at a desk after he'd shown up drunk one day. My dad was stuck on a phone call, so I struck up a conversation with Derek, and I was shocked by his honesty—he told me outright that he hated my dad. I remember saying, 'You do know I'm his daughter, right?' and he replied, 'Of course, beautiful, but you seem way too nice to rat me out.' I liked him immediately."

"You sure found a way to stick it to your dad, huh?"

She gave him an impish grin.

"How old was Derek?"

"Twenty-five." Hunter's eyebrows shot up, and Sophie continued, "Dad went ballistic."

"I bet. You were only eighteen."

"He ordered me not to talk to Derek, but I thought I was in love." She rolled her eyes. "My mom and dad yelled at me nonstop about it."

Hunter tilted his head to the side. "That must have been a nice diversion from yelling at each other."

Sophie looked puzzled. "Huh?"

"You said your parents fought constantly, and that your mom would complain to you about your dad all the time. So for them to yell at you instead—well, maybe that's what you secretly wanted."

She sat perfectly still on the sofa, absorbing his insight.

"What ended up happening between you and Derek?" Hunter asked.

"After he got fired for failing a drug test, things kind of faded between us. I realized he was a loser. Then I went off to college."

"So," Hunter ventured tentatively. "Have you dated other older men?"

She glared at him. "What's that supposed to mean?"

"I'll take that as a 'yes'?"

Frowning, Sophie realized she could not get much past this shrink. "I had a huge crush on my professor in grad school," she admitted. Her blush deepened when she divulged, "He was married."

"Did anything happen between you two?"

"Of course not. And that was the only older man I've been attracted to besides Derek, so whatever case you're trying to make for me seeking a father-figure boyfriend, you can flush down the toilet. The whole I-never-got-my-father's-approval-so-I'm-searching-for-a-daddy-husband thing just doesn't apply to me."

He couldn't help but chuckle. "Wasn't Logan Barberi older than you?"

"Well, yeah. He was about six years older than me, but it's not really that unusual for a twenty-eight-year-old woman to be involved with a thirty-four-year-old man."

"Logan was a bad boy, though, wasn't he?" Hunter pressed. "Just like Derek. And it was quite illicit for you to have sex with him since he was your psychotherapy client."

"What's your point?" she challenged.

"Why don't you tell me?" he challenged back.

"Arghhh! You're infuriating! You're making me do all the work! I should tell Jerry to have the DOC withhold your payment for this session."

"Sucks, doesn't it? Your cruel psychologist is making you think for yourself so the insights will have more meaning. What a jerk."

Her temper tantrum subsiding, Sophie flashed him a beguiling smile. She was imminently likable, even when she was frustrated as hell.

With a loud sigh, she plowed ahead. "Your point is that it was not surprising how I fell for Logan. When I couldn't get approval from my dad, no matter how hard I tried, I decided negative attention from him was better than no attention. So, I rebelled and chose male partners to intentionally piss him off: older men, bad boys."

She felt close to tears as she continued. "I was trying to show my dad that he didn't have any control over me, that his approval didn't matter to me."

Hunter was impressed. He couldn't have said it better himself. "Well done. I retract my earlier snarky comment that perhaps it was a good thing you lost your license. I think you would have made an excellent psychologist."

His compliment caused her emotions to erupt, and tears began sliding down her face.

"I guess your father's approval *does* matter to you," said Hunter. "As much as you don't want to care."

She nodded, sniffing and plucking a few tissues from the box on the coffee table.

"I guess we also know why you haven't called your father, then?" he added. "You're afraid he'll reject you again?"

She gave her answer by crying harder. Hunter let her sob for a while, her tears indicating they had arrived at the heart of the matter.

Softly he told her, "I have one more thing to add to your brilliant insights about what led to your mistake with Logan. It seems like trying to piss your dad off wasn't the only reason you fell for Derek and Logan. They both sound like very troubled men—both struggling with addictions of some sort. You said Logan was abused, and I wouldn't be surprised if Derek was too. But instead of their troubles repelling you, they actually attracted you. You wanted to help them."

"It's true." She nodded. "I was trying to help Derek to stop drinking."

"What the hell did an eighteen year old know about substance-abuse treatment?" he asked.

She smiled sheepishly. "Not a whole lot, as evidenced by his subsequent positive drug test."

"My sense is that your caring nature is drawn to wounded people. You attempt to help them just like you tried to help your mother and father with their unhappy marriage. You really sacrificed yourself for your family—attaching yourself to loser men to deflect the attention from your parents' conflicted relationship. But Sophie, you deserve a man who is healthy and strong, not damaged and dysfunctional. You don't have to settle for a Mafia criminal who uses you to get what he wants. You deserve a man who can care for himself, and for you, in a loving, honest way."

Sophie returned Hunter's gaze, blinking several times while taking in his words. All she could think about was Grant. He seemed caring and loving and healthy on the surface, but there was still so much she didn't know about him, beginning with his disturbing nightmares and apparent family history of abuse.

Hunter's words of encouragement circled in an endless loop in her mind. She deserved a good man. Was Grant that good man?

Grant removed the headset and placed it carefully in the drawer while Roger powered down the ship engines.

"Madsen, you got yourself a phone yet?"

"They just turned it on this morning," he replied.

"Good. Joe called last night to check up on you, and I didn't have a number to give him."

"Joe called last night?" Grant was pleased.

"Yeah, the fucker's back stateside for a few weeks, and he was wondering how you were doing."

"What did you tell him?"

"I told him you were shacking up with another parolee—"

Grant's mouth dropped open in protest. "Sophie is living with Kirsten, not me!"

"I also told Joe you have a drinking problem."

Grant's eyes widened with shock, making Roger feel guilty for goading him.

"Jesus, Madsen, can't you take a fucking joke? You are wound so tight, man. Of course I told Joe you're doing just fine. If I *had* said those things, you know he would've taken the first plane to Chicago and would be here this instant, trying to set your ass straight."

"Yeah, Joe would have gotten on my case, that's for sure."

Roger disdainfully eyed the bag of celery sticks on the counter of the bridge, then grabbed one. "Was the XO tough on you as a kid?"

"Yeah, tough but fair. You could say I did my share of military pushups as a teenager."

"I can imagine," said Roger, chomping his celery stick. "His PT sessions at Great Lakes were from hell. He liked to torture us enlisted men."

"Looks like you could keep up with his physical training a little better now," Grant suggested, eyeing Roger's slowly decreasing gut.

"I've lost ten pounds so far," the boss proudly announced.

"That's great, Rog. You and the veggies are getting along much better these days."

"Not really." He frowned. "I still fucking hate vegetables." He violently gnashed the celery stick. "Tasteless piece of shit. But maybe Joe wouldn't give me so much crap if he saw me now. Now that I'm super svelte."

Ignoring Roger's ridiculous assessment of his fitness, Grant inquired, "Is Joe going to visit Chicago?"

"Maybe. He said he had some stuff to take care of but he might make it up here next week. He wants to be the good uncle who visits his nephew, you know?"

Grant tensed, remembering Ben's birthday party tomorrow night. Was he going to be the good uncle who visited his nephew? He'd been wrestling with the decision for days.

He took a few steps toward the stern and glanced at the deck, noticing Sophie wiping down the benches with a wet cloth. She was leaning over a bench, which caused her black miniskirt to hike up on her creamy thigh. Grant felt aroused just looking at her.

"...the new place?"

Grant turned around, confused. "What'd you say, sir?"

Eyeing Sophie in Grant's line of vision, Rog exhaled derisively. "You are so fucking pussy-whipped, Madsen. Christ! I was asking how it was going in your new apartment!"

"Oh." Grant grinned. "Sorry. It's good. How's, um, how's it going at your place?"

"Much better now that I don't have fucking employees throwing books on the floor, waking me up in the middle of the night!" After a few moments Roger added, "Hey, you want to grab a bite to eat?"

"Oh, um, well Sophie and I are going out later, but it would be fine if you wanted to join—"

"Forget about it," Roger quickly interjected. "I'll pass on being the third wheel."

"It's fine, Rog, really."

"No thanks."

They awkwardly busied themselves with various clean-up tasks in the bridge before Grant tentatively asked, "I take it you didn't live with your wife before you got married?"

Roger looked up from his kneeling position by a storage cabinet. "Nah. Nobody did that back then. Didn't want to 'live in sin.' But maybe that would have been a good idea, sort of like a test drive of the marriage. Maybe then I wouldn't be paying fifteen-hundred bucks a month in alimony."

"Whoa," Grant grimaced. "Sounds like things ended badly?"

"Women are the motherfucking devil spawn!"

"C'mon, Rog, don't hold back. Tell us how you really feel."

But Roger was in no joking mood. "She cheated on me, Madsen. The bitch cheated on me."

Grant's face fell. No wonder Roger always seemed suspicious of women in general and Sophie in particular. "Sorry to hear that, sir." There was a moment of silence before Grant asked, "But if she had an affair, how come you have to pay alimony?"

"Excellent question. I got royally fucked over by the courts." Roger seemed pained. "I gotta go," he muttered. "Do yourself a favor, Madsen. Never get married. And never trust women."

With that advice, Roger exited the bridge and hustled down the stairs, leaving Grant leaning against the console, staggered by the weight of his boss' warnings.

He glanced down at Sophie again. She was almost finished wiping down the benches. She'd seemed distant when she arrived for work that morning, but he was starting to notice a pattern of her appearing tired and standoffish following her therapy sessions. He could definitely imagine how rough it would be to discuss family and feelings for an hour straight. Hopefully they could reconnect over dinner tonight.

He was bursting with excitement about something he'd done for her, and he hoped he wouldn't spill the beans before the surprise materialized. Grinning to himself, Grant removed the key from the ship engine and jauntily descended the stairs.

25. Unexpected Gifts

The next day, Sophie's mind was on overdrive as she walked home after the last evening cruise. She'd asked Grant where he wanted to go for dinner, which had become their routine, and was summarily dismissed. Now their conversation played over and over as she walked…

"I got plans," he'd brusquely informed her while stacking chairs on the deck.
"Oh," she replied, and an awkward silence descended. "What kind of plans?"
"I'd rather not get into it, Sophie."
She sighed. She'd been determined to take Hunter's advice and truly get to know Grant before rushing to trust him, but recently her questions had smacked up against a brick wall. Deciding to be direct, she spoke in a clipped tone. "I was hoping the evasiveness you showed at dinner last night would be gone by today."
"Well, it's not like I know everything about you either," he snapped.
Arching one eyebrow, she called his bluff. "What do you want to know? You can ask me anything."
He exhaled loudly. "Look, I'm not trying to be evasive, it's just … I have to go somewhere tonight, and I don't want to go, but I feel like I have to go. And there will be some people there that I'm not looking forward to seeing again."
"So then take me with you," she offered, entwining her fingers with his. "At least you'll have one friendly face on your side."
"No, I don't want you to go," he said forcefully, pulling his hand free. Seeing her wounded look, he backpedaled, "Sophie, you remember those bad people I told you about? They'll be there. It won't be safe for you."

She felt a flash of fear. "Then you shouldn't go, either, if it's not safe. Don't go, Grant, please."

Looking into her eyes, he was touched by her protectiveness.

She noticed him hesitate and continued, "You won't be in violation of your parole if you go there, will you?"

"No." Actually, he hadn't thought about his parolee status. "It…should be fine. I have to go, Sophie. I'll see you tomorrow." Grant leaned in for a chaste peck on the lips, then hustled off the ship. Sophie was left staring at his quickly departing figure, wondering what the hell he was hiding.

❧

"Hey, I'm home!" Sophie called to the empty hallway, pocketing her key as she entered the apartment.

She heard a muffled "In the bedroom!" and followed the sound of Kirsten's voice to find her kneeling, partially swallowed by the closet. Bare feet and legs stuck out from under a skirt, then Kirsten emerged from the dark depths, holding two different sandals.

"Okay." Kirsten smiled, hauling her tall body to a standing position, then precariously bending at the waist while balancing on one foot to slide on each sandal. "Which shoe looks better?"

Sophie eyed her stylish black shirt and denim skirt, tilting her head to one side as she evaluated a black wedge on Kirsten's left foot and a turquoise open-toed shoe on her right. "Definitely the black."

Kirsten exhaled nervously. "I thought so too. I'm so glad you're out, um, that you're back, to help me avoid fashion disasters."

"What are you getting all dressed up for?"

Bashfully Kirsten admitted, "I have a blind date."

"Eeeee! With who?" Sophie squealed. "Tell me!"

"My supervisor knows this guy from the suburbs, and she's setting me up with him."

"That's wonderful! What do you know about him?"

"Well, he's supposedly like six-five, and I like tall guys. And he's a fertilizer technician."

Sophie scrunched up her eyebrows. "What's that?"

Kirsten giggled. "I have no idea, but I guess I'll find out!" She looked at her watch and her eyes widened. "Oh, I gotta go or I'll be late." She quickly dumped her wallet, keys, and lipstick into a handbag. "I was feeling like a loser since you go out like every night with Grant, so I figured I'd give this dating thing a try myself. Wait a minute—why aren't you out with Grant now?"

"Because he blew me off," Sophie replied indignantly.

"What?" Kirsten halted. "Am I going to have to kick McSailor's ass?"

Now Sophie giggled. *That* was a funny visual.

"Relax, Laila Ali. I don't know. He's so hot and cold—I can't figure him out." She met Kirsten's blue eyes. "But let's talk about it later. This is your night. You gotta go meet your hot date!"

"Eek!" Kirsten shrieked. "If he's one-fifth as cute as McSailor, I might be in business." She waltzed out of the bedroom and was almost at the front door when she paused. "Oh!" she cried, turning back to Sophie. "I almost forgot—Anita called you."

"Anita?"

"Yes, Anita. Anita Green, your advisor? Hellooo, don't you remember her?"

"Of course I remember her. Why would she call?"

"I don't know, but she gave me her number, and she wants you to call her. Tonight. I left a note for you on the counter. *Ciao*, roomie!"

Sophie quickly picked up the note and was entirely absorbed in reading her roommate's scrawled handwriting: something about Anita leaving town soon and wanting Sophie to call her immediately.

Anita, her graduate advisor—the woman who had once heaped compliments on her, telling her she was astute, sharp, caring, a great writer, a real team player, a budding psychologist with a bright future. Sophie's cheeks bloomed pink with embarrassment. Why would Anita want anything to do with her now? She was a felon who had lost her license, bringing shame to her family and the entire psychology department at DePaul.

Pacing in the empty apartment, Sophie considered whether to make the call. She hadn't talked to Anita since she'd been arrested, and she couldn't imagine what they would discuss. *So, what was prison like? Exactly how demeaning was it to be on the other side of the bars after we interviewed so many prisoners for our study?*

Feeling a shiver of dread, Sophie set her jaw and crossed to the phone, quickly dialing the number Kirsten had left for her. She might as well get this over with.

"Hello?"

Sophie could not help but smile upon hearing the pleasing lilt of her advisor's voice. She could just picture Anita answering the phone, her beautiful, long red hair curling over her shoulders and her deep-set blue eyes blinking earnestly, taking in everything around her with a cerebral intensity.

"Anita?" She heard her voice tremble. "It's Sophie."

"Oh, Sophie, it's so good to hear your voice. How *are* you?"

"I'm okay." It seemed surreal to be conversing again with the woman who had been such an integral part of her life for four years of graduate school, back when she'd been on the professional fast track, back when life made sense. "How are you?"

"Well, I wish I'd heard from you sooner, because I'm about to head out of town. I got a grant! I'm going to Spain tomorrow to consult on their prison system. They're setting up psychological services for their women's prisons, and they really liked our manuscript published in *Forensic Psychology*. They want me to stay there for six months to help them get started!"

"Wow, that's great!" Sophie was swept up by the enthusiasm in her mentor's voice, as usual. That woman could convince her to try anything, to do anything—the sky was the limit. "I'm so happy for you, Anita."

"Oh, just wait, my dear. You haven't heard the half of it. I need to hire a visiting instructor to teach my fall-semester classes. We were interviewing some candidates but nobody looked promising. Then I got a phone call and the idea just came to me. I need somebody to teach my classes and, Sophie, that somebody is you! I talked it over with the department chair, and we want to hire you to be a visiting instructor."

Sophie collapsed into a chair, sitting in stunned silence.

"Sophie?" Anita's expectant voice filled her ear. "Did you hear me?"

"Yeah. I think so. Um, are you offering me a job?"

"Yes, precisely! We want you to teach in the psychology department."

"But the state board took away my license, Anita."

"I heard that, but you don't need your license to teach, just to practice."

Sophie took a deep breath. She remained mired in disbelief, but a tiny spark of possibility ignited inside her.

"I thought…" She gulped. "I thought I disgraced the entire psychology department when I went to prison."

"Oh, Sophie, why would you think that? You made a mistake, that's all. And when you tried to make up for it, you landed in a huge mess. You were one of our best and brightest grad students, and it would be impossible to mar your excellent reputation with just one mistake. But I didn't get the chance to tell you any of this because you never contacted me! Why haven't you called me this whole time?"

"I thought you'd be ashamed of me," Sophie said. "You worked so hard to train me, and then I went and messed it all up."

Anita sighed, feeling unsure what to say. Sophie had arrived at graduate school with little self-esteem, and it had taken Anita years to build up the young woman's confidence. It appeared her stint in prison had landed her back at square one.

"I'm not ashamed at all. I'm just happy to hear your voice again. I missed you."

"I missed you too." Sophie smiled wistfully, then asked, "Wait a minute—how did you get my number? I mean, how did you find out I'd been released?"

"Let's see, a man named Grant, um, Grant…Madsen, yes, that's his name. He called and asked if I knew of any job opportunities for you."

Tears sprang to Sophie's eyes.

Anita broke the silence. "He told me you were the smartest woman he'd ever met, and it would be a travesty if the field of psychology did not utilize your expertise. Who *is* he, Sophie?"

"He's…he's the man…" Her emotion-laden voice trailed off as she pictured his compassionate crystal-blue eyes boring into her. This was the kindest, most thoughtful gift she had ever received. Despite her earlier frustration, intense warmth filled her heart, and she realized how she really felt about him. Tears rolled down her cheeks. "He's the man I love," she finally managed.

"Why are you crying?" Anita inhaled sharply. "He doesn't have anything to do with the man who put you in prison, does he?"

"Oh, no," Sophie reassured her. "Grant has nothing to do with Logan Barberi." She sniffed. "It's just that nobody has ever done something so incredibly and unexpectedly nice for me."

"Sounds like Grant means a lot to you."

"Yes. I'm a little overwhelmed by this."

"Well, you deserve it, Sophie. You've had quite a string of bad luck, and it's time for things to start going right. Listen, I have to get back to packing. My flight is tomorrow night, but I want to meet with you before that to review some things. Can we meet in the morning? Let's say around nine?"

"Sure," Sophie agreed, still in shock. Then, after mentally thinking through her next day, she cried, "Oh, wait! Tomorrow is Wednesday." She sniffed and then bit her lip. Her voice lowered to barely above a whisper. "I have to meet with my parole officer tomorrow at nine."

"Well, how about right after that then?" Anita suggested, not fazed at all. "We need at least a few hours to get you settled with the teaching duties."

"A few hours? Hmm … I'm supposed to be at work at eleven."

"Really? What's your job?"

Sophie grinned. "Serving drinks on an architectural cruise."

"Oh, that sounds, um, nice." Anita was not sure how to respond, and Sophie rescued her with an attempt at humor.

"I still get to use my training, though. You know what they say—bartenders are just like therapists."

Anita laughed, and Sophie said, "I'll call my boss and ask for a day off tomorrow." She crossed her fingers that she'd find Roger in a good mood. Dieting had made him irritable and kind of depressed of late. "I'll be there, Anita," Sophie promised.

"I look forward to seeing you in my office, Sophie. Have a good night."

"Anita?" Sophie added. "Thank you."

"You're welcome. But you should thank Grant for calling me in the first place."

Sophie hung up and sat back with a sigh, slowly and thoughtfully running her tongue across her upper lip. Anita was thrilled to receive a grant, and Sophie was equally pleased to get *her* Grant. She would definitely thank him. Properly.

Logan crouched behind a line of bushes fronting a brownstone apartment building in the Gold Coast, Chicago's wealthiest neighborhood. He knew the area well. Across the street was his Uncle Angelo's mansion, alight with activity tonight: Ben's sixteenth birthday bash. Expensive cars rolled to a stop as parents dropped off the teenage guests. Logan was amused as he observed the low-riding, baggy jeans of the boys and the plunging halter-top necklines of the girls. Strains of Fallout Boy or Chris Brown blasted from the house each time Ben opened the door for one of his friends.

Catching a glimpse of his son in the doorway, Logan's jaw clenched. He should be there, celebrating this rite of passage. But as a man wanted by the police, Logan was stuck watching the festivities from afar. It crushed him that Ben didn't seem very happy as he greeted his guests. He wore a morose expression and didn't even crack a smile as he accepted haphazardly wrapped gifts from the arriving teens. Logan wanted to smack his son upside the head for his rudeness.

When a cute blond chick sashayed across the street, Logan zeroed in on her tight butt, admiring its curvy perkiness. Then she turned and he immediately recognized her profile: *Ashley Fredrickson.* There she was, the woman who had wooed him years ago, the mother of his child. He chuckled. Her butt still captured his attention seventeen years later. Too bad she was so goddamn opinionated or they might have made their fledgling relationship work. She disappeared inside the house as well.

But the guest he was waiting for still had not arrived. Logan had no idea if his brother even knew about Ben's birthday party, though he was sure Grant knew the date of Ben's entry into the world. Grant had been only fourteen years old when his nephew was born, but somehow Ben always received a birthday present from his uncle. Gifts had come from Qatar, Queensland, and Quito, depending on where Grant was stationed, but they always arrived safely and on time—except for the last two years when Grant had been in prison.

Logan waited another thirty minutes as dusk began settling into the summer sky. He was about to give up his Grant vigil when suddenly a tall, dark-haired man rounded the corner and headed toward Angelo's home. Logan drew a sharp breath. When the lean figure stole a nervous glance to each side, showing his face, Logan smiled.

He was about to stand up and intercept Grant when he heard a strange noise. Logan froze, honing in on the area to his right, and he finally located the source of the sound: the snapping shutter of a camera, held by a dark figure in the shadows. Who the hell was that? Whoever it was, Logan wasn't about to expose himself by stepping out of his hiding spot.

Oblivious to the camera, Grant strolled by, and Logan nearly burst with frustration after waiting for his arrival all night. He watched Grant hesitate before knocking on the ornate maple door. After a few moments Ben answered, and Logan saw his son smile for the first time tonight before Grant enveloped him in a bear hug. He felt a twinge of melancholy watching the scene unfold, once again reminded how remiss he was as a father. At least Grant was there for his son.

The bastard hiding to the right captured it all on film, snapping away as Grant entered the house. Logan watched the shadowy man continue taking photos, apparently aiming at license plates on the vehicles parked near the mansion on the tree-lined street. Logan felt violated. *Fucking feds.* Angelo wasn't kidding. The Barberi family was under surveillance like never before, and they would all have to watch their backs.

Wanting to get the hell away from the long arm of the law, Logan slunk out of the bushes and headed in the opposite direction. Evidently he would not be able to warn Grant about Carlo tonight. His brother had just walked into the lion's den, and there was nothing Logan could do about it.

"I didn't know you'd be here!" Ben grinned as they stepped out of their hug in the foyer.

"I wouldn't miss it for the world," Grant said, pretending he hadn't agonized over the decision for days. "I ran into your mom a few weeks ago, and she told me about your party."

"Wow, my mom, like, never gets out. Where did you guys run into each other?"

Grant affectionately studied his nephew, whose boyish features were beginning to shift toward manhood, although he remained rather short. Apparently, he'd inherited his mother's genes when it came to height. However, his eyes were a dead giveaway that he was a Barberi boy. Actually, Ben's light-blue eyes mirrored his uncle's much more closely than his father's. That similarity seemed to bond them, though it had been years since they last saw each other.

"Ashley took an architectural cruise, which is where I work now."

"Sounds like a sweet job," Ben said.

Grant chuckled. "Um, yeah, the job is maybe not so *sweet*. But it..." He looked at the floor. "It keeps my parole officer off my back."

Ben knew his uncle was embarrassed, and he felt embarrassed too. Grant had always shown him kindness and patience, unlike the stoicism and occasional gruffness his father displayed. And for the momentous occasion of his sixteenth birthday, Ben was not at all surprised that his uncle was here and his father was not. It seemed quite fitting.

Tentatively he asked, "Was it, like, scary or something in prison?"

Grant leveled his remorseful gaze with his nephew's. "It was awful." He swallowed hard and then sternly advised, "Don't ever put yourself in a position where you'll end up there too, Ben."

Though he hated being lectured to by adults, Ben sensed the gravity in his uncle's voice, and he nodded obediently.

Trying to lighten the dark mood, Grant handed over his gift. "I can't *believe* you're sixteen. Happy birthday, Ben."

The boy grinned and took the gift from his uncle, immediately ripping into the neatly wrapped paper to reveal a DVD case. "Ohmigod, is this a Wii game?" He exuberantly turned over the case and read the name aloud: "Ocean's Commander."

"I was hoping you already have a Wii," Grant said.

"Of course Ben has a Wii," an adult male voice responded snidely. Grant tensed as Carlo swooped into the room. "*I* bought the system for him after all."

Ben stopped grinning and tried to stand a little taller as Carlo draped his arm across his shoulders, snatching the game from his hand. "How sweet of your uncle to buy you another game, though." His voice was slick and sarcastic. "How many games does that make for you now, Ben? About two hundred?"

Shrugging, Ben replied, "Yeah. But I didn't have this one yet."

"Naturally. *I* certainly am not going to buy you this military shit." He returned the game to Ben and let go of his shoulder, sidling up to Grant instead. "What are you trying to do, *cugino*? Turn him into a Navy boy?" Carlo's lips curled into a derisive sneer. "He's got a much brighter future than *that*."

Grant felt his hands furling into fists, and he imagined the delectable fantasy of punching the weasel squarely in the nose, perhaps drawing blood in the process. However, he remained quiet, remembering how that same stunt in prison had led him to solitary confinement and antipsychotic medication.

"So, you're finally out of the state pen, huh, Grant?" Carlo grinned wickedly. "Doesn't look like prison toughened you up any, as far as I can tell."

"Sure it did," Ben butted in, eyeing his uncle proudly. "Prison makes you a badass."

Grant was horrified by his nephew's words. Ben had changed in the presence of Carlo. His eyes and face seemed darker, as if the Mafia evil seeped into his veins any time Carlo was present. Ashley had been correct in her assessment that his nephew thought his cousin and great-uncle were "cool."

"Benjamino, you're already a badass. I'm sure you'd do better at surviving prison than this one." Carlo gestured toward Grant, winking at him. "He became mentally unstable in there, from what I hear. Went a little insano."

Ben stared curiously at Grant.

Desperately trying to control himself as he glared at the man responsible for sending him to prison, Grant glanced from Carlo to Ben and told the younger Barberi in a measured tone, "How about you go back to your party, Ben? Your guests are probably waiting."

Ben hesitated until Carlo added, "Yeah, Ben, I'm sure your mother is wondering where her baby disappeared to. And my parents need your help keeping your little lawbreaking friends out of their extensive liquor cabinet."

With a smirk, Ben turned to leave—without a word of thanks about the Wii game he held in his hands.

Now that the two cousins squared off, an electric energy pulsed between them. Grant had the height advantage, but Carlo definitely edged him out in hostility and ruthlessness.

"Don't you *ever* again use Ben against me. You got something to say, you say it to me," Grant raged.

Carlo laughed scornfully. "You think you can order me around, Grant Pants? Think again, *cugino*. With your brother out of the picture, I'm the one in command now. Not some fucking Ocean Commander."

"I was a lieutenant, you asshole, and I couldn't care less about the little Mafia games you all play around here. Leave me out of it."

Carlo's smirk had long faded, and he shook his head disapprovingly. "You show disrespect, *cugino*. Not smart. Not smart at all."

"Are you threatening me, Carlo?" Grant asked. "Because you've already taken everything from me. There's nothing left to threaten or destroy."

"Ah, there I disagree with you. Everybody has something to lose. It just might take some time to find out what it is."

Grant suddenly panicked, thinking of Sophie. Perhaps the Barberis had moved on from their interest in harming Joe, but it was just a matter of time before they learned about Sophie. He realized in that moment that he loved her. And love was a dangerous feeling when it came to leverage and a crime family.

Carlo studied him intently and liked what he saw. Apparently, Grant did have something to lose—something or somebody, somebody he seemed to care about deeply. "Your brother owes us, Grant. And someone is going to pay that debt. Now that I know you're back in good ol' Chicago, maybe it will be you."

Sighing, Grant found himself in the exactly same situation he'd faced just over two years ago: his family dragging him into their criminal fold, threatening to hurt those he loved unless he joined them. But this time was different. This time they didn't know the identity of the one he loved. They could never know about Sophie. He had to keep her safe.

Grant stared into Carlo's black eyes, crisply demanding. "Stay away from me, and stay away from Ben." He silently added, *And stay away from Sophie.*

"Carlo!" An older voice called out from the depths of the huge house.

Carlo smiled. "In here, *padre*, by the front door!" he yelled.

Hearing Angelo's approaching footfalls, Grant took a step backward, toward the door. He had no desire to see the father of the monster standing across from him, the brother of the Mafia don—his father—who'd led this family into despair and shame.

"Tell Ben I'm sorry I had to leave."

Grant swiftly opened the door and slipped into the July night.

"But we were just starting to have fun," Carlo protested. He rubbed his hand across his spiked black hair, staring at the door his cousin had just shut in his face.

"What the hell are you doing?" Angelo asked, striding into the foyer. His slicked-back hair was the same shade as his son's, though gray was beginning to salt the temples. A lit cigar hung from his mouth.

"You'd be interested to know who I was talking to. He just left."

"Who?"

His face erupting into a smile, Carlo answered, "Grant."

"So, he *is* in Chicago after all."

Carlo nodded and licked his lips, mentally reviewing their conversation. His chest still felt tight at the audacious things Grant had dared say to him. But that was the past, and now he was focused on the future. Somehow, some way, he was going to put Grant Pants in his place. He was the heir now, and Enzo's sons were not going to stand in his way.

26. Perfect CONnection

Eventually determining that Grant wasn't going to show up early for his appointment, Sophie knocked on her parole officer's door. She'd been bursting with excitement since hanging up the phone with Anita last night and was *so* looking forward to thanking Grant for his incredible thoughtfulness.

Entering Jerry Stone's office, Sophie immediately realized something was off. A palpable heaviness pervaded the small space, and a weighty despair emanated from the man behind the desk. His expression was sour, almost hostile. "Sit," he barked.

Obeying his command, she noticed a flower arrangement perched on the filing cabinet—completely out of place in the drab, dingy office. There were violet and fuchsia carnations, pink snapdragons, and white amaryllis. "Your flowers are beautiful," she said.

"They're stupid," he countered gruffly. "I don't know why people spend so much money on the damn weeds. They always end up shriveled and dead, just like everything else."

A flash of understanding coursed through her. "Your mother?" she softly questioned. "The flowers—they're for her?"

He averted his gaze and Sophie had her answer. Jerry's mother had succumbed to her battle with cancer.

"I'm very sorry about your loss." She sighed. "No matter what kind of relationship you have with your mom, it's always devastating to lose the woman who brought you into the world."

He gave a half-smile. "When I misbehaved as a child, she used to yell, 'I brought you into this world, and I can certainly take you right back out!'"

Sophie returned his wistful smile. "I think every mother has said that at some point."

They were quiet for a few moments, and Jerry's well-defended crustiness seemed to shift into a vulnerable sorrow. He didn't know what it was about Taylor that put him in touch with his "softer" side—an aspect of himself he thought he'd buried along with his mother—but he found himself asking, "So, you said that it gets easier? This grief thing?"

She held his weary gaze a few moments, wondering whether to be truthful. "Not really," she admitted.

"Finally someone is honest with me," Jerry said, leaning back in his chair. "I'm so sick of hearing all the damn platitudes—it was her time, God needed her up in heaven, all that crap." He glanced at the floral arrangement. "As if flowers are going to make it better, as if flowers would make me forget her cries of pain …" His voice trailed off, and Sophie kept quiet. "I guess, um, when your mom died, uh, nobody could send you flowers in prison?"

Sophie drew a sharp breath and blinked rapidly, trying to stop the prickling tears threatening to erupt. She gripped the arms of the metal chair, fighting for self-control, still surprised by the sudden intensity of emotion that flooded her body any time she was reminded of that horrible December day when the warden had informed her that her mother had died. She'd snidely told Sophie she was *lucky* she had a clean record in prison, resulting in the DOC's *magnanimous* gesture of allowing her to attend the funeral—under heavy guard and in cuffs, of course. Sophie was supposed to feel thankful for the privilege.

Seeing her distraught reaction, Jerry backpedaled. "I'm sorry, I shouldn't have said that. I was feeling guilty that I was bitching about getting flowers from a coworker, when you couldn't even get flowers—"

"It's okay," she interrupted, taking a deep breath. She gazed at the arrangement, commenting absentmindedly, "The amaryllis sure is pretty."

Satisfied that she had not let herself dissolve into tears once again in Jerry's office, Sophie turned her thoughts away from painful loss toward hopeful gain, remembering what Grant had done for her. "Your coworker sent you flowers—well, now I have people in my life that do nice things for me too." She managed to smile while confiding, "Actually, I should probably report to you that I have a new job."

Reminded of his duties as parole officer, Jerry looked at Sophie as if seeing her for the first time today. She was dressed in a lightweight black pantsuit, and the silky halter top showcased the creamy skin of her neck and slender arms. Her blond locks were pinned back in a neat bun.

"A new job? I *was* wondering if your clothes would be suited for working on a ship."

She grinned. "Not quite. These long pants might get caught in the rudder or something. I'm actually going to be teaching psychology at my alma mater, DePaul."

"Really? How'd you pull that off?"

A slight blush colored her cheeks. "Grant made it happen."

Jerry arched one eyebrow. "Grant? As in Grant Madsen?"

She shyly nodded, and he deduced he was going to have to draw it out of her. "How did Grant get you the job?"

Her eyes took on a dreamy, enraptured glow as she explained. "Grant told me once about how much his Uncle Joe meant to him, and he asked me if I had anyone in my life like that. So, I told him about my graduate advisor, Anita. But I never in a million years expected Grant to *call* Anita and ask her to give me a job! I still can't believe he did that! It's the kindest thing *anyone* has ever done for me."

She's in love, it dawned on him. For all his colleagues' jokes about setting up a dating service for their parolees, these two cons had developed a tight connection, a budding romance, right under his nose. He was stunned. He had to admit they made a gorgeous pair, but for some reason he felt uneasy about their relationship.

"When do you start your new job?"

His question drew her out of her romantic reverie. "I'm not sure. I'm meeting with Anita today to set things up before she travels overseas. And I need to give my current boss, Roger, enough notice."

He nodded and took out her file, snapping the end of a ballpoint pen. "What's the contact information for your new supervisor?"

Now that they were all business, Sophie sat up in her chair and provided Anita's full name, address, and phone number, promising she would have her call Jerry today before leaving the country.

After taking down the data, Jerry studied Sophie, whose face was flushed with optimism. He felt a paternal tenderness toward her. "So, things are looking up for you then?"

"I guess so," she tentatively agreed. She still had a long road back to herself, but she was taking steps in the right direction.

He rose from his chair and plucked a white amaryllis from the arrangement. Slowly the stern parole officer walked around his desk and handed her the green stem. It just felt like the right thing to do. "Perhaps it does get easier?" he said.

Biting her lower lip, she carefully placed the delicate flower into her handbag. Feeling a little choked up, she stood to leave, murmuring, "Perhaps. Thank you, sir," before bolting out the door.

She emerged from the office slightly shaken, causing Grant to scramble to his feet.

"Are you okay?"

Sophie gazed into Grant's eyes and a bright smile spread across her face.

"Yes, especially now that you're here."

Suddenly propelling herself into his arms, she wrapped him in a tight hug while tilting her mouth upward to meet his. Though he was surprised, he quickly got on board and his full lips met hers with intensity and fire as his sure hands caressed the skin of her shoulders and upper back. Their deep kiss lasted several moments, and she felt her heart pounding with arousal, her chest pressed against his.

Finally, he peered down at her, his eyes dancing like droplets of sun skimming across a pool. "That was some greeting, Bonnie. Good morning to you too."

She giggled. "Good morning."

He took a step back to take in her elegant clothing. "And you look smashing this morning, I must say."

"Thank you, Grant."

"A new uniform for Rog's ship?"

She grinned and shook her head. "Nope." Coquettishly she patted her up-do. "I *may* be meeting with my new boss today." Her eyes narrowed playfully. "I got a call from Anita, and it seems *somebody* doesn't want me working with him anymore."

"Wait a minute, I—"

Giggling again, she cut him off by planting another smooch on his unsuspecting lips. "Relax," she assured him in a sultry voice, her face inches from his own. "You did good, McSailor. And this kiss is only the beginning of how I'm going to thank you for the best gift I've ever received."

His smile now matched hers. "I like the sound of that." He ran his fingertips across the smooth skin of her shoulder blades as they swayed gently together.

She peeked at her watch. "Listen, you have to meet with Jerry, and I have to get to DePaul to sort out the details. Rog gave me the day off, but I'll see you at your place tonight, okay? I'll be all ready for you then."

"What are you planning, you little minx?"

Chuckling, she said, "You'll just have to wait to find out." She reluctantly let go and grabbed her handbag. "You better get in there. You don't want to be late!" she called over her shoulder.

He watched her stroll away, her pantsuit flowing and billowing alluringly with each confident stride. Her bright countenance stood in sharp contrast to the darkness of his previous evening with Carlo, and Grant knew he would miss her light spirit immensely today at work. Taking a deep breath, he knocked on his parole officer's door.

"How's it going, Madsen?" Jerry asked once Grant was seated.

Grant stared across the desk piled high with papers and files. "Fine, sir."

"Anything to report to me today?"

"Nothing comes to mind, sir."

"So," Jerry began, leaning forward on his desk. "What's this I hear about you getting your girlfriend a job?"

Grant's shy smile did not hide his bubbling excitement, which made him look younger than his thirty years. "Oh, Sophie told you, huh? I'm so glad it worked out."

Jerry could not hide the suspicion in his voice. "Why did you do it?"

The question startled Grant. Why *had* he found Sophie a teaching job? Because he cared for her, of course. He wanted the best for her. He wanted to make her happy. But the real reason was niggling at the back of his mind: *because he loved her.* And because it wouldn't be a bad idea for her to spend her days far away from him and the threat of his family. But particularly after that kiss they'd just shared, he couldn't stay away from Sophie completely. That was just not possible.

He was not about to reveal any of those thoughts to his parole officer. "I did it because Sophie didn't have the courage to do it herself," he explained. "I know what it's like to try to make it on the outside after being totally humiliated in prison. It's not easy. And sometimes you need another person to help you see the strength in yourself."

Jerry was impressed by the young man sitting across from him. Suddenly there was a knock on the door.

"Enter!" Jerry yelled.

Expecting to tell an eager con to wait outside until his appointment time, Jerry instead found his colleague Sheila standing in the doorway.

"Officer Sarconi," he greeted her, rising from his chair. Grant craned his neck to catch a glimpse of the woman behind him, and he also stood as a sign of respect.

"What can I do for you?" Jerry inquired.

"Some photos just came in for you from HQ," Sheila explained in a voice deepened by years of smoking. Although the fortyish woman was somewhat petite, she came across as a tough bitch, and Grant couldn't imagine many parolees daring to give her a hard time.

"I thought you'd want to see these, pronto," she prompted, handing him an envelope.

"Thanks," Jerry replied, opening the clasp. "Madsen, take a seat."

"Yes, sir." As Grant watched Jerry extract the glossy photographs, he felt a heated glare from the female parole officer. What was her problem?

Jerry gasped, a photo in one hand and a typed report in the other. Grant was suddenly alarmed to find his parole officer also glaring at him with a menacing fierceness, looking back and forth between him and the photo.

Jerry swiftly rounded the desk and without a word grabbed him by the shirt collar, yanking him to standing.

"What the hell?" Grant blurted.

Jerry roughly spun him around and shoved him toward the wall. Grant's heart raced with panic and confusion. Under the force of Jerry's rough hold he felt himself falling and clawed for something to grab on to, unfortunately bringing down the vase of flowers when his hand hit the filing cabinet. Grant heard the crash just as his body slammed into the wall, knocking the air out of his lungs.

"You're under arrest!" Jerry shouted, his tone causing Grant to stop squirming immediately while his throat constricted with fear. The parolee felt two pairs of hands on him now as Sheila joined in to restrain him against the concrete.

"Hands on the wall. Spread 'em," Jerry ordered, and Grant quickly complied, feeling rough hands thoroughly frisk him. Desperately wanting to ask what the hell was going on, he wisely kept his mouth shut. Once he felt Jerry wrench one arm behind his back and snap a cold metal cuff onto his wrist, he closed his eyes with despair. Swiftly his other arm joined the first, his wrists now tightly manacled together.

There was dead silence in the office. Still facing the wall, Grant dared to glance down at the mess of broken flowers, spilled water, and shards of glass.

"Eyes forward!" Jerry yelled.

"Yes, sir." His shoulders were already beginning to ache and he'd been cuffed less than one minute. He'd forgotten how painful it was to be handcuffed—physically and emotionally.

"You're going back to Gurnee, Madsen," Jerry growled.

He simply had to know what had happened. "Why?"

Exhaling with disgust, Jerry stepped over the clutter on the floor and reached for something on his desk. When he returned, he shoved Grant's chest into the wall, causing him to twist his head, his cheek flush with the concrete. Sheila studied Grant disdainfully, her arms folded across her chest.

Leaning in behind him, Jerry thrust a glossy photograph in Grant's face. It was unmistakably an image of him on Angelo's doorstep. Rifling through the photographs, Jerry showed him the images one by one: Grant greeting Ben, hugging his nephew, then striding out the front door. Who the hell had taken those pictures?

"You tell me you got nothing to report to me, but you were at fucking Angelo Barberi's house last night?"

Grant blinked rapidly. "So what, sir?"

"So *what*? You're caught at a goddamn Mafia don's house, and you say *so what*? You're on fucking parole, you idiot! You don't associate with criminals, or you go straight back to prison!"

Closing his eyes again, Grant felt his stomach drop. His family was taking him down once again. Sophie's words of warning reverberated through his head: *You won't be in violation of your parole if you go there, will you?* How could he have been so damn stupid? He hadn't even considered visiting Ben as a potential parole violation.

"What were you doing at Angelo Barberi's house?" Jerry demanded.

Oh, God, what was he supposed to do? Tell the truth about his Mafia connection? His parole officer already hated him, mistrusted him, viewed him as a no-good criminal.

"Answer me!" Jerry commanded.

But Grant couldn't get the words out. He couldn't admit he was a Barberi—a name that sickened him. He stood pinned against the wall in complete stillness, astonished by how quickly he had flushed his future down the toilet once again. And what was he going to tell Sophie?

"Maybe it would help to have him sit down, Jer," Sheila said.

Taking a step back, Jerry peeled Grant off the wall and guided him back to the chair. He felt Grant's body shaking beneath his strong hold.

Dismayed by the shitty day this was turning into, Jerry gingerly stepped over the mess on the floor and returned to the chair behind his desk.

Jerry glanced at his colleague. "Sorry your flowers got trashed."

Sheila shrugged. "Hey, what are you going to do?"

Grant warily looked back and forth between the parole officers. "I'm sorry too, ma'am."

Sheila raised her eyebrows.

Jerry nodded toward his colleague. "Sheila, I think I can handle this one now. Thanks for your help."

"You want me to get some officers down here?" she offered.

Jerry studied Grant, who sat ramrod straight with a pained expression on his face. This con made him *very* curious. Knowing the reason Sophie Taylor went to prison, Jerry was determined to find out exactly how Madsen was connected to the Barberi family, even if he had to question Grant all day long. "Nah, I'll call them when I'm ready."

"Gotcha, Jer. I'll talk to you later."

Once Sheila had exited, Jerry returned his attention to the handcuffed con trembling before him. "I'll ask you again, Madsen. What were you doing at Angelo Barberi's house?"

Grant felt consumed by despair. "Do I have to go back to solitary, sir?"

"What? No, you'll go back to Gen Pop, unless for some reason you break the rules again at Gurnee."

He nodded. At least there was that.

Jerry tried another tactic, looking down at the documents Sheila had brought him. "You were hugging, um, it says here, Benjamin Barberi." He raised his eyes to meet Grant's. "Do you know him?"

Apparently the feds were also watching his nephew. Things just kept getting better. In that moment, Grant decided simply to give up. Why keep fighting? It never got him anywhere. Listlessly he answered, "Yes, sir."

"How do you know him?"

Grant averted his eyes. "He's my nephew."

There was a knock at the door, undoubtedly Jerry's next parolee, and he shouted, "Go away! Come back later!" Not surprisingly, the knocking stopped.

A perplexed expression colored Stone's face as he tried to regain his focus. "Benjamin Barberi is your nephew? How exactly are you related to him? Are—"

Resolving to end this pointless conversation, Grant butted in, "I was born Grant Barberi. My uncle Joe Madsen adopted me when I was twelve." Watching

Jerry struggle to understand this fresh information, he added, "Enzo Barberi, the Mafia don who shot a kid and got sentenced to life at Gurnee—he's my father." He exhaled derisively. "My family is a bunch of criminals. And I'm one of them."

Jerry was dumbfounded by Grant's explanation, but his mind remained on overdrive, sensing he was missing something. "Enzo Barberi is your dad? That means . . . Logan Barberi—he's your . . . your *brother?*"

"Yes, sir," Grant responded, trying to discern why his PO would care about Logan. *Enzo* was the name everybody knew. Enzo was the most shameful relative.

Jerry's eyes bugged. "Does Taylor know any of this?"

Grant looked down. "Sophie? No, sir. I didn't tell her about my family. I didn't think she would want anything to do with me if I did."

Jerry was almost speechless, but he soldiered on. "And do you know why Sophie went to prison?"

Now it was Grant's turn to look confused. "Not the details. Why? *Should* I know?"

They didn't know. Neither had any idea Grant's brother was responsible for putting Sophie in prison. Sophie loved Grant, and she had no fucking clue who he was. Jerry felt sick just thinking about it.

"Sir? Are you okay?"

Jerry looked at Grant. "Why did you pull that robbery, Madsen? Back in 2006?"

Grant looked away, protesting, "It doesn't matter—"

"Just answer my question," he insisted.

"My brother and cousin threatened to kill my Uncle Joe unless I stole the money."

Jerry inhaled sharply. "Jesus! Why didn't you go to the police?"

"Yeah, right," Grant scoffed. "That would have done a lot of good. Joe would have been in even more danger if the police had started sniffing around."

Jerry shook his head. What a mess. "Why the hell would you go to Angelo's house after what they did to you? Why would you put yourself in that danger?"

"It was Ben's sixteenth birthday," Grant retorted defensively. "He's my nephew, and they're already getting their claws into him. I've got to save him before it's too late—just like my uncle saved me."

Grant suddenly became aware of the handcuffs again—all trussed up, ready to return to prison—and lowered his head. "Well, like my uncle *tried* to save me. Obviously he failed."

Juxtaposing the shock of discovering Grant's criminal family with the injustice of his dark resignation to take the fall for crimes way beyond his control, Jerry felt a battle wage within him. Did this parolee deserve to return to prison? Or was he a good man trapped in bad circumstances? Sophie seemed to think the latter was true, but she didn't really know what those bad circumstances entailed.

Jerry grabbed one of the photographs from his desk. "What's that in your hand there?"

"Uh, a present for Ben?"

"So, you were there for a birthday party, and you only stayed…" He peered at the time stamps on the photographs. "Five minutes?"

"About that, yes, sir."

"Did you discuss or engage in any illegal activity while you were there, Madsen?"

"Um, I don't think so, sir. Well, my cousin Carlo Barberi approached me, but we pretty much just yelled at each other."

Jerry popped out of his chair and quickly circled the desk. "On your feet," he ordered.

Grant stood up, prepared to be hauled to a transport bus bound for Gurnee. Instead, Jerry unlocked his handcuffs.

Rubbing the raw skin on his wrists, Grant watched the PO clasp the cuffs back on his belt.

"I'm not returning to Gurnee?"

"You're not in violation of your parole," Jerry said. "You went to a family birthday party, that's all. You weren't attempting to associate with known criminals. It was a big misunderstanding."

Expelling a huge sigh, Grant gazed gratefully at his parole officer, who did not seem to share his happiness and relief.

"But, Madsen, stay away from your family while you're still on parole," Jerry sternly advised. "Hell, stay away from them forever. They're no good for you."

"Yes, sir, I can see that."

Swallowing hard, Jerry commanded, "And you should tell Sophie who you really are."

Grant absorbed his words. Testily he inquired, "Is that an order, sir? Is that a condition of my parole?"

How was Jerry supposed to answer that? He felt bound to protect Sophie, but he found himself wanting to protect the young man standing next to him as well. Once they learned of their connection, their fledgling love affair would be demolished.

Jerry stared into Grant's troubled eyes. "No, it's not an order. But it's the right thing to do, Madsen."

He took a deep breath and nodded.

"Now get the hell out of here. You've made me late for my next appointment."

"Yes, sir."

Grant left the office, his mind swirling. Despite his desperate attempts to escape his family's influence, they kept infecting his every chance at happiness. But now he had Sophie, and he was determined not to let his family ruin that love too.

27. Imperfect CONnection

Sophie struggled as she tried to fit the key into Grant's apartment door while juggling two sacks of groceries and a heavy bag of cooking supplies along with her large purse, which threatened to slide off her shoulder. Finally, she opened the door and made her way down the hallway into the kitchen, where she plopped down her purchases with relief.

A giddy excitement coursed through her as she glanced around the empty apartment. She'd just spent a wonderful morning with Anita preparing for the teaching assignment, and she was pleasantly surprised by the salary they offered. Anita's research grant afforded Sophie better earnings than expected, and she'd now be able to make the monthly payment for her student loans without begging her father.

As she began removing items from the grocery bags, she thought guiltily about her father. She hadn't spoken to him in more than a year, and she wondered how he was handling the death of his wife. Sure, her parents had argued, but over the years, Sophie had come to realize they needed each other in some incomprehensible way. She knew her father had to be taking his grief hard. Shaking her head, trying to elude the tormenting reminders of her family, she gazed down at the jar of Kalamata olives in her hand.

First, she set out the ingredients for the appetizer: olive oil, garbanzo beans, tahini, onion powder, and a garlic bulb; followed by the necessary elements for the salad: hearts of romaine, tomatoes, feta cheese, cilantro, and parsley.

Cucumber and pita bread were the next items she extracted from her grocery bag. Finally, she took out the leg of lamb.

Surveying the fresh food in front of her, she gave a satisfied grin. As she turned to the refrigerator, her smile spread even wider. Although Grant had not one piece of artwork on his apartment walls, he'd carefully displayed the note she'd written weeks ago on his refrigerator door.

Her dreamily scrawled handwriting also brought back steamy memories of their first sexual encounter. Perhaps they could ignite that sensual flame again this evening.

You should tell Sophie who you really are.

Jerry's words echoed through Grant's mind, causing his chest to tighten with dread. How would Sophie react? Would she run from him in fear? Was his family going to ruin yet another important relationship in his life? She was absolutely precious to him—a beacon of light amidst all the darkness—and the thought of losing her made his heart ache.

"Madsen!" Roger hissed, snapping Grant out of his vexed trance.

"Sir?" he nervously questioned, looking around at the bridge and finding his boss glaring at him from the controls.

"Turn off your microphone when you're speaking to me!" he ordered.

Grant winced as he shut off the headset.

"You've been silent for over two minutes, you douche bag," Roger fumed. "What the hell is your problem?"

Grant's eyes widened. Wonderful. Now his family was causing him to be derelict in his duty. "No excuse, sir. Permission to continue?"

Roger pursed his lips and nodded dismissively. Grant immediately turned the microphone back on and robotically launched into a description of the futuristic round towers of Marina City. He felt his boss' angry glare from across the bridge, and he swallowed hard.

Once the cruise had finished, Roger turned to Grant. "You didn't answer my question," he said. "What's wrong with you today? You're a major space cadet."

Grant looked down. "I'm sorry."

"I thought Sophie taking the day off would make your focus better, not worse."

"I guess I miss having her here," he admitted.

"Well, you're the one who got her the new job, right? And you're already regretting it?"

"I don't regret it—she was *so* happy about getting back into psychology, you should have seen her." A soft smile formed as he remembered her glee. "It's just…I, well, I had a rough meeting with my parole officer today."

"Yeah, that guy seems like a hardass. You don't want to mess around with him."

"No kidding." He sighed. "Officer Stone thinks I'm going to hurt Sophie."

Roger scrunched his eyebrows. "*Hurt* her? Have you seen the way she looks at you, Madsen? She thinks you're God's gift—the fucking cat's meow." He scratched his head. "I'm still trying to figure out why she likes you so much."

Grant chuckled softly, and Roger went on, "You should be more concerned about *her* hurting *you*. Remember what I told you about women, Madsen?"

"Ah yes, how could I forget?" Grant said, the lines of worry on his face quickly replaced by laughter. "They're the devil spawn."

"Damn straight," Roger confirmed. "Women: can't live with 'em, can't kill 'em." With a huge guffaw, the captain departed the bridge and walked down the stairs, undoubtedly headed off the ship to procure some hated vegetables for an afternoon snack.

☙

Ben grinned, high-fiving his buddy, after his virtual player scored a touchdown. He and two friends were engaged in a full-scale videogame frenzy at ESPN Zone, not far from his uncle's home.

"Ben!" Dylan yelled, causing him to glance away from the game. "Come on. Let's shoot some hoops, man!"

Nick nodded in agreement, and they slid out of their chairs facing the giant green screen and headed over to ESPN Hoops Hysteria.

"You are so going down, Dyl." Ben shook his head.

"Oh, yeah? What makes you think that?" the taller, shaggy-haired boy shot back.

Ben smiled wickedly. "'Cause when the pressure is on, Dyl, you freaking crumble."

Nick snickered. Last week the three had made their first drug deal, accepting two-hundred ecstasy pills from a well-known local dealer, Aaron Caldwell, then selling them to their classmates. Actually only two of them made the deal, as

Dylan panicked and hightailed it out of there when Aaron's huge German shepherd came to the door first.

Hearing Ben taunt him once again, Dylan realized he would never live down running away. Ben and Nick had each come away with a cool one-hundred-dollar profit, and they were already contemplating their next transaction.

"That was just one time," Dylan mumbled.

"I think it's a chronic condition, Dyllie-girl. Your freakout was *so* epic," Ben said. "But I gotta take a leak before I school you two in hoops. Be right back."

Ben turned away from his buddies and entered the men's room. Once he flushed the urinal, he glanced up at the mirror. His jaw dropped when he saw the reflection of the man behind him.

Staring back at him were two deep-blue eyes.

Whirling around to face his father, Ben's face was trapped somewhere between delight and anger. Finally, he aimed a lopsided smile toward the tall, black-haired man. "Hi, Dad."

Logan exhaled with relief and smothered his son in a bear hug. Though allowing his father to scoop him up like that was definitely uncool, Ben could not help but feel pleasure and safety in the sure embrace. It had been too long.

"Happy birthday, son," Logan said, his voice sounding uncharacteristically shaky.

As they shyly stepped back from one another, both immediately adopted more manly demeanors.

"Did you bring me a gift?" Ben asked.

Logan looked down. "Uh, I wasn't sure it would be safe to approach you, so, um, no." He licked his lips nervously. "But next time, okay?"

Crestfallen, Ben nodded. His father hadn't been around for his fifteenth birthday either, and he was slowly learning not to get his hopes up. "You, um, decided it was safe to talk to me? No cops around?"

"I'm more worried about the feds than the fuzz at this point."

"The feds?"

"They're watching you, Ben. Don't you know that?"

"They don't care about *me*," he scoffed.

Logan looked at his son like he was a complete idiot. "Of course they do. You're Enzo Barberi's grandson, for chrissake. The feds were parked right outside Angelo's place last night for your party."

Ben's light-blue eyes widened, then quickly narrowed. "You were *there?*" His tone was wounded. "But you didn't come inside?"

"Of course not! I would have been arrested on the spot!"

"But Carlo says the police aren't really after you anymore. He says you've just lost your edge—that you're too scared to be involved in the business. That's why you don't show your face."

Logan clenched his fists, infuriated by his cousin. But was it really a misrepresentation? Logan was supposed to meet Carlo in an hour to pull a job. And he'd been feeling sick about it—not because he was scared, but because he was disgusted by the whole thing. He was relatively certain Carlo would use him as muscle, meaning he would have to rough up anyone standing in their way, even if it meant murder. There had already been enough killing in Logan's thirty-five years. There was enough blood on his hands.

"Do you actually think I would hide myself away from you unless it was absolutely necessary?" Logan asked. "I've missed a whole year of your life, and you're my son! I hate this, but I have no choice."

Ben sniffed. "You didn't seem to care about that when you got in trouble with the cops." Logan watched his son look away. "Just like Uncle Grant. It's not like he cared about *me* when he went away to prison."

So, Grant had never told Ben about Logan's involvement in his arrest. Logan felt simultaneously relieved and ashamed. Quietly he asked, "How *is* your uncle?"

"Fine," the teenager responded petulantly. "At least *he* got me a gift."

Logan exhaled forcefully. "I said I'd get you one, all right?" Biting his lip, he added, "Did Grant say anything about where he lived?"

"Nope," Ben replied. "We didn't get to talk much before Carlo showed up. He and Uncle Grant got sort of pissy with each other."

"Did anything happen?"

"Dunno. I went back to my party and let them work out their little bitch-fight."

Logan was taken aback by Ben's snarky tone. His son was turning into a pint-sized punk.

"Why do they hate on each other?"

"That's a conversation for another day, Ben. How did Grant find out about your party?"

"Oh. He said he ran into Mom on an architectural cruise. That's where he works now or something."

"Really." The wheels in Logan's mind started turning. "Listen, I should go, but before I leave, I want to ask you why you were at Aaron Caldwell's house."

"Were you spying on me?"

"You're damn lucky the feds didn't trail you there," Logan replied. "Answer my question. Why the hell were you on a drug dealer's doorstep?"

Staring defiantly into his father's disapproving glare, Ben answered, "None of your business, *Dad*."

Logan took a menacing step forward, making the difference in their heights more obvious. "It *is* my business," he countered. "I'm your father."

"I don't have a father," Ben insisted, his voice filled with fury and hurt. "He left a long time ago."

"But I'm here now," Logan pointed out. "And I don't want you around drug dealers."

"That's rich, Dad. You're on the run from the police, and you're telling me to obey the law. Classic."

His son's sarcasm made Logan's throat tighten with regret. Swallowing guiltily, he stared at his only child. "You're right. I have no room to tell you how to live your life. Just please, try to learn from my mistakes. Being a fugitive, in trouble with the cops—it's no way to live." He ran a hand through his cropped jet-black hair and sighed. "I always wanted a better life for you."

Ben had no idea what to say.

Clearing his throat, Logan murmured, "I gotta go. Be careful, kid." Then he slunk out of the men's room, disappearing from his son's life again. Ben jammed his hands into his pockets and gazed into the mirror for a second before returning to his buddies in the game room. His father had left him once again.

❧

As soon as Grant walked into his apartment, he was overwhelmed by the enticing aroma of garlic and spices. His stomach growled as he closed the door and glided around the corner, following his nose toward the heavenly scent. All vestiges of fatigue and stress vanished the second he saw her.

Sophie stood by the kitchen counter, chopping a cucumber while she swayed her hips to the Gap Band's infectious "You Dropped a Bomb on Me." She hadn't heard him over the din of the radio, and he held back laughter as her carefree dance moves filled his kitchen with energy and grace.

She turned to grab a towel and nearly jumped out of her skin when she caught him standing there, watching her with amused eyes, his hands on his hips. "Oh!" she squeaked, quickly reaching over to turn down the radio. "You're early!"

He chuckled while moving toward her, drawn in by the endearing flush of her cheeks and the striking figure she cut in her silky black pantsuit. "And you're adorable," he responded, leaning in to plant a feathery kiss along the curve of her neck, sending goose bumps cascading down her arms. His warm breath lingered on her skin for a moment before he lifted his head.

His hand rested protectively on the small of her back as he gestured to the feast she was compiling on the counter. "What's all this? Smells incredible, by the way."

Her eyes sparkled. "I wanted to do something nice for you, to thank you for being my personal employment agency. So, I'm cooking you a Mediterranean meal."

"My favorite food! I can't wait to try it."

"Well, don't get too excited. It's my first time making these dishes, so they might be a total disaster. And I'm not done yet. I didn't expect you home so soon!"

"Yeah, Rog didn't make me swab the deck tonight. But I still got kind of grubby on the ship." He glanced at his watch. "How about I take a quick shower before we eat?"

"Yes!" she responded enthusiastically. "That would give me some time to finish up."

"Wow. Are you trying to get rid of me, Bonnie?" He grinned.

Sophie blushed. "Not at all, Clyde. It's just that I want this dinner to be perfect and having you here, hovering over me, is kind of, um, *distracting*."

"Say no more," he advised, leaning in to graze his lips across her warm cheek and holding her spellbound with his tantalizing touch.

As Grant headed for the shower, Sophie felt her cheek and neck on fire from his lingering kisses. Slowly she turned her attention back to the cucumber, sighing happily.

"That was simply amazing," he murmured appreciatively while surveying the table covered by remnants of their feast: rich garlic hummus with pita and slices of cucumber and tomato, then shish kebabs featuring succulent lamb, grilled onion, and green pepper, along with fattoush salad drizzled with lemon vinaigrette.

Sophie beamed. "I'm so glad you liked it. Are you ready for dessert?"

"Whoa, dessert too?" He clasped her hand in his, and the electricity that crackled between them only intensified. "What kind of dessert did you plan? Food or flesh?"

Her mouth dropped open, and he felt enticed by the parting of her pink, luscious lips. Heat stirred below his belly as she slowly slid her tongue across her bottom lip, leaving a moist trail.

"Hmm," she mused. "I had planned some baklava to end our Mideast feast, but it sounds like you have something else in mind?"

Keeping hold of her warm hand, Grant rose from the table, drawing her out of her chair. "Maybe later for the baklava," he suggested. He gently cradled her other hand in his and they faced each other, inches apart. His fingers slid softly over her smooth hands, which rested by her side.

"The flesh kind of dessert then?" She tilted her face up and leaned in to meet his smiling lips with her own. Their kiss started as tentative and sweet, an exploratory union holding the promise of deeper passion. Grant let go of one hand to cradle the back of her head, his hand pressing into her strawberry tresses while his lips bore down on her mouth.

Between gradually intensifying kisses he whispered, "Your delicious dinner was a wonderful thank-you gift."

Snaking her hands up his back and cradling them over his broad shoulders, she gazed into his eyes and pledged, "My thank you is just getting started, McSailor."

He raised his eyebrows and his typically cool eyes smoldered. Abruptly he squatted and hoisted her body in one swift movement.

Sophie squealed as he slung her over his shoulder.

"I'm taking you to my bed, woman," he announced.

She continued giggling, feeling blood rush to her face. "Oh, McSailor, you've got me. I'm at your mercy."

"Glad you see things clearly," he responded as he took sure strides into the bedroom, his precious cargo slung like a sack of potatoes across his back. The bed was neatly made—traces of his military training—and he gently unfurled her body from his, resting her on the leafy sage bedding. He feasted his eyes on the rosy skin of her arms and neck.

"As sexy as you look in that getup, I'm going to have to strip it off of you right now."

"Well, what are you waiting for?"

He grinned. "Ah, I love a feisty Bonnie lass." Crawling onto the bed, he undid the clasp of her halter top while simultaneously planting a scorching kiss on her lips.

She pulled down her halter top, exposing her bare breasts. No bra! He swiftly lifted his light-blue polo shirt over his head, then straddled her reclining form.

He slid his long fingers up her ribcage, kneading and massaging her firm breasts and hardening nipples with his adept touch. Feeling his hardness near her, on her, around her, she desperately wanted him *in* her, and she reached down to unzip his jeans.

He was zoned in on the flesh cradled in his hands, however, and he would not be deterred. Her breath hitched as his tongue swirled across her sensitive skin. She gave up on removing his pants and allowed her arms to fall by her side, useless.

Grant paused and peeked up, smirking. "Is my little chef tired from all her cooking today? Just leave the work to me. I'll take good care of you."

She grinned as he scooted himself toward her feet while he peeled off her pantsuit. Always a gentleman, he popped off the bed to hang the pantsuit carefully on a chair before returning to his beauty.

Grant admired her black panties. "You are one sexy woman, Sophie Taylor."

She sat up and grabbed the waistband of his unbuttoned jeans, noticing the tightening bulge beneath the zipper. "And you are wearing entirely too many clothes, Grant Madsen." She helped him shimmy out of his jeans, then beckoned him back to the bed. He sat on the sheets and she cuddled up on top of him, her long legs wrapped around him as they continued kissing, reveling in their closeness.

Moving easily together, she helped him shed his boxers a split second before he removed her panties. Having spent several evenings naked in each other's company, their self-consciousness was gone.

Grant nestled himself into the covers, resting on his back and panting with anticipation, as Sophie unrolled a condom over his rock-hard erection. There was no need for words as they synchronously flowed together, reading each other's intentions through hungry looks or sensuous touches. He reached down to her core and let his fingers do the talking as he prepared her for entry, reveling in her delectable moans.

Crawling up his body, her eyes glowed with desire. The faint smile on her lips disappeared the moment she guided him into her wetness. Her lips separated and a staccato gasp stole the air around her as he filled her completely.

She rested her weight entirely on top of him and he bucked into her, his hands all over her glorious body as they thrust together. Somehow managing to corral his roving hands with her own, she held on for dear life as he took her screaming upward to the height of arousal—higher, faster, climbing to a soaring zenith as both reached a shuddering peak. They held onto their high for a magnificent moment, suspended in time. Then their bodies collapsed into each other, and Sophie tried to catch her breath, her lungs heaving and quivering against his strong chest.

Their eyes met again and she gave a brilliant smile, watching beads of sweat form on his forehead and enjoying the feel of him below her and inside her. "I love your widow's peak," she said, still trying to resume normal respiration.

"You do?"

"Very much," she confirmed, shifting up to kiss the peak softly. "And I love the cute little mole you have over here." She moved her mouth to plant a sweet kiss on his right temple. "I find your luscious, full lips irresistible." He lifted his head to meet hers, and their tongues danced and dipped playfully.

"But most of all," she continued, "I adore your beautiful eyes. I could get lost in those sparkling sea-blue eyes, McSailor." She leaned forward and feathered a soft kiss on each eyelid in turn.

She finally rolled off him to rest by his side. They were contentedly quiet for a few moments until she remembered a question she'd been meaning to ask.

"So, how was your meeting with Jerry this morning?"

The high he'd been riding swiftly bottomed out with a crash, his lilting romantic fantasy abruptly ruined by his dark family reality. She noticed him tense instantly.

"Hey," she softly cried, reaching out to cup his chin with her hand. "What's wrong, Grant?"

Staring into her eyes, he knew what he had to do. This gorgeous woman deserved to know the truth about him and his family. She'd given herself to him, and he needed to be totally open with her. It was only fair.

"I…" He cleared his throat, his voice raspy from their intense lovemaking. "I need to tell you something, Sophie."

Watching a resigned expression darken his features, suddenly she didn't want to hear what he had to say. She didn't want anything ruining their perfect connection: lying here naked, snuggled close, relishing in post-coital bliss.

"Shh," she responded, lifting herself up on one elbow and laying her index finger on his lips. "I've been thinking about us, and I realized it's unfair for me to be mad at you for withholding information, when I myself have not been entirely forthcoming."

"Huh?" Grant replied.

"I feel closer to you than anyone in my life," she said, a slight tremor in her melodious voice. "Yet I realized there's a significant piece of my past that I never shared with you. I want to tell you what happened to me, Grant. I need to tell you why I went to prison." She couldn't help but turn her eyes downward as her face reddened with shame.

Reading the pain in her body language, Grant gently brushed his fingers across her cheekbone. "You don't have to tell me, Sophie."

"Yes, I do," she responded with increasing confidence, raising her eyes to peer into his once again. "I need to be completely honest with you if I want to make this relationship work. At least that's what my shrink told me. I just hope, um, I hope you'll still want to be with me when you know the truth."

Grant flinched upon hearing her words, shocked that she'd been experiencing the same doubts as he had—fears that if the truth was revealed, one of them would leave. He felt deeply saddened that she thought he would cast her aside so easily. He would never allow that to happen.

He grasped her hands in his, stroking the soft skin of her palms lovingly. "Sophie, no matter what you tell me, I would never leave you. Don't you understand?" He waited until she met his eyes. "I love you."

She drew in a sharp breath and felt the sting of tears as her heart thumped furiously. Oh God! Her eyes glistened. "I love you too," she declared. She was sure of it.

He squeezed her hands in his. "Don't you see? We love each other, and we won't let anything come between us, okay?"

She nodded. "Okay."

He gently leaned forward and kissed the tip of her nose, tasting the salt of her tears. They studied each other for a moment before she plunged ahead, determined to tell her story before she lost her courage.

"I was seeing a client in my practice," she began. "He was court-ordered for treatment related to a, uh, an addiction."

Grant nodded and drew her hand to his mouth to kiss it encouragingly.

"My client was a well-known criminal," she continued, feeling her cheeks flush. "Well-known to everyone except for me, that is. I don't know how I could have been so stupid."

Grant frowned and smoothed his fingers down her long blond tresses. He carefully tucked a strand of strawberry hair behind her ear, then resumed caressing her cheek.

Sophie sniffed. "I'd been meeting with him for more than six months, and he wasn't getting any better. I wasn't helping him. Then this one session, he was telling me an awful story about his childhood—I was trying to comfort him—and he—he…kissed me. He did other things to me too. And…" She gazed down in shame. "And I let him. I liked it."

"It's okay, Sophie."

"No, it's not, Grant. It's not okay! I was his psychologist! I shouldn't have let it happen. I exploited the situation. I broke every ethical guideline in the book."

"That's why you went to prison?" he asked incredulously.

"No, what I did could have put my license in jeopardy, but it couldn't have put me in prison." She sighed. "There's more. He stashed stolen money in my office. When I found the cash—there was a lot of it—I freaked out, and I called him and yelled at him. He was going to come pick up the money but before he got there, the police arrived. They had a search warrant. I tried to tell them the money was my client's, but when they searched the office, they found…they found…" Her voice trailed off, and she seemed miles away.

Grant snuggled closer and planted a soft kiss on her collarbone, nudging her to continue. "It's all right."

"They found a stash of guns," she choked out.

He lifted himself up on his elbow and stared at her, alarmed. "Guns?"

She nodded and felt her tears resume. "Guns. One of them had been used in a…murder." Her last word was a whisper.

"But they weren't your guns!" Grant objected. "Why should you have to go to prison?"

"Because my client skipped town—nobody knew where to find him. And somebody had to take the fall. At least that's what my attorney said."

Grant suddenly realized his hand had ceased caressing her face and instead was balled in a fist, pressing down on the pillow next to her head. He was infuriated.

Watching his eyes cloud over, Sophie ventured, "What are you thinking? Do you hate me for what I did?"

"*Hate* you? Of course not. I hate the man who did this to you, though. He's never been brought to justice?"

"No. I don't think the police have found him."

"What's his name?"

Sophie hesitated. "It doesn't matter."

Grant's voice was low and tight. "Yes, it does. I want to hurt him like he hurt you."

She now recognized that the intensity in his eyes represented furious vengeance, and it scared her. "Listen to you, Grant. What exactly are you planning? What are you going to do if you find him? Beat him up?" Her voice sounded harshly derisive, and she added in a softer tone, "Anyway, how would you find him? Have you forgotten that you're on parole, not allowed to travel anywhere without Jerry's permission? If you got yourself in so much as one fight you'd be back at Gurnee immediately. Have you thought of that?"

For Sophie's sake, Grant tried to take a deep breath, studying her with a quiet intensity.

"I had to tell the police my client's name, but other than that I should keep his identity confidential," she said. "I may appear totally unethical but I can at least keep that one promise of privacy."

It dawned on Grant that she felt as guilty and insecure about her situation as he felt about his. Unlike him, however, she had the decency to take responsibility for her lapse in judgment. In his weaker moments, Grant still blamed his brother for forcing him into prison. He couldn't even step up and be accountable for his crimes.

Shaking this off for now, Grant tried to lighten the mood. "So, now I know about the guns and money leading to your arrest, Bonnie. Now it all makes sense, my little lawbreaker."

Gently he gathered her in his arms and held her tight, protectively wrapping himself around her, skin on skin, feeling the wetness of her tears on his shoulder. "And I still love you."

He felt her body shudder into his, leading him to squeeze her tighter, swathing her in his compassionate love. Sophie unleashed a torrent of sobs. Grant gently rubbed her back, and her body gradually stopped trembling, her breathing eventually evened out.

A loud knock on the door broke the mood. Grant looked into Sophie's questioning eyes and gave a dismissive shake of his head. "I'm not answering it. Nobody knows where I live."

She nodded and they continued holding each other, but the knocking resumed, louder this time.

"Maybe you should see who's there?" she said, pulling back from his embrace.

The person was pounding now, and Grant sat up. "Oh! Maybe it's my Uncle Joe!" Swiftly he rose from the bed and slid on his boxers and jeans, jogging out of the room shirtless.

Sophie scrambled out of the bed as well, sliding on her underwear and pantsuit. There was no way she wanted Grant's father figure to catch her naked in his apartment.

Grant's broke into a smile as he strode down the hallway. Joe was finally coming to visit him! He flung open the door and immediately gasped, his face morphing from exhilaration to shock in one second.

Standing on his doorstep was a dark-haired man, just his height, staring back at him. *Logan.*

"I have to talk to you," Logan said.

"No!"

"Grant—"

"You're not welcome here!" Grant's eyes flared with rage.

Logan stepped forward and was inside the apartment before Grant could stop him. "I know you're angry with me. Just hear me out," he pleaded.

Clasping her halter top in place while straining to hear the conversation, Sophie froze. *I know that voice.* She stopped breathing and didn't move a muscle. It felt like her heart stopped beating as well.

"Get out of my home!" Grant yelled, trailing after his brother. Logan had strolled into the living room and was taking in the two plates on the messy kitchen table, covered with leftover food.

"Did you hear me?" Grant hollered, placing a hand on Logan's muscular shoulder and spinning him around. "You can't be here. I'm on parole! I can't associate with known criminals!"

Suddenly Grant noticed Sophie quietly step out of the bedroom. The look on her face made him instantly drop his hand from his brother's shoulder and go to her. All color had completely drained from her face, and her lips were parted in shock as her body visibly trembled.

Logan turned to look, and his jaw dropped at the sight of the elegant woman in the doorway.

"Sophie?"

"Logan," she numbly acknowledged.

Grant gaped at the man and woman to his right and left.

"You know my brother?"

It took a second for his question to register, then a look of abject horror crossed her face. She drew her hand up to cover her mouth, feeling like she was going to faint, collapse, vomit, scream, punch, slap, explode, disintegrate . . .

But she did none of those. Instead, she tore ahead on wobbly legs and sprinted down the hallway, rushing past both men with such velocity that they had no chance to stop her. She was out the door before Grant knew what hit him, and he took a tentative step toward the exit before deciding he would never catch her in her frantic state.

He turned back to his brother, and a lifetime of hurt and fury poured into his seething words. "How the *hell* do you know Sophie?"

28. Fathers

Reeling from Sophie's swift, unexplained departure, Grant's bare chest heaved with strained attempts to get air.

"I'll ask you again," Grant fumed, glaring at his brother. "How the hell do you know Sophie?"

Logan continued to feel at a loss for words. That was Sophie? Coming out of what had to be Grant's bedroom? They'd probably just had sex, although her haunted mahogany eyes had not looked sated but terrified. Logan knew that fearful look well. He'd seen it many times on the faces of men he was about to kill. She'd been afraid of him, and he felt sick with remorse.

But Sophie had seemed scared of Grant too. How did they know each other? Turning the tables, Logan inquired, "What was she doing here?"

Refusing to be redirected, Grant spat, "She knew your name! She knew you!"

Logan tried to figure out how to play this situation. He wasn't about to share that he'd been in therapy. "Why do you care, man?"

"I'm the one asking questions here! How do you know each other?"

Running his tongue along his lower lip, Logan began cautiously. "We met about two years ago. At a, um, game. A Cubs game."

"You met at a Cubs game?" Grant's eyes narrowed with suspicion.

"Yeah," Logan confirmed, making it up on the fly. "We randomly sat next to each other at a game and found ourselves talking about the players. She really knew her stuff—first time I met a chick who actually knew anything about baseball. We went on a date or two, but nothing really happened."

"That's a lie," Grant said, his lips curling into a sneer. "You're lying."

Damn. He thought it had been a good story. "What makes you think I'm lying?"

"Because Sophie is a Sox fan, you fraud." Nostrils flaring, he inched closer to his brother, refusing to be intimidated. Dressed only in jeans, Grant's lean upper body seemed almost scrawny compared to Logan's bulk. "I'll ask you one more time. How do you know her?"

Silence. Logan's deep-blue eyes met his gaze with a calculated stare.

Grant threw his arms up. "Why can't you just tell the truth for once? You've destroyed me, Lo! You forced me to commit that robbery, to go to prison! Why can't you just help me for once? Why?"

Logan sighed, gritting his teeth. He was once again hurting his brother, which had not been his intention at all. In a low voice he confessed, "Because I didn't want to tell you she was my shrink."

Grant stood perfectly still, listening intently.

Watching Grant's non-reaction, Logan wondered if he had heard him. "She was my shrink, okay? The fucking judge made me go to therapy after the Great Lakes thing. I had to see a goddamn shrink! How embarrassing! Are you happy now?"

Instead of a satisfied expression on his brother's face, there was a stunned paralysis. Grant's tanned olive skin was rapidly losing color, and he looked almost green. Logan watched with fascination as his brother began trembling, crossing his balled-up fists before him and clenching his stomach.

Grant gave an anguished cry. "It was you! You—you stashed money in her office."

"What?" Logan replied, dumbfounded. "How did you know that?"

A sickening realization took hold. "She knows we're brothers," Grant whispered.

Suddenly he made a mad dash to the bathroom. He yanked open the toilet and retched violently. Remnants of the dinner Sophie had cooked for him came rushing up, the reminder of her kindness making him even queasier. His whole body quivered as waves of nausea pulsed through him, and he gripped the counter for balance. Evidently his stomach of steel was a thing of the past.

Logan started to follow but stopped short, disgusted by the sound of his brother getting sick. He had no idea why Grant was so upset. "You okay in there?" he hollered, hearing nothing but heaving from the small bathroom.

Finally, the torturous vomiting ceased, and Grant pulled himself to the sink. Scooping handfuls of cold water into his parched mouth and onto his hot face, he dared to look into the mirror. Dead, glassy eyes stared back at him, and he fought the urge to claw violently at his skin, his hair—anything to remove the identifying markers bestowed upon him by his family. He wanted nothing to do with them.

"What's your problem, dude?" one of those family members called from the living room. "Are you sick or something?"

Seeing red, Grant abruptly spun and charged out of the bathroom like a bull. He lowered his head as he hurtled forward, colliding into Logan's unsuspecting torso with an immense force that threw the muscular man backward.

"What the f—?" The force of landing on his back pushed the air out of Logan's lungs in a vigorous whoosh. Grant crashed on top of him and wound his right fist high in the air before smashing it into his brother's jaw.

The blow seemed to awaken the older brother, and he groped above him to try to restrain Grant's wrists before he received another strike.

"Get off me!" Logan ordered.

Grant's white-hot rage powered his attack, and his right hand wriggled free to land another punch on his brother's face. Logan snarled and met his attacker's anger with the same intensity and strength. He shoved Grant off and scrambled to his feet, panting.

No longer holding the advantage of surprise, Grant warily scooted to a standing position as well. Tension crackled as the brothers fluidly circled each other, seeking any weakness to exploit. Grant felt his body trembling with the lingering aftereffects of vomiting, and he knew he was overmatched. His older brother beat people up for a living.

"Don't do this," Logan warned in his deep baritone. "I didn't come here to hurt you."

Grant exhaled with disgust. "Well, you've done a bang-up job so far." He wiped his mouth with the back of his hand as they continued prowling the small apartment, and his eyes narrowed once again. "Do you even *care* that you sent Sophie to prison?"

"Prison?" Logan repeated, bowled over by the weight of the word.

His eyes widening, Grant shouted, "You didn't *know?* You didn't know she went to prison because of *you?* Because of the guns you planted in her office?"

Logan's arms fell to his side. "But I thought she'd get off. Those were our guns, not hers. That's why I got the fuck out of town."

Grant's blood was boiling. "And when you left, who do you think had to take the fall, you selfish bastard?"

Swiftly Grant charged his brother again, only this time Logan was ready. He ducked when Grant took a big swing at his head, and retaliated with a powerful uppercut to the lighter man's face, sending him reeling to the side. Staggering, Grant cradled his cheek.

"How the hell could you not know what happened to Sophie?" Grant demanded as he recovered from the blow to stand upright and face his brother once again.

"Dunno. Once I saw the cops at her office, I hightailed it outta town. I kept in touch with Angelo, but all I told him was that the cops were after me. He didn't know anything about Sophie."

Grant swallowed the bile rising in his throat. How could his brother be so fucking clueless?

"I figured Sophie would be a big hero for turning in the cash and guns."

"A *hero*?" Grant's fury clouded any sense of reason as he careened forward again, arms flailing, craving a pound of flesh from his brother, desperately wanting to hurt him like he'd hurt Sophie—like he'd hurt Grant too.

Logan expertly fought off Grant's attack, grunting as he deflected several blows before throwing him to the ground, trying to subdue him. But Grant would not be deterred and quickly got on his feet again, managing to deliver a quick jab to Logan's solar plexus in the melee.

Grant's hand throbbed from hitting the solid wall of muscle, but Logan barely seemed to feel the punch as he swiftly struck back, delivering a devastating blow to Grant's ribcage that left him groaning, panting while he listed to the right, painfully clutching his ribcage.

"Stop this!" Logan yelled. "I don't want to hurt you!"

Miraculously Grant came at his brother yet again, though he now realized the futility of attacking the muscular man in his weakened state. This time Logan just spun him around and wrapped him in a bear hug, restraining Grant's squirming sinewy body in his powerful arms.

They remained glued together, both breathing hard. Although this was not exactly a warm brotherly hug, it was the closest the two had come physically in more than twenty years. Logan wondered if they would ever be this close again. "Oh, Grant," he said softly, refusing to release his brother.

Grant felt tears spring to his eyes as hopelessness enveloped him. He would never win. He would never be free of the harmful hold his family had over him. He had already lost his career, his freedom, his dignity, and now they'd taken Sophie away from him as well—and that was a loss he simply could not sustain. No wonder she'd looked at him with such terror. She now knew he was one of *them*.

"Let me go," Grant begged, dismayed to hear his voice cracking. He took a deep breath and promised, "I won't fight you anymore." He had lost his will to fight. It was useless.

Logan weighed his options before reluctantly releasing his hold. Grant put some distance between them, and rested his shoulder against the living room wall.

"I hope you fought better than that in Gurnee," Logan said. "It's a wonder you didn't get killed. Of course, you did have Dad to protect you in there."

Grant sniffed. "How could you?" he pleaded, turning to look at Logan, sounding much younger than his thirty years. "How could you put me in there, with *him*?"

Logan looked down, his head bowed by shame. While going to prison for a three-year stretch was a horror for any man, only Grant would experience the additional devastating betrayal: Logan's botched blackmail attempt forced his baby brother to cohabit with their abusive father in Gurnee.

Daring to meet those wounded light-blue eyes, Logan muttered, "I'm sorry. I know that doesn't mean anything to you, but I am truly sorry. I never meant for you to be inside with him."

Grant yanked his head to the side, angrily breaking their gaze. He twisted his hands in front of him, trying to ward off the images of intense charcoal eyes staring him down, threatening to drown him.

In a quiet voice Logan asked, "Did he hurt you?"

Drawing a shuddering breath, Grant felt shame flush his face. The pressure of handcuffs encircling his wrists, the kind gray-haired doctor sitting next to his bed, the empathic embarrassment of the psychiatrist's words: *You were catatonic, Mr. Madsen. And you, um, well, you had urinated all over yourself in the cell.*

Darkly Grant confessed, "Let's just say you're not the only one who needed therapy."

Logan smirked. "Oh, that's how you met Sophie, then. She was your shrink too?"

"No! She lost her psychologist license. Because of you! You ruined her career."

Logan's face fell. He felt waves of hostility from his brother. Hostility that was well-deserved.

There was a tiny trace of jealousy in Logan's voice as he ventured, "So how *did* you meet?"

Grant shook his head disgustedly. "We have the same parole officer. We met outside his office." Watching Logan absorb this explanation, it suddenly dawned on Grant that if not for Logan forcing him to pull that job and get arrested, he would have never met Sophie. Logan was the reason he'd found the love of his life. And now, Logan was the reason he'd lost the love of his life.

His steely eyes set with resentment, Grant seethed, "We were in love. Love! Something you know nothing about, Lo. And now she won't want anything to do with me—knowing I'm a Barberi, knowing my brother is the man who ruined her." The wicked sarcasm returned. "Thank you *so* much, Lo. Thank you for coming here."

Logan clenched his jaw. "I fucked up, Grant. Big time. But I'm going to try to make it up to you. I'm going to be a better brother—a better father too. I've changed."

This load of bullshit dropped Grant's jaw. "You've changed?" he scoffed.

"I've changed, Grant. No more running drugs. No more hits. I'm supposed to be doing a job for Carlo right now, and I refused. Hell, I haven't even gambled in over a year."

"Sure, you've changed," Grant replied, his voice dripping with derision. "What prompted this miraculous *change*?"

He considered the question for a few moments. Then he chuckled, low and deep.

"What the hell could be remotely funny right now?"

"I just realized," Logan said, "why I wanted to change. It was Sophie. She helped me see I could be a good person. That I…that I…that I once was a kid who tried to do the right thing, who tried to protect his younger brother…" Logan's voice trailed off, lost in memories of his childhood. Shaking off the painful images, he exhaled loudly. "It was Sophie. Kind of ironic, huh?"

"Get out," Grant fumed. "Get out of my life!" He crumpled onto the rented sofa and held his face in his hands. "You already ruined my life once, and now you're doing it again. I wish you weren't my brother. I wish—"

"Don't say it, Grant." Logan stopped breathing.

His frosty eyes were as cold as ice. "I wish you were dead."

A stunned silence settled between them, and Logan swallowed hard. So, there would be no chance to redeem himself to his brother. He should have known as much.

"Please leave," Grant whimpered, refusing to look at his brother.

Logan had no choice. He quietly rose and shuffled down the hallway, hearing the door shut behind him. As he stole away into the night, he realized he had forgotten to warn Grant about Carlo. Ah well, maybe another time. It wasn't like Grant was in the mood to listen to anything he had to say. All he seemed to care about was losing Sophie. Logan felt a stabbing sensation in his chest, thinking of her. They had both lost Sophie.

Sophie walked numbly through the streets of Chicago, having no idea where she was and not caring in the least.

How could she have been so incredibly, undeniably stupid? She was devastatingly dense, naive, obtuse, foolish—the biggest idiot in the entire city of nine million people. The skyscrapers hovered over her, closing in on her, mocking her imprudent attempt to start over, her ill-advised endeavor to find love.

She had allowed herself to be duped yet again, and the intensity of the rage and humiliation stirring in her gut made her want to throw up. They were brothers! How the hell had she not seen that? It was right in front of her face! Grant and Logan standing next to each other in that damn apartment—looking alike, sounding alike, acting alike—it was the most obvious thing in the world! She had been fucking blind.

Anita's worried voice floated in her mind: *He doesn't have anything to do with the man who put you in prison, does he?*

Sophie screamed. She was walking in the middle of downtown Chicago, the streets teeming with nightlife, yet she screamed out loud. Sophie emitted a wail of utter despair and regret. A few passersby gave her strange looks, but Sophie forged ahead, aware of nothing but the pain pressing on her heart.

How had she let this happen? How had she failed to realize that Grant was part of a Mafia family? His name was Grant Madsen, not Grant Barberi, wasn't it? Or had he lied about that too? Then she remembered their conversation about his mother dying and his uncle adopting him. Uncle Joe must be Joe Madsen. Smart man to try to separate his nephew from the destruction of the Barberi bunch—too bad he didn't succeed, given that Logan walked into Grant's apartment like he owned the place, like they saw each other all the time.

There had been hints all along. *She* had started the whole dishonest ruse, almost begging him to deceive her on the courthouse steps outside Jerry's office:

Let's not talk about our families. Let's talk about something else.
And then later:
Um, why did you go to prison?
Well, if we're not talking about families, then I can't really answer that.

A momentary curiosity about how his family was involved in his imprisonment flashed through her mind, quickly replaced by her anger toward herself and Grant. No wonder he had encouraged them to make a pact not to discuss their pasts. No wonder he had wanted to hide his past from her. He was damaged goods.

Addictions run in my family, he'd told her. Like gambling, she mused. And alcoholism. And lying. Logan had lied to her so he could use her office as an illegal dumping ground. Why had Grant lied to her? What was he hoping to gain? How was he planning to use her? Perhaps she would never know.

She kept walking, her mind as numb as her feet. A scowl settled over her features. With uneasiness, she realized she had slept with both brothers. Once he found out, Grant would probably think she was a whore. Who was she kidding—she was as damaged as he was.

Suddenly Sophie stopped dead in her tracks, remembering the awful story Logan had told her in therapy—the horrible trauma that made her try to comfort him, leading to their first kiss, the heart-wrenching family tale that appeared to undo Logan and left Sophie furious with parents who abused their children.

She cried silently on the street. That little four-year-old boy locked in the closet all night—that was Grant! Grant, who was scarred from the undoubtedly plentiful beatings delivered by his father. No wonder he had nightmares, growing up with a bastard father like that, a father now serving a life sentence in Gurnee, according to the newspapers.

Sophie gasped again. Grant had been imprisoned with his father! He'd been thrown into the same penitentiary as his abuser, and her heart ached for him.

Aware of her surroundings for the first time in hours, Sophie looked around, trying to discern her location through a veil of tears. She noticed large homes with ornate facades, lush landscaping, and gated entryways. She'd stumbled into the richest section of Chicago: the Gold Coast.

It was probably time to return to Kirsten's and attempt to pick up the pieces of her shattered life. Reaching for her handbag to find cab fare, she inhaled sharply. She did not have her purse. She'd left it at Grant's in her haste to get the hell out of there. Now what was she going to do? She had no money, no phone, and no energy to walk all the way home.

Sighing wearily, a new batch of tears cascaded down her cheeks. She fought the urge to collapse on the sidewalk and never move again. But then another idea entered her mind.

Tonight had been a complete disaster. Did she really want to risk adding to the pain and rejection she'd already endured? But Hunter's pesky encouragements nagged at her, and she found her feet moving, as if they had a mind of their own.

The streets looked more and more familiar. She attempted to quell the butterflies flitting about in her stomach by telling herself no matter what happened, things could not get any worse for her tonight. She'd already lost one man she loved, why not go for two? She might as well get it over with.

Entering the code on the keypad, Sophie sighed with relief when the heavy metal gate clicked open. He had not changed the pass code in the past year. Was that a sign?

She trudged forward, her feet throbbing from walking miles in high-heeled shoes, and paused in front of the opulent cherry door. Taking a deep breath and shaking her hair out a bit, Sophie pressed the doorbell. She closed her eyes and waited, detecting dead silence from within.

She was not wearing a watch but figured it had to be after midnight. Was this really the way she wanted to see him again after all this time? Would he be angry with her for waking him? Biting her lip, she pressed the doorbell again and fidgeted as she waited.

Finally a light flipped on inside. She swallowed hard as the deadbolt unlocked and the door slowly opened, revealing a man in his early sixties with graying brown hair and intense blue eyes. His expression became shock and concern once he saw her tearstained cheeks.

"Daddy?" she choked out.

"Oh, Sophie," he said, swiftly gathering her into his arms. As she clutched her father, Sophie bawled with utter relief. At least one man she loved would not hurt her tonight.

29. You Only Realize What You've Got When It's Gone

For the first time since his mother's death, Jerry Stone did not feel immensely sad. He had actually fallen asleep quickly the previous evening, and even more miraculously, he had awoken before his alarm this morning. There was a slight bounce to his step, and a strange optimism that maybe he could help at least one of today's parolees stay out of prison. He didn't know how to explain this break in the dark cloud hovering over him for the past five days, but he welcomed the reprieve.

Turning the corner inside the courthouse, he noticed a con already waiting for him, though it was a full twenty minutes before his day began. Parolees were *never* this early for their dreaded appointments. As he got closer, he recognized Grant's lanky physique and midnight-black hair.

"Did you get your days mixed up, Madsen?" he called. "Today's Thursday—"

He stopped short once he got a good look at the purple bruise blooming on Grant's left cheek. "Where'd you get that shiner?"

Grant ducked his head. "May I talk to you, sir? Do you have a couple of minutes?"

Apparently, yesterday's almost-arrest hadn't scared the parolee away for long. Intrigued, Jerry unlocked his door and held it open, gesturing into his office, "After you."

"Thank you, sir." Grant stepped inside.

After they were both seated, Jerry asked again, "What happened to your face?"

Grant took a deep breath. "You remember how you told me to stay away from my family?" His full lips formed a sad smile. "I didn't listen very well. Logan Barberi visited me last night."

Jerry scrunched his bushy eyebrows. "Madsen, are you telling me you've been associating with criminals again, violating your parole?"

Sighing, he replied, "Yes, sir."

"Why are you telling me this when you know it can land you back inside?"

"I was up half the night worrying about what happened, and I already ran along the lake and did pushups this morning, but I couldn't get my head straight. I had to get out of that apartment. I didn't know what to do. I didn't know where to go. So I asked myself, what would a member of my family do in this situation? What would Logan do if he had broken the law? And I tried to do the exact opposite." Grant shrugged. "That's why I'm here."

"Because your brother, Logan, would never report himself to a police officer like you're doing now."

"Precisely, sir."

"Logan gave you that shiner?"

"Yes, sir."

"I hope you gave him something in return."

Grant's only reply was a slight smirk.

"Do you know the whereabouts of your brother, Madsen?"

"No, sir."

Jerry had no choice but to believe him. They sat in silence as Jerry tried in vain to understand the parolee sitting across from him. Grant finally spoke up.

"Aren't you going to arrest me, sir?"

"What about Sophie? Won't you miss her if you return to prison?"

Hearing her name made Grant flinch, and he struggled to compose himself. "That was another reason I wanted to see you, to let you know I followed your advice to tell Sophie who I really am. Well, Logan showed up before I had the chance to tell her myself, but she knows now all the same. She knows the truth."

"Taylor knows Logan Barberi is your brother?"

"Yes, sir," Grant said. "And I, um, now I know why you wanted me to tell Sophie who I was. Now I understand Logan's involvement in Sophie's arrest." Grant looked sickened. "I finally get why you seemed so freaked out when you discovered my real identity."

Jerry studied the young man sitting ramrod straight, fighting to maintain self-control. Grant radiated such melancholy and resignation that the parole officer felt strangely protective of him. Every fiber of Jerry's being strained against the idea of throwing him back in prison.

"Your real identity?" Jerry gently inquired. The parole officer reached his right hand across the desk and held it out expectantly.

Confused, Grant stared at the outstretched hand for a moment before grasping it in a firm handshake. "I know your real identity," Jerry said, looking Grant in the eye while continuing to clasp his hand. "You're not Grant Barberi. You're Grant Madsen."

Grant felt a lump form in his throat. He had to pull his hand back from the older man's grasp lest he start crying, and he clenched his teeth to keep the tears at bay.

"I've lost her," he said in a heartbroken voice.

Jerry leaned forward on the desk. "You don't know that for sure. What did Sophie say when she found out?"

Grant bit his lip. "She didn't say anything. She just looked at Logan, and then at me. She seemed so shocked, so devastated. But the worst part was how completely afraid she looked. *Afraid*—of *me*." He exhaled an anguished breath.

"Maybe you still have a chance, if you talk to her, explain things," Jerry said.

"You didn't see the look on her face!" Grant argued. "She wants nothing to do with me!"

Jerry had no idea what to say, and he nervously fidgeted in his chair, playing with a paperweight on his desk. How the hell had he become embroiled in this mess? He didn't care about romances between fucking parolees! He glanced at the clock.

"Madsen, it's almost nine o'clock, and I need to start seeing parolees on today's docket. Maybe you came here to turn yourself in, maybe you came here seeking advice, I don't know, and frankly I don't care. The truth is I don't have time to arrest you—too much goddamn paperwork—and besides that it isn't even your day to see me. Just get the hell out of my office, and let's both get started with another thrilling day."

Grant panicked. He hadn't thought through any plans beyond reporting to his parole officer. "What should I do now?"

"Well, your instinct to do the opposite of what your brother would do sounds pretty damn good to me."

"But I don't know what that is! I don't … really know my brother." He looked down. "I don't know what to do."

Jerry grew frustrated as the clock ticked forward and this miserable parolee still had not departed. It was obvious Grant needed some fatherly guidance, but Jerry simply didn't have the time, and his typical grumpiness was quickly returning. "Here's what you do, Madsen. You get your head out of your ass, and you go to work just like everybody else on this planet. And you stay out of trouble."

Grant sat up a little straighter upon receiving the admonishment. He was familiar with being chewed out by superiors—this he could understand. "Yes, sir," he sharply replied and rose from the chair. "Thank you, sir." Then he was gone.

☙

"That smells so good." Sophie smiled tentatively, smelling freshly brewed coffee as she entered the kitchen.

Will Taylor looked up from the newspaper and felt a stabbing pain in his heart as he watched his daughter lean on the marble countertop. Her hair was mussed from sleeping, as if she was still a little girl, but what hit him most poignantly was the emerald-green silk nightgown she wore. Laura's nightgown. He'd almost started crying when he extracted the gown from the untouched chest of drawers last night, wordlessly handing it to Sophie.

He cleared his throat. "It's actually the second pot of the morning, sleepy-head. Justine put it on before she left for the grocery store."

"How *is* Justine?" Sophie thought fondly of the Jamaican woman who had been her parents' housekeeper for fifteen years.

"She's, well, she's Justine. Already complaining about the upcoming winter even though it's only July."

Sophie smiled as she poured herself a steaming cup of coffee. After adding creamer, she stirred the hot liquid nervously, sensing her father's eyes on her. She had some explaining to do. She'd fended off his questions about her tears the night before, begging him to allow her to sleep and promising they'd talk in the morning. Now that morning had arrived, she had no idea where to begin.

She shut her eyes momentarily, feeling overwhelmed by the previous evening. *You know my brother?* Grant's stunned question still pierced her.

Sitting across from her father at the kitchen table, she asked, "Aren't you due at work by now?"

"I cancelled my meetings this morning," he replied. Will Taylor also felt a pressing need to explain himself, to make her understand why he'd avoided her for the past year. He had no idea how their reunion would proceed, and he swallowed anxiously. "Construction can wait."

Sophie stared down at the swirling steam rising from her coffee. Her father couldn't see the skeptical arch of her eyebrows. Construction could *not* wait. At least it never had before. Work had *always* come before family. Feeling her shoulders tighten, Sophie took a deep breath and tried to remember Hunter's encouragement about reconnecting with her father. He was all she had now.

"I'm sorry for barging in on you last night," she began. "I didn't have my purse, and I had, um, no place else to go."

"You left your purse somewhere?"

His accusatory tone made her sit up a little straighter in her chair. Worried questions tumbled out of his mouth.

"You lost your phone? Your wallet? Do you need to cancel your credit cards?"

"Dad—"

"Here, let me get the phone—"

"Dad!" Sophie practically yelled, causing him to sit back down in his chair. She took another deep breath. "I don't own a cell phone. I don't have any credit cards, okay? I just got out of prison!"

His face fell at the cold reality of his daughter's situation. He lived in a luxurious home, and she didn't own a credit card? His cheeks flushed as he looked down at the cherry table and quietly inquired, "When did you get out?"

"A little over a month ago."

"Where are you staying?"

"At Kirsten's."

"Kirsten's?"

"Kirsten Holland. She was my roommate at DePaul, remember?"

After a few tense moments, he asked, "Why didn't you come *here*?"

Sophie dared to look into his eyes, framed by lines of worry. Her father appeared to have aged ten years since she last saw him, and noticing his emerging fragility she wondered why she'd been so intimidated by him all her life. "Because I didn't think you wanted me here," she said.

"What? Why on earth did you think that?"

Her brown eyes flared with year-old fury. "Oh, gee, Dad. I don't know, maybe because you didn't visit me *once* in prison?" Will averted his gaze, but Sophie wasn't going to let him off the hook that easily. "Or maybe it was the fact that you didn't say *one word* to me at her funeral." She felt her chest tighten and added, "Anyway, I got the message loud and clear."

Sophie felt the hole inside her grow larger with each second of continued silence. She would never earn her father's approval, and it was stupid to come to his house when she needed comforting. Will Taylor: construction magnate, coldhearted businessman—he would never be able to comfort her. "I should go," she muttered, scraping her chair across the expensive tile.

"No," Will said, standing with his daughter. "Please don't go, Sophie."

She glanced angrily at his face and was stunned to see tears.

"I—I—I'm sorry," he stuttered. "That was inexcusable, what I did. Please, sit back down. I—I want to talk. I need to talk to you. Please, Sophie?"

Swallowing hard, she paused, then slowly felt herself buckling back into her chair, never taking her eyes off him. After Will resumed his sitting position as well, he folded his hands on the table, taking a deep breath.

"I thought it would be easier," he began, talking to the table. "Easier…not to see you. You look just like her," he choked out, gazing lovingly at her thick strawberry-blond hair and intelligent brown eyes. "You remind me so much of your mother."

Sophie took in his words, listening and evaluating, unsure how to react.

He went on. "But when you came here last night, looking so heartbroken, so troubled…I realized how wrong I've been. I need you here, Sophie. I shouldn't be pushing you away. I should be reaching out to you. I'm sorry, so sorry I haven't been there for you."

She was dumbfounded. "When you avoided me at the funeral—that's because I reminded you of Mom?"

"Yes."

"I thought…" Her voice trailed off, and she didn't know if she should finish her sentence, though her father looked at her expectantly. "I thought you blamed me for Mom's heart attack."

His eyes widened with horror. "God, no! How could you think such a thing?" He ran his hands through his hair, anguished. "No wonder you didn't come here. No wonder you didn't call." He exhaled forcefully. "I'm a horrible father."

"No, you're not," she said. "I'm the one who got arrested and sent to prison. I'm the horrible one."

"You're not horrible," Will corrected. "You just got involved in the wrong profession."

"Oh, God, not this again."

"If you had joined my business, if you had agreed to work with me, this never would have happened, Sophie. I never would have let some mobster ingratiate himself with you like that."

"Dad!"

"But obviously I was not persuasive enough to make you follow the right path. Like I said, I'm a horrible father."

"No, you're not," Sophie argued again, but as she heard the words, she was infuriated. He was making this all about *him*. What about *her?* Why the hell was she taking care of his emotions instead of her own?

He rebutted, "Yes, I—"

"This is bullshit!" she yelled, causing Will to pause midsentence. She rushed ahead. "You weren't *persuasive* enough? You kicked me out of the damn house! You stopped paying for my college. Now I have major student loans hanging over my head, thanks to your *persuasion* for me to major in accounting instead of psychology."

He looked astonished, but Sophie could not stop her wounded diatribe. "I was so hurt when you cut me off like that! I was so scared of being all on my own. And then, when you didn't visit me in prison…when you looked at me that way at Mom's funeral…"

She felt herself shaking, her cheeks flushed with the release of pent-up emotion. She turned her furious eyes on him.

"Do you know how *awful* it was in prison? Do you know how scared I was? How hard it was to go a whole year without talking to you once? Did you think about me at all that entire year?"

She finally paused long enough for Will to get a word in.

"I worried about you every day in there. Your mother was sick with fear—"

"She's not here anymore, Dad!" Sophie exploded. "She's not here to be a buffer between us. I need a father in my life, okay? I need you. I keep making really bad decisions, and I need your advice, okay? I'm sick of choosing men who hurt me! I'm sick of you never being there for me!"

Suddenly tired, Sophie found her father cautiously studying her. She withdrew, preparing for him to yell back at her for her disrespect and unladylike behavior.

Instead, Will continued staring with a curious look that bordered on admiration. "You've never talked to me like that before."

"Sorry."

"Don't be sorry," he said. "I deserved that."

Sophie stared. He reached across the table and grasped her slender hand in his.

"Thank you for giving me another chance."

"You're not mad?"

"I wish I was. Pastor Tom told me anger was a healthy part of grief, but I can't seem to get angry, no matter how hard I try." He sighed. "But I wouldn't be mad about you telling it to me straight up like that. Contractors go off on me all the time, and I don't mind. It's just business. I'd rather people be honest so we can solve the problem. If I'd known you could be so direct, I'd have been even more eager to hire you."

"Dad," she warned.

He chuckled. "Relax, I won't incite your wrath again on the subject. I know you're a psychologist. Um, I mean, uh, you were a psychologist." An awkward moment passed between them and he asked, "Have you gotten yourself a job?"

"Yes, I just got a new job, but before that I was working on a ship—oh, shoot, what time is it?"

"A little before ten."

"Oh, no, I've got to get there soon to talk to my boss…" She swallowed hard, silently finishing her sentence, *before Grant gets there.* "I have to quit."

You know my brother?

"You're not giving notice?" Will asked.

"What?"

"You're not giving two weeks' notice before you quit? That's not a wise idea, Sophie."

"Dad, I can't! I have to quit today. I have no choice." *I can't work with a man who lies.*

Seeing the fear on her face, Will demanded, "What's wrong? Why do you have to quit *today*?"

She bit her lip, feeling too overwhelmed to confess she had fallen in love with Logan Barberi's brother. "It's complicated," she said.

"Sophie? Are you in trouble?"

"No, Dad. Well, I won't be in trouble once I quit this job." *You know my brother?* Her chest tightened. She knew it was over with Grant. She just wished it didn't have to hurt so much. "It's complicated," she repeated. "I may not have made the wisest choice when it came to my last boyfriend."

"Shocker."

Momentarily stunned, she could not stop her smile. "You're never going to let Derek Bowden go, are you, Dad?"

"Sophie, Sophie, Sophie. You and your bad boys." Will shook his head disapprovingly.

"Don't worry. I'm swearing off men for the rest of my life." She was determined to lock up her heart. She simply could not get hurt again.

Will stroked his chin. "Don't call it quits on men yet, or else some lucky guy will miss getting to call you his wife one day." He looked wistful. "I sure am lucky your mother married me."

"But, Dad, you and Mom argued all the time."

"I know, I know. I guess—you know what they say, 'You only realize what you've got when it's gone.' I didn't truly appreciate your mother until too late." Sophie was shocked when her father's voice thickened with emotion. Without excusing himself, he quickly left the kitchen.

She stared after him. *You only realize what you've got when it's gone.* But she'd known very well what she had with Grant. She *had* appreciated what they shared for one glorious month. Even though he'd hurt her irrevocably, she didn't know if she'd be able to make it without her McSailor.

Grant plodded toward the ship, grateful that his workplace was not far from the courthouse. A shooting pain seared through his left side any time he shifted the wrong way. He wondered if Logan had caused permanent damage with that last jab. But despite the pain, he had punished his body with a grueling workout. Perhaps he'd overdone his early-morning exercise regimen, but pushups were strangely calming for him, reminding him of his orderly days in the military. And running was all he knew to do when the demons of his family started chasing him again.

A paroxysm of anger and regret seized him. Recalling his heated exchange with his brother the night before, Grant ran his hand across his jaw, careful to avoid the tender bruise on his left cheek.

He hated how he'd acted like a child around his big brother the previous evening. He'd behaved like an eight year old, crying and telling Logan he wished he were dead. Grant winced as that wounded comment looped through his mind once again. What a horrible thing to say—but at least he'd gotten Logan to leave his apartment.

"You're early!" Roger bellowed when Grant stepped onto the deck. He squinted into the July sun and saw his boss descending the steps from the bridge.

"Where's your better half?" Roger inquired jovially.

"How should I know? I'm not her keeper," Grant responded testily.

"Whoa. Trouble in paradise?" He noticed his employee's battered face. "Yikes, did you let yourself get hit by a woman, Madsen? Should I call the cops and report domestic violence?"

Observing Grant's distraught expression, Roger stopped kidding around. In a softer tone, he asked, "What's wrong?"

Grant gulped. "Nothing. I'm going to go clean toilets." The shit had hit the fan, and now it was time to start cleaning it up.

Roger watched him hustle aft, appearing eager to clean the restrooms for some bizarre reason. Shaking his head, Roger muttered, "Fucking parolee."

About an hour later, Roger was reading the food section of the *Chicago Tribune*, drooling over a recipe for Italian sausage meatballs, when he heard his name being called. Peering down his nose, he saw Sophie looking up at him nervously.

"Is Grant here?" she asked while Roger made his way down the stairs.

He was bamboozled by her sexy black pantsuit, and he ogled her while inquiring, "How are you going to serve drinks wearing *that?*"

Sophie glanced down at her pantsuit. It was nothing special, particularly since she'd been wearing it two days in a row now. She hadn't had the courage to put on one of her mother's outfits, even though her father kept Laura's entire wardrobe hanging in the closet.

"Rog, I, um, I can't work today."

"What?" he countered angrily. "I gave you yesterday off, Taylor. One day. I expect you to work today."

"Actually, I can't work any day. I have to, um, resign. I'm sorry."

Roger's jaw dropped. "You're quitting? Why?"

She bit her lower lip. "I'm sorry, Rog. I hate to do this to you—you've been so kind to take me in when I really needed a job, but I…" She stopped talking as she sensed another presence on deck and felt intense gemstone eyes on her.

Swallowing hard, Sophie looked to the left, confirming that Grant had indeed emerged from wherever he'd been hiding on the ship. He looked pained and had a deep bruise on his left cheek, which made him look even more like a criminal. Her heart pounded furiously as she carefully stepped back toward the railing.

Perplexed by her fear, Roger studied Sophie, then Grant. Grant took a step forward, and Sophie inhaled sharply, her eyes growing wider.

"Sophie," he pleaded.

"Stay away from me!"

Roger continued to stare back and forth between them. "What the fuck is wrong with you two?"

Seeing her so sickeningly scared of him made Grant want to run, to give her the sense of safety she desperately seemed to need, but he felt compelled to speak. He couldn't help himself.

"Please, Sophie. I need to talk to you."

"I have nothing to say to you," she insisted. "Go run your con on some other woman."

"It's not a con," he protested. "I had no idea what Logan did to you—I promise. I . . . I *love* you."

"You lied to me!" she cried.

"I didn't know what Lo did to you! How can I lie about something I know nothing about?"

"Stop playing games, Grant Barberi. You lied to me every time you pretended to be someone other than the son of Enzo Barberi. You lied to me every time you failed to admit you were the brother of Logan Barberi!"

Grant looked over to see Roger staring at him with an apparent new understanding, a look bordering between fascination and respect. Grant felt sick.

There was nothing he could say to refute her words, and he hung his head low. He felt utterly defeated, like a little boy who'd just been scolded. Sophie's throat constricted, picturing him as an innocent four year old, beaten within an inch of his life. She had to look away, drawing her hand to her mouth to stifle a cry.

Grant noticed her distress and fought the urge to scoop her into his arms. She would never let him hold her now. How had this all gone so wrong?

Sophie backed up another step, and it was obvious she was about to flee. She delivered her last words in a seething tone, masking the tears in her voice. "I don't want *anything* to do with you and your family! Your brother ruined my life!"

She leaped from the ship, running as fast as her legs would carry her.

Heartbroken, Grant held his head in his hands. "He ruined my life too."

She was gone.

30. CONsequence

Logan rubbed the sleep from his eyes as he made his way down the deserted warehouse-district street. It wasn't the first time he'd slept outside on a bench by the lake, but for some reason it seemed he'd sunk to an all-time low. He was responsible for putting two people—the only two people he cared about besides his son—in prison. A man responsible for such pain certainly did not deserve the finer things in life, like a warm bed or fresh, laundered clothing.

Although undeserving of others' help, he'd still reached out for some financial assistance with the hope of affording a warm bed tonight, maybe in a hotel room somewhere. He'd called the one man who could not refuse him: his godfather, Angelo. Although Angelo had not sounded pleased about shelling out even more money, Logan knew he couldn't turn away his nephew and godson.

Entering their rendezvous point, an abandoned warehouse on the west side, Logan stopped short when he saw who was waiting for him. It was not the calm, grizzled patriarch of the Barberi family. Instead, it was his menacing, envious, black-haired son, flanked by two imposing Mafia thugs. Logan eyed his cousin Carlo and the muscled men standing at a respectful distance behind him.

Logan nodded to the behemoth on Carlo's left, who had somehow added to his bulk in prison. "Didn't know you were out, Meat."

Mario, known as "Meat" inside the family, simply grunted in return.

"And of course you know Tank," Carlo said with a sugary smile, gesturing to the man on his right. Logan studied the six-foot-three, brown-haired bodybuilder Anthony Tanketti, whose eyes narrowed upon meeting his gaze.

Both remembered the incident three years ago. Angelo had ordered Logan to "take care of" Tank after he'd unknowingly attracted the FBI's attention by falling in love with an undercover agent. Angelo had luckily discovered her true identity, and he'd commanded Carlo to kill the federal agent and Logan to rough up Tank. The feds had been on the Barberi family like sauce on spaghetti ever since, hoping to avenge the murder of their agent yet unable to prove the family had anything to do with her death.

Eyeing Tank's transformation from lean to large, Logan surmised he'd decided to familiarize himself with the inside of a gym following such a humiliating beating. Tank crossed his arms in front of his substantial chest, smirking at Logan.

"Where's Angelo?" Logan asked.

"He sent me instead," Carlo replied, recalling their heated argument an hour ago. Carlo was incensed that Angelo overlooked Logan's absence in the latest drug deal, and he'd become even more furious when he discovered his father was planning to loan some cash to his archrival. He'd used all his charm to persuade his father to let him take his place.

Maintaining his saccharine smile, Carlo added, "Angelo's busy. You know, making money for the family? A concept that seems to be lost on you, *cugino*."

Logan cleared his throat nervously. "Yeah, I couldn't make it last night. I had someone I needed to see."

Carefully studying his cousin's bruised face, Carlo scoffed. "Apparently that someone kicked your ass."

Logan wondered if he'd said too much. "So, is Angelo showing up or not?"

"Not," Carlo said.

Trying to appear nonchalant, Logan said, "Well, I guess I'll leave then." His subtle step backward caused the human guard dogs to tense behind Carlo.

"Not so fast, cuz," Carlo warned, taking a step toward Logan with his two sentries by his side. "We got some things to discuss first."

Despite the pleasant expression on his cousin's face, Logan sensed the threat immediately, and his mind raced with options. Should he run? No. He quickly dismissed that act of embarrassing cowardice. Should he fight? He didn't like the odds. Three men at once was a losing bet. The only choice was to try to placate Carlo until he could get the hell out of here and perhaps start a new life—one far away from Chicago.

"What do you want to discuss?" Logan asked evenly, sticking his hands in the pockets of his black leather jacket.

His apparent cooperation seemed to calm Carlo, whose shoulders relaxed slightly. "We got lots to discuss," he began, ticking off each topic on the fingers of his left hand. "Where your brother is, for one. It's about time the fucking coward joins the family. Why the hell the cops are after you, for another. Then there's the matter of two hundred thousand dollars you owe us." He smiled smugly. "But we'll start with a discussion about job absenteeism. You took an unauthorized vacation day, leaving Tank over here high and dry if the police had caught wind of the transaction and shown up last night. The boss ain't happy at all about you just deciding not to follow orders."

"I'm sorry," Logan replied in a conciliatory tone. "It won't happen again."

Carlo turned to Tank and mocked, "Aw, he's sorry." They shared a smirk before Carlo returned his attention to his cousin. "Where were you, Lo?"

Remembering the scene in his brother's apartment, he winced. "I had some business to take care of." *Some lives to ruin.*

"What kind of business?" Carlo edged imperceptibly closer to Logan.

"None of yours," Logan assured him.

Tilting his head to the side, Carlo swept a questioning look up and down Logan's tense body. His cousin behaved so protectively when it came to only one person.

"Were you with Grant?"

"No," Logan responded a little too quickly, a trickle of sweat trailing down his spine. "Why would you think that?"

Carlo licked his lips and stepped in even closer. He had his answer. "Where is he?"

Logan felt the hairs on the back of his neck bristle. "I have no idea. This isn't about Grant. This is between you and me—"

Carlo must have given some sort of signal because suddenly Tank and Mario lunged for him. Surprised, Logan recoiled to get off a hard punch and a swift kick, but before he knew it, he had both arms pinned behind his back, held in place by the inordinately strong men at his side. Logan managed to kick the side of Tank's knee, making the big man groan and stumble, but not lose grip of his prey.

"Get him on his knees," Carlo ordered.

"Get your goons the fuck off of me," Logan snarled as they wrestled him to the floor. "Angelo is not going to like this."

Carlo laughed derisively, yanking Logan's chin and forcing him to look up into his black eyes. Though the motion was harsh, it reminded Logan of Sophie cupping his chin once, lovingly caressing his face as he cried in her office. However, there was nothing comforting about Carlo's unyielding grip, his fierce gaze, or his livid words.

"You think my father would choose *you* over *me?* Think again, cuz." His grasp tightened and his fingers dug into the bruises lining Logan's jaw. "Where is Grant, you piece of shit? If you're not going to do your job, I'll find somebody who will!"

Logan gritted his teeth and shut his eyes, refusing to look at his cousin, which infuriated him.

Carlo cocked his right arm and sent his fist careening into Logan's gut. "Look at me!" he screamed, clutching Logan's chin once again.

Defiant blue eyes stared back at him, and Carlo desperately wanted to wipe the insolent smirk off his cousin's face. "You and your brother—hell, your father too—the lot of you, you've never helped this family *once.* You only pull us down."

"Speak for yourself, Carlo," Logan retorted in his deep baritone. "Should I remind you how badly you fucked up Blackfoot?"

"You son of a bitch," Carlo sneered, whaling another punch across Logan's face. A trickle of blood oozed from Logan's nose, dripping onto his white T-shirt.

"Carlo," Mario cautioned. "*Stare attento.* He's Enzo's son, for chrissake!"

"*Silenzio!*" Carlo hissed. "What the hell can Enzo do, locked up in Gurnee?"

"You're right to be concerned," Logan told Mario. "Angelo's going to discipline you both when he finds out you held me down."

Tank twisted his arm tighter, and Logan grimaced in pain. "Shut the fuck up, Barberi," Tank commanded.

"That's the spirit, Tank." Carlo smiled, then returned his attention to Logan. "The only person Angelo will be disciplining is *you*, you spineless good-for-nothing. You *will* start pulling your weight in this family, Logan. Or I will beat you down every day until you do."

Logan boldly jutted out his jaw. "You'll have to threaten me with something a little more real than that, cuz. Your fairy punches are even weaker than Grant's."

Feeling blind fury, Carlo unleashed another jab, this time aiming for the contusions already adorning Logan's jaw. Logan grunted when the blow glanced off his chin, and he swayed to the side, trying to catch his breath. Beads of sweat formed on his forehead.

Staring at the profile of his cousin's damaged face, Carlo suddenly stood stock still. "Grant punched you," he said, the realization dawning on him. "He's the one who gave you those bruises."

A malevolent smile crept onto Carlo's face. He'd just identified a way to get both of the damn brothers, the *chosen ones*, out of his way for good. He'd never have to compete for Angelo's attention again, and he could finally assume his proper place in the family. A flash of excitement coursed through him, followed by a stab of fear. He didn't know if he could carry out his plan.

Quickly whipping a knife out of his boot, Carlo held the weapon in front of Logan's face and made sure his quarry watched him as he slowly unsheathed the blade, which gleamed in the slats of sunlight shining through the dirty windows of the warehouse.

Struggling against his captors' hold as his cousin held the blade inches from his face, Logan felt his heart thump rapidly. Carlo ignored his associates' reactions to the knife—a look of consternation on Meat's face and an expression of smug triumph on Tank's—and leaned in to hold the sharp edge against Logan's throat.

"Tell me where Grant is," he quietly seethed.

"Fuck you," Logan retorted. He felt the pinching sting of the blade on his throat as Carlo allowed the knife's edge to dig into his skin. The wound was not deep but elicited blood all the same, mixing with the crimson trail dripping from his nose.

"You really want to protect that pansy?" Carlo asked incredulously. "You want to risk your life for that lightweight? For *Grant*?"

Logan pictured Grant at their mother's grave, his eyes welling up as he placed flowers near her headstone. Logan's deep voice was wistful. "He's a better man than any of us here."

"Oh, come *on*," Carlo scoffed, distractedly removing the knife from Logan's throat and waving it around emphatically. "Grant has no fucking clue. He's a weakling. That's what you get when your real dad goes to prison and you go live with your pussy uncle."

Feeling rage build up in his chest, Logan spat out, "*You're* the reason my dad went to prison! He got arrested trying to protect *your* sorry ass!"

Carlo's black eyes flared with fury. "It wasn't my fault!" he insisted. "I got shot! I could have died."

His restrained arms aching, his skin bruised and bleeding, Logan glared at his cousin. "My dad should have let you die. It would have been better—for everyone. I know for a fact that Angelo would much rather have his brother with him than his screw-up son. You fucked everything up, Carlo."

Carlo's throat tightened as he fought for air, and his vision clouded over, veiled by a deep red that matched the blood leaking from his victim's body. Suddenly he had no qualms about what he must do. Logan had just begged him to carry out his plan. It was the burden of his position of leadership in the family. He had a great responsibility—responsibility to rid the family of anything standing in its way, responsibility to take out the trash, just like his father had taught him to do.

Without another moment of hesitation, Carlo lunged forward, sinking the knife into Logan's abdomen. Once the tip of the blade pierced his rock-hard solar plexus, it slid into his internal organs with a sickening sluicing sound. The shocked gasps of three men—Logan, Meat, and Tank—met Carlo's ears, followed by dead silence.

Logan felt a burning tear while a fiery heat spread into his lungs and stomach. The pinch of the foreign body inside his twisted and turned, taking his breath away. Struggling to maintain consciousness, he stared dumbly up at Carlo, whose shiny black eyes looked equally stunned.

Horrified, Mario let go of Logan's arm and took a step away. The smug grin had quickly departed Tank's face. Despite his desire for revenge, he could not believe what he'd just witnessed. He too unleashed Logan from his vice grip. Once free, Logan wheezed for air and crumpled forward, the knife still lodged between his abdomen and chest.

Now Carlo didn't know what to do. After a few surreal moments, he decided to remove the knife. As he jaggedly jerked out the blade, Logan felt a searing pain cleave him, and he moaned loudly. Carlo gaped at the leaking hole left in Logan's flesh, then stared mesmerized at the seeping red stain flourishing on his white T-shirt.

"Shit, I'm outta here!" Mario said, slowly backing away.

"You're not going anywhere, Meat!" Carlo yelled angrily, halting the big man's progress. Carlo then turned to Tank, who shook his head disapprovingly.

"You went too far, Carlo," Tank said, also taking a step backward to distance himself from the crazy man facing him.

"You've got to help me!" Carlo cried.

"Only if you don't tell Angelo I was part of this," Tank ordered in a strange role-reversal of boss and employee.

"Just don't leave," Carlo pleaded, stealing a glance at Logan. "Help me do something with the body, man."

Tank frowned and whispered to Mario, now standing about twenty feet away from the cousins.

Dark spots entered Logan's field of vision as he clutched his upper abdomen, his breathing labored and his sudden physical weakness maddening. Carlo stood right above him, paralyzed by what he'd just done and presenting the perfect opportunity for Logan to beat the living hell out of him. He wanted to rip his fucking heart out! But Logan could not find the strength to move.

"I—I—I didn't mean it, Lo," Carlo offered in a quivering voice, reduced to a sniveling boy by the life-or-death circumstances. "You're my cousin … I—I love you, man. Do you, um, do you love me?"

Logan looked at Carlo with disbelief. Then, sensing a sticky wetness pouring over his hands, he peered down at his wounded torso. An abject sadness flooded him. He knew he was dying. "Grant," he gasped.

"Grant?" Carlo knelt down curiously, prompting his victim to say more despite himself.

"Stay … away." Although losing his thin grasp on consciousness, Logan willed himself to keep talking, "Stay away … from Grant."

Carlo watched his cousin's hands redden with blood. His tone was frantic. "But Lo—you love me, right? You know I didn't mean it?"

Logan stared at his cousin incredulously, feeling a stab of sympathy for the pathetic man kneeling next to him. Carlo had been irrevocably damaged from the moment he witnessed Tony Fanocelli dying at his Uncle Enzo's hand—at the hand of Logan's father. Feeling himself slipping away, Logan murmured, "I know. You've taken my dad … and me. Just … don't take Grant too."

Hearing the weakness in the once-formidable man's voice, Carlo gulped. As he stood, a flash of anger coursed through him. Who the fuck cared about Grant? He just wanted to know if Logan forgave him. Surmising that his cousin would not be conscious much longer, Carlo took one last look at Logan, whose deep-blue eyes bore into him with a surprising intensity.

Turning on his heel, Carlo joined his two bodyguards and started hissing commands. After a plan was hatched, all three waited for Logan to die and get it over with.

Helplessly Logan fell backward. The back of his head hit the concrete floor with a thud, and his arms flopped to his sides. He no longer had the strength to apply pressure to his bleeding wound. It was just a matter of time now, and he found himself welcoming the cool release of death. He was never much good at life, only bringing pain to those around him.

He'd heard the old adage about your life flashing before your eyes when you were dying, but Logan only had one scene replaying in his mind. He saw only pleading aquamarine eyes, the smell of scotch, the feel of a small hand curling in his. He was eleven years old again.

"Leave me! Go to your room!" his mother begged, her voice muffled by the bulk of the man pinning her to the floor, flat on her back. All Logan could see was his father's hunched back crouching over her, straddling her waist as he held down her wrists. The gleaming knife lay on the linoleum kitchen floor, inches from Karita's balled-up hand.

Logan was frozen in fear, as his father exploded in violence against his mother once again. Karita, Logan, and Grant had experienced such a fun afternoon, but the second they walked in the door, Logan knew immediately it was all turning to shit. Their father was waiting for them, his face beet red with rage and alcohol. Grant had cowered behind his big brother, flinching at their father's screamed accusations, but once they saw Enzo extract a knife from the wood block, the six year old had sidled up to his brother and grasped his hand.

"You little bitch!" Enzo seethed. "How dare you go to see him when I expressly forbade it? How dare you take my boys to that place?"

"He's my brother!" Karita softly cried. "The boys need to see their uncle."

"I'll determine what my sons need!" Enzo slapped her across the face, and the sharp noise snapped Logan to action.

He sprang forward and leapt onto his father's back. "Stop it!"

Enzo quickly shrugged the boy off his shoulders, pushing himself up and off his wife's prone frame and standing. Angrily he backhanded Logan, who hit the floor with the force of his father's strike.

"No," Karita moaned, sitting up. "Go to your room, boys! I'll be okay—just leave!"

"Shut up," Enzo commanded, quickly pushing his wife back to the floor as he straddled her again. Logan watched with horror as his father scooped up the knife in his trembling grasp. The distinct odor of scotch wafted through the air.

"I'll show you who's in charge in this family," Enzo growled, holding the edge of the blade to Karita's throat. She shuddered in fear below him, trying not to whimper.

Glancing at Grant, wide-eyed and shaking uselessly by the wall, Logan pushed himself up off the floor and lunged at his father once again. "Get off her!" he wailed.

"Goddamn it," his father muttered, and the knife clattered to the floor. Enzo groped behind him, trapping the boy's wrist in his strong hold and yanking his body around so he was staring into his father's unfocused eyes. "You are such an idiot, Logan. You're just dying for me to beat you too, huh?"

Logan met his mother's worried crystal-blue eyes before his father violently shook him to draw his attention back. Enzo shoved Logan, and he stumbled toward Grant near the kitchen doorway.

"I'm going to give you boys five seconds to get the hell out of here," Enzo warned, reaching to unbuckle his belt. Logan watched his mother quietly stand up, unbeknownst to his father, and mouth "Go!" as she crept out the other entrance to the kitchen.

Once Logan saw her escape, he grabbed Grant's hand and yanked him toward the hallway, just as Karita had predicted. She'd known Logan wouldn't leave her alone with Enzo.

"Let's go, Grantey!" Logan ordered, and they ran for the stairs, grateful their father wasn't following them with his belt looped in his hand.

Enzo had turned to find his wife gone, and they heard him holler, "Get your ass back in here, Karita! I'm not done with you yet!"

As the boys scampered up the stairs they heard their father pounding on the locked door of the first-floor bathroom, assuring Logan that his mother was safe for now.

"C'mon," he instructed, panting as they entered their bedroom, "Let's play Battleship."

Also out of breath from their hasty exit, Grant nodded his head, "'Kay."

They laid out the board game on the yellow shag carpet, and Grant picked up one of the ships, absentmindedly twirling it in his hands.

"Is Dad gonna kill Mom?"

"C'mon, Grant." Logan gestured to the game. "You gotta set up your battleships so I won't find them."

Grant blinked rapidly, undeterred. In a quieter voice he asked, "Is he gonna whip us?"

Logan bit his lip. These were questions he didn't know the answer to, questions he couldn't think about just now. Ignoring the stinging red blotch on his cheek, he feigned cheerfulness. "What's this ship?" he quizzed, holding up a small gray boat. "What did Uncle Joe tell us about this one?"

Eyeing his brother suspiciously, six-year-old Grant dutifully answered, "It's a frigate."

"Yeah," Logan confirmed. "The one we saw today at Great Lakes. A Perry-class, an FFG-7."

"Uh-huh," Grant responded. "A fig-seven."

"A fig what?" Logan inquired.

"A fig-seven!" Grant insisted, his eyes beginning to recapture their twinkle. "'At's what Uncle Joe told me when you were in the bathroom. 'At's what they call an FFG-7."

Logan stared admirably at his intelligent younger brother. They began the game, somehow able to drown out the disturbing noises from the floor below, somehow not hearing their mother's cries.

Whispered conversation between the three men behind him brought Logan back to the present. He'd never had the chance to tell Sophie that story in therapy. What would she have said if he had? *You bravely tried to save your mother. You tried to save your brother. You tried to be a good man.*

But I failed, he'd respond, if he could. He knew he'd never see Sophie again. Grant was better for her anyway, much better.

He stared at the grimy warehouse ceiling, unsure if the encroaching dimness was due to fading daylight or his eyelids drooping. He was tired, so tired.

He'd been unable to save his mother when he was a child, and he hoped by some grace of God he might be able to join her soon, to apologize for failing her so completely, to make her understand how he'd simply lost his way. He had failed so many people. A pang of sadness pierced his heart when he realized his own son Ben was going to grow up without a father, just like he had. Hopefully his son would fare better than he had. Perhaps it was a blessing for Ben that his fucked-up father was leaving him for good.

Finally succumbing to his fatigue, Logan allowed his eyes to flutter shut. All was quiet in the warehouse.

31. Until Morale Improves

Grant sighed heavily and felt hot tears well up in his eyes. Great. He was crying. Again. Some kind of mobster he made—no wonder Lo had called him a wuss when they were kids.

He was supposed to be preparing the ship for the day's sold-out cruises, but instead he was standing by the controls, staring into space and thinking about Sophie, only Sophie. Her look of fear and mistrust, the betrayal evident in her clipped tone, the finality of her parting words—it all had haunted him for the past twenty-four hours.

Roger brusquely entered the bridge, and Grant quickly swiped at a wayward tear, hoping his boss hadn't witnessed his little display of weakness. He pretended to clean the steering mechanism, methodically running a wet rag over the gleaming silver wheel.

Disdainfully studying his employee, Roger set a plastic bag on the counter and grumbled, "I see you're still moping around, Madsen."

He halted his cleaning charade and looked down, trying to prevent any more tears. "Sorry."

Roger sighed. "Why don't you talk to her, try to explain things?"

"I did try!" Grant insisted, lifting his chin and staring at Roger defiantly. "After work last night I took her purse to her apartment, and I freaking begged her roommate to let me talk to her. But Kirsten told me Sophie was at her father's, which I *know* was a total lie."

"How do you know that?"

"Because Sophie hates her father; she would never go there. I'm sure she was hiding right inside the apartment, refusing to see me." He sighed. "There's nothing I can do. It's over."

Roger had no idea what to say, and Grant leaned down to extract the window-cleaning solution from the cupboard.

Perking up, Roger offered, "Screw Sophie. Why don't you just go to your Uncle Angelo's club and find some hoochie-mama to cuddle up with?"

Grant popped up immediately with a look of incredulous anger.

"Or not," the older man amended.

"Please do not *ever* discuss my uncle, my dad, my brother ..." Grant's indignant voice trailed off, and he found himself fighting tears once again. He was so sick of his family, so sick of them ruining his life.

"When I first hired you, Joe told me you'd be fine if you just stayed away from your family," Rog said sympathetically. "I didn't understand that then, but I'm finally getting the picture now."

"You probably shouldn't have hired me in the first place."

"You're right," Roger snapped. "I would never have hired you if I knew what a fucking Debbie Downer you'd turn out to be. I'm so sick of this mopey shit—all over a damn chick! Pull it together, Madsen."

Grant sniffed. "Yes, sir."

Emphatically pointing his index finger in the air, Roger continued. "That reminds me! I bought a sign announcing a new policy for all employees, effective immediately." He shot a disappointed glance at Grant. "It was your sulking ass that prompted me to get this."

Roger scooped his bagged purchase off the counter and turned to the console, taking out a hammer and nail before banging the drawer shut. Grant studied him curiously for a moment, but decided to get back to work.

Roger stuck his tongue out the corner of his mouth as he nailed the plaque to the wall, then stood back to admire his handiwork.

"Let's see if ROTC boy learned anything in college," Roger called. "Come over here and read this."

Dutifully Grant came over to the plaque, which was adorned with a skull and crossbones, and read aloud, "The beatings will continue until morale improves."

Despite himself, he felt a slight grin coming on.

Roger smiled too. He'd finally succeeded in cheering up the morose boy. "Maybe that bruise on your face, which looks even worse today, by the way, will send a message to those lazy-asses Tommy and Dan."

Grant absentmindedly drew his hand to his face, and his smile quickly faded. With another sigh, he grabbed the spray bottle and listlessly went back to clean the next window.

Roger turned and descended the stairs to see if Tommy and Dan had arrived yet. If those fucking sloths were late again, they were definitely in for quite a beating. The boss was going to improve morale around here if it killed him.

"Come, Lucky!" Lieutenant Jo Ann Jemison hollered, clapping her hands to emphasize the command. With his tongue lolling happily, the black Springer Spaniel-Collie mix came bounding out of the shallow waters of Lake Michigan, a piece of driftwood clutched in his teeth.

"Good boy!" Jo Ann cooed, grasping the end of the wet wood. But Lucky continued to hold on. Jo Ann frowned. "Lucky," she admonished. "Drop."

Mischievous black eyes stared back at her as the dog clamped down harder and swiftly wagged his tail.

"Drop!" Jo Ann ordered again, taking a sweeping look around her to make sure that none of her superiors was observing her utter lack of control. Jo Ann and Lucky were only a quarter-mile south of the Naval Station Great Lakes, and it would not be unusual to find a commander or two jogging along the lake before it became too hot later in the day.

His owner gave the stick one more jerk, and Lucky maintained his vice grip, adding a playful growl. Refusing a game of tug-of-war, which the dog seemed to crave, Jo Ann trotted ahead and strolled along the waves lapping the beach, pretending to ignore him. Lucky galloped to catch up and nuzzled her hand with his snout, offering her the wood once again.

Casually looking down, Jo Ann swiftly grabbed the wood from the unsuspecting dog and this time managed to swipe it clean. "Ha!" she cried, victoriously holding it high in the air, while Lucky danced at her feet. Grinning, Jo Ann tossed the driftwood into the lake, where it was followed immediately by the black-and-white dog. He pursued the wood with tenacious glee before locating the floating piece and clamping it into his mouth.

They played this game for fifteen minutes as they headed back north toward the base. Lucky was finally getting the hang of releasing the wood on command, but Jo Ann was pretty sure his progress would be forgotten when they took their walk tomorrow. The dog was incorrigible. Suddenly Lucky veered away from the water toward several canoes roped together at a dock just outside the perimeter of the base.

"Lucky, get outta there!" Jo Ann chastised, hustling to the canoes once the dog poked his head under the canvas tarp. Lucky snatched his head back and barked frantically, puzzling his owner. As she approached the canoes, Jo Ann felt an unexplained creepy sensation quiver up her spine. She slowed her pace and cautiously took the last few steps.

"What is it, boy?"

The dog continued barking, poking his head into the canoe, then backing out. Jo Ann had no idea why she dreaded looking inside the canoe, but she could ignore her insistent pup no longer. Peeling away a section of the tarp, she stopped breathing when she saw the sleeve of a black leather jacket. Following down the length of the sleeve, she stared disbelievingly at a gray human hand.

Jo Ann let out a bloodcurdling scream.

☙

"Get a hold of yourself, Lieutenant," Captain Archibald Lockhart commanded, watching his subordinate's trembling hands clutch the leash of her spunky black dog.

Jo Ann gulped. "Yes, sir."

Archie's deep-brown eyes glanced toward the canoes, which were now guarded by two military police officers thanks to the lieutenant's frantic call to the base from her cell phone. They were all waiting for local police to arrive. Gesturing to the canoe closest to the water, Archie asked, "The body is in that one?"

Lucky barked as if to provide his own answer, and his owner confirmed, "Yes, sir."

Taking a deep breath, the captain strode to the canoe and, without a moment's hesitation, peered inside. Once the sunlight hit the corpse's pallid face, Archie inhaled sharply and took a step away.

"I know this man," he quietly informed the MPs, thinking immediately of his friend Commander Joe Madsen. Then his mind quickly flashed to an image of Grant Madsen's frightened face, imploring Archie to let him pass at the foot of that basement stairwell, his arm trembling as he held the gun. Archie felt sick.

"You do, sir?" one MP incredulously inquired.

"I know this man," Archie repeated, in a stronger voice this time. "His name is Logan Barberi."

"Well, that will save us some time identifying the body then," a voice announced behind him.

Archie swiveled around and found a petite woman staring back at him, her neat, reddish-brown bob framing her face and her green eyes flashing intensity and intelligence. She wore a fuchsia blouse underneath a black suit-jacket and pants, giving her a no-nonsense, business-like appearance. "You're the commanding officer on this base, sir?" she asked.

"Captain Archie Lockhart, ma'am," he confirmed, reaching out to shake her hand.

"Detective Marilyn Fox, Great Lakes Police," she responded, pumping his hand with a surprising strength. Archie then noticed two men just behind her, who appeared to be equipment-laden crime-scene techs.

Lucky began barking and wagging his tail, anxious to meet the newcomers. Glancing at him, Marilyn asked, "That's the dog that found the body?"

"Yes," Archie replied. "Along with his owner, Lieutenant Jo Ann Jemison."

"Okay, I'll need to interview her. Could you please join the lieutenant over there, Captain, while we get to work on the scene? I'd like to look things over before talking to you further."

"Of course, Detective," Archie replied. "The lieutenant could use a little support right now anyway. She's rather freaked out."

Marilyn smirked. "Yeah, it's not every day you find a dead body while walking your dog."

As Archie rejoined his subordinate, he heard the detective tell one of her techs, "Smell's not too bad yet. TOD must be recent."

About ten minutes later, Marilyn interviewed Lieutenant Jemison while Archie observed the techs hovering over the scene—snapping photos, brushing for fingerprints, and conversing with the coroner who had recently arrived.

"Okay." Marilyn sidled up to Archie, her voice friendly and engaging, "I'm finally ready to ask you a few questions, sir. How do you know the deceased?"

"How did he die, Detective?" Archie asked quietly.

Marilyn paused, unsure whether to share such information with a potential suspect. Just about everyone was a suspect at the moment. But wanting to see his reaction, she informed Archie, "Looks like he was stabbed in the chest."

A look of pure sadness washed over him as he cleared his throat. "Very well. To answer your question, I'm good friends with Logan Barberi's uncle, Commander Joe Madsen."

She jotted down some notes. "I see, so Joe Madsen is the brother of Mr. Barberi's mother, then?"

"Yes, ma'am."

"You said you know Mr. Barberi's uncle—that's what helped you identify Mr. Barberi?"

"Joe brought his nephews and his sister to live with him on the base back in, when was that, 1986? Back when Enzo Barberi was sent to prison for life."

Marilyn scribbled furiously. "So that's when you met the deceased?"

"I met Logan once in the O Club back then, but he didn't stay here long. He ran away to live with his other uncle, Angelo Barberi." Archie looked wistful. "Joe was crushed when Logan ran away. Anyway, Logan was only about thirteen when he lived here. I recognized him as an adult because his picture was in the paper during Angelo's trial."

Archie gave the detective some time to get all this down before he added, "You should also know that Logan and his brother were arrested near this base a little over two years ago."

"Really?" Marilyn said. "So Mr. Barberi had a brother."

"Yes, ma'am—Grant Madsen."

Catching her questioning glance, Archie explained, "Joe adopted Grant after his sister, Karita, died from cancer. Karita was the boys' mother."

Nodding her head, Marilyn continued, "Why were the brothers arrested?"

"I caught Grant trying to steal a bag of cash from a bar nearby." He rubbed his jaw. "Grant pointed a gun at me, but I subdued him, and then he was arrested."

Arching her eyebrows, Marilyn asked, "And Logan?"

"Logan was arrested in the bar's parking lot, but somehow he wasn't tied in to the attempted robbery. Grant wasn't talking, and Logan had a good attorney, I guess."

Marilyn's green eyes narrowed. This certainly did not sound like a slam-dunk homicide case. "And Grant is still in prison, sir?"

"Yes, he was sentenced to three years at Gurnee."

"Unless he's out for good behavior," she speculated, wondering if one brother had exacted revenge on the other.

"I haven't heard whether Grant got out." Archie shrugged. "It's been a while since I spoke to Joe. Things got a little weird between us after Grant's robbery."

Archie thought again how devastated Joe would be upon learning his nephew had been murdered.

"And Joe Madsen lives in town?"

"No, ma'am. He's probably out to sea right now, but if not, he's stationed in Norfolk." While the detective was writing, Archie asked, "Are you going to call him about this, or should I?"

Marilyn paused. "Looks like I have a growing list of next-of-kin to notify. Let me see if I got this straight: Mr. Barberi had two uncles—Joe Madsen and Angelo Barberi, one father serving a life sentence in Gurnee, one brother who may or may not still be serving *his* sentence in Gurnee…anyone else I should know about?"

Archie bit his lip. "I think Joe mentioned once that Logan might have a kid of his own? I'm not sure."

"I'll check it out. I'd like to do the notification of death myself, but if you have Joe Madsen's contact information, I would appreciate it."

"You have my full cooperation, Detective. I was much closer to Joe than I was to Logan, but I want to find the bastard who did this and bring him to justice."

"Good. And may I ask, Captain, your whereabouts for the past twenty-four hours?"

Archie was startled. She had charmed him into believing they were a team, then *wham*! She was good.

He nodded. "I was actually in Washington, DC, yesterday, Detective," he said. "Meeting with Admiral Kearney. Just returned last night. I'd be happy to show you my travel itinerary and give you the Admiral's number, as well as Joe's information, if you'd like to accompany me to my office."

"That would be lovely," she smiled, pocketing her notebook.

Archie waited for Marilyn to check in one last time with the techs before they headed to the base.

❧

"Carlo!" Angelo yelled, entering the foyer of his opulent house. He was shaking with rage and had no idea what he would do once he saw his son's fucking face.

"In the kitchen, *padre*!" He heard a faint reply from the interior of the mansion.

Making his way to the large kitchen, Angelo was greeted by the sight of his son sitting at the table, stuffing pasta into his mouth. Noticing the fury in his father's black eyes, Carlo put his fork down and slowly stood up, taking a few uncertain chews.

Angelo crossed the room in a second and slapped Carlo across the face, causing him to reel to the side, coughing and sputtering. Somehow, Carlo managed to avoid choking on the pasta, and he cradled his burning cheek while righting himself, staring at his father with utter shock and disappointment.

"You promised you would never hit me," he softly cried.

The Mafia boss looked at him incredulously. Since they'd just completed a scan for listening devices in the house this morning, he decided to speak freely. "That was before you decided to murder my godson."

Carlo's eyes widened. "What? Logan?" He looked horrified. "He's, he's *dead?*" The last word came out as a shocked whisper.

Thinking he should hand his son a fucking Oscar for *that* performance, instead Angelo gave him a slashing punch to the gut. Carlo doubled over, breathing laboriously for a few moments before moaning, "I didn't do it!"

Angelo looked at him disgustedly. "Unless you want me to keep beating the shit out of you, you'd better stop. You've been gunning for Logan since you two were kids. I *know* it was you."

Still doubled over, Carlo was glad his father couldn't see his face, which bought him some time to decide how to play this. Acting stupid about Logan's death clearly wasn't working. Carlo was simply too intelligent to play dumb convincingly. There was also something appealing about finally being able to discuss his victory with someone who would listen. Tank and Meat had refused to talk about what happened in the warehouse yesterday.

Slowly returning to standing, Carlo tried to ignore the throbbing pain in his stomach and face. Although Angelo was fifty-four years old, he still packed a wallop. Carlo silently scolded himself for underestimating his father—he was the boss of the family, after all.

"I didn't mean it, *padre.* I went in there planning just to get Logan back in the fold like you told me to, but he wouldn't stop insulting me. It just, um, happened."

"How the fuck does a man getting fatally stabbed in the gut just *happen,* Carlo?"

Carlo blinked several times. "So, they found the body, then?"

"The police just interrogated me at my club, you fuckwit! I appreciate you giving me the heads up, by the way. I could be sitting in a goddamn holding cell right now! Thank God I was at the club yesterday, with witnesses. I told them you were there too, and you're lucky the guys backed me up on that. What the fuck were you thinking, stuffing the body in a *canoe*?Right out in public?"

"I—I freaked out," Carlo retorted, feigning fear. "I wasn't thinking straight."

"You drove all the way up to fucking Lake County, and then you don't even finish the job right? Hell, the lake was right there. You could have weighed down the body and put it in the water. No boaters are allowed near that naval station anyway…"

Angelo's voice trailed off as something dawned on him. He peered disbelievingly at Carlo. "You're trying to pin this on Grant," he said slowly. "That's why you left the body up there, not even bothering to hide it."

Fuck. Carlo indeed had underestimated his father. Angelo could see right through his plans.

"So, you're jealous of both brothers, then," Angelo added, shaking his head. "You wanted to take them both out with one fell swoop. Son of a bitch, Carlo. Logan was worried about you hurting Grant, and now I know why."

"Great. Now you're siding with Logan and Grant against me?"

Angelo felt exhausted, and he refused to engage in this discussion. He didn't think Carlo would like the answer anyway. Rubbing the bridge of his nose, he asked, "Who was with you in the warehouse?"

"Tank and Meat."

"Don't tell them I know you it was you. Enzo would kill me if he found out what you did." He sighed loudly. "This was a fuckup of massive proportions, Carlo. You have made me so goddamn furious. I don't know what to do with you."

"I thought you'd be proud of me," Carlo whined.

"*Proud* of you? Why the *hell* would I be proud of you?"

"Because I took care of things for the family," Carlo explained in a small voice. "Logan was hurting our profits, so I did the brave thing to protect the family."

"Don't you understand, Carlo? Logan *is* the family. Or, I should say, he *was* the family." Now that Angelo's rage was mostly spent, he felt a lump in his throat thinking about his godson, a man who understood and admired Angelo like none other. He would never see him again.

Clearing his throat, Angelo demanded, "Give me your weapon."

"What? Why?"

With a menacing glare, he took a step toward his son. "Give it to me. Now."

Grimacing, Carlo reached into his jacket and pulled out a handgun, reluctantly handing it over to his father. Angelo took the weapon and seethed, "I can't trust you with this right now. Try not to fuck anything else up in the next few days, got it?"

Carlo gritted his teeth. "I help this family, *padre*. I do everything in my power to help this family. When are you going to give me the respect I deserve?"

"When you start earning it," Angelo replied.

"Just like Logan earned it?" Carlo sneered. "Even though he lost the family hundreds of thousands of dollars, you always treated him better than me. You always wished he was your son instead of me, didn't you?"

Suddenly Angelo couldn't take his son's childish jealousy a moment longer. He raised the weapon over Carlo's head and crashed the handle into his skull. Carlo threw his hands up, but he wasn't fast enough. His body folded like an accordion onto the marble floor.

Angelo looked down at his son, lying crumpled on his side. With dismay, he leaned down and verified that Carlo was still breathing, with a steady pulse. Staring into his son's now-peaceful face—his permanent sneer gone now that Carlo was unconscious—Angelo hoped his son had finally learned his lesson. It was glaringly obvious that sparing the rod had *not* turned him into a respectable man. Once upon a time Angelo had desired to be different from his own bastard of a father, but eyeing his beaten son on the floor, he realized he was not different at all. He was a Barberi man through and through.

❧

"Sophie, please just talk to him."

Her roommate's pleading tone was evident, even over the phone, but Sophie angrily stared at the books lining the shelves in her father's study. "What, are you on *his* side now?"

"No," Kirsten insisted. "It's just that Grant looked so broken. You don't even want to talk to him at all? Even for a few minutes?"

"He lied to me."

"But he didn't know, Sophie! He didn't know his brother was the reason you went to prison."

"Listen to yourself, Kir. Do you really think I should trust the brother of the man who ruined my life? They share fifty percent of their DNA, for heaven's sake!"

Kirsten suppressed a giggle. DNA? Who the hell discussed DNA in the middle of a conversation about man trouble? "But he's a different guy from his brother," Kirsten argued. "You told me Grant was raised by his uncle, right? That he's been trying to get far away from his family?"

"Not far enough, evidently," Sophie spat. "He was convicted of aggravated robbery—that's why he went to prison. I bet he was doing a job for his family. What's to say he wasn't working some con for them by trying to seduce me? I bet he was working a game on me."

"Oh, come on, Sophie. That was no game. You can tell he loves you—"

Kirsten's voice suddenly cut off, and she was quiet for a moment. "Hey, wait a second. I have another call coming in on call-waiting."

"Okay." Sophie tried to take some deep breaths. Talking about Grant only upset her, and she hoped to change topics when Kirsten got back on the line. She should ask Kirsten how her dissertation was coming along...

"Sophie?" Kirsten returned to their conversation. "That was actually a detective from Great Lakes calling for you. Her name was Marilyn something?"

"What?" Sophie asked, totally confused.

"They're coming to your dad's house to talk to you."

"Kirsten! My father is going to freak if police officers show up here."

"I'm sorry. She made me tell her where you were—I didn't have a choice. She said they were conducting a murder investigation, heading into the city to interview a suspect. They need to talk to you ASAP, and your dad's house is on the way."

Sophie inhaled sharply. A *murder* investigation? Who had been murdered? She felt tears spring to her eyes, instantly knowing it was Grant. She felt it in her gut. *They're bad people*, he'd told her. *They've already destroyed my life.* Oh, God. Had they killed Grant? Had they taken away the man she loved?

"Sophie?" Kirsten's concerned voice rang out in the silence.

"I gotta go," she replied hoarsely, hanging up the phone as the tears began. The Barberi family had already taken so much from her. They couldn't take Grant too. She'd spoken so harshly to him the last time they saw each other. *Please, don't let it be Grant*, she silently prayed, and the intensity of hurt in her heart surprised her.

Plucking tissues from the box, she dabbed at her tears, as Grant's wounded gaze swam before her eyes. Sophie braced herself for the detective's arrival.

32. Complicated Grief

Perched by the docks of the Chicago River, Joe Madsen could hear Grant's smooth, confident voice before he could see him. Eventually Joe could make out Roger's ship, chugging toward him at the end of the five o'clock cruise.

Joe strained to hear Grant's voice—was that *singing?* Grant had been delivering some sort of monologue before, but now he was definitely singing, and it only took a few notes for Joe to identify the familiar tune: "My Kind of Town."Joe smiled brightly, but his smile faded when he thought of his sister Karita, Sinatra's biggest fan. Joe knew it wasn't by coincidence that Grant had chosen that particular song.

A charge of upbeat energy filled the air as the ship backed into its place along the concrete walkway. The boisterous singing of everyone on board certainly drew attention from the passersby and local businesses. Joe could see his buddy Roger adeptly working the controls, bringing the ship right alongshore. Then two young men jumped over the gunwale and tied the ship in place.

While passengers disembarked, flowing off the ship in a steady stream, Joe kept his eyes trained on the bridge. Occasionally Roger appeared to make a remark or laugh, but Grant never even smiled. He looked exhausted, gaunt, and sadder than Joe had seen him since Karita died eighteen years ago. His physical appearance did not at all match Roger's recent reports of Grant flourishing outside of prison, and Joe wondered what was going on.

Finally all the lively, chatty passengers were off the ship, and Roger descended the stairs, chomping on a piece of fruit.

"Holy shit, are you eating an *apple?*" Joe called disbelievingly.

"Joe!" Roger grinned and beckoned his friend onto the deck. Proudly holding the apple aloft, Rog gestured to his belly. "Heeuh?" he pointed to his body, standing in profile and sucking in his gut. "Heeuh? Don't I look skinny?"

"The very picture of fitness," Joe agreed, stifling a grin. "How's your heart doing?"

"Good," Roger replied, glancing up to the bridge. "Much better than your nephew's, anyway."

Joe watched Grant move slowly around the windowed interior of the bridge, doing some sort of cleanup task. His head seemed weighed down by some invisible force. "What's with him, Rog? He doesn't look good."

"Yep, Debbie Downer up there is having some chick issues. I got on his case about how depressing he was as a docent, so he livened it up a little, but I think it really takes it out of him to fake being all peppy. He barely says a word to me between cruises."

Joe frowned. "Chick issues?"

"Yeah, we had this good-looking girl working for us—another parolee he met named Sophie—but when she found out about his family, she ditched him. You never told me his name was Grant Barberi, by the way."

Tensing immediately, Joe tersely replied, "It's not. His name is Grant Madsen."

"Well, Sophie Taylor ain't buying it. She was one pissed-off woman, let me tell you—screaming at Grant about how he lied to her, acting all scared of him."

Joe grimaced. No wonder Grant was so upset—his family had taken him down once again. But losing his girlfriend would be nothing compared to the loss Joe had to share with him next.

"Listen, Rog, I've got to give Grant some bad news, and I don't think he's going to take it so well. Can you cover for him if he can't fulfill his docent duty for your next cruise?"

"What the hell do you have to tell him that would knock him on his ass like that?"

"Just give us some time while I go talk to him."

"Sure," Roger said.

Joe made his way to the bridge and stood in the entryway for several moments before Grant noticed him. Finally cracking a smile, Grant uttered a relieved "You came back" before allowing his uncle to draw him into a hug. The younger man leaned into his father figure, comforted by the familiar sight of his khaki uniform and the smell of Safeguard soap.

"Of course I came back. I had to see my favorite nephew." Joe swallowed hard. *The only nephew I have left.*

"Rog did say you might be coming for a visit. It's great that you made it."

"Yeah, I had a flight planned for tomorrow, but I bumped it to today."

"Why?"

Joe cleared his throat. "I needed to tell you something." Looking steadily at his nephew, he added, "Captain Lockhart called me today."

"How is the captain, sir?" Grant asked warily.

"Not too good after what he saw today. Listen, Grant, there's no easy way to say this, so I'll just come out with it." Joe drew in a deep breath and averted his gaze, suddenly unable to look into his nephew's cool gemstone eyes. "Logan is dead," he said quietly.

Grant gasped, slowly taking a step backward, his horrified eyes blinking not once. "What? How?"

"They found him near Great Lakes." Joe swallowed again, and his jaw flexed forcefully, attempting to hold in his emotion. He'd already cried enough on the plane, his face turned to the window. "Somebody stabbed him to death, Grant."

Joe watched his nephew's face crumple. His lips quivered, and his eyes filled with glassy tears. "No," he moaned, still stepping back to rest against the console.

Joe desperately wanted to take the pain away, but he couldn't. "I'm sorry," he mumbled, feeling helpless.

"When?" Grant rasped.

"They found his body this morning." Joe leaned against the wall and closed his eyes. "I couldn't believe it when Archie called me—I still don't believe it."

Grant didn't believe it either. "Why?"

Joe stared into his glistening eyes. "I don't know. I assume his gambling debts finally caught up with him."

Feeling his legs give out, Grant slid down the console onto the floor, just like he'd done during his tequila stupor a month ago, and his body folded onto itself, his elbows settling on his knees and his forehead resting on his crossed arms. He looked down, watching his tears plop onto the white floor. His brother was gone. The brother he hated—the brother he loved.

Suddenly a paroxysm of guilt pierced him as he remembered his last words to Logan: *I wish you were dead.*

Grant's body shook with wracking sobs.

❧

Parole Officer Jerry Stone met Detective Marilyn Fox in the Gold Coast district, on the cobbled street outside the Taylor home. She had a uniformed police officer accompanying her, and the three made their introductions while taking surreptitious glances at the large home on their left.

"Thank you for your help with this case, Jerry." Marilyn nodded while shaking his hand.

"It's not too often a parole officer becomes part of a murder investigation, but I'll do what I can," he said.

"Well, you've saved me some time already by providing addresses and background information over the phone. Speaking of time, I still have to get to my key suspect before the afternoon is over, so let's head in there."

The three were buzzed through the heavy wrought-iron gate, and once they climbed the stairs to the porch, the front door was opened by a nervous woman with long strawberry-blond hair and classy clothing. Behind her stood a distinguished, graying man.

Sophie's eyes widened when she saw her parole officer on the doorstep, and she anxiously opened the door wider, stepping back to allow the police to enter the foyer.

Jerry shut the door behind them. "Taylor, this is Detective Marilyn Fox from Great Lakes. Detective, Sophie Taylor."

"Jerry, it's Grant isn't it?" she cried immediately. "He's dead."

"Grant? No, it's not Madsen," Jerry said.

Sophie breathed in huge gulps air, overwhelmed by her relief, and she grabbed her unsuspecting parole officer in a hug. Jerry stood awkwardly for a moment before giving her a few light pats on the back, trying to comfort her. Over her shoulder Jerry aimed an embarrassed glance toward the older man glaring at him. "I'm her PO," he explained.

Will felt a mixture of sadness, anger, and confusion as he watched his daughter turn to another man, seeking solace. *He* should be the one soothing her, not that damn parole officer. But he had no idea why Sophie needed comforting in the first place. Who the hell was this Grant character? Will had just arrived home from work, and Sophie had not had time to explain why the officers had come to question her.

Marilyn watched the scene with curiosity, unsure why a parolee would be so familiar with her parole officer.

"Why did you think Grant was dead?" she asked once Sophie released her hold on Jerry.

"Who is *Grant?*" Will demanded.

Sophie bit her lip and avoided her father's stare. Marilyn and Jerry realized the construction magnate had no idea about the love triangle his daughter was embroiled in. This could get interesting.

"Mr. Taylor, is it?" said Marilyn. "We need to interview Ms. Taylor. Is there some place we could speak with your daughter privately?"

"Uh, I guess you could use my office," Will offered tentatively. "Um, no, wait, it's too much of a mess in there," he quickly amended with a nervous smile. "How about we go to the living room? This way." He pointed to a room off the foyer.

The detective gave him an unnerving stare. "We need to interview your daughter separately, sir," she clarified.

"I'm not letting you talk to these cops without my attorney present, Sophie."

But Sophie felt comforted by Jerry's presence. He would look out for her. "It's okay, Dad. I haven't done anything wrong." *Except fall in love with another criminal,* she thought.

"Mr. Taylor, we'd also like to speak with you after we question your daughter," Marilyn informed him. "Could you please get some coffee for us in the meantime, sir? Officer Gonzalez can help you." She exchanged a knowing glance with the uniformed officer next to her. He was to babysit Will Taylor without allowing him to overhear the interrogation of his daughter.

Will hesitated. "Do you know why my daughter went to prison, Detective?"

"Yes, sir." *That is why we're here,* Marilyn mentally added.

"Then you'll understand my reluctance to have her implicated undeservingly in yet another legal matter." He gave his daughter a stern look. "Sophie is a good girl, a law-abiding citizen. She just falls in with the wrong boys."

Watching Sophie roll her eyes, Jerry stifled a laugh. *That* was the understatement of the year.

"And I will *not* have her carted off to prison again when she's totally innocent."

"I understand, Mr. Taylor," Marilyn said. "We just have some routine questions for her. Please, sir, the sooner you let us begin, the sooner we'll be out of your hair, and you can both get back to your lives."

Reluctantly, Will nodded. "I'll be in the kitchen—just holler if you need anything."

"Okay, Dad."

Once the three were settled on the overstuffed floral-print sofas, Marilyn extracted her notepad from her jacket and repeated her previous question. "Ms. Taylor, why did you think Grant Madsen was dead?"

"Because his family is Mafia, and I thought they might hurt him," Sophie responded. "They're bad people. His brother is Logan Barberi."

"Do you know where Logan Barberi is right now?"

"No," Sophie said. "I wish I did, so I could tell the police where to find him. He needs to go down."

Marilyn raised her eyebrows at Jerry.

Oblivious, Sophie sighed deeply, and then seemed to notice Jerry staring at her. "Oh, God!" she exclaimed. "Did I just get Grant in more trouble?"

"Relax," Jerry said. "I already knew about his Mafia connections. Once I realized his brother Logan was the man who put you in prison, I told Madsen he should come clean with you about his identity."

Sophie nodded sadly, remembering how Grant had needed to tell her something, but once again she'd thwarted his efforts at honesty, insisting on sharing her own story first. She wished she'd allowed Grant to tell her about his family—that would have been a much better way to discover the truth. Or *would* it? The news of the brothers' connection was devastating no matter how she learned of it.

"And then Madsen came back to see me yesterday morning," Jerry added.

"He talked to you?" Sophie asked.

"Yeah, he came to tell me about his brother showing up at his place. He was basically turning himself in for associating with a known criminal." Jerry watched Sophie's eyes widen with alarm. "But I didn't have the heart to arrest him." He paused and then added, "He was too torn up about losing you."

Sophie looked down.

Marilyn took it all in and glanced skeptically at the parole officer. What the hell was going on here? Choosing not to dress down the PO in front of a suspect, Marilyn asked him, "What time was Mr. Madsen in your office yesterday, Officer Stone?"

"Let's see, about eight-forty in the morning."

"And what time did he leave?"

"A little before nine."

"Why are you asking these questions, Detective?" Sophie butted in. "If Grant wasn't the one who was murdered, who was?"

Marilyn finished writing, then trained her green eyes on Sophie. She gave the obligatory Miranda warnings, making Sophie's expression even more frightened, and then ordered, "Ms. Taylor, please account for your whereabouts the past twenty-four hours."

Sophie looked questioningly at her PO, who returned her stare. "Answer the detective's question, Taylor."

"Yes, sir," she gulped, realizing she was being questioned as a suspect. This overwhelmed her so thoroughly that she was unable to figure out who the murder victim could be. One of her father's associates? A former client?

Sophie took a deep breath. "I, um, Wednesday night I left Grant's—"

"You left Grant's?" Marilyn interrupted. "Was Logan there?"

"Yes," Sophie confirmed. "I left Grant's apartment, and I walked around downtown for a few hours until I landed on my dad's doorstep." A blush feathered her high cheekbones and she continued, "We hadn't talked for over a year, but luckily he let me in. I spent the night here, and then we had some coffee the next morning."

"What time did you wake up Thursday morning—yesterday morning?" Marilyn inquired.

"It was kind of late," Sophie said. "Almost ten I think?"

"And what did you do then?"

"I came down to the kitchen and was surprised to find my dad still here. He took the morning off of work. We talked for a little bit"—she grimaced—"he told me yet again that my taste in men was horrible and I should have gone to work for him, blah, blah…" She met Marilyn's gaze and cleared her throat. "Sorry, that's probably irrelevant information. Anyway, I realized how late it was getting, and I needed to get to work to tell my boss I was quitting before, um, before…" Her voice drifted off and she looked at Jerry.

"Before what?" Marilyn prodded.

"Before Grant got there. I didn't want to see him."

"You and Grant work together?" Marilyn asked curiously.

"Yes, he got me a job on an architectural cruise." She sighed fondly. "And then he got me another job teaching psychology at DePaul. I start in a couple of weeks. But after what happened…" She looked down at her hands, twisting them nervously in her lap. "After I found out he was Logan's brother, well, I couldn't work with Grant anymore. I just wanted to quit and leave and never see him again."

"And did you manage to avoid Grant when you got to work?"

"No," Sophie replied, feeling a pang of sadness. "He was there."

Marilyn turned a page in her notebook. "What time was this?"

"Um, right around eleven, I think? The time our shift would normally start."

"What happened when you saw him?"

Another sigh. "He begged me to talk to him, but I couldn't. It, ah, hurt too much." She looked away. "I told my boss, Roger, that I was resigning, then I got the hell out of there."

"And what did Grant do?"

"Stayed on the ship, I guess. He had to work."

Marilyn nodded. "Where did you go next?"

"I went to DePaul to try to work on the syllabus for one of my classes."

"Can anyone verify that you were there?"

Sophie looked up, startled, and her heart rate increased. Anita was already in Spain—who could vouch for her? "Oh! Yes, the department secretary gave me the keys to the office I'm using. I was going to stay there all afternoon, but I wasn't getting anything done." Grant's pleading crystal eyes had haunted her all day, mixed in with distracting images of his brother's deep-blue gaze.

"So, I came back here. It was around three or so," Sophie added.

"Was your father here?"

"No. He got home around six-thirty, I think."

"So, you were here alone from three to six-thirty, then. What were you doing?"

Sophie looked down and bit her lip. She continued to wring her hands.

"Ms. Taylor?" Marilyn prompted. "What were you doing between three o'clock and six-thirty yesterday afternoon?"

Finally, Sophie lifted her eyes to meet the detective's, revealing her tears. "I was in my mother's room," she confessed quietly. "I was looking through some of her clothes, her jewelry, remembering when I was a kid and she would dress up to go out with my dad..." Her voice faded and a tear dropped onto her cream-colored skirt.

Jerry fought the urge to place a consoling hand on her arm. "When Taylor was in prison, her mother died," he explained.

Marilyn nodded, wondering how Sophie was going to take the news of yet another death.

"Ms. Taylor, I'm investigating the murder of someone you know, I'm afraid."

Sophie stared at the detective and blinked rapidly, trying to clear her eyes of tears.

"Logan Barberi was killed yesterday."

Sophie sat completely still. She thought of Logan's head bowed in her office, tears falling as he related the awful tales of his father's abuse. "What happened?" she managed.

"I can't say anything more until I interview all the suspects," Marilyn replied calmly. "Though the media is bound to get hold of this soon."

Sophie's muddled mind ticked through various thoughts and questions, one at a time. Quietly she asked, "Does Grant know?"

"I'm not sure. We're headed there next."

Sophie's eyes widened. "Is Grant a suspect, Detective?"

"Do you think he should be, Ms. Taylor?"

"No! I—I—I don't know." Sophie shakily drew her hand to her face, placing the heel of her palm against her forehead. Logan was dead! Logan was dead, and all she could think about was Grant. How would he react? Did he have motive to kill his brother? Could he be *capable* of murder? *No, never,* she thought. Not the man she knew. But did she know him really? What else had he been hiding from her?

"We'll need to interview your father now," Detective Fox said. "Check his story against yours, see if your alibi pans out."

Sophie sat up with a start. "Am *I* a suspect, Detective?"

"You certainly have motive, Ms. Taylor. The deceased's actions led you to prison, as I understand it."

"But I could never kill him!" she responded indignantly, then continued in a softer tone. "Logan was, well, he was trying to turn his life around. He was abused by his father—awful, horrible stuff—but he did everything he could to protect his little brother back then." She sniffed, feeling a lump in her throat. "To protect Grant."

Sophie stared off into the distance, thinking of Grant and how he would take the news—if it were indeed news.

"I'm an awful person," she said. "I can't believe I don't even feel that badly about Logan dying. All I can think about is Grant."

"You're probably in shock," Marilyn said. "You probably feel numb right now."

Sophie nodded. "I guess you have to notify lots of people about loved ones dying, huh?"

Marilyn gave a faint smile. "Probably not as many up in Lake County as the Chicago detectives have to contend with." Her green eyes pierced Sophie. "So, were you in love with Mr. Barberi, then?"

She had once thought so, but the man she truly loved was not Logan Barberi—she now knew that for sure.

"I'll have to pass on that question, Detective," Sophie said. "Just please find Logan's killer."

"Uh-oh, time for the PO's surprise inspection again!" Roger boomed, his voice full of amusement.

Jerry looked down at Madsen's boss. He was irritated with himself for forgetting the man's name, but given the outrageous number of parolees he supervised, he guessed it would be unreasonable to expect to remember all the details. And then there was the murder investigation weighing on his mind…

"Parole Officer Jerry Stone," he said formally, pumping Roger's hand.

"Yeah, I remember you, but it looks like you have no fucking clue who I am. It's Roger Eaton." Peering behind the taller man to find a sharp-dressed woman about his height, Roger inquired, "And who do we have here?"

Jerry stepped to the side and swept his arm toward Marilyn. "Detective Marilyn Fox of the Great Lakes Police, this is Roger Eaton, Grant Madsen's boss."

"Pleasure to meet you, sir."

"A detective, eh?" He nodded appreciatively. "So, what's Madsen done this time?"

Neither officer laughed at his joke, but Marilyn smiled pleasantly. "Where is Mr. Madsen, sir? We need to talk to him."

"Well, get in line, then," Roger brusquely retorted, gesturing to the bridge. "His uncle has been up there with him for awhile already."

Roger then turned and looked up to the bridge, but saw only Joe's silhouette outlined by the setting sun—no sign of Grant. "At least I *thought* Grant was up there with his uncle."

Marilyn pursed her lips. Her key suspect better not have gotten away before she had the chance to question him. "Stay here, Mr. Eaton," she commanded, heading up the stairs to the bridge. "We'll need to talk to you next."

Roger watched her scuttle up the stairs, admiring the alluring sway of her cute derriere before Jerry's body blocked his sweet view. Roger was left on deck with the uniformed police officer. They stared at each other awkwardly.

"So," Roger began, rocking back and forth on his heels. "What's *your* fucking deal?"

Arriving at the bridge, Marilyn was relieved to find a man curled up on the floor, soft moans of despair emanating from his coiled form. That had to be Madsen. Another man wearing a decorated Navy uniform turned to her as she entered.

"Detective Fox?" the older man inquired. His striking blue eyes caught her off guard.

"Um, you must be the uncle, sir? Joe Madsen?"

"Yes, ma'am, Commander Joseph Madsen." They grimly shook hands.

Hearing their voices, Grant looked up at the three adults blocking the doorway. A familiar man was shaking Joe's hand … Grant stared for a moment before registering that his parole officer was onboard. Why was Jerry here? Grant's fuzzy brain tried to understand what was happening.

"Thank you for looking after Grant, Officer Stone," Joe said as they shook hands.

"It's been my pleasure, sir," Jerry answered.

Marilyn studied the suspect, noticing the multihued bruise on the left side of his face. He swiped wet trails from his cheeks, focusing on Jerry and Joe, then he rested his penetrating gaze on her, tilting his head to the side, failing to recognize her.

Grant finally placed his hands on the deck and pushed his body into a squat, then upward to his full height. Even Marilyn was taken in by his dazzling aquamarine gaze.

"Officer Stone?" Grant's confused voice cut through the conversation.

"Madsen," Jerry acknowledged. "I see your uncle already told you about Logan?"

Grant's voice cracked. "Yes, sir."

Jerry cleared his throat. "This is Detective Marilyn Fox from the Great Lakes PD. She needs to ask you some questions."

Grant gave her a dumbfounded look. Joe watched him anxiously, wondering how he would react. Then Grant began nodding. "You think I did it," he said, glaring at Marilyn and Jerry. "You think I killed him! My own brother!"

Jerry stepped forward. "Madsen—"

"Fuck you!" Grant snarled. "Fuck all of you!"

"Grant!" Joe sharply admonished.

Seeing his uncle's disapproval, Grant felt the heat in his veins dissipate slightly, replaced by intense dread. His breaths came in panicked gasps, and he glanced back and forth from one appalled face to another. They were disgusted by him because he was part of *them*—the criminal element, the Mafia. He was born into evil. He knew it, and they knew it. It was in his blood.

"Just fucking arrest me and get it over with," Grant muttered. "You've already made up your minds about me anyway!" His eyes flared. "It's fucking useless to pretend I can make it out here. I clearly belong in *there,* with my father."

Grant looked at Joe, the only family member he had left. "They've taken *everything* from me!" He suppressed a cry. "They've taken everything," he continued, his raspy voice growing softer. "What's the difference if they take my freedom again? It doesn't matter anymore."

"Hey!" Joe crossed the bridge and grasped Grant's biceps, forcing him to look at him. "It matters to *me,* damn it! It tore me up when you were in prison, and I'm not going to let it happen again. Now you sit your ass down and you talk to the detective, and she will figure out that you're innocent—that you're a good man despite your bad family." Joe's imploring eyes locked on the matching blue of his nephew's, and he shook Grant with each word. "You stop this little pity party right now! You got it?"

Grant swallowed. Slowly he nodded, and his voice sounded more like himself as he replied, "Yes, sir."

Realizing he had his nephew in a vice grip, Joe released his hold and stepped back, trying to regain his bearings. He pointed to the seat by the controls and ordered, "Find some leather."

Grant quickly slid into the chair and folded his hands in his lap, his back perfectly straight, eyes forward.

He sat in his chair expectantly awaiting his interrogation, but Marilyn thought for a moment before she began. Madsen was probably furious with his brother for making him take the fall for the Great Lakes heist, but he also seemed devastated by his death.

"Mr. Madsen, um, Commander Madsen, I'd like you to wait down below while we question your nephew."

"Yes, ma'am." He nodded.

"Just tell them the truth, Grant, and you'll be okay."

"Yes, sir."

When Joe left, Marilyn sat on the console in order to be eye-level with the suspect. She wanted him to feel at ease, but he certainly looked anything but peaceful at the moment. After a perfunctory reading of his Miranda rights, she said, "Mr. Madsen, I'd like to ask you some questions. Are you capable of responding at this time?"

Surmising she must think he was a total wimp, he quickly nodded. "Yes, ma'am."

"Then please account for your activities the past two days."

Jerry watched Grant carefully as he responded.

"Starting when, ma'am?"

"How about Wednesday night?"

"Um, Wednesday night was when Sophie—Sophie Taylor? Do you know her?"

"Yes, Mr. Madsen. We were at her father's questioning her before we came here."

Grant was incredulous. "Questioning *her?* Surely you don't believe Sophie killed Lo, ma'am."

"I've learned not to rule out any possibilities too soon. But it surprises you that we questioned Sophie Taylor? You think she's innocent?"

"Of course she's innocent," Grant said. "She's one of the most honorable individuals I've ever met."

Marilyn hesitated a second before continuing with the next statement that flowed naturally from her detective's brain. It would be a potentially low blow to pit the two suspects against each other, but such a technique often worked to nail the killer. And Marilyn always got the killer. Taking a deep breath, she went for it. "Funny, she didn't say the same thing about you, Mr. Madsen. In fact, when I asked Ms. Taylor if she thought you should be a suspect, she didn't give me a clear answer. I think she believes you killed your brother."

Grant's face fell, and he dropped his head with hopelessness and shame. Sophie thought he was capable of *murder?*If he hadn't realized it before, he now knew he'd lost her forever.

Jerry's mouth tightened as Grant folded over in agony. Marilyn had taken some creative liberties with that last statement.

Marilyn felt a little guilty watching Grant react to her cruel words, but like a good detective, she soldiered on. "Do you wish to change your earlier statement about Sophie being completely innocent?" she asked.

"No, ma'am," Grant choked out.

"Okay then. You were saying about Wednesday night?"

Grant closed his eyes and nodded, clenching his teeth. "She, um, Sophie, cooked me dinner, and we were having, uh, dessert when Logan showed up."

Scribbling notes, Marilyn urged, "Go on."

"Sophie had just told me about the man who stashed money and guns in her office, leading to her arrest, but I had no idea that man was Logan. And Sophie had no idea Logan was my brother. That all changed when he showed up. We all figured out the connection—and Sophie ran out of there as fast as she could.

"Logan actually didn't know Sophie went to prison and lost her license because of him. What a freaking idiot." Then realizing he'd insulted a dead man, Grant added, "Sorry."

"You were angry with your brother for what he did to Sophie?"

"I was furious, ma'am," Grant said.

"You two had a fight?"

"Yes, ma'am."

"He gave you that shiner?"

Grant brushed his fingertips across the bruise, and suddenly his eyes got big. "I know how this looks, but I didn't kill him, I swear!"

"Relax, Mr. Madsen," Marilyn said. "I was already aware of the bruise from Officer Stone. You told him about it on Thursday morning, remember?"

Grant nodded, relieved.

"Did your brother hit you anywhere else, Mr. Madsen?"

Grant reluctantly nodded again. "Yeah, on my side."

"May I see the damage?" Marilyn asked. It was a routine question, but she could not deny her eagerness to see the sculpted body hidden beneath his white button-down shirt.

Grant loosened his shirt from his black pants and lifted the shirt-tail to reveal an angry deep-purple contusion over his left ribcage.

Jerry whistled through his teeth. "Maybe you should see a doctor about that, Madsen."

"I'm okay," he countered, tucking his shirt back in. His father had done worse to him as a kid.

"The bruises on Mr. Barberi's face—you gave those to him?"

"Yes, ma'am," he said.

"Did you hurt him anywhere else?"

Grant looked sick. "I punched him in his stomach once, but he probably didn't even feel it. He was the muscle in the family—he fought for a living." As Marilyn noted this information, in a small voice Grant asked, "Did Lo feel any pain, ma'am?"

"I don't really know." Taking a deep breath she added, "The autopsy will tell us more."

The coroner had informed Marilyn that time of death was somewhere between 0900 and 1300 on Thursday morning. They would likely narrow that window after the autopsy, so her next questions about Wednesday night were crucial.

"What happened after you and Logan fought?"

"I told him to leave, but he wouldn't. Then I told him …" Grant stared out at the water for a few moments. "I told him I wished he was dead."

Marilyn watched his eyes well up with tears again. *Complicated grief*, she thought. She didn't know if Grant would ever recover from Logan's death, given his last words to his brother. And both Sophie and Grant were either not guilty of murder or they were the dumbest criminals known to humankind. Between Sophie informing the detective that Logan needed to "go down" and Grant telling her he wished his brother was dead, both parolees had completely shot themselves in the foot.

"We all say things we regret," Marilyn offered, trying to get the suspect back on track. "I suppose Logan left your apartment after that comment?"

Grant swiped at his cheek and nodded. "Yes, ma'am, he left." He took several deep breaths, trying to compose himself. "After that I tried to go to sleep, but I finally gave up around oh-five-hundred and went for a run on the lake. I took a shower, and I still didn't know what to do. That's when I went to see Officer Stone."

"And *I* told you to go to work," Jerry chimed in. "Did you do that?"

"Yes, sir. I came straight to work, and I was here until my shift finished at twenty-hundred."

"What time did you arrive here yesterday morning?" Marilyn inquired.

"Uh, however long it takes to walk here from the courthouse—maybe nine-twenty-five or so?"

"Can anyone verify that you were here?"

Grant nodded vigorously. "Yes, ma'am. Roger was here too."

"We'll be speaking to him shortly to check that out." Marilyn snapped her notepad shut and returned it to her jacket pocket. She looked into Grant's troubled eyes. "So, Mr. Madsen, despite you having two powerful motives, it appears you have an alibi for the time period in which your brother was murdered."

Grant's shoulders drooped and he exhaled loudly. He looked out the window to the deck below, finding Joe looking up at him. Grant nodded, trying to reassure his uncle.

Marilyn bit her lip. "I'm wondering, who do you think might have killed your brother?"

"I don't know, ma'am. Joe thought it might be somebody Lo owed money to. He, uh…" Grant looked down. "He had a gambling problem."

"Any ideas who he owed money to?"

"You found him near Great Lakes, right?" Grant asked. When Marilyn nodded, he said, "I was wondering about the lieutenant who won a hundred-thousand in a poker game at Angelo's club that night two years ago. That was the money I was supposed to go and steal back when I screwed up and got arrested."

"Yes, Officer Stone was telling me you were extorted by Logan to pull that crime? That he threatened to kill your Uncle Joe unless you complied?"

Grant swallowed, looking at Jerry. "Yes, ma'am."

"Why didn't you report that to your attorney? Or to the prosecutor?"

"It's water under the bridge, Detective."

"But it's not too late to see if you can get your sentence revised. Perhaps you could even get your parole dropped if you get a sympathetic judge."

Grant contemplated her words, then aimed a sardonic half-smile at Jerry. "But then I wouldn't get to see Officer Stone every week, ma'am. I wouldn't get to be slammed up against the wall, handcuffed, drug tested. I wouldn't get to hear how I better not hurt Sophie…" His smile abruptly vanished. He had indeed hurt Sophie, just as Jerry predicted.

"It *does* sound like good times you've shared with Officer Stone," Marilyn teased. "I can see why you wouldn't want to give that up." Then she advised, "I want you to be careful in the next few weeks, Mr. Madsen. Until we find Logan's killer, nobody is safe."

Grant nodded, looking again at Joe on the deck below. "I think my Uncle Joe will stay with me for a few days, at least."

"I need to get down there to interview your boss," Marilyn said. "Well, Mr. Madsen, I'll keep in touch as the investigation continues. Take care of yourself."

"Yes, ma'am."

After Marilyn left the bridge, Jerry turned to Grant. "Madsen, what Detective Fox said about Taylor—it wasn't entirely accurate."

"Sir?"

"When we arrived at her house, I guess all she knew was we were there to question her about a murder, and for some reason she thought *you* were the one who'd been killed. She was freaked out, but once she found out you weren't the murder victim, she was totally relieved. She even, uh, gave me a hug." Jerry blushed.

For one blessed moment Grant felt the heavy load, which had been crushing him from the second he found out about Logan's death, lift off his chest. Sophie still cared about him!

"Are you trying to steal my girlfriend, sir?"

Jerry grinned. "I just thought you'd want to know."

"I did. You just made one of the worst days in my life a little better," Grant replied, staring solemnly at Jerry. "Thank you."

They both looked down at Marilyn talking to Roger and Joe.

Grant sighed. "I guess Joe and I will have to plan the funeral."

33. Casting a Pall

Grant had not seen his uncle in his dress blues since he was a teenager, and he felt a childlike awe at how distinguished and powerful Joe looked in his commander's uniform: gleaming silver buttons and all the insignia and honors befitting the Vietnam War hero. No longer a lieutenant, Grant was relegated to the black suit, light-blue shirt, and black tie Joe had purchased him for the occasion.

Uncle and nephew—father and adopted son—walked the center aisle of St. Monica's basilica. Joe had not left Grant's side since Friday afternoon, and he continued to hover, guiding Grant toward one of the front pews on this Monday afternoon. Grant could not help but scan the mourners scattered across the pews, but there was no sign of her. He knew Sophie was unlikely to attend Logan's funeral, but he searched for her all the same.

"Are you sure you can do this?" Joe asked as they were seated.

Grant sighed. His uncle had been second-guessing their decision to serve as pallbearers once the mass was finished. "I have to do it."

"No, you don't," Joe countered.

"I already know you don't like me near my uncle and cousin," Grant assured him.

"That's not what I'm worried about." Grant looked at him quizzically. "It's an honor to be a pallbearer, Grant. But it's also … it's tough. It stays with you. For a long time."

Grant looked down at his hands, knowing immediately what his uncle referred to. Joe had been a pallbearer at Karita's funeral, while twelve-year-old

Grant watched from afar, too young to participate. Seventeen-year-old Logan and fifteen-year-old Carlo had joined Joe in carrying his mother's coffin, though, along with three other men from the family. Grant had never felt more alone.

"I *want* it to stay with me," he quietly responded.

In the narthex of the church, Angelo stood in the shadows and watched his son haughtily stare at the pews in front of him, a small smile on his face as he observed Grant conversing with Joe. Just as Carlo shifted forward, ready to pounce, Angelo stepped out and caught him by the elbow.

Surprised, Carlo hissed, "Let go."

"I told you not to go anywhere near Grant," Angelo said. "What part of *maintain a low profile* don't you understand?"

Carlo's eyes smoldered. He *hated* a low profile. He was the reason behind this funeral, and he craved the spotlight to showcase his cunning and bravery. Instead, he had to slink in the shadows. It was so unfair!

"Grant Pants has no fucking clue, *padre*," Carlo reasoned. "He's too blinded by his pussy tears to see what really happened."

Angelo slid his firm grasp up his son's arm a few inches and clutched the skin and bone there tightly. Carlo gasped and his father knew he'd located the scar tissue on his son's arm—where he'd been shot twenty-two years ago, when he'd been ten years old. When he'd screwed everything up for Enzo.

"Grant has a college degree," Angelo whispered.

Carlo clenched his teeth. *This again.* His father would never shut up about him dropping out of college.

"Don't underestimate him. Once things settle down, he might figure out it was you."

"*He* should be the one in prison, charged with murdering his brother," Carlo grumbled. "Anyway, I can't stay away from him if we carry the fucking casket together."

"It would be too obvious if you backed out now, and that's why you're going to remain a pallbearer. But play it cool. That broad over there is the detective investigating the murder, remember?"

Carlo shifted his gaze and caught a glimpse of reddish-brown hair. The woman subtly scanned the funeral guests, taking in everything. Carlo swallowed hard.

"Unless you want to end up like Enzo, I suggest you take my advice," Angelo hissed, squeezing the scar one last time before releasing his son's elbow.

Carlo straightened his black suit-jacket and whispered, "Will Uncle Enzo be here today?"

Angelo sighed. "Word is he's in solitary for hitting a guard—the one who told him his son was murdered."

Carlo felt his neck tense, as if his uncle's strong hands were holding him by the scruff of the neck like they had when he was ten, when Enzo found him in the Fanocelli house. Carlo's one regret in murdering Logan was the possibility that Enzo might find out he was the killer. He knew he was a dead man if that ever happened.

"He's going to miss his own son's funeral," Angelo muttered.

But Enzo's grandson would not be missing the funeral. Ben entered at the rear of the church, a few steps ahead of his mother, who frowned when she saw her son making a beeline toward his relatives.

"Ben," Angelo said. "*Come è il mio* favorite sixteen year old?"

Ben closed his tired eyes as his great-uncle wrapped him in his strong arms. "Fine."

Carlo grabbed the boy next, thumping him on the back. "You haven't been over to the compound all weekend, *ragazzo*."

"Sorry," Ben said, glancing furtively behind him as his mother approached.

"Ashley." Angelo nodded respectfully at the blond-haired woman. "My condolences."

She stared warily at the men, and Carlo added, "We have seats saved for you next to us."

Ashley nervously wrung her hands. Meeting Angelo's coal-black gaze, she pleaded, "Please, um, Godfather. Please give us some time. We need some time alone…some time to grieve."

A flash of anger coursed through the Mafia don. Ben was part of the family—the only connection left to his beloved Logan, now that Carlo had so unceremoniously wiped his godson from this earth. But the fear and worry evident in Ashley's begging blue eyes dissolved his anger into a feeling that bordered on sympathy. Angelo's own son had caused Ashley and Ben such pain, and perhaps they deserved some time to recover.

"Of course, Ashley." Angelo smiled and took a slight step backward. "We are here for you and Ben, though. Please know that."

"Thank you." Turning to her son, she gently urged, "C'mon, Ben."

"But I want to sit with the family," Ben argued with a twinge of whine.

Carlo jumped in. "Yeah, we need to stay together."

Angelo placed his arm across Carlo's chest. "It's okay, Ben," he assured him. "Go with your mother. We'll see you after the mass."

Ben hesitated for a moment, then followed his mother down the center aisle.

Marilyn watched this interaction between the Barberi men, wishing she could've heard what they said. Her interviews with Angelo and Carlo Barberi had not been fruitful, and she sensed they were hiding something. Her investigation was at a standstill, and with each passing hour the odds of finding the killer decreased substantially. Former Lieutenant Adam Gottlieb, the officer who'd won money from Angelo's club and had stashed it in the bar near Great Lakes, had been discharged from the Navy following Grant's break-in, and no one had heard from him since. He was her only remaining lead, and it was turning up cold.

Swiftly passing, Ashley barely registered seeing the detective—the woman who had informed her and Ben of Logan's death two days ago. She'd witnessed Ben begin to destroy their apartment upon learning of his father's murder, furiously throwing books and vases and candles against the wall before collapsing to the floor in a heap, weeping uncontrollably.

Ashley blocked Ben's breakdown from her mind as she moved toward the one man who seemed like a haven amidst the Barberi family. She had noticed his closely cropped black hair the moment she entered the church, and his presence calmed her immediately.

"Grant?" She approached his pew with her son in tow.

He glanced up and drew her into a hug. "Ashley."

She melted into his strong arms, instantly comforted by his masculine sandalwood scent and tender yet firm hold. She then stepped back to allow uncle and nephew to reunite. They had not seen each other since Logan's death.

Grant studied his nephew, and Ben felt a hitch in his throat upon meeting his uncle's desolate stare. He averted his gaze, angrily stuffing his fists into his stupid black suit-jacket, feeling strangled by the even dumber black tie.

"I don't know about you, Ben, but I've been a total mess since Friday. I, um, I can't stop crying," Grant said.

Ben was astonished that his uncle—a grown man, a man who'd been in the Navy, who had gone to prison—would admit to *crying* like a little boy. But as Grant's eyes began to mist over with tears, Ben's welled up also.

"I'm so sorry, Ben." Grant sighed, emotion coloring his smooth voice. "I'm sorry we both missed out on having Lo in our lives. But I do know he loved you, his only son—he loved you so much, Ben."

Ben took a shuddering breath and shuffled forward, pulled into the waiting embrace by his uncle's soothing words. Watching the tall man clinch the boy in his arms, both Ashley and Joe felt a lump in their throats.

Grant took a deep breath as he gestured behind him. "I want you to meet my Uncle Joe. Um, Joe Madsen, this is Ashley Fredrickson and Ben Barberi."

Joe shook Ashley's hand. "I wish we'd shared the pleasure of meeting before today."

"Me too." Sadness filled her eyes. "I wish Logan would have stayed with you, instead of running to Angelo. Maybe we wouldn't be at his funeral right now."

Ben narrowed his eyes at his mother—why was she ragging on Angelo like that? "I deeply regret letting Logan go," Joe said. "But if he'd stayed with me, he might never have met you, Ashley. And then you wouldn't have created this wonderful young man here."

Ben shifted from one foot to another, embarrassed with three sets of adult eyes trained on him. Joe offered his hand, and Ben extended his tentatively. "I've heard so many good things about you from Grant, Ben," Joe said, smiling warmly.

Taken aback by the kind words, Ben abruptly withdrew his hand and returned it to his pocket. Remembering his late night with Nick and Dylan, Ben hoped he didn't smell like pot now that he was standing by the uniformed man.

"Please join us," Grant offered, and Joe and Grant scooted down the bench to make room for mother and son.

The priest, dressed in a black cope, began singing the introit, signaling the start of the requiem mass. Grant laid his hand reassuringly on Ben's knee, and both looked to the altar, where the coffin rested.

The priest welcomed the congregation, then began a prayer. Mired in choking sadness, Grant was barely aware of what was happening.

Ashley rose and made her way to the pulpit for the first reading. She drew a deep breath, leaned toward the microphone, and with a trembling voice began reading from Romans 12.

> Let love be without pretense. Avoid what is evil; stick to what is good. In brotherly love let your feelings of deep affection for one another come to expression and regard others as more important than yourself. In the service of the Lord, work not halfheartedly but with conscientiousness and an eager spirit. Be joyful in hope, persevere in hardship; keep praying regularly; share with any of God's holy people who are in need; look for opportunities to be hospitable. Bless your persecutors; never curse them, bless them. Rejoice with others when they rejoice and be sad with those in sorrow. Give the same consideration to all others alike. Pay

no regard to social standing, but meet humble people on their own terms. Do not congratulate yourself on your own wisdom. Never pay back evil with evil, but bear in mind the ideals that all regard with respect. As much as possible, and to the utmost of your ability, be at peace with everyone.

Carlo tensed beside his father, then quickly recomposed his face in a look of appropriate sadness. Ashley's eyes glistened with tears as she returned to the pew.

The priest began the responsorial psalm, and Grant's mind drifted from present to past and back. He tried to focus on the priest's voice, on the words of the twenty-third Psalm, on the steadying presence of his uncle beside him—but he kept remembering. He was twelve years old again, attending his mother's funeral at the exact same church.

Grant had stood outside the church, alone in his grief. The big, strong men had just eased Karita's coffin into the hearse, and Grant watched Uncle Joe gruffly take Uncle Angelo aside, appearing to exchange tense words. Logan snuck away from the hearse and miserably slouched against the stone wall.

Carefully, timidly, falteringly, Grant crept toward his brother. He had not seen Logan for four whole years, and the seventeen year old was now huge, probably six feet tall, towering over Grant.

"Lo?" His voice sounded frustratingly small and needy.

Logan looked down. "Hey."

They stood quietly for a few moments, neither knowing what to say. Grant hesitantly backed up and leaned his shorter body against the wall, nestling himself beside Logan. Their substitute fathers continued to quarrel near the hearse, and when Joe pointed his index finger toward Angelo's chest, two beefy men stepped forward to flank the don.

"Your Uncle Joe looks pretty pissed off," Logan said.

"He's your uncle too," Grant pointed out.

"Nah, he wants nothing to do with me."

Grant frowned. He'd often overheard his mother and Joe lament losing Logan to Angelo, and it seemed more like Logan wanted nothing to do with them. Gulping, Grant asked, "Lo? How come you didn't visit Mom in the hospital?"

Logan exhaled loudly and licked his bottom lip. Grant wondered why his brother seemed to have trouble breathing.

"She kept asking for you," Grant added, having no idea how his words sliced through his brother's heart.

"I didn't know she was going to die!" Logan said, clenching his fists.

"Oh."

Grant chewed on his lip, wondering if he should ask his next question. Logan was in a horrible mood, but Grant didn't know when he would see him again.

Finally mustering the courage, he asked, "Lo?"

"What?"

"Um, will you, um … will you come live with me and Joe now? Please?"

The lines around Logan's mouth tightened. "I can't."

"Uncle Ange won't let you?"

"No, that's not it. I, uh, I can't live with you 'cause," Logan swallowed guiltily, "'cause I have to go to juvie. My sentence starts tomorrow."

"What's juvie?"

"Dunno. Juvenile detention or something like that. It's like jail for kids."

Gasping, Grant asked, "Do you gotta go to jail with Dad?"

Logan smiled at his worried brother. "No, he's in an adult facility. Juvie's different."

After a couple of seconds Grant asked, "Why you gotta go?"

Kicking at a rock, Logan looked down. Eventually he muttered, "'Cause I got caught selling drugs."

Grant's mouth formed a small "o" and he remarked automatically, "Drugs are bad."

Logan found himself smiling. "That's right, Grantey. Drugs are bad."

Joe hollered for Grant, interrupting the brothers' conversation. Looking up at Logan, Grant whispered urgently, "I gotta go."

"'Kay." Logan looked really sad. "Be good, Grant."

Grant nodded solemnly, and Logan's arms gathered him in a firm embrace. Suffocated by Logan's brawny hold, Grant barely heard him say once more, "Be good."

Feeling his uncle's hand patting his knee brought Grant back to the present. He looked around through blurry eyes, taking in the cream, blue, and gold of the church. He realized he was crying openly. Joe gently nudged him, handing him his handkerchief, which Grant scooped up gratefully.

Arriving late, a woman in a simple black dress and a not-so-simple wide-brimmed black hat quietly crept down the side aisle, walking on the balls of her feet to prevent her patent-leather heels from clicking on the floor. She slid into an empty pew at the rear of the church and breathed out, relieved that she seemed to go unnoticed. However, Detective Fox smirked when she saw the woman glide gracefully into her seat. She'd been wondering if Sophie Taylor would attend.

Feeling protected by her ridiculously large hat, Sophie took in the somber surroundings. Her eyes swept over the mourners sitting quietly as the cantor sang, and as soon as she determined her father had not followed her here, she allowed her shoulders to drop, releasing the tension she'd been carrying the past two days. She welcomed a brief respite from the conflict with her father, who had exploded upon learning of her relationship with Grant. He had forbidden her to attend Logan's funeral, and she prayed he would not discover her presence.

Noting the closed coffin near the altar, Sophie felt a sickening heaviness. Such a wasted life. Logan had been only thirty-five years old. As a woman with twenty-nine years already under her belt, Sophie could not imagine having only six more to live. Prison had stalled her goals, and she still had so much she wanted to accomplish...

Her eyes wandered to the left of the altar, and she saw the back of his head about twenty rows in front of her. She held her breath and instinctively slouched down in the pew. That perfectly shaped skull, covered in buzzed black hair, could be none other than Grant. Her father had warned her to stay away from him, and she desperately wanted to follow his advice. But she couldn't. She just had to see him—she had to know how he was coping with the loss of his brother. It must have devastated him.

Sophie watched as he protectively draped his arm across the shoulders of a boy sitting next to him. To the boy's right was a blond woman, who anxiously turned to her son. In profile, Sophie recognized her from the ship. Ashley was her name?

The priest gestured to the congregation, and all stood on cue as the priest sang the antiphon, wishing everlasting rest for the recently departed.

Sophie clenched the church program in her hand. She remembered Logan's edgy deep-blue eyes, darting around her office, avoiding her stare, fighting off tears as he told her stories from his painful childhood. She hoped Logan had finally found some rest.

The crowd returned to sitting or kneeling as several men made their way to the center aisle and toward the coffin. Grant and the boy, who must be his nephew, were among them, as well as a man dressed in a military uniform, who must be Grant's uncle. Sophie thought she recognized Angelo Barberi in the mix as well.

The six men arranged themselves around the raised coffin—Joe, Grant, and Ben on one side, and Angelo, Carlo, and Tank on the other. Angelo glanced at Tank, the wrong sixth man. *It should be Enzo*, he thought. Angelo felt the familiar hatred when he aimed his icy stare at the back of his son's head. Carlo had taken his brother from him, and now he'd stolen his godson too.

The men hoisted the coffin over their shoulders, attempting to accommodate the shorter sixteen year old among them. Feeling the weight of his brother's body on his shoulder, Grant's knees almost buckled. It wasn't only the physical weight burdening him, but also the emotional load—the burden of never feeling good enough for his older brother to want to be with him, and the weight of his brother's dysfunctional addictions, which Grant had been helpless to fight. Logan may have failed Grant, but Grant believed he had failed him in return. The heavy loss crushed his fragile spirit, and he cried once again.

As the subdued group proceeded down the aisle, Sophie's eyes never left Grant. He looked devastatingly handsome in his black suit and tie, but what took her breath away were his glistening tears. She longed to touch him, to try to comfort him, but he passed her row without a glance in her direction. She looked at her hands in her lap. Maybe she'd missed her chance with him. Maybe it was too late.

Once the men placed the coffin in the hearse, they dispersed, preparing to drive to the cemetery for the burial.

Grant, Joe, Ben, and Ashley stood in a foursome. Eyeing the corner of the building where his brother had hugged him eighteen years ago, Grant felt pulled to that spot. "Um, Joe? I need a minute."

"Sure, Grant. Take all the time you need."

He approached the grassy spot, then leaned his back against the stone and allowed his eyes to flutter shut. Grant was *so* tired, yet standing here also infused him with some sort of spiritual energy. He felt closer to Logan in this spot.

Ashley watched Grant retreat. "I guess it would be hell to lose your only sibling," she mused. "Still, I'm kind of surprised how destroyed Grant seems to be, especially after what Lo did to him."

Joe studied her curiously. "What Lo did to him?"

"You know, forcing him to pull that robbery."

Ben morphed from bored teenager to piqued young man, and he leaned in to hear their conversation.

"What do you mean?" Joe asked. "*Who* forced Grant to steal that money?"

"You don't know?" Ashley's voice lilted with surprise. "You don't know about Logan's threat if Grant didn't pull that job?"

"I assure you I have no idea what you're referring to, Ashley."

She stared at Grant's uncle. He'd never told him? Why? Glancing at the man slumped against the church wall, Ashley stammered, "Um, maybe I—I shouldn't tell you. Maybe he should—"

"Tell me, Ashley. Tell me what Logan did."

His commanding voice startled her. Meeting Joe's strong stare, Ashley confessed, "Logan told Grant they would kill you if he didn't help them rob that club."

Joe blinked several times, gazing at Ashley and then over at Grant.

"You're lying!" Ben hissed, his eyes narrowing with rage. "My dad would never do that!"

"Ben, I'm sorry," Ashley placed her hand on his shoulder, but he quickly shrugged it off. "But it's true. Logan admitted it to me himself."

"No!" Ben retorted, sounding younger than his age. "You know what? I can't take this shit anymore!" He pivoted and furiously strode away, heading toward Carlo and Angelo.

Ashley drew in her breath. "Should I go after him?"

"Just let him be for awhile, Ashley. Give him some space." Joe sighed sadly, still shaking off Ashley's news. "His father wasn't all that different. Looks like Ben inherited Logan's short fuse."

"Don't I know it," Ashley said.

Joe glanced at Grant, still glued to the wall, looking down at the grass. His heart felt heavy, realizing his nephew's sacrifice for him. He guiltily remembered yelling at him at the courthouse visitation booth before his sentencing hearing, feeling utterly disappointed that his nephew had flushed his future down the toilet. Grant had silently absorbed his uncle's tirade, never saying one word about what led him down that dark path.

After everyone had filed out, Sophie emerged from the church, self-consciously adjusting her hat. Her eyes nervously skimmed the crowd, and she bit her lip when she didn't see him. She knew she should probably leave.

Be good, Grant. Logan's voice reverberated in his head, and Grant forced himself to open his eyes. He looked back toward the entrance to the church and noticed a young woman standing there, looking for someone among the lingering guests. Her wide-brimmed hat obscured her face, but Grant knew that lithe, sexy figure. He pushed his body off the wall and stared at her, wondering what she would do next.

With a frustrated sigh, Sophie turned to leave but stopped short when she saw Grant standing by the corner of the church, his eyes bearing down on her. She nervously brushed her hands down the sides of her dress. If she followed her father's advice, she would turn right now and flee. But seeing Grant's mournful expression, she knew there was no way to flee from him. Quite the opposite. Those soulful eyes sucked her to him like a magnet.

Making sure he was still waiting for her, she took a tentative first step and then swiftly crossed to him, holding her hat on her head with one hand.

Sophie came to rest right in front of Grant, the tension so palpable she was almost grateful the wide brim of her hat blocked most of her view. Grant was not so grateful for her obscured face, and he gently reached out to touch the black fabric, his lips curling into a small grin at the ostentatious head-covering.

Peeking up at his amused expression, Sophie gave an apologetic shrug and swept the hat off her head, freeing her strawberry curls to rest on her shoulders. His eyes remained moist with tears, and he seemed to stop breathing as he fixed them on her. She could not take her eyes off his tortured face.

When they'd first met, Grant had reached out in her time of need to swathe her in a hug, providing immense comfort. Sophie knew she must now return the favor. He was hurting deeply. Her trembling hand reached up to caress his cheek. Their eyes remained locked as she gently wiped away a tear. Then she dropped her hand and stepped into his body, wrapping her arms around his lean waist.

Grant had been frozen, desperately wanting to touch her but afraid to do so. When she melded her body into his, he shuddered with relief and immediately enfolded her in his arms, wrapping her up like the most precious gift he'd ever received. He was stunned that she'd returned to him, and despite his utter desolation at losing Logan, he felt like the luckiest man on earth.

Sophie's cheek rested against his chest and she sighed contentedly, inhaling his characteristic scent. Withdrawal symptoms for the drug otherwise known as Grant quickly abated.

Striding toward his Lexus, Carlo's steely black gaze swept across the lingering mourners, wondering if anyone was admiring his sweet ride. He caught a glimpse of a couple by the corner of the church. That was no platonic hug of sympathy. This was something much more.

"Hold on, Tank," he called, halting the big man from sliding into the passenger seat. His eyes glued on the couple, Carlo took a few steps forward, observing their embrace.

Tank joined his boss in gaping at the couple, and felt a pang of longing. He'd felt the same way about Irene, the woman who turned out to be a fucking undercover cop. He was lucky to be alive after that.

"I already got Meat tailing Grant after the burial," Carlo whispered. "And that smokin'-hot chick he's hugging—I want *you* to find out who in the hell she is."

"Okay, boss," Tank responded agreeably.

Suddenly a Mercedes Benz squealed into the church parking lot, and a man leapt out, almost before it stopped, and stomped toward the church. He searched the crowd, then stormed toward Grant and the woman as Carlo and Tank looked on.

"Sophie!" Will yelled.

She instantly stepped away from Grant, her eyes widening with alarm.

"What the *hell* are you doing here, young lady?" After glaring at his daughter, he trained his hostile gaze on Grant, who anxiously bit his lip.

"Dad!" Sophie said. "I—I had to come. You don't understand."

"To hell I don't! You *want* to return to prison, don't you? You're doing this just to spite me. You just can't let go of that criminal Logan Barberi."

"This has nothing to do with him!" Sophie countered. "Or you … I came here for Grant."

Will turned to glare at him. Placing his face inches from Grant's, he jabbed his finger into Grant's chest. "You're just like your brother! You stay away from my daughter, you got it?"

Completely embarrassed, Sophie looked at the ground, but Grant met Mr. Taylor's wild-eyed stare. "I won't hurt her, sir."

"What's going on here?" Joe interrupted, coming to stand by Grant's side.

"Oh, so now you got a military man on your payroll too, huh?"

Grant stared at Will incredulously, and Sophie gasped. "Dad! That's Grant's uncle!"

Will was frantic. "You're not safe here, Sophie. Come home with me now."

"Yes," Joe said evenly, stepping in front of his bewildered nephew. "Perhaps you should go home."

Shooting Joe and then Grant an evil glare, Will warned, "Leave my daughter out of whatever you've got going on here." He grabbed her wrist and yanked Sophie away.

She had not seen her father so angry or shaken in years. Sophie looked over her shoulder and mouthed *Sorry* before allowing herself to be carted away like an errant schoolgirl caught drinking at a high-school kegger.

As Joe watched the father and daughter exit, Grant took his head in his hands, feeling as if he'd been hit by a truck. "So, now you've met Sophie," Grant said.

"And that was some first meeting," Joe said. After a moment they shared a smirk.

Carlo took it all in without moving a muscle, fascinated by the soap opera playing out before his eyes.

Tank grinned. "So, my assignment is already done then, boss."

"What do you mean?"

"That guy who came to haul that chick outta here? I'd recognize him anywhere—Will Taylor. That must be his daughter or something. You asked me to find out who she was. Well, there you go. Chick Taylor." He smiled smugly.

"How do you know the guy's name?"

Tank gave Carlo a curious stare. "Huh, I'm surprised you don't know. I guess you don't work that side of town. C'mon, I'll tell you on the ride over."

Both men slid into Carlo's car, and he gunned it, heading to the cemetery. As Tank began to talk, a wicked grin spread across Carlo's dark face.

34. Family Tree

The amber liquid swirled against the thick rectangular glass as Grant, sitting alone in his apartment early Monday evening, tilted the unopened bottle in his lap. Staring intently at the bottle's label, he heard his own unsteady voice read aloud, "José Cuervo."

So, here he was again: contemplating opening the damn bottle, pondering whether or not to give into temptation. Should he allow the Barberis' clutches to advance along one more branch of the family tree, like creeping ivy—strangling the solid trunk and weighing down the limbs until they were all destroyed? Should he open the bottle? Should he accept his fate as a Barberi man?

Joe had been behaving strangely ever since they returned from the cemetery this afternoon, and when he'd decided to help Roger with his last cruises of the day, Grant had told him he was too tired to join him. But the truth was Grant had wanted to be alone—alone with his hidden bottle of tequila, alone just like he'd been three nights ago when he'd lost Sophie. Since then even more devastating events had occurred, and he was back in the same place—back to square one, back to holding the bottle in his trembling hands, teetering on the edge of obliterating his mind and body with alcohol.

Had his father, Enzo, ever hesitated like this, wondering if he should take that first drink? Grant doubted it.

After Sophie had rejected him on the ship three mornings ago, running away in fear, he had purchased a bottle of tequila on his way home. If he couldn't have

Sophie, at least he could have the memories they shared. She had introduced him to tequila, after all.

But his corruption had actually begun long before he met Sophie. Grant frowned as he trained his gaze on the liquor. A sterile, solitary shot of tequila now would be nothing like the experience he had shared with Sophie, though he'd still get the mind-numbing effects of the alcohol.

Although he longed to be numb, a small part of him did have to admit that his circumstances with Sophie had improved. She'd attended Logan's funeral—not for Logan, but for *him*. And, miraculously, she'd hugged him. But would she ever look at him and see Grant Madsen? Or was he doomed to be Grant Barberi, tagged and weighed down by fear and mistrust?

He held the neck of the bottle tightly. Alcohol had a long and storied role in his family. He could remember that history in the making.

Seven-year-old Grant lay splayed out across his bed, making swooshing light-saber sounds as Luke Skywalker and Darth Vader action figures battled in his hands. Across the room, Logan made his own noises—frustrated sighs as he slogged through his sixth-grade science homework. Suddenly their father burst in, a folded belt coiled in his hand.

"All right, which one of you hid my vodka?" Enzo snarled, his wild black stare threatening each boy in turn.

Logan's surprised gaze darted from the instrument of punishment in his father's hand to his brother's wide, frightened eyes, which flashed with obvious guilt. Shit. Logan knew in an instant Grant was to blame for their father's missing bottle.

Enzo's eyes narrowed as he fumed. "Goddamn it! You stay out of my stuff, you hear? If I don't hear a confession this instant, you'll both get it!"

He raised his right arm in a wide arc, preparing to strike his trembling younger son when Logan shouted urgently, "It was me!"

Enzo swiftly spun around.

Gulping, Logan shakily admitted again, "I did it."

Grant drew his hand to his mouth, strangled by fear. What was Lo doing? Grant should be the one confessing, not Logan. But his throat was suddenly tight, and he was unable to squeak a sound.

"Logan," Enzo began, his voice smoother now that he had the situation under control. "Tell Grant where you hid the bottle, and then he'll go put it back while I teach you a lesson."

The twelve year old gave his little brother with a desperate glance. "It's in the basement," Logan guessed.

Enzo turned and glowered at Grant. "That bottle better be returned to my cabinet by the time I'm done here, or you'll be learning the same lesson as your brother."

Grant flew out of the room as the first crack of the belt rang out. He felt the hairs on the back of his neck stand on end as he ran down the stairs, trying to distance himself from the horror in their bedroom. He did not hear Logan cry out in pain. Unlike Grant, Logan never cried.

Grant had stopped breathing, and he had the bottleneck in a death grip. Clouds rolling in had blocked the sun, and it seemed late in the evening, though it was only the afternoon. Blinking quickly, Grant looked around, trying to orient himself, and he finally sucked in a gasping breath.

How many times had Logan tried to save him? How many times had he attempted to protect their mother? Too many to count. But nobody had ever tried to save or protect Logan. Grant's mind kept replaying the past:

With their father safely snoring away in an alcoholic stupor on the sofa downstairs, Grant and Logan lay sprawled on their respective beds, the room dark and quiet. But neither boy was sleeping. Since Grant had returned after replacing the bottle of liquor, Logan refused to talk to him, a decision that left the younger brother consumed by anxiety.

The bedroom door creaked open, slanting a triangle of hallway light across the yellow carpet. "Are you boys okay?" Karita whispered.

"Yeah, Mommy," Grant called out. Logan remained silent.

Creeping toward their beds, Karita softly rubbed the black hair on Grant's head. In the dim light, he could make out the contours of her beautiful face, the lines of worry creasing around her mouth, and the bright turquoise eyes framed by wavy blond hair.

"Grant," she whispered tenderly, sitting at his side. "I know you're trying to help, but, honey, you cannot hide your father's vodka."

He frowned and looked like he was about to cry. "I'm sorry."

She cradled his cheek. "You can't provoke him like that. He's an adult, and he's the only one who can control his drinking."

Logan could remain quiet no longer. "But he doesn't!" he hissed. "He doesn't control his drinking at all. That's the problem!"

Karita sighed and placed her hands in her lap, helplessly gazing across the room at her hostile older son. "How are you feeling, Logan?"

Logan rolled over in bed, turning his back on his mother.

Grant watched his mother look down, seeming to choke back a sob. "We're going to leave him someday," Karita promised. "We'll go live on our own."

Logan sat up and turned to face her with a bitter sneer. "You always say that, Mom! But we're still here, aren't we? He's still beating the crap out of us!"

Grant pleaded, "Don't be mad, Lo." He watched his mother cover her face with her hands, sitting there helplessly, and realized Logan was probably right. They weren't going anywhere. His father would hunt them down no matter where they went.

Logan sighed. "It's okay, Grant. I'm not mad at you. Just go to sleep, okay?"

Still clutching the bottle, Grant closed his eyes, picturing his big, strong brother taking care of him. He swallowed hard, recalling the heavy wood coffin on his shoulder. Logan hadn't had one person to save or protect him. Grant desperately hoped his brother hadn't died all alone.

Hearing a sharp knock on the door, Grant sat up straighter on the couch.

Kirsten's face lit up when she saw Sophie come through the apartment door. "Hey! I thought you were going to stay at your dad's for a while."

Kirsten relieved her of one of her bags as Sophie juggled the keys back into her purse and managed to shut the door behind her.

"That *was* the plan," she replied bitterly. "Until my dad started acting like a first-class jerk. He treated me like a total child!" She plunked her bags on the kitchen table before grasping Kirsten in a grateful hug.

"I wondered how long the Taylor détente would last." Kirsten grinned, stepping out of the hug. "What was it this time?"

"Guess."

"Let's see, it's always men or career—I'll go for men?" When Sophie nodded, Kirsten's eyes widened. "You told your dad about Grant? Being Logan's *brother*?"

"I had no choice," Sophie insisted, plopping on the couch. "After the detective came to my dad's house, I had to come clean."

"Oh, yeah, the detective." Kirsten nodded, joining Sophie on the sofa. "What was that all about?"

Sophie raised her eyebrows. "You don't know? Haven't you watched the news?"

Kirsten shook her head.

"I'm sorry. I should have called you—it's just, everything got so crazy and then my dad freaked out. Logan Barberi was murdered."

Kirsten's mouth dropped open. "When?"

"Thursday morning." Sophie's lips tightened. "And I know that because apparently I have an alibi for that time."

Kirsten's eyes opened wider. "You were a *suspect*?"

"Yes. Logan did screw me over, as you know. I had a big, fat motive."

"How did he die?"

Sophie averted her eyes. "He was stabbed to death."

"How did Grant take it?"

"Not well, as you can imagine. He was also a suspect, although Detective Fox told me he has an alibi as well. You should have seen him ... he was so crushed. I went to the funeral today—huge mistake in my dad's opinion—anyway, Grant looked devastated. He was a pallbearer for his brother."

"Oh, Sophie." They were both quiet for a moment before Kirsten inquired, "How are you feeling?"

She smiled softly at the shrink-style question. "I don't know ... confused maybe? Definitely sad for Logan—what a horrible way to die. I just know there was some good in him, despite all the awful things he did. I mostly feel so badly for Grant. I, um, against my better judgment I gave him a hug at the funeral."

"Good!"

Sophie arched an eyebrow. "*Good*? Weren't you the one warning me off McSailor in the first place?"

"Well, yeah ... and I know his family is evil and stuff, but Grant just made you so happy, Sophie. You were getting back to yourself. You know, to how you were before prison. And look how much he's done for you, getting you not one, but *two* jobs."

"I don't know," Sophie said. "I don't know if I can trust him." She exhaled loudly. "I need some time."

"And," Kirsten continued, as if Sophie had not spoken, "McSailor *is* incredibly hot."

"Are you coming after my boyfriend, roomie?"

"Well, he's a much better choice than the fertilizer technician."

"Oh, no. What happened with him?"

Kirsten sighed. "He was very nice, it's just that he, uh, he kind of…" She wrinkled her nose. "He kind of *smelled.*"

A tiny giggle escaped Sophie's lips. She grinned evilly. "No shit?"

They began giggling, and soon their shoulders shook with hysterical laughter. Finally, they fell into the sofa cushions, sighing after a good cleansing laugh.

❦

After rapping on the door, Carlo shook his head as he stood outside Grant's apartment. Fucking Tank and Meat had both bailed on him, making up some bullshit excuse about how Angelo had ordered them to return to the compound. Oh well, it would probably be better to approach Grant alone. Grant Pants might spook easily. Besides, Carlo was much better at manipulating people than anybody he knew. He didn't need their help.

Waiting patiently, holding a small cardboard box, Carlo noticed a shadow fall across the peephole and tried to make himself appear appropriately mournful. "Grant?" he called.

"What do you want, Carlo?" Grant asked from the other side of the door.

"I've got some of Lo's possessions to give you."

Grant paused, feeling uneasy. Why the hell was Carlo here? How had he discovered where he lived? Mustering his best authoritative voice, he instructed, "Leave the box and I'll get it later!"

"Aw, c'mon, *cugino*," Carlo said. "Don't shut me out. I'm grieving, man. I need to talk." The door remained shut. "We carried his casket together, Grant. We're family."

His hand resting on the deadbolt, Grant considered what to do. Could he turn away one of his last remaining family members? Could he ignore his own blood? He was just so tired…

"Please?" Carlo implored, his strong voice resonating through the door. "I won't stay long, I promise."

With a frustrated sigh, Grant finally unlocked the door and swung it open, peering down at his shorter cousin. Carlo managed to hide the victorious smirk threatening to emerge. Without a word, Logan's brother stepped back to allow Carlo to enter the apartment.

Grant trailed him into the living room. "Sorry it's kind of a mess."

Carlo glanced at the spotless room. He noticed the bottle of booze and gravitated toward it, setting down the box and picking up the bottle from the coffee table.

"Drowning your sorrows, eh? But why is this bottle unopened, Grant? We should toast your brother."

Grant collapsed into the sofa, scooping the cardboard box onto his lap and ignoring his cousin's suggestion. He hardly wanted to get chummy with Carlo.

Studying Grant intently, Carlo slid into a chair next to the sofa and watched him extract some photographs from the box. Grant's face fell as he flipped through pictures from his nephew's childhood. "Poor Ben," he lamented.

Carlo's jaw clenched. Everyone was feeling so sorry for Logan's son, but Carlo knew Ben *needed* to experience this loss of his father to make him tougher, to breed the proper loyalty to the family so he could become a capo one day. Logan had been growing soft and might have led his son astray if not for Carlo.

Tapping his foot with restless energy, Carlo looked around at the bland apartment. "Man, I could really use a drink."

"Glasses are in the cupboard," Grant mumbled distractedly, still absorbed by the photographs.

Miffed that he had to retrieve his own glass, Carlo rose from the chair and headed into the small kitchen. He could not locate any shot glasses but did find two tumblers in the cupboard.

"Don't suppose you got a lime?" he shouted. Preparing to open the fridge, he noticed a written note stuck to the door with a magnet. His eyes narrowed with curiosity, then he inhaled sharply.

He glanced behind him at Grant, who thankfully was still riveted by the pictures cradled in his hands. Who the hell was Bonnie? He thought her name was Sophie. Setting his jaw with resolve, Carlo determined to look into this. He lifted the magnet and removed the paper, quietly folding it and sneaking it into the pocket of his black pants.

Confidently striding back to the seating area, Carlo set the glasses on the coffee table and opened the bottle, pouring a sizeable amount of tequila into each tumbler.

"*Salute!*" he announced, holding the glass aloft and inviting Grant to do the same.

Grant put down the photographs and grasped his own tumbler, halfheartedly raising the glass and meeting Carlo's intense black eyes. "*Salute,*" he listlessly replied.

"To our brother who was taken from us much too young." Carlo shook his head, feigning heartfelt grief. "May he find peace in heaven. *Cent'anni!*"

May you live one hundred years. Grant frowned. Why would anyone want to live one hundred years of this miserable existence? Perhaps if he still had Sophie in his life… He brought the glass to his lips and sipped, feeling fire slide down his throat.

Carlo had knocked back the entire glass. With disdain, he eyed the substantial amount of liquor still present in his cousin's glass and decided to get down to business. He couldn't stand to be around this vanilla angel any longer than he had to—Grant might rub off on him or something.

Noticing the fading bruise on Grant's cheekbone, Carlo inquired, "How'd you get that shiner?"

Grant gazed at the glass in his hand. "The man we just toasted. He and I got in a fight before he died."

Carlo whistled through his teeth. "That must not have looked too good when the cops showed up to question you."

"Yeah. Fortunately I'd been to my PO's that morning, so I had an alibi."

"Lucky," Carlo responded, his smile of relief not quite genuine. "I was at my dad's club," he quickly added. "So I have an alibi too."

Grant glanced at him curiously. Why was Carlo volunteering that information?

"Speaking of my parole officer…" Grant suddenly sat up, coming to his senses. "You should go. I can't associate with known criminals or I'll be in violation of my parole."

"Oh, I'm not leaving yet. We got some business to discuss."

"What kind of business?"

"I'm here to make you an offer you can't refuse." Carlo's black eyes glistened with delight.

"What the hell does that mean?"

"We need you, Grant. The family needs you in the business. Whatever rift you had with your brother will no longer prevent you from taking your rightful place. Logan lost us a lot of money, and it's your turn to help us get it back."

"I can't believe you're asking this on the day I buried my brother."

Sneering, Carlo pulled back the lapel of his suit-jacket to reveal a gun in a holster. "This ain't a request, *cugino.*"

Grant's eyes widened, never leaving Carlo's. "I—I—I'm on parole… for a crime *you* made me commit." His voice became stronger. "There's no way in hell I'm pulling another job for you." He looked down and scoffed, "Threaten me with whatever you want."

Carlo gave him a saccharine grin. "Who's Sophie, Grant?" Suddenly he had his cousin's attention. "Sophie Taylor?" Carlo tilted his head to the side with feigned naïveté. "The girl who hugged you this afternoon?"

Grant's heart was pounding so loudly he couldn't hear himself think. His Bonnie! Carlo knew about his Bonnie! "She's—she's nobody. Just a friend of Joe's—"

"Save your lies for someone less intelligent," Carlo interrupted. "I know who she is. She's that shrink who got the cops chasing after Lo. She's the whore who seduced both brothers. How sweet. So, Lo was banging her too, huh?"

Grant's eyes flared, and before he knew what he was doing, he'd lunged for his cousin. Carlo was ready for him. Despite his smaller stature, Carlo swiftly dominated, whipping out his weapon and somehow spinning and twisting Grant's arm around his back. In less than two seconds, he held the weapon flush against the taller man's temple. A dead quiet spread through the apartment—the only sound their panting.

Grant felt his cousin's hot breath on his neck. "That bitch turned over a lot of money to the fucking cops," Carlo hissed. "Our money. And we want it back."

Grant closed his eyes, feeling the cool metal on his skin.

"But I promise I won't go after her, *if* you work for us. You choose, Grant. You choose if she lives or dies."

It wasn't a choice at all. Grant had no choice.

"What will it be, *cugino*?" Carlo prompted, twisting Grant's arm tighter.

Grant wondered if he was going to throw up. "I'll do it," he said. "I'll do whatever you and Angelo want. Just please don't hurt Sophie."

A satisfied smile spread across Carlo's face. "That's what I want to hear. It would be a pity to kill such a beautiful chick." He released his hold on Grant, and the younger man immediately broke away. But he could not escape the cloyingly sweet scent of Carlo's aftershave. It was as if his cousin had infiltrated his every pore, seeping into his system, infecting him, owning him, and Grant had the strong urge to take a shower.

Carlo carefully replaced his gun. "You be at the compound by nine o'clock tomorrow morning, Grant. We'll discuss your career opportunities then."

Grant nodded. If he had to show up at Angelo's, at least the feds might catch him violating parole again, landing him back in prison and far away from Carlo. But then, gripped by despair, Grant remembered his father awaited him back in Gurnee. And if he was in prison, he couldn't protect Sophie. Wherever he went, he was trapped by his destructive family. Hopelessness washed over him.

Sliding his hands into his pockets, Carlo's fingertips brushed the folded paper with the address for Bonnie, surely a nickname for this Taylor girl.

"I gotta go," Carlo announced, not sure if Grant was listening. "I got people to talk to, to um, consult with."

When Grant finally glanced up, Carlo added, "See you tomorrow, cuz. Don't be late."

With that last instruction, Carlo disappeared, letting himself out.

Grant crumpled on the sofa, holding his head. Sophie! Should he warn her? She would be safe with her father's protection. But what if she returned to live with Kirsten?

He closed his eyes, remembering her soft lips brushing over his eyelids. His Sophie. She was gone to him forever. He would never put her in that kind of danger again. She was much too precious.

Drawing an anguished breath, he glanced around the empty apartment, which grew dimmer by the moment. Joe would be back soon. What in the world would Grant tell him? Eyeing the bottle and glasses, he swiftly gathered them up. Joe had never approved of liquor in the house.

Dumping the tequila from his glass into the sink, Grant turned to the refrigerator to hide the bottle in the cabinet above it. Once he stood on his tiptoes and placed the tequila bottle in the far recesses of the cabinet, he glanced at the fridge. Something seemed a little off.

Suddenly Grant gasped. Sophie's note! It was missing. His stomach flipped with fear as he realized only one person could have taken it. Grabbing his jacket, Grant rushed out of the apartment.

35. Scar Tissue

Wow, I love what you've done with this!" Sophie exclaimed. She looked from Kirsten's computer screen to her roommate, who bit her lip nervously as she sat on her bed. Sophie had just finished reading the last ten pages of Kirsten's dissertation.

"You do?" Kirsten asked.

"You pulled it all together wonderfully in the discussion section," Sophie said, tucking a strand of hair behind her ear. "This study definitely makes a contribution to the counseling literature. You could totally publish this!"

"No shit?"

Sophie began giggling immediately, remembering their conversation about the occupation of Kirsten's last date. Kirsten snorted with laughter once again.

"Yeah, you just have to edit out about fifty pages before you submit the manuscript to a journal," Sophie advised.

"Arghhh!" Kirsten collapsed on her bed. "I'm so sick of this damn dissertation! I can't look at it anymore!"

"Oh, I know the feeling. I wanted to burn the stupid thing when I was done with mine."

Kirsten abruptly lifted her head, resting on her elbow. She listened intently to something, then quietly asked, "Did you lock the door after you came in?"

"Um …" Sophie tilted her head, trying to remember. "I don't know. I, uh, had a lot of bags."

Alarm crossed Kirsten's face, causing the hairs on the back of Sophie's neck to bristle. "I just heard something," she whispered. "I think someone is in the apartment."

Sophie's eyes widened. "I—I—I'll go look," she offered, feeling responsible.

"No—I'll join you," Kirsten insisted, grabbing hold of Sophie's elbow as they inched toward the living room.

When they were almost to the door, Sophie realized how preposterous this was. It was probably nothing. "We're being ridiculous," she whispered, giggling.

They emerged to the empty living room, and after looking around, Kirsten breathed a sigh of relief.

Sophie scoffed, "You see? Ridiculous."

She gave her roommate a reassuring smile, but from the corner of her eye, she caught movement. Sophie's smile froze as she watched a black-haired man spring from behind the futon, uncoiling his body and aiming a gun at both women.

Kirsten screamed.

"Shut up!" Carlo snarled. He squeezed the weapon tighter. "You scream again, and I'm putting a bullet in you."

Gesturing with his gun, Carlo ordered, "Both of you, take a seat, *now.*"

They slowly sidestepped over to the sofa, neither taking her eyes off the gleaming weapon. Sophie was mesmerized by the circular black muzzle of the handgun. Her shaky legs folded under her as she and Kirsten crumpled onto the sofa. *Deescalate,* she thought. How could she calm this menacing stranger?

"W-w-what do you want from us?" Sophie asked, trying to steady her rapid heartbeat. "You can have whatever you want—my purse is over there on the table."

Carlo smirked. "Unless your purse has one hundred grand in it, Sophie, I'm not interested."

Her eyes widened. This creep knew her name? And the amount of money he specified—that was what Logan had left in her office. She felt sick to realize her past was still haunting her. "You're Logan's friend?" she asked.

His coal-black eyes smoldered. "Logan is no friend of mine. Or should I say, he *was* no friend of mine." Relaxing his hold on the weapon slightly, he grinned triumphantly. "But I'm glad you know why I'm here. You *must* have known there'd be consequences for letting the cops steal our cash, didn't you?"

I know all about consequences, Sophie thought. *Going to prison, losing my career, my dignity, my mother…* Apparently there were even more consequences coming her way. "You want the money back," she said numbly. She would never stop paying for her mistake.

"Very perceptive," Carlo grinned, lowering his gun an inch yet again. Two pretty women, trembling, giving him their complete attention, riveted on his every word, seeming to appreciate his handsomeness—he was enjoying this immensely. "I know who your father is, Sophie."

The syrupy sweet way he said her name made her shudder. His snake-like intonation was worlds away from Grant's tender pronunciation—caressing the "s" softly with his smooth, velvety voice.

"Therefore, I know you can get that money," Carlo continued.

"I—I—I didn't know it was your money," Sophie explained. "Please, please leave my father out of this. He's paid enough for my mistakes."

Carlo paused, and he stared at her curiously.

Hearing her roommate's pleading tone, Kirsten's fear morphed into anger. Who the hell was this stranger to come into *her* home and intimidate them?

"Listen, whoever you are," Kirsten began, her voice growing stronger with each word. "We don't have your money. I suggest you get out of my apartment right now before I call the cops."

Carlo looked amused. This bitch thought she could threaten him? He took a step closer, shifting the weapon from Sophie to Kirsten. "You think you can get a call off to the cops before you bleed out?" he inquired. "Let's give it a test. I'd probably only hit my target, say, three or four times before you reached a phone."

Sophie was horrified. Kirsten clearly didn't know who they were dealing with. "She didn't mean it!" Sophie yelled frantically. "We won't involve the police, okay?"

"Oh, I know you won't," Carlo said, pointing the gun back at Sophie. "Because if you breathe one word to the cops about my friendly visit today, then Grant is dead."

Sophie gasped. He knew Grant too? Of course he did—they were all part of the family, weren't they? She studied the stranger more closely and recognized him from Logan's funeral. How were they all related?

"How do you know Logan and Grant?" she asked.

"That's none of your concern, bitch," Carlo growled. "All you need to worry about is getting one hundred Gs to me ASAP. I'll return in two days, and you better have that money for me, if you want to live."

"You promised!" The livid voice made all three of them jump, and Carlo spun around to find Grant in the hallway of the apartment. Sophie had never seen her McSailor so furious. "You promised you'd leave Sophie alone if I agreed to your plan!"

Sophie stared at Grant. What had he agreed to?

Carlo's eyes narrowed as he trained the gun on his cousin. "Grant Pants has joined us, I see." He waved the gun toward the sofa though his eyes never left Grant's incensed crystal glare. "Get over on the sofa with your bitches."

"No," Grant said, ignoring the gun. He stole a glance at Sophie, whose abject fear ripped into him. He was putting her in danger, like he promised he'd never do. "Let's take this outside," Grant offered in a placating tone. "This has nothing to do with them. This is between *us*."

Quickly checking his female prey, Carlo returned his gaze to Grant. He did not feel so smug anymore. Three hostiles outnumbered him, even though he was the one with the gun. "Do you want to die, *cugino*? Get your fucking ass on that sofa!"

Carlo gave the gun a definitive shake, aiming it straight at Grant's chest.

"No!" cried Sophie.

Frantically training the gun on the women and then back to Grant, Carlo screamed, "Get over there now!"

"We'll resolve this outside," Grant said again, refusing to budge from his position. He had to keep Sophie safe. "I'm not going anywhere."

"No, Grant!" Sophie cried again, clutching Kirsten's arm in terror.

"I'll give you five seconds to get over there, Madsen, snuggled right up next to your whore. Five seconds before I shoot you dead."

Grant's heart thumped, and he frantically searched for a way out of the situation.

The sound of blood pumping in her ears nearly deafened Sophie, and she desperately tried to clear her head. She was missing something important. Watching the menacing stranger threaten Grant without hesitation, seeming to enjoy the impending kill, a realization suddenly dawned on Sophie.

Over Carlo's menacing count—"Five … four … three …"—Sophie shouted, "It was you!"

Carlo and Grant couldn't help but turn their heads from their tense standoff. "What?" they asked in unison.

"It was him!" Sophie announced, meeting Grant's blue eyes while emphatically pointing at Carlo. "*He* killed Logan!"

Carlo's eyes widened with stunned guilt before he quickly composed himself. "What the fuck are you talking about?" he screamed at Sophie. Wheeling around to face Grant, he insisted, "I didn't *touch* Logan!"

But the performance didn't fool Grant. He'd seen Carlo's initial reaction to Sophie's accusation and knew she was right. "It *was* you!" he echoed. Taking a step toward Carlo, Grant growled, "You killed my brother. Of course it was you."

Carlo shook his head vehemently. "*Cugino*, I would never be so stupid as to cap Enzo's son!"

They were not buying his denials. With the infuriated stares of three people on him, Carlo felt caged in. Grant took another step forward and Carlo thrust the gun in his face. "Stay back!" he cried.

"How dare you," Grant snapped, his fury blinding him to the gun. "How dare you kill Lo!"

"Swear to God, Grant. You get any closer, you'll be sorry."

Grant felt a boiling rage, and all he wanted to do was lunge for Carlo's throat, the gun be damned. He took another step closer, unknowingly crossing the invisible line Carlo had drawn.

Swiftly, decisively, Carlo rotated toward Sophie and lowered the gun an inch before firing a deafening shot.

Grant gasped and Kirsten screamed.

Sophie felt the astonishing impact of the bullet ripping into her, sending her reeling back into the sofa cushions. Her left arm was on fire. She gasped for air, unable to move, totally overwhelmed by shock and a searing pain above her elbow. Kirsten reached across her friend, frantically scanning her body. She felt warm stickiness when her hand encountered Sophie's left elbow, and Kirsten pulled back in fear.

Carlo instantly trained the weapon back on Grant, who gaped at Sophie and moved to go to her when he felt the hot muzzle of the gun on his temple.

"On your knees," Carlo ordered. "Or the next shot goes straight through her heart."

Grant complied immediately. Kneeling on the carpet, he lifted his arms to the side in a gesture of surrender and begged, "Please don't kill her. I'll do whatever you want, just please."

Carlo smiled, delighted to hear his cousin's pleas.

"We need to call an ambulance!" Kirsten shrilly demanded.

"Shut up," Carlo snarled. "No cops."

Sophie groaned as a spasm of pain raced up her arm. Grant flinched at the horrific sound and closed his eyes. His fear for Sophie was so overwhelming he barely registered the gun pressing into the side of his head.

If Carlo had killed Logan, surely he and Sophie had no chance at surviving this. And Kirsten was likely going to die too. She was completely innocent—her only fault was befriending Sophie. And Sophie's only fault had been falling in love with him. He waited for the blinding flash of a gunshot to pierce his brain, praying his own death might somehow save them.

Carlo's mind raced as he considered what to do. He longed to pull the trigger and end the family competition forever. But his father's incensed black eyes haunted him. How would Angelo react if Carlo killed *both* brothers? He glanced at the girls on the sofa. Sophie's face was drawn in anguish, and Kirsten applied pressure to her wound, which oozed blood. Her eyes begged him for help.

"Please, Carlo," Grant implored. "Please let us call for help. I won't tell anyone it was you. All I care about is saving Sophie. We'll keep it a secret, okay?"

Wrenching his eyes from the blood on Sophie's arm, Carlo stared down at the unmoving crown of his cousin's head. Could he just walk away? Bouncing his eyes back and forth from Grant to Sophie, Carlo clenched his jaw. Of course they would go to the cops. His little extortion game was now out in the open, as Grant and Sophie knew he was pitting one against the other, so nothing would stop them from reporting him to the police. And there was no way he'd submit to being on the run the rest of his life like Logan. He was going to have to kill all three of them. There was no way around it.

The jarring ring of a cell phone filled the air, freezing all four in place. The phone's cheery ring kept going for three, four, five seconds, interfering with Carlo's concentration and making him tense. "Whose fucking phone is that?"

Finally, the phone stopped ringing, only to resume the incongruous happy melody seconds later. "Goddamn it!" Carlo fumed. "Whose phone is that?"

"It's mine," Sophie gasped, swallowing pain. "It's my father. He's…he's going to hunt you down if you hurt any of us."

"Then I'll kill him too," Carlo retorted.

"Please let me get the phone," Kirsten said. "I'll turn it off."

"You stay right where you are, bitch," Carlo said, taking the gun off of Grant for a split second before returning the muzzle to his temple. "Nobody is going anywhere."

The phone rang incessantly, fraying Carlo's nerves. Kirsten inched forward on the sofa. "I'll just stop it from ringing," she negotiated, training her gaze on the unpredictable murderer in her living room.

"Don't you fucking move one inch!" Carlo yelled.

"It will be fine," Kirsten snapped back, feeling on edge herself. "You can watch me the whole time." She was now perched on the edge of the sofa and exchanged a glance with Grant. Kirsten quietly got to her feet, taking tiny steps toward the table.

A realization hit Grant: Carlo was going to shoot Kirsten. He'd already shot Sophie! Why the hell was Grant allowing the love of his life to bleed out on the sofa? What the hell was he doing on his knees, succumbing to his cousin—capitulating to Lo's *murderer?*Logan was not here to protect Grant from a menacing Barberi man like he always had. Grant had to step up and be the protector now. Carlo had taken his father and brother from him. He simply was not going to allow him to steal Sophie too.

"Goddamn it!" Carlo yanked the gun off Grant and pointed it toward Kirsten. "I told you not to move!"

With one graceful move, Grant leapt to his feet and lunged for Carlo, taking him by surprise. His left hand fumbled for the gun in Carlo's grasp, and his right hand groped for the skin above Carlo's left elbow, where Grant knew there was scar tissue from the gunshot wound his cousin had sustained twenty-two years ago. Carlo yelped in pain, giving Grant a sliver of satisfaction, before twisting his right wrist away in an attempt to regain control of the handgun.

Fiercely digging his fingers into the scar tissue again, Grant felt Carlo give way—leaning to his left to shy away from the painful grip—and suddenly they were on the floor, fighting and clawing for control of the gun.

"Son of a bitch!" Carlo hissed breathlessly as they tussled on the floor.

Sophie's face drained of color as her throbbing wound continued to bleed, and Kirsten could only stand by, frozen, watching the battle play out in front of her.

Grant had both hands on the gun now as he attempted to wrestle it away from Carlo, and he could feel the shorter man weakening under him. The wrath of avenging his brother's death and Sophie's injury had infused Grant with strength. He might not have the ruthlessness or cunning of his cousin, but he certainly had the determination.

Now crouched above Carlo's prone body, Grant sensed he had the upper hand. He forced the gun down between their chests, away from Sophie, and his long fingers wormed their way to the trigger. Watching panic creep into his cousin's eyes, Grant felt Carlo's hand wriggle and grope for the gun. Suddenly the weapon discharged, sending a second deafening roar through the apartment.

His ears ringing and his body thrumming, Grant's eyes widened as he slowly peeled himself off of Carlo and saw a red stain on the white shirt beneath his White Sox jacket. Was he hit? Then his eyes found the deep crimson stain on Carlo's chest, from which leached thick blood, spreading quickly.

Oh my God, Grant silently repeated, sitting back on his heels. *I shot him. I killed a man.* He shoved the gun, sending it sliding across the carpet.

Carlo gasped for air, each breath like a knife twisting in his lungs. Was this how Logan had felt after he'd stabbed him? He clutched the carpet, feeling searing pain rip through his chest, though his lower body was already numb. Black spots crowded his vision, and he called out shakily, "Grant?"

Grant crawled forward, and Carlo saw a pair of frightened eyes peer down at him. "Tell my father—tell him I loved him," Carlo wheezed. "Even though he didn't ..." Carlo's eyes glazed over, and all he could see was blackness. Determined to finish his sentence, he panted, "Even though he didn't love me. He only loved *Logan.*"Carlo's last word came out in a sneer.

Grant winced, hearing his cousin's dying words. "Why, Carlo? Why'd you have to kill Lo?"

Carlo stared back with unseeing eyes. His body shuddered and somehow he found the energy to draw his mouth into his characteristic smirk. "It was you. Logan died trying to protect you."

Stunned, Grant pulled back and sat up. Hearing Kirsten's voice, he looked up to see her on the phone and gathered she was talking to emergency services. He then looked across the coffee table to his love, whose pale skin and pained expression brought a stab of guilt.

Carlo's moan drew Grant's attention back to him. Grant hovered over his cousin, flooded by conflicting emotions—the most palpable being relief that Carlo could no longer hurt Sophie. He thought about putting pressure on his horrific chest wound, but Grant knew there was no hope for his cousin.

"I'm sorry," Carlo whispered. Seconds later, Grant watched the light fade from his black eyes, and he realized he was gone. Another Barberi man had died.

I shot him. I killed a man. Grant knew he would return to prison now. His short-lived parole was a thing of the past.

Drawing a trembling hand toward his cousin's face, Grant brushed his fingertips over the eyelids, closing the lifeless black eyes. "I'm sorry my father ruined your life," he whispered back, feeling the sudden urge to cry.

Sophie. He longed to wrap her in his arms and keep her safe until the paramedics arrived. But she'd rejected him after learning about his family, and now she was possibly dying from a wound inflicted by that very family. How could he even look her in the eye?

She felt his longing look and said softly, "Grant? Please bring me my purse."

He was up like a shot and returned to the sofa instantly, handing her the bag as he sat on the low armrest. "Thank you," she whispered. Her eyelids drooped, and she just wanted to fall asleep, but she forced herself to rummage through her bag until she located her cell phone. Gingerly holding her left arm motionless, she searched in her purse once again.

"Can I help you with that, Sophie?" Grant asked, feeling useless. Gazing worriedly at her bleeding arm, he could no longer prevent himself from taking action. He reached down and unbuckled his belt.

"This is something *I* need to do," she said. She *had* to make this phone call. Finally locating the business card, Sophie flipped open the cell phone and painstakingly dialed the emergency number listed on the card.

"Yes, hello?" She spoke weakly. "I need to get an emergency message to Officer Jerry Stone."

Sliding the belt out of his pant loops, Grant listened to her end of the conversation.

"This is Sophie Taylor. Please tell him Grant Madsen had to shoot a man in self-defense tonight. We need his help."

"Sophie—" Grant objected, but she shushed him and resumed her conversation.

"Yes, thank you."

Ending the call, she looked at him with glassy eyes and a small smile. "I can't have my McSailor return to prison now, can I?"

"It's where I belong, Soph—"

"Please," she interrupted. "Please hold me, Grant. I'm so cold."

"First we have to stop the bleeding." He slid next to her and looped the belt around her bicep, tightening the tourniquet as she winced in pain. "Sorry."

He then wrapped his arms around her carefully. Closing his eyes as he felt the familiar comfort of her melting into him, he murmured, "I'm so sorry, Sophie." They held each other for several moments, and then he looked at his watch. "Where are those damn paramedics?"

Silent tears slid down her cheeks as she wondered if she'd ever get to experience this pleasure again. She had no energy left. "I missed this," she murmured. "You smell so … good." Her last word was barely a whisper.

"I don't deserve you," he said. "I brought danger to you and Kirsten tonight, and—" He glanced at Carlo's lifeless form, "I just killed a man. I *am* Grant Barberi."

Every fiber of her being wished to protest his words, but instead she slipped into a deep, peaceful blackness.

36. Restraint

A throbbing ache formed in his shoulders and radiated down the length of his arms, culminating in a tingling numbness in his manacled hands. Grant had been sitting in the apartment with his wrists cuffed behind his back for over an hour now.

His mind flashed repeatedly to the horror of feeling Sophie slump against him as he'd held her...

Realizing she was unconscious, Grant had shouted at Kirsten to tell them to hurry. Her voice rose with fear as she continued speaking to the 911 dispatcher. Fortunately, a banging on the door immediately followed his plea, and Kirsten let in two police officers.

One officer knelt by the handgun, carefully placing the weapon in an evidence bag, while the other moved toward the couple on the sofa. He was a barrel-chested, balding man with a fleshy face and beady black eyes, and over Sophie's shoulder Grant read the name on his uniform tunic: Dirkson.

"Get away from her," Officer Dirkson ordered.

Nodding, Grant fully intended to comply but found he could not let go of Sophie. This might be the last time he would ever hold her. He simply couldn't detach himself.

"I said," the officer snarled as he stepped forward and rested his right hand on the gun in his holster, "get away from her."

Grant could not believe he was disobeying an officer of the law. "Not until the paramedics arrive, sir."

"Hey, idiot!" yelled the other officer, now standing near Kirsten. "We won't let the paramedics in here until we subdue you. Let go of her!"

Grant immediately released Sophie, resting her gently on the sofa cushions. Quickly Dirkson was on top of him, shoving him off the sofa and onto the floor, burying his face in the carpet.

Turning to stare at Carlo's peaceful profile, Grant felt his arms wrenched behind him and the painfully familiar cool-metal sensation of handcuffs closing on his wrists.

"You're the shooter, right?" Dirkson growled, clasping the cuffs tightly.

Grant closed his eyes, wishing to erase the vision of Carlo's dead body. "Yes, sir," he quietly confessed.

"Stay down then and don't move, asshole," Dirkson replied, roughly frisking the length of his body.

Grant heard the bustle of paramedics arriving. He listened to Kirsten insisting she was fine and begging the paramedic to join her colleagues attending to Sophie.

He heard snippets of conversation between the EMTs: "Vitals 130 over 70, pulse 68, sat 90 percent, one medial entrance wound above the left elbow…Get some O2 and an IV for her on the rig…Damn, BP's dropping. Let's get moving."

He badly wanted to raise his head to look, but the big black boot of Officer Dirkson, perched right next to his nose, convinced him to stay still.

As Sophie rattled out of the apartment on a stretcher, Kirsten followed closely. "I'll stay with her, Grant," she called as she left. "She's going to be okay!"

Grant gulped. She had to be okay. He could never live with himself if he'd caused the death of his Bonnie…

The pulsating ache of rigid restraint filled his mind once again as he stole a glance at the two officers babysitting him. He could tell they were pissed off that they had to wait so long in the apartment—waiting for what, Grant wasn't sure. But nothing compared to the pain of worry and regret piercing his heart. He had waited interminably to hear news of Sophie's recovery, and he could bear it no longer.

"Please, sir, can you get an update on Sophie Taylor?" he asked.

The two Chicago PD officers, standing fifteen feet away, paused their conversation long enough to send him hostile glares. Grant immediately regretted opening his big mouth.

Officer Dirkson strode across the room and towered over Grant.

"You want to find out if you murdered two people, not just one?" he glowered.

Grant said nothing.

"Even if that little *señorita* makes it, which it don't look so good for her, you're still going away for life, con."

The officer had searched Grant's wallet and discovered his driver's license with *Registered Offender* stamped on it. Grant being on parole did not exactly endear him to Officer Dirkson.

"I did not shoot her!" Grant insisted.

"Shut the fuck up, you murderer," Dirkson sneered. He grinned wickedly before surprising Grant with a devastating punch to the midsection. Grant instantly doubled over, groaning from the blow.

"What's going on here?" an irate voice demanded from the entryway. Through his pain, Grant located Detective Marilyn Fox standing with her hands on her hips, glaring at Officer Dirkson. Accompanying her was a man dressed in a business suit. "Why are you assaulting my suspect?"

"Who the hell are you?" Dirkson retorted, eyeing the petite woman suspiciously. "This is a crime scene. You can't just walk in here—"

"Detective Marilyn Fox, Great Lakes PD," she brusquely informed him, whipping out her badge.

"I'm Detective Bruce Hammond, Chicago PD," the fortyish, brown-haired man added, also showing his badge. "And *anyone* could walk in here, you dipshit. Where's the crime scene tape on the door?"

"You're the detectives?" Dirkson avoided looking at Bruce and aimed his comments at Marilyn. "We were ordered to wait for *you*, sweet cheeks. What took you so damn long? Did you stop for a manicure on the way?"

Marilyn's green eyes narrowed, then focused on his nametag. "Officer Dirkson, did you listen to one word I just said? I was coming from *Lake County*." She enunciated the words carefully, as if explaining a concept to a child. "Detective Hammond was gracious enough to wait for me—naturally it took awhile to get here."

"Yeah." Dirkson grinned. "They probably couldn't sacrifice their *only* detective for the whole day, huh? Let's hope no crimes are committed in Disturbia while you're downtown, darlin'. Your superior might not like that."

Detective Hammond watched the exchange, a look of amusement on his face.

"Speaking of superiors, what's your sergeant's name, Officer?" Marilyn asked calmly.

"Why do you care?" Dirkson countered.

She smiled sweetly. "Because I'd like to report your misconduct to your supervisor, once I'm done here."

Dirkson's grin quickly faded. "Now wait a minute, Detective—"

"You touch my suspect one more time, and I'll have Internal Affairs all over your sizeable ass," Marilyn leaned in and whispered, causing Grant to miss the end of the conversation.

There was a clanging in the hallway, and Marilyn backed off, turning to smile at the forensic techs. "Come on in, guys," she said. Turning back around, she maintained her congenial expression as she told Dirkson, "I suggest you join your partner over there and get out of our way, Officer."

Dirkson silently followed her command.

Bruce had agreed that Marilyn would be the first to interrogate Grant, since she'd already questioned him once. He efficiently took charge of the crime scene as she turned her attention to the suspect on the couch. "How are you holding up, Mr. Madsen?"

"I'm fine, ma'am. Please, do you know how Sophie is doing?"

"When Officer Stone called me, he said he was going to try to track down which hospital she was taken to. I'm sure he'll let me know once he finds out anything."

Grant nodded, though her answer had not smoothed the lines of worry on his face at all. His heart remained crushed by guilt. He had done this.

A tech joined Bruce in pulling on latex gloves before stooping down to examine Carlo's body. Cocking his head toward Carlo, Grant resolutely informed her, "I shot him. I killed my cousin."

She blinked several times before extracting her notebook from her jacket pocket. The air was heavy between them as she jotted down his quote. "His name is Carlo Barberi?"

"Yes, ma'am."

"Mr. Madsen, I need to ask you some questions." Even though he was a parolee, she read him his Miranda rights, just to be clear. Then with a nod from Grant, she began her questioning.

"Why did you shoot him?"

Grant shifted uncomfortably, trying to ignore his throbbing shoulders. "He shot Sophie, and he was going to kill us all—"

"Wait a minute. Back up. Why did Mr. Barberi shoot Ms. Taylor?"

Drawing a deep breath, Grant launched into the story. "Carlo found out about the money Sophie had turned over to the police, and he came here, demanding that she get it for him. By the time I arrived, he already had the gun on Sophie and Kirsten."

"This is Kirsten's apartment?"

"Yes, ma'am."

"How did you know Mr. Barberi would be here?"

"Because Carlo came to see me first," Grant said. "Sophie had left a note with her address on my fridge, and after Carlo took off I realized he'd stolen the note. I got here as fast as I could, but I was … too late."

"This the note?" the tech called out. He held up piece of paper he'd removed from Carlo's pants pocket, and Grant immediately recognized Sophie's flowing scrawl.

Bruce's gloved hands took the note from the tech and read it. "Who's Bonnie?" he asked.

Although he'd just admitted to killing another human being, Grant looked endearingly cute as he blushed. "Private joke, sir?"

Marilyn nodded. Getting back to business, she looked down at her notebook as the forensic tech bagged the note and resumed his duties. "Mr. Barberi had the gun trained on the two women?" Marilyn prompted.

"Yes," Grant said. "He ordered me to join them on the sofa, but I refused. I was just trying to get him out of here, away from Sophie, but he wouldn't leave."

"He had a gun on you, and you didn't do what he said?" Marilyn asked.

"Yes, ma'am." He shrugged, wincing in pain as he moved his sore shoulders. "He had the gun on me at my apartment too. It wasn't a big deal."

"Why did he threaten you in your apartment?"

Grant paused, wondering if he should share that he'd agreed to join his Mafia family.

"Mr. Madsen?" Marilyn urged.

Sighing, Grant admitted, "Carlo threatened to kill Sophie unless I started working for the family."

Marilyn arched her eyebrows, and a hint of sarcasm crept in her voice. "Let me guess. You agreed to do it and didn't even think of calling the police."

"How could I call the police when I had to race over here?"

"You never would have called them. Let's face it, Mr. Madsen."

"Don't you understand how my family works, Detective? You can't go against them, no matter how hard you try, and I've been trying all my life. Believe me. You can't go to the cops—nobody can keep you safe. Hell, my father would have killed the man who was informing on him if not for Carlo messing it all up."

"But the informant lived, and your father got caught."

In the last few days Grant had not thought once about his father, holed away in prison for the rest of his life. How would Enzo react to all that had happened? How would his father treat him when they reunited at Gurnee?

"The good guys won that time," Marilyn continued. "I suppose we should thank Carlo here for that one."

Grant glanced furtively at the pallid body surrounded by busy techs. He would *never* feel thankful toward Carlo.

Bruce stood with his arms crossed in front of him, supervising both the collection of evidence and the interrogation.

"So." Marilyn resumed her questioning. "What happened when you refused to join Sophie and Kirsten on the sofa?"

"Carlo was counting down before he put a bullet in my head, and that's when Sophie…" Grant's voice faded. He had not allowed himself to consider Carlo's confession since it occurred—it was too overwhelming to acknowledge that his own cousin had killed his brother. It was unfathomable.

"What did Sophie do?"

"Sophie…" He trailed off again, feeling hot tears in his eyes. He didn't want the detective to see him crying *again*. "Sophie—I don't know how she figured it out, but she knew." His voice thick with tears, he leaned forward. "And once she said it, I knew too."

"You knew *what*?"

As much as his restrained arms would allow, Grant's head sunk lower and lower. His tears were flowing freely now, just as they had that afternoon at Logan's funeral. "Carlo killed Logan," he said. "He killed my brother."

Marilyn sat completely still, running through various scenarios in her mind.

Grant rocked as he sobbed, refusing to look up, and Marilyn eyed him sympathetically.

"Carlo murdered Lo," he bawled. "I know y-y-you don't believe me, but he was the k-k-killer. He did it." He sniffed and took a shuddering breath. "And he said…he said that Lo died t-t-trying to protect me. Lo wouldn't give me up."

Marilyn took a deep breath, watching the parolee writhe in pain before her. She stood up and conferred with Bruce for a moment before approaching the two police officers.

"Madsen's in the mob?" Dirkson quietly asked.

She looked at him with disdain. She was glad this idiot worked for the Chicago PD, not for Great Lakes.

"How long has Mr. Madsen been handcuffed, gentlemen?"

Dirkson glanced at his watch and shrugged. "Hour and a half?"

"Remove the cuffs."

"You're not letting him go, are you?" Dirkson hissed.

"I didn't say I was letting him go. But I want to question him without having him wince in pain every five seconds." She quickly grabbed Dirkson's beefy arms and drew them behind his back, clasping his wrists together with her small hands.

"Can you imagine holding this position for five minutes, Officer?" she spat, leaning in toward his ear. "What about ninety minutes?" She shoved his arms forward. "Uncuff him now."

Feeling the glares of both detectives, Dirkson reluctantly walked over to the sofa. "On your feet, Madsen."

Embarrassed to feel his nose running despite copious sniffing, Grant kept his head down as he rose.

The officer released his wrists, and Grant exhaled gratefully. Through shooting prickles of pain, he covered his face with his tingling hands and tried to wipe away the evidence of his crying.

"Sit," Dirkson barked, then left Grant alone in his misery.

"Thank you, Officer." Marilyn nodded, then returned to the futon, scooping up a box of tissues along the way and placing them next to Grant.

"So, after Sophie accused Carlo of killing Logan, then what happened?"

Still looking down, Grant smiled sadly. "I hated him so much for what he did to Lo, and I stupidly moved toward him. I—"

"Mr. Madsen, I want you to look at me as you answer my questions."

He snapped his head up, showing her his startled glassy eyes, and he nodded, "Yes, ma'am." With difficulty, he kept his eyes trained on her. "I—I moved toward Carlo, and that's when he ..." She watched his hands twist nervously in his lap. "He shot Sophie. It was all my fault—I provoked him."

"Go on."

"Then he, uh, he had the gun to my head, and he forced me to my knees. And Kirsten begged him to let us call an ambulance, but he wouldn't listen. He just let Sophie keep bleeding." Grant's jaw clenched and his hands tightened into fists.

"And then Sophie's cell phone started ringing. It annoyed the hell out of Carlo, and Kirsten kept saying she would go turn off the phone, but Carlo told her not to move. At one point, Kirsten and I looked at each other, and we just knew we had to do something or Sophie would die—we would all die. So, when Kirsten went for the phone, I went for Carlo. We—we wrestled for the gun, and we were on the floor, rolling around, when I forced the gun between us, between our chests, and I, um…" His eyes remained glued on her but he seemed far away, in the recesses of his mind. "I pulled the trigger." He swallowed hard. "I killed him."

Marilyn stared at Grant for several moments, watching the kaleidoscope of guilt, fear, remorse, and relief spin and swirl in his eyes. Jerry Stone had relayed Sophie's message to Marilyn, and it certainly did sound like a self-defense situation. But the fact that Grant was on parole for aggravated robbery and was a recent suspect for murder meant she could not let him go. She also hadn't interviewed Sophie or Kirsten yet, to corroborate Grant's story. *If* Sophie was still alive.

"Do you have anything else to tell me about what happened tonight?" she asked Grant, her face perfectly neutral.

Grant thought for a moment. "No, ma'am."

"Stay put, Mr. Madsen."

He nodded and continued kneading the tingling out of his hands. He knew he'd be back in the cuffs soon enough.

Grant watched Marilyn join Bruce, who was listening to the officers recreate the scene as they found it. They pointed to the spot where they'd found the gun on the floor.

The sound of a body bag being zipped up diverted Grant's attention to the techs, and he stared at the crimson stain left on the carpet once they hauled the body away. He wondered if Kirsten would ever be able to remove that evidence of the trauma that had occurred in her apartment tonight. Even if she could, she was probably emotionally scarred for life, and it was totally his fault.

Suddenly Detective Fox stood before him, flanked by Detective Hammond and both police officers. "Mr. Madsen, I'm afraid we have to arrest you now."

He nodded. "Yes, ma'am." He'd expected this outcome.

"Please stand up and place your hands on this wall."

"We already frisked him, Detective," Dirkson said.

"Just being thorough, Officer," she said. Detective Hammond frisked Grant quickly.

Grant's stomach dropped with the sick realization that he was returning to prison.

"Let's go," Hammond commanded, taking hold of his arm as Detective Fox's cell phone rang.

"Can you hold for a second?" she asked. She spoke into the phone. "Hi, Jerry."

Grant felt dead tired. But he perked up instantly when he heard Marilyn ask, "How is Ms. Taylor?"

In the hospital waiting area, Jerry glanced at Kirsten Holland before resuming his phone conversation with Detective Fox.

"Taylor just got out of surgery to repair the Basilic vein," Jerry told her, glancing across the small waiting area at Kirsten Holland. "They removed the bullet and gave her a blood transfusion. She's reportedly stable."

He exchanged a few more words with the detective before Kirsten heard him say, "Yeah, I'm here with the roommate." He listened for a moment, and then nodded. "Will do. Keep in touch, Detective."

After hanging up, Jerry turned his attention to Kirsten. "Detective Fox wants to question you after she books Madsen. You're not to leave the hospital before she arrives to talk to you."

Kirsten's eyes widened and she nodded. The whole situation was so unreal, like being stuck in the middle of some crime movie. But Sophie's blood had been real, as well as the horrified shouts from Sophie's father when Kirsten called him to say his daughter had been shot. She was not looking forward to Mr. Taylor's arrival to the hospital.

"So, Grant was arrested?" Kirsten asked.

"Yep."

"But he'll get off, right? I mean, it was total self-defense!"

Jerry sighed. "I don't know. I don't have the facts, Ms. Holland."

"It's Kirsten, Jerry," she said warmly.

"And it's Officer Stone to you," he corrected gruffly. He watched her blush at his admonishment. "I only let Taylor call me by my first name."

After a few moments of tense silence, Jerry asked, "How's the dissertation coming along?"

"Pretty good?" Kirsten said, puzzled. "Did Sophie tell you about that?"

"Yes, she did."

"She talks about *me* in her meetings with you?"

"Well, I have to find out who my parolees are living with, if they have roommates—it's protocol." He smiled. "She laughed pretty hard when I asked her if you had a criminal record."

Kirsten blushed again. "I can imagine. Nobody is more law-abiding than me, except for..." She looked embarrassed.

Curious, Jerry prompted, "Except for?"

Kirsten ran her hand through her long, brown hair. "I was going to say, 'except for Sophie.' She's as goody two-shoes as they come—before she got arrested, of course." Her determined eyes bored into Jerry. "Officer Stone, you've got to believe me. Sophie is a really good person. She just got lost there for a while, led astray by Logan. She was only trying to help him."

Jerry rubbed his jaw. "And is she being led astray again, this time by Madsen?"

Hesitating, Kirsten eventually said, "I don't know Grant very well, I have to admit. But I do know Sophie. And she's been so happy with Grant. Here she was just getting out of prison—she should have been totally devastated, depressed, aimless—and instead, she couldn't *wait* to get out of bed to go to work every morning, to a job *he* got for her. And when she found out he was Logan's brother, she was devastated, but she loved him so much she was willing to give him another chance."

Kirsten looked down and picked at her fingernail. "I know Grant comes from an awful family, and I don't want to see Sophie get hurt again. But he seems like such a sweet guy. He's not like them. I kind of wish I had a boyfriend like him, to tell you the truth."

Jerry gave a wistful sigh. He kind of wished he had a friend who would stand up for him like Kirsten. "I'm gonna get some coffee," he announced, rising to his feet. "Do you want any?"

"No, thanks. Um, Officer Stone, do you make a visit every time one of your parolees goes to the hospital?"

He paused. "Not usually."

"So, why are you here for Sophie, then?"

Now it was Jerry's turn to blush. "Maybe I agree with you," he said. "Maybe I think Taylor is a good person too." His face flushed deeper and he set his mouth in a frown. "But don't tell her that I said that."

Like a shot he was gone, leaving Kirsten looking after him with a grin.

☙

A half-hour later, Sophie's father had still not arrived, but her parole officer and roommate were led to the hospital room where Sophie was waking up from the anesthetic.

Kirsten rushed to her bedside, dismayed to see Sophie's left arm heavily bandaged and immobile at her side. "Kirsten," she mumbled groggily, smiling.

Leaning in to pull the sheet up higher over Sophie's skimpy gown, Kirsten whispered, "Your PO is here."

Despite her fatigue, Sophie's eyes grew round, and she allowed her roommate to draw the sheet up to protect her modesty. When Kirsten stepped back, Sophie could see Jerry in the doorway. "Please come in, Jerry," she called weakly.

He tentatively entered the room, taking in the machines surrounding her, making her appear small and defenseless on the big bed. "Just wanted to make sure you were okay, Taylor," he said awkwardly.

"I'm fine," she said. "More importantly, how is Grant?"

"He wasn't the one who got shot," Jerry growled.

"But he's the one who had to shoot," Sophie countered. "And I know it must be killing him. What's happening with Grant?"

"Detective Fox is taking him in for booking."

"Oh!" Sophie drew her right hand to her mouth, and the movement jarred her body, making her wince. She gritted her teeth and begged, "Please, Jerry, you have to go there. You have to convince them it was self-defense."

"I don't have to convince them of anything, Taylor. If he's innocent, he'll be released."

"But that's not how it works!" Sophie insisted. "Once they find out he's Enzo Barberi's son, they'll crucify him. He won't be given a fair chance. You have to fight for him. You know the way they think. Please."

"Sophie!" Will Taylor cried, rushing into the room. "Oh, God! Are you okay?" He dashed to her side, his wild eyes sweeping over her.

"I'm okay, Dad," she replied calmly. "You remember Officer Jerry Stone and Kirsten Holland, right?"

Will barely acknowledged them before returning his attention to his daughter. "What happened? Kirsten said you got shot? Oh, no—your arm is all bandaged!"

"I'll tell you everything, Dad. Just a second." She returned her eyes to her parole officer. "Thank you so much for being here, Jerry. But please go to the station. See? My dad is here now. Grant needs you much more than I do. Please?"

Will's face reddened and he shouted, "Is Grant involved in this?"

Ignoring the angry man to his left, Jerry met her imploring gaze and nodded. "Get well soon, Taylor. I'll give you a break on Wednesday, but I expect to see you in my office Thursday morning. You have a couple of days to get better."

"Yes, sir." She gave him a half-smile as he left. *I hope Grant makes his next parole appointment too.*

"Sophie? Answer me, young lady. Did Grant Madsen have anything to do with you getting shot?"

Sophie exchanged a nervous glance with Kirsten. "Well, yes," she said.

"I knew it, Soph—"

"But not in the way you think," she butted in. "Grant saved my life."

Will's eyes narrowed. "How? Start talking now, young lady."

"Will you stop this 'young lady' stuff? I'm freaking twenty-nine years old, Dad!"

"Is it okay if I explain, Mr. Taylor?" Kirsten jumped in. "Sophie's pretty wiped out from surgery."

He folded his arms across his chest and looked warily at Kirsten. "Okay. Just somebody tell me what happened tonight after my daughter decided to leave my house. Which was obviously not such a bright move," he added snidely.

Sophie rolled her eyes as Kirsten launched into a blow-by-blow description of the evening's events.

"And then Grant used his belt to make a tourniquet, which the paramedics said was really smart," she concluded.

Will frowned. "So, Grant's in jail right now?"

"Yes," Sophie confirmed.

"That's where he belongs."

"It is *not*, Dad!"

"The way I see it, you would never have been in danger if not for your association with Grant Madsen. You need to stay away from him, Sophie. Or you'll get yourself killed."

Even through her anesthesia haze, she knew something wasn't right with her father's conclusion. She tried to concentrate despite the throbbing in her arm. She felt a vicious headache coming on. Finally she argued, "No, Dad. The reason Carlo came after me had nothing to do with Grant. He wanted the money the police confiscated—the money Logan left in my office. And he was going to make me go to you to get it. So, if Grant hadn't shown up, we'd both be in a lot of trouble."

Will absorbed this information. "I still don't like him, Sophie. I don't trust him! Out of all the men in this city, can't you find yourself one boyfriend who is *not* in the Mafia?"

She smiled. "Sorry, Dad. You might not like Grant, but I do. I really do. And if you give him a chance, you'll like him too."

"Fat chance in hell," he scoffed.

"Grant's already won over Kirsten, right, Kir?"

Kirsten returned Sophie's grin. "I do like McSailor. He's yummy."

Already loopy, Sophie found herself giggling, and her laughter only increased when her father asked, "What the hell's a McSailor?"

37. Back Inside

Detective Marilyn Fox was concerned. She kept her eyes glued on the closed-circuit-camera monitor, which provided her a sharp view of the jail cell. She could see the emptiness of its inhabitant's eyes as he stared into space, seeming far away. The prisoner sat on the thin, striped mattress, his long legs pulled up to his chest with his elbows resting on his knees.

Marilyn sighed heavily and looked back at her paperwork.

Inside the cell, Grant was beholden to a series of flashes in his mind, punctuated by sharp intakes of air when his body reminded him he was unconsciously holding his breath.

A dark space—utter quiet—a rough wool coat scratching against his cheek—blackness—his own whimpering. "I'll be good. I promise, I'll be good."...

"It was you," said Carlo's raspy voice. "Logan died trying to protect you."...

Eyes the color of midnight searing into him, emanating anger—blinding sunlight in the prison yard—aching shoulders—numb, prickly hands...

A proud youthful voice, "Prison makes you a badass."...

Deep cerulean eyes. "Don't say it, Grant."...

Joe's devastated face, staring at him across the visitation glass...

A thunderous explosion—her body slumping on the sofa...

Grant rocked a bit on the mattress, his mind stuck in the horrific past.

"She's right in here, sir." Marilyn glanced up from her report to find Jerry Stone being led into the observation room by a uniformed police officer.

She rose and nodded. "Thank you, Officer." The desk sergeant left the room and Marilyn smiled warmly at the parole officer, extending her hand to shake his. "Good to see you, Jerry."

"It surprises me you're still here, um, Detective." Jerry referred to everyone by their last name, but he blushed when *Fox* almost slid out of his mouth. "I thought you'd be off to interview Taylor and her roommate."

"Paperwork," Marilyn replied, sweeping her eyes to the half-written report on the counter. "Detective Hammond had to run off on another call, but he's going to meet me later. The prosecutor refused to come in after hours so I want to get my interview with Mr. Madsen written down before I forget the key points."

Jerry had already begun peering at the camera monitor, and after a few seconds he frowned. "I was going to ask you how Madsen is doing, but from his cell and the camera setup I gather he's on suicide watch?"

She returned his frown. "That's right. I'm worried about him—he's taking this all really hard."

"Taylor getting shot? Having to shoot his cousin?"

"That, as well as discovering his cousin killed his brother."

Jerry's eyes widened. "Madsen's cousin was the one who stabbed Logan Barberi?"

"Yes." Her mouth tightened. "At least that's what Mr. Madsen claims. I need to verify that with Ms. Taylor and Ms. Holland—find out if they also witnessed Carlo Barberi's confession."

Jerry studied Marilyn. Her face was drawn with fatigue, and it was strange to see the normally spunky detective so down. "You've had a long day, with the funeral and all, huh?"

She nodded.

"You sound rather certain you've found Logan's killer, though."

"If you'd witnessed Grant, um, Mr. Madsen, describe how he discovered his cousin killed his brother, you'd be convinced too. He was a total mess." She glanced at the monitor and then at her report. "I've been so wrong about him."

With a sigh she sat back in her chair. "The truth is I'm stalling. I don't want to go visit Ms. Taylor because I don't want to face my failures."

"What do you mean, Marilyn?"

"Jerry, is she going to be all right?"

He nodded.

Marilyn sighed with relief. "Still, Ms. Taylor would not have been shot tonight, and Mr. Madsen would not have been arrested, had I done my job right the first time. I was off pursuing the wrong lead while the true murderer, Carlo Barberi, was terrorizing innocent people."

Not sure what to say, Jerry was quiet for a moment before venturing, "It was a tough case. You did your best, Marilyn."

"No, I didn't! I totally screwed up the investigation by assuming Grant Madsen was the killer. Once I heard he was from a prominent Mafia family, on parole, formerly a sailor at Great Lakes right where we found the body, I knew it had to be him. I *knew* it." She sighed again. "But when I interviewed him, and he had an alibi…" Her voice trailed off and she looked down.

Resting a hand on her shoulder, Jerry smirked. "Madsen's not your typical con, is he?"

His hand felt soft and comforting on her shoulder, and it surprised her, given his hard, gruff demeanor. She let out a half-chuckle. "Hardly. I've never had a murder suspect address me as 'ma'am' so many times."

"Taylor's not quite like any of my other parolees either," Jerry added, letting his hand fall from her shoulder.

Marilyn stood and faced Jerry with a look of tenderness. "I'm glad, um, I'm glad they found each other in the midst of all this mess."

Jerry returned her gaze and suddenly felt nervous. Darting his eyes away, he looked at the monitor, finding Grant with his forehead resting on his crossed arms, almost folded onto himself.

"I better go talk to him," Jerry said. "Taylor begged me to help him if I could."

Marilyn also focused on the monitor. "After I go to the hospital, Detective Hammond and I have to inform Angelo Barberi that his son is dead. That should be interesting." Still studying Grant, she felt a sadness wash over her. "I guess Mr. Madsen has been trying to get away from his family his entire life."

Jerry nodded. "Let's hope he finally succeeds."

❧

Frowning at the grown man huddled in a ball on the makeshift bed, Jerry stood outside the metal bars a few moments before asking, "You okay, Madsen?"

Grant lifted his head with a start to find Jerry watching him. Once he got his bearings he asked, "Is Sophie all right?"

Jerry nodded. "She'll live." A long, heavy sigh escaped Grant's lips as he tilted his head back and closed his eyes.

"Thank you," Grant murmured, and Jerry wasn't sure if he was talking to him or God. Opening his eyes, Grant scrambled to his feet to approach the bars.

Jerry's eyes narrowed. Sensing his disapproval, Grant asked, "What is it, sir?"

"Why the hell are you wearing a White Sox jacket? You told me you were a Cubs fan!" Jerry practically shouted.

Right then a wonderful thing happened to Grant Madsen: a refreshing sensation welled up from within, building and spreading throughout his body, and he found himself actually wanting to laugh. Despite all the horrific events still fresh in his memory, Jerry learning the truth about his baseball allegiance finally made him smile.

Shrugging his shoulders, Grant said, "I lied?"

Jerry's mouth dropped open. "You *lied* about being a Cubs fan? That's blasphemous! Why the hell did you lie to me?"

"Calm down, sir," Grant said, attempting to keep a straight face. "When I first met Sophie outside your office, I was wearing this jacket. She saw it and told me you were a huge Cubs fan—and that you were grumpy that day, so I'd better not admit I cheered for the Sox."

Jerry took a step back from the bars, warily studying Grant.

"Are you okay, sir?" Grant asked nervously. His smile faded as he noticed his PO's angry expression. "Sophie didn't mean anything by it. She just told me to take off my Sox jacket, and I did."

Jerry shook his head. "Christ, even then she was trying to get you to take off your clothes, Madsen."

Grant was pleased to see a smirk pierce the veneer of the older man's sternness. "So, she's really okay, sir?"

"Yes. I talked to her after her surgery, and she couldn't get me out of the room fast enough. She wanted me to come over here and check on you."

"Really?" Grant beamed. "She's not mad at me?"

Jerry looked incredulous. "You saved her freaking life, Madsen! You landed yourself back in jail, all for her. I'm thinking 'mad' isn't topping the list of how she's feeling right now."

Looking down, Grant twisted his hands nervously. "How long before I return to Gurnee, sir?"

"I don't know. Detective Fox needs to speak to the prosecutor, and there will probably be some sort of hearing."

Grant nodded. After a beat, he looked up and asked, "Will you tell Sophie I miss her?"

"What the fuck? I'm not your damn relationship counselor! Tell her yourself. You had your phone call, right?"

"No, sir."

"You haven't gotten your call yet? You gotta be more assertive, Madsen. The squeaky wheel gets the grease. Didn't you learn that in Gurnee?"

"I was trying to fly under the radar there. I was hoping not to let on that I was Enzo Barberi's son." Grant sighed and jammed his hands into the pockets of his jacket. "The truth is, I don't really want to make that phone call. They haven't offered it to me, and I'm not chomping at the bit."

"Why? Who are you going to call?"

"My Uncle Joe." Grant chewed on his lower lip. "I can't believe I have to tell him I've been arrested again. He's going to be so disappointed."

"Better now than never, Madsen. He's going to find out one way or another."

Grant nodded.

"I'll go get some boys in blue to let you make that call."

"Okay, thanks." He glanced around him at the cell. "I, um, I guess I'll stay right here, then."

Jerry grinned, shaking his head as he walked down the hallway.

❧

Smoothing a hand over her hair, Marilyn took a deep breath and knocked gently on the door before cautiously pushing it open. She walked into the room, expecting to find the patient conked out while her loved ones nervously paced around her. Instead Marilyn was greeted by Sophie's inquisitive brown eyes staring from the hospital bed. Kirsten was sprawled out, sleeping on a nearby chair.

"Hi, Detective," Sophie whispered.

Sitting next to the bed, Marilyn whispered back, "I thought you'd be sound asleep."

"This pain medication makes it hard to sleep, I suppose," Sophie said. "I'm dead tired, but I can't sleep. At least I stopped shivering—I couldn't stop shaking after the surgery."

"They say the anesthesia can do that to you." Marilyn smiled, and then the questions she was expecting began.

"Did you have to arrest Grant?"

"I'm afraid so. He confessed to shooting Carlo Barberi. Is that what you saw?"

Sophie nodded. "But it was self-defense!" Her voice trembled. "Is he back in Gurnee?"

"No, he's in a holding cell for the moment. We'll sort it all out starting tomorrow. Now, Ms. Taylor, are you able to answer some questions for me?"

Sophie nodded.

"How did this all begin tonight? Can you tell me the events from your perspective?"

"Kirsten and I were on her computer, in her bedroom, when we heard something in the living room. We went to investigate." She gulped. "And there was a man by the futon holding a gun on us."

"Carlo Barberi?"

"Yes." Sophie shuddered.

"How did he get in?"

She looked down. "I forgot to lock the door when I came in."

Marilyn arched one eyebrow, and Sophie lamented, "I know, I know. It was really stupid of me. I was just so flustered by my dad that I wasn't thinking straight."

"And where is your father now?"

"He's talking to his attorney on his cell phone somewhere in the hospital. He thinks he can get me out of parole now that I got shot."

"Not likely, Ms. Taylor."

"That's what I told him, but it's like talking to a wall once he gets his mind set on something."

Marilyn's stern look softened. "You can stop beating yourself up about leaving the door unlocked. Mr. Barberi was Mafia. If he wanted in, he was getting in, and a little lock on the door wouldn't have stopped him."

Sophie gave her a grateful smile and continued explaining the events of the evening. Eventually she said, "Suddenly I just knew Carlo had killed Logan."

"*How* did you know?

Sophie thought for a moment. "Carlo wanted the money Logan had hidden in my office, so obviously he knew Logan, but he also said that they weren't friends or something like that." Her heart raced at the memory. "When he held the gun on G-G-Grant, I realized he was going to kill him. He would have done it without a second thought. And it hit me then that Carlo was ruthless enough to kill Logan too."

The detective was quiet, and Sophie studied her worriedly. "You probably don't believe me, but I swear that's how it happened."

"Oh!" Marilyn interjected. "I believe you. I, um, I just wish I could have identified the killer before you had to. Then maybe you wouldn't be lying here in this hospital bed."

Sophie stared at her incredulously. A police officer believing her? Treating her nicely?

Getting back to business, Marilyn clicked her pen and held it poised over her notepad. "What happened when you accused Carlo of murder?"

"At first he looked *so* busted, but then he tried to deny it. Grant wasn't about to believe his lies." She closed her eyes. "Grant kept walking toward him, and Carlo was shouting at him to stay back. They were yelling at each other, and then all I remember is feeling like a speeding train slammed into my arm." She swallowed hard, trying to slow her breathing. "The next thing I knew, Grant was on his knees…" She felt tears behind her eyes. "And Carlo had the gun to his head."

Sophie clenched the sheet as a tear slid down her cheek, and the heart-rate monitor beside the bed beeped as the number on its display climbed higher and higher.

"Take your time," the detective encouraged.

Sophie nodded. "My memory is kind of fuzzy. I think Kirsten was trying to get to the phone, but Carlo wouldn't let her, and then Grant and Carlo were wrestling on the floor and… the gun went off. I was so scared, thinking Grant was the one who was shot, but then he got up, and I could see it was Carlo."

"What happened next?"

"Kirsten called 911, and I called Jerry. I, um…" She blushed. "I asked Grant to hold me. Then I woke up here."

"Speaking of waking up," Marilyn nodded toward Kirsten stretching in the chair, blinking her blue eyes at them. "I think your roommate just joined us. I'm Detective Marilyn Fox, Ms. Holland."

Kirsten finished removing her earphones and frowned at Sophie. "I told you to wake me up when the detective got here!"

"Actually, I wanted to talk to Sophie on her own first," Marilyn said.

"Oh," Kirsten responded, bleary-eyed. "That makes sense."

"And now I need to interview *you* separately, Ms. Holland, so why don't we let Sophie get some rest?"

Kirsten stood and followed Marilyn.

"You can call me Kirsten, Detective. Is it all right if I call you Marilyn?"

"Of course, Kirsten."

"Oh, good," said Kirsten. "I thought you were going to be all cold and standoffish like Officer Stone."

"Oh, he's not cold at all," Marilyn protested as they left the room.

By the time Marilyn and Kirsten returned, Sophie's father had resumed his place at her bedside. He gently held Sophie's hand as she snoozed and gazed apprehensively at her, seemingly worried she'd stop breathing at any moment.

"It took you long enough to get here, Detective," Will quietly seethed, ignoring Kirsten.

Marilyn raised her eyebrows. "It's nice to see you too, Mr. Taylor."

He released his daughter's hand and tenderly placed it on the sheet, turning expectantly to the detective. "So, what's the update?"

"Well, sir, I arrested Grant Madsen—"

"Good."

"Although Sophie's and Kirsten's stories corroborate that he was acting in self-defense."

"That's bullshit! You have to keep that man away from my daughter, Detective."

"Dad?" Sophie's weak voice made him swivel and find her sleepy eyes staring up at him. "Please be nice."

"You can't be serious, Sophie. He's from a Mafia family!"

"But he isn't a criminal like them. He doesn't work for them."

"Actually," Marilyn interrupted, "he told me that before Carlo came to your place, he'd been at his and threatened him. Grant agreed to start working for them so Carlo wouldn't hurt you, Sophie."

Sophie's heart ached even more for Grant.

"This is great, just great," Will sputtered. "You know what, Sophie? Just go to your Mafia boyfriend, I don't care. You two can commit your little crime spree together, Bonnie and Clyde style. But when you go back to prison, don't expect me to come visit you."

"Visit me in prison?" Sophie cried. "I've already learned not to expect that, *Dad*."

In the midst of the family squabble, a grin of recognition spread across Marilyn's face. "Bonnie," she said out loud, causing Will and Sophie to pause their argument. "I finally get why Grant called you that." She winked at Sophie.

Sophie's cheeks flamed.

Suddenly Marilyn seemed to come to her senses, and she officiously announced, "I have to leave now. I have to make a notification of death. You two need to let Ms. Taylor rest, and I'll be in touch." Smiling briefly at Sophie, Marilyn quickly left the hospital room, taking a deep breath as she strode down the corridor. She was headed to a Mafia compound, the home of one Angelo Barberi.

Joe stood by his chair as his nephew was brought into the interrogation room. Grant's hands were cuffed in front of him and his eyes were huge. He held his breath, waiting for Joe's reaction.

"Sit, Madsen," the officer barked, and both Madsen men took their seats.

"You have fifteen minutes," he informed them before exiting.

"I think we've done this once before," Joe said.

Expecting to receive a tongue-lashing, Grant was surprised when instead Joe asked, "How are you doing?"

"Fine." Grant nodded. "Now that I know Sophie is okay, they can do whatever they want to me. I don't care."

"Well, *I* care," Joe insisted, more loudly than he intended. Lowering his voice, he continued, "I'm going to get you an attorney."

"It's too expensive," Grant countered. "I'll just take the court-appointed guy."

"Yeah, 'cause that worked out so great for you last time."

Grant looked down at his cuffed hands. He hated putting Joe through this again. "Maybe I won't have to go back inside for as long this time," he mumbled.

"Maybe you won't have to go back inside at all. It was clearly self-defense."

He forced his eyes upward to meet Joe's. "I killed Carlo, Joe. I killed my cousin."

"He held you at gunpoint! He shot Sophie! H-h-he murdered your brother!"

But Grant looked guilty as hell, and Joe became even more incensed. "Goddamn it!" he shouted, rising from his chair.

Grant cringed.

"Why do you blame yourself for all of this?" Joe raged. "It's not your fault! You can't help which family you were born into!"

"I'm sorry," Grant said.

Watching his nephew tremble, Joe rested his hands on the back of his chair and tried to take a deep breath. Yelling at Grant wasn't going to help anything.

Joe realized he had buried one nephew and found the other arrested for murder, all in the span of ten hours, and he suddenly felt exhausted. He took his seat.

"I know what you did," Joe said after a moment.

Grant's heart beat faster.

"I know why you went to prison before. Ashley told me Logan and Carlo threatened to kill me unless you pulled that robbery."

Grant looked away. When he finally looked back at Joe, he found his uncle's blue eyes glistening with tears. "Why didn't you tell me, Grant?"

"I didn't want to drag you any further into this mess. It wasn't your fault your sister married my dad. You already had to take care of me all my life—you didn't ask for that burden. And then I went and screwed it all up. I must seem so ungrateful for all that you've done for me."

"Don't you understand?" Joe pleaded, grasping Grant's arm. "You were *never* a burden to me. When your mother died…" He felt tears prickle the back of his eyes, and he tried to blink them away. "When Karita died, the only thing that got me through was *you*. I was so proud to adopt you and have you as my son. Never forget that."

Grant didn't know what to say. Joe's powerful grip on his arm finally released.

"Karita fell in love with her 'tall, dark, and handsome Italian man,' and I tried to talk her out of marrying him, but she was determined. She had no idea what he was—she had no idea what she was getting into. But you know what? I'm glad she married Enzo."

Grant looked startled.

"I'm glad she married your dad because they produced two amazing boys. I have loved you both all my life."

Feeling a lump in his throat, Grant acknowledged, "I love you too."

"And this is awful to say, but I feel a sense of peace knowing Logan's murderer got justice," Joe admitted. "You did that, Grant. I hate that you have a man's death on your hands, but you had no choice. You had to protect yourself and Sophie… I would have done the same thing."

Grant sat silently, absorbing his words.

"So, what did they threaten you with this time?"

"Sir?"

"Did Angelo or Carlo threaten my life again unless you joined the family?" When Grant said nothing, he continued. "It's their way, Grant. They threaten and extort their way through life. I've been around the Barberi family almost forty years now. I know what they do."

"Carlo told me he'd kill Sophie unless I showed up to Angelo's tomorrow."

Joe nodded. "Do you think Angelo is going to come after you now that Carlo is dead?"

"I don't know. I guess he can't get to me if I'm in prison."

"But your father can," Joe said, sickened by the prospect. "I've got to keep you away from them. They seem hell bent on bringing you down. If it's not Carlo framing you for murder, it's another way to try to hurt you."

"What?" Grant asked. "Carlo framed me?"

Joe gave him a bewildered look. "Yeah, by planting Logan's body at Great Lakes. Why else would he put the body there? I bet Carlo saw Lo's bruises and found out you two had fought, giving him the perfect opportunity to pin it on you."

Grant shook his head. Carlo's evil nature astounded him.

"Time's up," the officer announced, striding into the room and hauling Grant to his feet in one swift motion.

"I'll be back when I can," Joe promised.

"Thank you, Joe," Grant called over his shoulder as he was led away.

As his nephew left, Joe Madsen's jaw clinched determinedly. He would not let the Barberis hurt his nephew ever again.

38. Uncles

A shrill ring began competing with the deafening snores rocking the studio apartment. Bolting upright in bed, the snore producer looked all around, snorting and snuffling, until he identified the cause. Roger Eaton noticed his alarm clock said 6:30 a.m. as he reached for the phone.

"What is it?" he barked.

"Rog? Is that you? It's Joe."

With a yawn, Roger retorted, "Of course it's me. Did you forget who you were calling, numbnuts?"

"You didn't sound like yourself," Joe said.

Another yawn. "Yeah, I'm losing my voice from being the docent on every cruise without your nephew there to help. Good thing he's coming back."

"Um, Rog? That's one of the reasons I'm calling. Grant won't be able to return to work today."

"Why the hell not, sir?"

Joe was quiet a moment before revealing, "He's been arrested."

Roger drew in a sharp breath. "I thought he was cleared for his brother's death."

"He was." Joe paused. "But then Grant shot and killed Logan's murderer." Hearing Roger's gasp, Joe continued, "It was self-defense. His cousin Carlo came after Sophie, and Grant saved them both by tackling him to get the gun. The gun went off, and Carlo died—right after confessing to killing Logan."

Roger didn't know what to say. Madsen's screwed-up family belonged on Jerry Springer or something. "He's gotta get released if it was self-defense, right?"

"I hope so, but I don't really know. It's not good that he's already on parole."

"I'm sorry Joe—that fucking sucks. Is there anything I can do to help?"

"Um…" Joe seemed startled by the question. "Do you know any good attorneys?'

"Ah, yeah, he needs to lawyer up, doesn't he? Hmm, I certainly would not recommend the douche bag I hired for my divorce!"

Joe sighed. He didn't have the energy to laugh. "Well, don't worry about it—"

"Wait! That bitch who represented my wife—she obviously knew what she was doing. She was as tight as a camel's ass in a sandstorm."

This time Joe did crack a smile. "But I need an attorney specializing in criminal cases, not divorce."

"She worked for some high-powered firm. I bet they got all kinds of ambulance chasers there. It's called McCallister, Abrams, and Mitchell if you want to check it out."

"Great, I'll give them a call before I head out."

"Where ya headed? Are you gonna help me with the cruises today?"

"I wish I could, Rog, but that brings me to the real reason I called. I wanted to tell at least one other person where I'm going this morning, in case anything happens to me."

"That don't sound good, sir."

Joe took a deep breath. "I'm going to the compound—the Barberi home. I need to talk to Grant's uncle, Angelo. So, if you don't hear from me, you might want to call the detective working the case."

"Don't do it, Joe. At least don't go alone. Hell, I'll go with you—let me hop in the shower—"

"No," Joe countered grimly. "Angelo won't talk if he feels at all threatened, and I need to have some words with him. It's a, it's a family matter."

Roger was quiet for a moment. "I don't like the sound of this, Joe. Not one bit. But you're a stubborn son of a bitch, and I'm sure that I can't talk you out of it."

"You know me well, Rog." Joe hesitated and then added, "Oh!" He sighed deeply. "I've got some more bad news, I'm afraid. Sophie Taylor worked for you too, right? Grant told me she got shot in the standoff with Carlo, and now she's in the hospital."

"What the fuck?" His heart pounded. "Is she at Northwestern?"

"I think so. Apparently she's doing okay now—Carlo shot her in the arm. Grant feels horribly guilty about the whole thing."

"I bet. His family is a bunch of *fucked up* crackerjacks. Stay safe, Commander. I don't want you to end up swimming with the fishes."

"Thanks, Rog. Thanks, um, for looking after Grant these past two months."

"I wasn't much help, obviously. But our boy does not belong in prison."

"You and I both know that. Let's hope the prosecutor agrees with us. Gotta run, Rog."

Roger stared at the phone. Madsen was in jail and Taylor was in the hospital? What a shitstorm this had turned out to be. He frowned, thinking about running his cruises without them. Who was he going to insult all day long? Who was going to tease him about his vegetable diet?

❧

Sophie's eyes fluttered open and panic gripped her. She had no idea where she was. Then the antiseptic smell and white, sterile room began to orient her, just as a shooting pain in her immobilized left arm brought it all back. Her breathing slowed as she looked all around her, wondering where Kirsten and her father were. She was pretty sure it was Tuesday morning.

Hearing a soft knock on the door, Sophie looked up and smiled brightly at the short man with a huge floral arrangement entering the room. "Roger!" she cried. "Those flowers are beautiful."

Once he set down the massive vase, she could detect a blush forming on his cheeks. He tentatively approached her bedside. "You, uh, you look great, Taylor."

She'd never seen her former boss try to be so civil, and she narrowed her eyes suspiciously. "No, I don't. I've been shot, Rog, and stuck in this hospital bed without a shower or any makeup. I'm a mess."

"Hey, you said it, not me," he said, holding his hands out in mock surrender. Despite her protests, she still looked beautiful to him.

Sophie bit her lip. "I guess *I'm* the one in the hospital and *you're* the one visiting this time."

"Yeah, kind of a role-reversal, huh?" He glanced around him excitedly. "Is that hot nutritionist chick gonna come see you?"

Sophie grinned. "I don't think they send dietitians for gunshot wounds."

Frowning, Roger peeked at her left arm. "Joe told me what happened. You gonna be okay, Taylor?"

She nodded. "Did Grant's uncle say anything about how he's doing?"

Her voice was etched with concern, and Roger was blown away that she still loved Madsen despite him nearly getting her killed. Some guys had all the luck. "Joe was trying to get an attorney for Grant, and I gave him a name. It'll be pricey though."

"Well, my dad will help pay for Grant's legal costs," she offered.

Roger scrunched his eyebrows. "He will?"

"Yes," Sophie confirmed. "He doesn't know it yet, but he will."

Shaking his head, Roger chuckled. "You got him wrapped around your finger?"

She smiled wryly. "Obviously you haven't met my father. He's not exactly thrilled about me dating Grant."

"Well, that's what dads are supposed to do—protect their kids. I bet that's why Joe is headed off to have words with Angelo Barberi, to try to protect Grant."

Sophie drew her hand to her mouth. "I hope he'll be okay." She was consumed by worry for Grant's uncle, though nothing compared to her fear for Grant himself. He was locked up, unsure of his fate, and all alone.

❧

The guard led Grant into the interrogation room, and he found himself staring at a slender brown-haired woman with piercing hazel eyes, dressed in a tailored navy business suit and lavender silk blouse.

She eyed his manacled hands and glared at the guard. "Take off those cuffs."

"No can do," the officer retorted. "If you want the surveillance cameras off, the cuffs stay on."

The woman gave the officer a puzzled glance—why all the precaution? She then realized the prisoner must be on suicide watch. She had a live one here, evidently.

"Fine." She gave a tight smile. "Have a seat, Mr. Madsen."

His polite "Yes, ma'am" threw her a bit, and his sea-blue eyes almost took her breath away.

"I'm your attorney, Mr. Madsen. No need to kiss up. Your uncle hired me."

Grant offered her a guilty grimace.

"My clients are invariably thrilled to see me," she said. "What's *your* problem?"

Grant looked down. "I told Joe not to do that. It's too expensive."

"I *am* expensive," she said. "But I assure you, Mr. Madsen, I'm worth it."

"You can call me Grant," he offered.

"Okay, Grant, then let's get started."

"I didn't catch *your* name, ma'am."

"Nicole McCallister, and you can call me Nic. Now," she said with barely a pause. "Tell me everything about your involvement with the Barberi family, and don't leave out a single detail."

Grant took a deep breath.

℘

Joe attempted to ignore the thumping of his heart as he stood outside the gated entrance to the massive stone house. He glanced down at his khaki uniform and bit his lip. He'd debated about wearing civilian clothes, but in the end decided his military garb might make them at least pause before they tried to kill him.

Holding on to the image of Grant's angelic eight-year-old face, Joe rang the bell on the stone pillar. Within seconds a strapping black-haired man appeared, and Joe marveled at the speedy response; the bodyguard must have been perched outside the mansion, on patrol. Joe also noticed that despite the stifling warmth of the August day, the guard wore a suit-jacket, most likely to hide the weapon strapped in his holster.

"What do *you* want?" he questioned in a deep voice.

"I need to speak to Angelo."

His black eyes danced with disbelief as the bodyguard gave Joe the once-over. The visitor seemed almost as insistent as the scrumptious little brunette who'd come knocking with a guy in a suit late last night, but this guy didn't have a badge like they did. "Nobody gets to speak to Mr. Barberi."

"Listen, meathead, go tell your boss Joe Madsen is here to see him, and quit wasting my time." Joe felt a catch in his throat at the heat of the broad-shouldered goon's glare, but then the guard turned and slowly ambled toward the house.

About five minutes later the door buzzed, and Joe turned the knob and entered. With no one to guide him, he headed to the front of the house.

As soon as Joe reached the porch, the solid front door opened, revealing two more large men in the foyer. "Come in, Commander," Tank said, limping slightly as he stepped back and exchanging a nervous look with Mario. This was Logan's uncle on his mother's side, and Angelo had demanded he be treated with respect.

But respect did not negate the need for safety. Mario held his meaty paw against Joe's chest. "We gotta frisk you first."

Joe sent the bodyguard an irritated glance but nodded. He'd expected this. He stood ramrod straight as the two men expertly searched him. Tank paid special attention to patting down his chest, and Joe muttered snidely, "I don't think a weapon would fit in there, gentlemen."

Tank gave a perfunctory smile. "Just making sure you're not wired."

"This way," Mario instructed, and Joe followed with Tank lurching on his heels. The naval commander was in the middle of a goon sandwich.

They entered a luxurious study, darkened by rich paneling and cherry bookshelves, and Joe found himself face to face with Angelo, whose tired, red-rimmed eyes were visible through a thick haze of cigar smoke. Angelo wearily rose from a leather recliner and sent a questioning glance at Mario.

"He's clean," the big man confirmed.

"Leave us," Angelo ordered.

Joe heard the door softly click shut. There was palpable tension in the room as Joe ventured, "So, you've heard about Carlo, then."

A flash of sadness crossed his face. Angelo had aged tremendously in the past few days. "The detectives came by here last night."

Wondering if they'd made it out alive, Joe furtively glanced around the study but found nothing awry. It took all of his self control to mutter, "Sorry for your loss."

"We've all experienced some losses lately," Angelo said. He gestured to a chair. "Want to take a seat?"

Sitting casually and comfortably in this lion's den was the last thing Joe wanted to do, but he needed Angelo to feel at ease. He crossed to the other leather recliner and both Grant's uncles took a seat. Angelo looked at Joe expectantly.

"Do you know why I'm here?"

Angelo shot him a curious glance. "To gloat?"

Joe looked horrified. "*No.* There's no happiness in Carlo's death for me. You lost your son, and I can't imagine what pain you're feeling right now … Well," he swallowed, "I can imagine how much it would hurt to lose Grant."

Angelo clenched his teeth. Joe adopting Grant behind Enzo's back was still a sore spot.

"That's why I'm here," Joe said. "Grant. I assume the detective told you who killed Carlo."

"Of course."

"I need your word that no harm will come to Grant. Inside or outside of prison."

Angelo looked into Joe's pleading blue eyes, noticing his resemblance to Logan. Logan and Grant had never truly fit into the Italian family because of those blue eyes from their fair-skinned mother. Though Logan sure had tried to make it work as a mobster. "You're asking me not to seek revenge on my son's killer?" Angelo asked quietly.

"What good would revenge do, Angelo? You mentioned how many losses we've all endured. You in particular have lost so much. Your brother is in prison, your godson is dead, and now your son is gone too. Don't lose your nephew as well."

A stabbing pain cut through Angelo's numbness. Joe was right. But how could he let his son's murder go unpunished?

A vision swam before his eyes of Carlo at age ten, small and defenseless in that hospital bed, the gunshot wound on his left arm bandaged tightly. Carlo hadn't been the same since, and truthfully, Angelo hadn't been the same either. Every time he looked at his son, he thought about his older brother rotting in prison—all because of Carlo's stupid, childish mistake.

"I know you loved Carlo," Joe said, cutting through the silence. "But he had Grant and two women at gunpoint—Grant had no choice."

"Carlo was just trying to motivate him. He never would have killed Grant."

"You of all people know what Carlo was capable of!" Joe countered. "The detective told you about his confession, right? About what Carlo said to Grant right before he died? Admitting he killed Logan?"

Angelo shifted his eyes away and swallowed guiltily. "Isn't that convenient? Grant tells the authorities Carlo confessed to killing the man *he* is suspected of murdering."

"It's not only Grant who heard him say that—there are other witnesses too!"

"As if Carlo would kill his own cousin," Angelo protested weakly, still not meeting Joe's eyes. He stood abruptly. "I need a drink," he said. But his journey to the bar was halted when Joe leapt to his feet in a moment of epiphany.

"You knew," Joe said.

Angelo froze, then slowly turned to meet Joe's appalled gaze. "Knew what?" he asked, trying to sound casual.

"You knew Carlo killed Logan!"

Fuck. He'd coolly led the detectives to believe he had no idea Carlo was the killer, but apparently Joe could read him more easily than he thought. "Of course I didn't know that," Angelo said evenly.

"Save your bullshit for someone else," Joe seethed. "You could have prevented all of this from happening. You could have turned over your son and stopped the bloodshed."

Besieged by Joe's attack, Angelo felt overwrought. He'd been awake all night, and his brain was too muddled to argue with this incensed military man, this man who thought he was too good for the Barberi family.

Angelo was still reeling when Joe yelled, "You knew how evil Carlo was! He pretty much *forced* Grant to shoot him—it was the only way to stop him! And now Grant has blood on his hands. You could have prevented it all."

"Shut the fuck up!" Angelo screamed back, feeling his hands furl into fists. "He was my son!"

Joe studied Angelo, ready for his next move. Mario stuck his head in the door, but his boss impatiently waved him off.

Suddenly another image from Carlo's childhood flooded Angelo's brain. Remembering Carlo's handsome, youthful face at his first communion, he felt his fury dissipate, replaced by sadness and guilt. "He was my son," he repeated, more softly this time. He coughed loudly. Worn out, Angelo slowly returned to his chair and slumped into the leather. He stared at the plush carpet.

Carefully, Joe also resumed sitting, never taking his eyes off the Mafia boss. Angelo sighed and looked up, shooting a dirty look at his guest. "So, that's the game you're playing, huh? Either I promise not to pursue Grant or you go to the cops and tell them I knew Carlo killed Logan."

Joe was surprised, but maintained a cool façade. Eventually he said, "No. I will not blackmail you. That's your way, not mine." He sighed. "I came here, man to man, to ask you to do the right thing. Grant is not a ruthless criminal—he never has been and he never will be. And if you coerce him into that role, he'll get killed. Please. There have been enough deaths already. Please, Angelo."

There was silence, the only sound the ticking of the grandfather clock. Angelo shook his head, feeling the burden of heading the powerful family. He missed Enzo's leadership. Enzo would know what to do.

Finally Angelo looked up, and the uncles' gazes locked. Angelo appeared pained as he pledged, "You have my word that I won't go after Grant. But if he ends up back in Gurnee, I can't control Enzo."

Despite his relief, Joe pressed on. "Why not? You're the head of the family now, right?"

"You don't understand Enzo." Angelo shook his head sadly. "What my father did to him…" His voice trailed off.

"What happened to Enzo?" Joe asked.

It was a rare window of vulnerability, and just as quickly as it had opened, it slammed shut. "None of your business."

A sharp rapping on the door made Angelo frown. "What?" he yelled.

Mario entered the study. "You got a phone call, boss."

"Take a damn message!"

"It's, uh, urgent. She made me come get you. She said it was an emergency."

Angelo yanked the cordless phone to his ear. "Yes?"

"Ben's missing!" Ashley's frantic voice filled the phone line.

"He's missing? Calm down, Ashley," Angelo ordered.

His instruction did not diminish her panic at all. "He wasn't here when I woke up, and I thought he went to school early, but the school said he isn't there! He's not answering his cell phone. I've called all his friends, but he's not with them." She forced herself to ask, "Is he at the compound?"

"Not that I know of, but we'll look for him. Relax, Ashley." Angelo handed the phone back to Mario. "Have you seen Benjamino, Meat?"

"No, boss. But he knows the code so he could have snuck in."

Joe did not like the thought of a sixteen-year-old boy coming alone to this house. "Ben looked really upset at the funeral yesterday. He doesn't know about Carlo yet, does he?"

"No," Angelo acknowledged, looking guilty. "I'll go myself to see if he's up in his room."

"I'm coming with you," Joe insisted. "We're both his great uncles. I'm worried about him just like you are."

Angelo narrowed his eyes but did not protest when Joe trailed him out of the study and up the stairs. Meat followed closely behind. They walked down a long, ornate hallway and arrived at a closed door.

"Ben?" Angelo called, knocking on the heavy wood. "Are you in there, son?"

Hearing no answer, Angelo turned the knob, grateful the door was unlocked. Smoky vapors hit both men like a sandstorm, swirling and enveloping them. Joe peered through the smoke to locate Ben, propped up on the bed, puffing away happily on a joint.

Angelo turned to Mario and quietly instructed, "Call his mom back and tell her we got him. But don't mention anything about the weed."

As Mario hurried down the hallway, Joe looked angrily at Angelo. "Don't tell his mom he's been smoking pot? A *sixteen* year old? His mother deserves to know her son is using an illegal substance!"

"It's no big deal. Lo smoked all the time at his age."

"And look where that got him," Joe sneered. "Six feet under."

Their argument was interrupted by Ben, who finally realized he had guests in his room. "Hey, the military dude is back," he said slowly, sending Joe a relaxed smile. Noticing Angelo, he amended his statement. "Oh, actually both my great uncles are here. Bitchin. I got both, uh … gruncles her wit me, yo."

"Gruncles?" Joe asked.

"Yeah, military dude. Great uncle takes too long to say. I'll call you my Gruncle. You down with that?"

"I'd be more down with taking you to rehab," Joe muttered.

"You want some of this?" Ben invited, holding out his joint. "It's great stuff. I sell only the best."

Joe wondered if he was getting a contact high from the secondhand smoke. So, not only was Ben using drugs, he was dealing too? Angelo was allowing this to happen? Had he learned nothing from Logan's experience in juvenile detention? From Logan's lifelong struggles with addiction?

Watching Angelo just stand there, Joe marched over to Ben's bed and extended his hand. "Sure, I'll try some."

"You're cooler than I thought, military dude," Ben smiled woozily and reached into the backpack next to the bed, extracting a large plastic bag. "Let me just roll you a toke."

Joe swiftly swooped in to grab the bag of pot.

"Heyyy," Ben protested, his grin fading.

"Did you honestly think I was going to light up a doobie with a sixteen year old, Ben?" Joe hid the bag behind his back with one hand while ripping the lit joint out of Ben's grasp with the other.

"Give it back," Ben whined.

Joe fought the urge to order the boy to drop and give him twenty. He glanced at Angelo standing uncomfortably by the door. "You knew about this too, didn't you?" Joe asked. "You let a teenage boy use drugs—*deal* drugs? Out of your house?"

"Hey, he's cool with it," Ben said. "Why do you gotta be such a jerk?"

"Because I care about you and your future, Ben," Joe responded gruffly. "And your father had a lot of wonderful things about him, but getting busted for selling pot as a teenager was not one of them."

At the mention of Logan, Ben immediately felt tears. He clenched his jaw, attempting to hold them in, but his bloodshot eyes glistened.

Noticing the boy's emotional torment, Joe sighed and sat down in a chair next to the bed. Ben drew his knees to his chest and wrapped his skinny arms around his legs. Grant had sat on his bed that very same way as a teenager, trying not to cry on his deceased mother's birthday. Joe sighed again. "It was a long, difficult day yesterday."

Ben nodded and angrily swiped away the tears that had begun to cascade down his cheeks.

"Why did you leave your mother's house?"

Looking down, the teenager mumbled, "'Cause my stash was here."

"Getting stoned will not help anything."

"Who c-c-cares?" Ben sputtered angrily. "No one cares anyway." He looked angrily at Angelo in the doorway. "*You* don't care."

"What do you mean, kid?" Angelo asked.

"You don't care that your son killed my dad!"

Angelo drew in a sharp breath, too stunned to speak.

"I was here!" Ben said, his tears falling in earnest now, "I was here when those detectives showed up. I heard the whole thing. Carlo k-k-killed my dad, and then my Uncle Grant killed Carlo."

Ben crumpled onto himself and sobbed. Joe ached for him. No wonder the boy had smoked himself into oblivion. It was more than anyone should have to bear—to find out his father was murdered, then discover his idol was the one who killed him.

Realizing Angelo was still too floored to speak, Joe took action, attempting to gather the weeping teenager into a hug. Ben resisted, then gradually melted into the man's firm embrace, continuing to sob. "I'm so sorry you lost your dad," Joe murmured, patting Ben's back. "It's going to be okay. You'll get through this."

They held each other for several minutes while Angelo looked on, appearing uncomfortable. He knew how to run a business by cheating, stealing, and killing, but comforting a crying teenager was not in his repertoire.

"How about I take you home to your mother's?" Joe suggested.

He was surprised when the boy readily nodded. Joe could only hope that learning of Carlo's evil might make this compound less appealing. Hiding the bag of pot behind his chair, Joe picked up Ben's backpack, and they walked out of the room.

"You're welcome anytime, *ragazzo*," Angelo told Ben as he headed down the hall.

"Okay, godfather," Ben responded.

Once the boy was out of earshot, Joe said, "Get those drugs out of here."

Angelo bristled. "This ain't over between us, Madsen."

"You bet it's not," Joe agreed. He'd successfully extricated Grant from the family's clutches, and that was a good start, but he wasn't done yet. He had to free Ben as well, if the boy was to have any chance of becoming a good man. Joe knew Angelo wasn't going to let Logan's son go easily. The battle for Ben was just beginning.

39. Bonnie and Clyde

Suppressing a yawn, Grant smoothed his hands across his chest, feeling the rough black T-shirt provided to him by a police officer. The cotton was coarse and heavy. He much preferred the soft, supple feel of a well-worn shirt, but he might as well get used to scratchy clothes issued by the state. The prison blues bestowed upon him at Gurnee would be even more uncomfortable, if memory served.

He'd been puzzled when the guard gave him the shirt but told him to continue wearing his own jeans after his shower earlier that morning. This was his third day of captivity, and he thought surely he'd be dressed in an orange prison jumpsuit by now, awaiting his hearing. He wondered if they didn't quite know what to do with a parolee-turned-murderer.

The click of heels on the concrete caused him to push his body off the bed. Just then Detective Marilyn Fox rounded the corner.

"Mr. Madsen," she nodded, taking in his lean arms and freshly scrubbed appearance.

"Good morning, ma'am." He smiled shyly. "Is there any word on my hearing?"

"Actually, I'm here to escort you to your attorney, and she will tell you the deal."

Grant nodded and immediately stuck his hands through the small opening to be cuffed. He was dismayed to find submitting to restraint becoming routine once again.

Marilyn paused, contemplating whether or not to cuff him. She looked up into Grant's expectant eyes and searched them for a moment, finding only warmth and gentleness reflected there.

Clearing her throat, she muttered, "No cuffs. We're walking just a short distance." She unlocked the cell, and Grant hesitantly stepped out. Looking up at him and suddenly seeming to doubt her largesse, Marilyn added, "Don't even think about making a move, though, Mr. Madsen, or I'll have you on the ground so fast you won't even know what hit you."

"Yes, ma'am," he smirked, loping along next to the feisty shorty with his hands in his jean pockets.

Once Marilyn dropped him off in the interrogation room, she waltzed into an adjacent conference room where Jerry Stone sat waiting. "Okay, let's synchronize watches," Jerry said playfully, pinching the face of his watch on his left wrist. "Nine-thirty-seven ... mark."

Marilyn rolled her eyes and also glanced at her watch. "In fact, it's nine-thirty-eight, Jerry. Just to make sure we're on the same page, you're saying Mr. Madsen is going to accept the prosecutor's deal within five minutes, right? And if he does, I owe you twenty dollars. If it takes him more than five minutes to accept the deal, you owe *me* twenty bucks."

"You got it," Jerry nodded, looking smug.

"But what if he doesn't take the deal at all?"

"Then he's dumber than I thought, and his ass belongs in Gurnee."

Inside the interrogation room, Grant waited until his attorney sat down before he took a seat as well. Nic was positively beaming.

"Grant," she began. "The prosecutor just offered us a deal. A damn good one, I might add."

"A deal? I thought I was going to have a hearing?"

"No!" she exclaimed. "Haven't you been listening? The deal negates the need for a hearing or a trial."

"Okay," he responded tentatively. "So, what is it? The deal, I mean."

Nic leaned in as if disclosing a juicy piece of gossip. "They're offering one more year—"

"One more year?" he repeated instantly, sitting back in his chair. He felt undeniably relieved. He'd been expecting a much longer sentence. Carlo's blood was on his hands.

One year without seeing Sophie. Could he do it? He seriously doubted the DOC would allow a parolee to visit him at Gurnee, and she had a good ten months left on parole.

One more year of his uncle's intense worry while he was behind bars with his father. Could Joe handle it?

Despite his misgivings, Grant had to admit it would be quite liberating to know that in one year's time, this whole ordeal would be over. Nic had expressed concern about a longer sentence if they ended up with a tough judge, and eliminating that nerve-wracking uncertainty would be quite a bonus.

Nic watched as Grant pondered the pros and cons of the deal, deliberating intently. He drummed his long fingers on the weathered wood table. Finally he asked, "Do you think I should take it?"

She squinted her eyes and peered at him as if he were the daftest, most dim-witted specimen in the universe. "Um, *yeah*," she replied. "Your PO and Detective Fox think you should too."

"They—they know about the deal?"

Again she shot him an incredulous look. "Of course they know about the deal—they were instrumental in getting the deal!"

"Wow" was all Grant could say.

"I'm good at what I do," Nic asserted proudly. "But I'm not *that* good. To get a deal this sweet, we definitely needed their help to grease the wheels with the prosecutor, who agreed to knock the charge down to a parole violation: consorting with known criminals. You sure know how to win people over, Grant."

He took a deep breath and rubbed his temples with his forefingers. He just wanted this to be over, and he felt quite alone at the moment. His attorney seemed thrilled with the idea, but only he knew what it would be like to serve another year in prison. "Maybe I should talk to my uncle about this first?"

Nic arched one eyebrow. "I'm *sure* he would tell you to take the deal, Grant. And once you do, you'll be seeing him soon enough."

Grant tilted his head. "They'll let him visit me here again, ma'am?"

Her expression was equally perplexed. "Why would Joe come here?"

"To visit me before I'm transported."

"Transported?"

Grant had the distinct feeling he was missing something. "To Gurnee?"

Nic sat frozen for a moment, then she burst out laughing. Grant was offended by her amusement, seemingly at his own expense, until she finally choked out, "N-n-not Gurnee! One more year of *parole*, not imprisonment. The deal is an additional twelve months of parole, to be added to your remaining eight months!"

He stared at her, speechless. "Parole? I—I—I don't have to go back inside?"

Her face glowed with pleasure, heartened by his look of pure joy as the reality of his freedom sunk in. Reactions like his made her career well worth it. "You can leave here anytime," Nic confirmed.

Startled by the immediate scraping of his chair on the floor as he bolted upright, Nic watched his eyes glow even brighter with happiness.

"I can go to Sophie?"

As he turned to fly out of the room, she called, "Grant, hold on! You have to sign these papers first!"

Almost to the door already, he spun around and returned to the table. Pointing to each signature line, Nic frowned. "You really should review these first. You need to know the conditions of the deal."

"Who cares about the conditions—I'll do anything as long as I don't have to return to prison. Will you, um, mail a copy to me, ma'am?" he asked, frantically scribbling an illegible signature on each line.

"I think I can handle that. And it's Nic, not ma'am." She grinned, meeting his excited gemstone eyes. Damn, the man was hot. She found herself devising evil plans to dispatch this Sophie woman he'd mentioned.

Finishing his last signature with a flourish, Grant set the pen down and took her hand in his warm, firm grasp. "Nic, thank you." He gave her a crooked smile, then spun on his heel, making a hasty departure.

As Grant emerged from the interrogation room, he was startled by Marilyn's triumphant voice in the hallway, "I win!" She beamed at him while Jerry frowned as he peered at his watch.

"Ma'am?" he asked nervously.

"You took the deal, Mr. Madsen?"

When he nodded Jerry inquired grumpily, "What took you so fucking long?"

Grant started to explain, but instead just shrugged. He wanted to hightail it to the hospital as quickly as possible.

Marilyn answered for him, winking at Jerry. "Mr. Madsen wasn't sure he wanted to see your sorry mug every week for another entire year, Jerry. It took him awhile to agree to that."

"Thank you both so much," Grant broke in. "Nic told me you were instrumental in getting the deal." He wanted to ask them why they'd helped him, but he had more pressing matters to attend to at the moment. He nervously offered Jerry his hand. "Thank you, Officer Stone."

Jerry pumped the extended hand, grumbling, "Now you have no excuse to miss our appointment tomorrow morning. I'll harass you then."

"I look forward to it, sir."

He went to shake Marilyn's hand as well, but feeling a wellspring of gratitude, he awkwardly leaned in and gave her a chaste hug instead. "Thank you, ma'am," he murmured.

Pleasantly surprised by the impromptu hug, Marilyn whispered in his ear, "Bonnie is in room 1165. Go get her."

He stepped back and a look of stunned anticipation crossed his face. Nodding, he gulped. "I'm free to go?"

"Yeah, the bulls down there know you're to be released," Jerry said. "Just don't get into any trouble between now and tomorrow morning. Okay, Madsen?"

Grant nodded, then practically ran down the hallway.

Marilyn leaned against the wall, a smug look on her face. "Eight minutes and twenty-three seconds," she gloated. "What made you think he would take the deal faster than that?"

"I *knew* I should have picked ten minutes instead of five. Those damn attorneys always milk it for every billable second." He turned to the detective, and she could see his indignant anger was all for show. "Well, I thought the horn-dog would jump at the chance to get back with Taylor. And I was right—did you see his happy dance out of here?"

Marilyn chuckled.

"What made *you* think it would take longer than five minutes?"

Her smile faded. "The boy has the self-esteem of a gnat, Jerry. I was worried he would feel like he *belonged* in prison or some such nonsense. His family has really done a number on him."

She thought back to the two occasions when she'd interviewed Grant's uncle, the slippery and malicious Mafia don, at his club and then at his house. There'd been something not quite right with Angelo's responses, but she hadn't been able to pinpoint the problem. It was incredible to her that Grant was related to people like Angelo and Carlo Barberi.

Jerry nodded. "Well, let's hope they stay away from him. I *will* put him back in prison if he commits a crime, even if he's forced to do it."

"You'd only be doing your job," Marilyn said, resting one hand on his arm. "Speaking of jobs, I'm sure we both have to get back to ours. But before we go, I do want to know how you're planning on paying up. You're not going to welsh on our bet are you?"

"I—I—I don't have any cash on me!" Jerry stammered.

Marilyn narrowed her green eyes.

"But I can do you one better," he amended. "Um, I could take you to dinner? You know, uh, to pay off the bet and all."

"Hmm, dinner," Marilyn said, letting the word linger on her tongue while she stroked her chin pensively. She finally flashed him a bright smile. "That would be lovely."

Jerry returned her smile. "Great, uh, Marilyn. I'll call you."

She nodded and they parted ways. The cool detective felt her face flush with warmth as she strode down the hallway. It had been quite a good day!

As Grant neared Northwestern Memorial Hospital, his pace slowed. He'd run all the way from the police station, dodging meandering shoppers, and now that he finally had Sophie's location in sight, he should have been sprinting to the elevators. Instead, his gait morphed from a run to a jog to a walk.

A niggling question played at the back of his brain, dancing and nudging, poking at his consciousness with an irritating reverberation.

What if she doesn't want me back?

Sure, Sophie had once told him she loved him, but that was before she found out he was related to Logan. Just thinking about his brother made Grant's stride decelerate even further, and a wave of regret once again crashed over him.

Willing himself to stop thinking about murders and funerals, Grant instead conjured up the image of Sophie's beautiful face, intelligent and compassionate, chestnut-brown eyes and flawless porcelain skin framed by wavy strawberry-blond curls. The depth of his love for her seized him with a ferocious intensity. He'd never felt this enamored of a woman. Did she feel the same way about him?

Grant placed his hands on his hips and sighed deeply. Whether she would have him or not, he had to go in and find out. If she never wanted to see him again, at least he might derive some comfort from knowing she was safe and on the mend. Taking a deep breath, Grant pushed forward and the revolving door conveyed him inside.

Emerging from the elevator, he scrutinized a sign on the eleventh floor and turned to his left, his anticipation building as he drew closer to Sophie's room. Reaching the door, he knocked softly. Hearing no response, he peeked inside.

He took in her prone form, lying on her right side, evidently sleeping. With a guilty wince he noticed her bandaged left arm in a sling over her shoulder, but his expression lightened considerably at the soft, peaceful look on her resting face. Grant was so mesmerized by her vulnerable beauty that he didn't notice the shadowy figure rising from a chair by the window.

He looked up at the last minute to find Sophie's father right next to him with a scowl on his face. Will gestured to the hallway. Pushed backward by her father's brusque advance, Grant backed out of the room and almost crashed into an orderly wheeling an IV stand down the hallway.

Will pointed to an empty spot near the water fountain and they stood, eyeing each other warily. Grant was dog-tired and full of dread about conversing with this man who seemed to hate him, but if he had to fight to have a chance with Sophie, he would. She was worth it.

"How's she doing, Mr. Taylor?"

"Why are you here?" he countered. "I thought you were locked up."

Taking a deep breath, Grant responded, "Yes, sir, I was."

Will glared at him. "Then how did you get out?"

"The prosecutor agreed it was self-defense and knocked it down to a parole violation. They let me off with another year of parole."

The news did not please Will. "Call it self-defense, call murdering a man whatever you want. The truth is my daughter would not be in *there*"—he pointed to the hospital room—"recovering from a gunshot wound if she hadn't gotten involved with *you*."

"You're right, sir."

Expecting the young man to argue with him, Sophie's father paused. He wanted to fire off another question but didn't get a chance before Grant continued.

"I can understand why you don't want Sophie to be with me, sir." He stuffed his hands into his jean pockets and looked down. "I come from a criminal family, and you don't want her associating with people like me."

He looked up to find Will staring at him blankly.

Grant sighed. "I knew what my family was capable of, and I promised myself I would never put Sophie in danger. But I failed." His hands tightened into fists. "I never meant for any harm to come to her, but she almost … *died*. Because of me." Swallowing hard, Grant confessed, "If I were you, I wouldn't want a man like me with your daughter either."

Will kept gawking at Grant. If he was trying to win the older man over, he was doing a piss-poor job.

"I know I can't guarantee that Sophie will be safe. But then again, can *you* guarantee her safety, sir? I wasn't involved in her life when she went to prison, you know."

"What?" Will shot back angrily. "You're trying to tell me your entire family wasn't involved in setting up my daughter?"

"No, sir," Grant replied nervously. "Uh, truthfully, I don't know if anyone besides Logan was involved in Sophie's arrest. All I know is I didn't have anything to do with it. The first time I met her was outside our PO's office. I swear."

Will's only response was "Humph."

Longing to get to Sophie, Grant pressed on. "I'm sure you don't believe me. Why believe a criminal, right? And I know if you had your way, I'd leave here and never come back. But this is Sophie's decision, sir. I have to hear it from her. If she doesn't want me here, I'll leave." *It will hurt like hell, but I'll leave,* he silently promised himself. "But please, let *her* make the decision. Please, sir."

Rubbing his jaw, Will glared at Grant. Then he dropped his arm to his side and let out a defeated sigh. Looking down, he stated quietly, "She's all I have now."

Grant winced, thinking about Sophie's deceased mother. Her recent death must be much fresher in both their minds than the loss of his own mother.

"I know I can't control her," Will admitted. "I can't stop her pain. But don't you dare put her in danger again. If she's at risk, you must leave her. If she's in danger, you have to walk away to keep her safe. Can you promise me that?"

Considering his demands for a moment, Grant said, "Yes, sir." He would be the first to walk away if it meant protecting Sophie from danger. Will examined his face for any sign of dishonesty, but found none.

Standing up taller with his shoulders pressed back, Grant asked, "May I go in now?"

Nodding his head, Will frowned and walked away.

This time Grant did not hesitate when entering Sophie's room.

❧

She was still sleeping, and he crossed with soft steps to sink into the chair formerly occupied by her father. Quietness blanketed them as he watched the steady rise and fall of her chest. She looked so calm and comfortable, and he longed to join her, to wrap his body around hers in that thin hospital gown and drift off to sleep. Would they ever be together again? Or would she flinch in fear upon seeing him?

He leaned forward to investigate the gauze bandage peeking out from under the tan-colored sling and felt utterly disgusted. The crack of the gunshot echoed in his head, followed by the vision of Sophie slumping back against the sofa. Grant shuddered.

Sophie rolled to her left side, and the pain from her wound startled her awake. Her cry of anguish pierced Grant's guilty heart. She managed to sit up without further jarring her injury, and her right hand instinctively cradled her left elbow. Her shoulders hunched and a tear rolled down her cheek. She was still so exhausted, completely worn out from physical pain and unremitting emotional worry for Grant. She was not surprised to find herself crying yet again.

"Please, Dad, don't bother the nurse again. It's feeling better today, I promise."

"You're in pain," Grant said in a choked voice. *And it's my fault.*

Sophie whipped her head around to find Grant with a white-knuckle grip on the chair's armrests. Inhaling sharply, she felt tears begin to flow as she gazed into his clouded blue eyes.

"If you want me to leave, just say so, Sophie."

She gave him a baffled look. How could he ever think she'd want him to leave? "I, um, I—these are tears of *joy*, Grant. You're here. You're free. You're not in prison." Smiling through her tears, she added, "How did you get here?"

"Thanks to your quick thinking in calling Jerry, I only got another year of parole."

His silky smooth voice and good news was a salve for her wounds. For once she did not feel the throbbing ache in her elbow. "So, you probably have another year with Jerry, then. Can you handle it?"

Grant was finally able to breathe again. "I'm not sure I can tolerate that Cubs fan for another whole year, but I'll do my best."

They felt drawn to each other by a palpable force. Finally Sophie asked, "Why aren't you holding me?"

Grant was next to her bed in a second. All he needed was an invitation, yet he still hesitated before touching her. "I—I—I don't want to hurt you anymore."

"The only way to hurt me is if you don't get your butt in this bed this instant."

"Yes, ma'am." Grant gingerly climbed in, taking painstaking care not to bump her left elbow. There was just enough room for him to fold his body around hers, resting his hand on her hip. As her back met the warmth of his chest, a happy smile danced across her face.

Their right hands stroking and caressing, Grant nuzzled into her strawberry tresses and planted a soft kiss on the back of her neck, which elicited shivers of excitement up and down her spine.

"Your dad is going to love this," he whispered.

"Where *is* my dad?"

"Probably standing outside your room like a vicious guard dog. I had to fend off his snarling threats to get in here."

"Oh, Grant, I'm sorry." She blushed.

"That's okay, Bonnie. You're worth it."

She sighed. "He doesn't like me being with bad boys." Then she chuckled. "Though I don't know why he thinks *you're* one."

As they lay together, Sophie recalled the last time they'd held each other—in Grant's bedroom after she cooked him dinner. So much had happened since then. It had all gone to hell. She cringed, remembering Grant's anguished expression when she'd screamed at him on the ship the next day.

"I'm sorry for yelling at you," she said.

"What?" Grant's body tensed.

"On Rog's ship—when I accused you of lying to me. I just was so overwhelmed to find out about Logan—"

"Shh," he tried to soothe her. "It's not your fault, Sophie."

"I'm sorry. I'll never doubt you again."

Grant's voice filled with remorse. "Please don't say you're sorry, when I'm the one who should be apologizing to you. I never should have dragged you into this mess." He sighed guiltily. "I never should have involved you in my family's affairs."

"No, I did that all by myself, Grant. I'm the one who got involved with Logan." She felt his body tense again. "I've been beating myself up for not recognizing that you and Logan were brothers."

She drew a deep breath, and Grant's body seemed frozen, listening to her intently. "When I saw the two of you together, you looked so alike!" She took his trembling hand into hers. "But then it finally dawned on me why I didn't see it."

He studied the back of her head nervously, steeling himself. "Why was that?"

"You may look like Logan, Grant, but you're *nothing* like him. You're nothing like your family. You're a good man." She drew his right hand to her lips and kissed his fingers softly.

Grant closed his eyes. He didn't quite believe he was a good man, but at least she did. She believed in *him*. He wanted to be worthy of her grace.

Then she grinned, thinking about her father. "It's kind of ironic that I had to date a convict to find a good man."

"Thank God you went to prison, Bonnie. I never would have met you otherwise."

"And I'm grateful you're a criminal thug as well, Clyde." They snuggled closer and both felt sheer exhaustion from their crime spree—a crime spree that had finally come to an end.

Pacing the hospital hallway, Will decided he'd waited long enough. Surely Sophie had kicked that Mafiosi to the curb by now? What was taking so damn long?

Will burst into the room only to stop short right inside the door. His eyes burned at the sleeping figures on the bed, curled around each other so tightly that there was not one inch between them. Will had never seen such a look of serene bliss on Sophie's face, and his own face curled into a scowl.

Apparently this Madsen man was here to stay.

40. Going Home

Still asleep, Grant unconsciously brushed off whatever was nudging him on the shoulder. However, the hand continued joggling his arm, and Grant's eyes opened to stare directly into the ample bosom of the nurse leaning over him.

"Get out of that bed, young man!" she hissed.

His eyes widened and he quickly extricated himself from the wonderfully warm cocoon he and Sophie had created. At his departure, she groaned, shifting in the bed while yawning and extending her toes like a cat stretching after a nap.

"What were you thinking?" the nurse chastised, glaring at Grant before hovering over Sophie to dress her bandage. "This is a hospital, not a hotel—unless you need to be admitted too?"

"No, ma'am," Grant said apologetically. He felt a little disoriented. That was the best sleep he'd had in a long time.

Feeling groggy herself, Sophie scrunched her forehead. The nurse had been very kind to her during her stay, and now she was harshly reprimanding Grant for sleeping? Something didn't seem quite right.

The solidly built nurse began bustling around the bed. "C'mon, honey, we need to get you dressed. You're being discharged and your father is waiting for you."

That was it. Sophie sat up and glanced at Grant standing a respectful distance from the bed. "Did my father send you in here, Chavonne?"

Nurse Chavonne appeared surprised, but then averted her eyes, bending down to the overnight bag on the floor. "These are the clothes your roommate brought for you?" she asked innocently.

"Chavonne," Sophie said, not fooled by her misdirection. "Answer me. Did my dad tell you to come in here?"

Reluctantly the nurse looked up from unzipping the bag. "Yes."

Rolling her eyes, she inquired, "What exactly did he say?"

"I'm sorry, Sophie. He grabbed me and asked if it was hospital policy to allow our patients to have sex with their visitors."

Sophie's jaw dropped. "We were *not* having sex!" She glanced at Grant, whose eyes danced with amusement.

Chavonne continued. "Your father said he was going to lodge a complaint with my supervisor if we didn't discharge you right away like we promised. So, I need to get you dressed and out of here."

Scooting off the bed, wincing slightly from the movement to her arm, Sophie muttered, "He is some piece of work. I'll dress myself, thank you very much."

"No can do, Ms. Taylor." Chavonne shook her head firmly. "You need somebody to help you. I want that elbow completely immobile for at least a week."

Quiet up to this point, Grant stepped forward. "I'll help her."

Chavonne and Sophie looked over, and he reciprocated with a smoldering gaze that made both women weak in the knees.

"Um, uh …" Sophie stammered, a blush coloring her neck.

Grant sidled up behind Sophie, placing his large hands on her small hips. He leaned in, his warm breath feathering her ear as he whispered, "Let's teach old Will he'd better not try to come between us."

Feeling goose-bumps travel up her spine, Sophie's blush grew deeper. She closed her eyes and leaned against his muscular frame, bolstered by his strength.

Chavonne hesitated, unsure what to do, but certain she felt like an intruder.

"It's okay, Chavonne," Grant nodded reassuringly. "You can tell Mr. Taylor it would be unwise to come in here for awhile, as his daughter will not be decent."

"Maybe you could go get my discharge instructions?" Sophie suggested.

Rolling her eyes, the nurse exited.

"Now," Grant asserted, kneeling down by the bag, "Let's get you dressed, shall we?"

"Grant, thanks but I can do it myself, really …"

He stood, holding some folded clothing in his grasp, and gave her a disapproving look. "And what would Dr. Hayes say about that, hmm? I thought you were supposed to work on asking for help?"

Her eyes narrowed. "I'm never telling you *anything* about my therapy sessions ever again!"

He chuckled and clasped her right hand in his, stroking her skin softly. Finally Sophie said, "It's embarrassing. I can't even dress myself."

"Let me take care of you, Bonnie. Please. After all the hurt I've caused you, it will make me feel good to take care of you."

Searching his eyes, she finally nodded. He gently loosened the belt of her sling and carefully freed her arm.

"It doesn't really matter," he added, circling around behind her and slowly untying her hospital gown. "I'm only going to rip these clothes right off of you once we're alone, anyway."

He slid the hospital gown off her shoulders, leaving her standing in the cool air-conditioning clad only in her lacy pink panties. Her creamy smooth complexion gave him pause, wanting to take her right then and there, but seeing her shiver slightly, he quickly grabbed her bra from the pile of clothing on the bed.

"Uh, *this* should be interesting," he commented as he faced her, holding up the bra and trying to figure out the best way to put it on.

"I usually clasp it in front and then slide it around," she suggested.

He gulped and reached around her, weaving the bra around the small of her back, bringing his sturdy body closer and causing Sophie's breath to hitch. She was glad Chavonne had helped her to shower the evening before, and she hoped she smelled as good as he did, his clean soapy scent flooding her senses. Sliding the ends of the lacy garment to the front, right above her navel, he concentrated as his long fingers hooked the eyelets. Skimming and twisting the bra across her skin, he began shimmying it up her ribcage but halted for a moment.

"Sorry." He shook his head. "I just can't resist." He leaned down to graze his lips across the baby-soft skin between her breasts.

Her shivers were less about feeling cold and more about thrilling anticipation, and she inhaled sharply as he tenderly kissed her sternum, his nose nuzzled between her breasts. Her right arm snaked around his back and held on tightly as his lips ravaged her. Finally he returned to standing and gently looped the bra straps over one shoulder, then the other.

He gave her a jaunty smile. "That wasn't so difficult now, was it?"

Reaching for the thin, scoop-neck white T-shirt, Grant draped the neck opening over her ponytail, one hand unleashing her thick hair from the collar and the other lovingly stroking her cheek. He was mesmerized by the flecks of gold and copper in her brown eyes.

His voice was husky. "There are going to be lots of kisses involved in getting you dressed."

"That would be just fine."

He inched closer and his lips lingered tantalizingly near hers. Then his full, sensuous mouth caressed hers, passing a jolt of electricity through them both.

Grasping her right hand while continuing to plant zealous kisses on her lips, he entwined his fingers in hers, fondling the smooth skin of her palm with his thumb. Reluctantly pulling away, he instantly locked his lips to her right shoulder and proceeded to glide his mouth down the length of her arm, leaving a hot, pulsating trail from shoulder to wrist.

He helped her lift and fold her left arm gently into the short sleeve. His soft lips loitered on the clean bandage above her elbow, and she whimpered only once as he carefully nudged her wrist through the sleeve. He drew the collar over her head then repeated the process with her right arm.

Her heart raced when he tugged her pink underwear down her legs. Once the panties passed over her ankles she nervously stepped out of them. Sensing her embarrassment, he had a fresh pair waiting for her to step into. A fiery red flushed her face as he guided the silky undergarment over her knees—would he continue his pattern of kissing the body part he dressed?

Glancing up at her with a mischievous smile, Grant craned his neck around her hip and planted a loud smooch on the curve of her bottom. Chasing her derriere with his lips he managed to connect with another kiss before she shrieked with laughter.

"Ticklish, Taylor?" he smirked, rising from his knees as he pulled her panties up and promising himself he would soon return to this enticing area (perhaps when her father wasn't right outside the door!). He gave her a playful swat on the bottom before reaching for her jeans.

To Sophie's delight, McSailor skimmed his mouth up and down the length of her legs like a vessel gliding across a body of water, and soon her jeans were also in place. He stood admiring his work, amazed that the casual ensemble looked so classy. She could make any clothing look stylish and chic, such was the grace of Sophie Taylor.

Her entire body hummed from the heat of his warm lips. With a woozy look, she confessed, "I never want to dress myself again." He laughed heartily. "Will you dress me every day?"

"That can be arranged, Bonnie."

Delicately replacing her sling, Grant then gathered magazines and books into her bag while Sophie stepped into her flats. She nervously glanced at him, knowing her father was likely waiting in the hallway. "Ready to face the music?"

Nodding confidently, Grant reasoned, "He can't be as bad as a Mafia don."

"We'll see about that."

They emerged from the room, hand in hand, with Sophie's overnight bag slung over Grant's shoulder.

"What took you so long?" Will demanded. Grant felt Sophie's hand tense in his.

"What's the rush?"

"I have the limo waiting outside for us. Let's go."

Sophie took a deep breath. "Dad, I'm not going home with you."

"Of, of course you are!" he sputtered. "Where else are you going to live?"

"Kirsten's."

"You can't stay in that blood-stained hovel! Kirsten is at her parents' right now, and that's where you should be too. Home."

Sophie had not considered the damaged state of Kirsten's apartment, and she dropped her head. Where was she going to live?

Grant gave her right hand a soft squeeze. "Sophie? Um, would you like to live, um, to stay, with me?" He leaned in closer and whispered, "How else would I dress you every morning?"

She smiled. "Yes. I would love to live with you, McSailor."

Grant and Sophie shyly grinned at each other while a storm cloud passed over her father's face.

"Y-y-you can't live with *him*!He's a felon!"

Sophie's grin vanished. "I'm a felon too, if you haven't noticed, Dad." Giving Grant's hand a reassuring squeeze, she promised, "We'll just have to be felons together."

"But you're not married! Your mother would not approve of this at all."

She felt like he'd punched her in the stomach. Grant felt her body trembling next to his, fighting for control. He pulled her closer, as if to shield her.

"It's hard to know what Mom would want for me," she said. "But I *do* know she'd want me to be happy, to be in love. And Grant is the one person in this world who brings me happiness. I am in love with Grant, whether you accept it or not."

Will sighed. "I just worry about you, Sophie."

She instantly felt guilty, and stepped forward to give her father a hug. "I love you, Dad," she said, feeling comforting fatherly pats on her back. "But I can't live with you right now."

"Why not?"

"Because you're being a helicopter parent."

"A *what*?"

"You're hovering!"

He peered at her peculiarly. "Damn shrink talk," he muttered.

She tossed her head and her ponytail swayed. "That's right, Dad. Our family is enmeshed with generational boundary-crossing and emotional over-responsibility. I'm trying to break the dysfunctional communication dyads, but you're not making it easy."

Will groaned, and Grant got the distinct impression they'd argued this way before. Will turned to him and pleaded, "Can't you do anything with her?"

Taken aback, Grant faltered. "Um, I have no idea what she just said, sir. I'm afraid I'm not much help."

"Good luck with that, then." Will anxiously cleared his throat and reached into his pocket, extracting a folded check. "I was going to give this to you, uh, at home. But I guess I have to give it to you now."

She warily placed the check in the pocket of her jeans. "Thank you."

"I gotta go," her father quickly announced. "Don't be a stranger." With those parting words, he strode quickly toward the elevator, leaving them standing in the hospital hallway.

"Well, that wasn't too bad," Sophie said once he was gone.

"It *wasn't*?"

"What do you mean? My dad and I argue constantly—well, when we're speaking to each other anyway—and this is one of the first times I actually won."

"I *never* argued with my dad," Grant said, feeling his cheeks redden with shame.

A frightened look ghosted his handsome features, and Sophie remembered the awful stories Logan had shared about their father. Grant was free of prison but evidently not free of his past. She hoped eventually she could help him heal.

She hooked her right arm into his left, attempting to distract him. "Time to go home?"

"Definitely. But do you mind if we make a stop first?"

The sunlight bounced off the rolling green waves of the Chicago River as Sophie and Grant sat on a bench by the dock, his arm protectively draped over her shoulders.

"You're sure he's on the ship?" Sophie questioned.

"Yeah, I had the police officer call my apartment from the station, and he wasn't there, so I bet he's helping Rog again. I don't know where else he'd be."

On cue, an awful sound hit their ears. They could make out a raspy, off-key shouting, like nails on a chalkboard, and to Grant's horror he realized Roger was *singing*. Or rather he was *trying* to sing, croaking out the ugliest, most abrasive Frank Sinatra interpretation known to humankind. The ship slowly chugged into their line of vision.

"Oh my God, what is he *doing*?" Sophie wondered, also aghast. Roger sounded like a dreadful karaoke Elvis.

"This is bad," Grant agreed, shaking his head. "If this is his kind of town, I don't want to live anywhere near it."

"Join in, everyone!" Roger called gleefully over the microphone as the ship began docking. His encouragement was met with stunned silence, the passengers cautiously glancing at each other, having no idea what caused the auditory assault on their eardrums.

Just as he eased the ship alongside the dock, Roger realized there was dead silence onboard. He nervously cleared his throat. "Thank you for choosing Eaton Tours! Please come back soon."

Once the ship had docked, passengers streamed down the gangway as if they could not disembark fast enough. Watching the melee, Grant and Sophie shared a bewildered smile. "Sounds like Rog missed you," Sophie smirked.

"Grant!" Joe's thrilled voice filled the air, easily audible over the din of the chattering passengers.

Grant popped up off the bench, finding his uncle leaping over the gunwale and rushing toward him. Meeting him halfway, Grant launched himself into his uncle's awaiting embrace and they thumped each other on the back soundly.

"You're out! What happened?"

"They dropped the charge to consorting with known criminals while on parole, and I got an additional year of parole, that's all."

Joe could only smile, the creases of worry lining his face finally smoothing away. "You don't have to go back inside with your father," he said, feeling liberation from the vice grip of the Barberi family.

Grant met his uncle's clear blue eyes and felt overwhelming gratitude. "I'm already with my father," he said.

Joe finally noticed Sophie standing a few feet behind his nephew. Grant turned to bring her forward. He rested his arm across her shoulders while she wrapped hers around his waist, and they faced Joe together.

"So, she's the one, huh?"

"Yes, sir," Grant nodded, nuzzling in to sneak a kiss on her cheek.

Joe's smiling eyes found Sophie's. "I'm glad you're here to take care of him, because I have to get back to my captain in Norfolk. We're shipping out soon."

"I'll try to keep him out of prison for you, Joe."

"Hey," Grant protested. "You're on parole too."

"Yeah, but I'll be done long before you will," she teased.

"Holy fuck!" A voice rang out from the deck, and all three immediately knew who it must be. Roger stood at the ship's railing, hands on his hips. "The parolees busted out! It's about damn time!"

"How are you doing, Rog?" Grant asked, boarding the ship with Sophie in tow.

"Just trying to keep afloat," he replied. "Since you left me in the lurch, you asshole, I've had to take back the reins as docent."

"So I heard," Grant said. Desperately attempting not to laugh, he tried to avoid Sophie's gaze. "You're, um, you're singing now too, huh?"

"Yeah," Roger smiled proudly, puffing out his chest. "I thought I'd do a little Frank Sinatra myself. He's more from my generation than yours, anyway. How'd I sound?"

"Uh…"

Sophie cleared her throat, glancing at Grant. "I'll take this one." Looking back at the captain, Sophie began, "You know I love you, Rog, and I'm very grateful that you gave me a job. But if you sing again, your business will go straight down the tubes." Her brown eyes were warm but her message was firm. "Rog, please promise me, *never sing again*."

His face fell, and Sophie immediately felt guilty. "But you do such an awesome job navigating, um, running the business…" She quickly tried to cover.

"Is she right? I'm not a good singer?" Roger pointedly asked Grant and Joe, who exchanged nervous glances.

Joe attempted a placating tone. "Rog, um, Sophie is a very wise woman. Her father is a successful businessman. Maybe you should take her advice."

Just then Grant noticed a teenager in navy-blue coveralls emerging from the lower deck. "Ben?" he called.

The boy appeared startled. "Uncle Grant!"

"What are you doing here?"

Joe answered for him. "Ben wanted to make some extra money before school begins, so he's helping out on the ship." The two exchanged a knowing glance.

The truth was Ashley had hit the roof once Joe informed her about Ben's drug habit, and she'd threatened to cart him off to rehab immediately. Ben had screamed that he'd run away before he went to rehab.

Somehow, Joe had helped them forge a compromise: Ben would see a local therapist and work on Roger's ship for a month, and if his subsequent drug test was clean, he wouldn't have to go to rehab.

Grant went over to rest his arm on Ben's shoulders. "So, you're chief toilet cleaner now!"

Out of earshot, Roger glared at Joe. "I'm gonna go check the shitters. He better have actually cleaned them this time or he's getting an earful."

Joe stifled a grin. "Give him a few days. He'll get on board with the program, Rog."

Once the ship's captain headed aft, Joe and Sophie were left alone while Grant and Ben chatted nearby. Joe cast a worried look at Sophie's sling. "How's your arm feeling?"

"Sore," Sophie admitted. Her right hand reached into her pocket and she felt the folded check. Pulling it out, she offered, "I uh, have some money for Grant's attorney fees. Will ten thousand cover it?"

Joe looked shocked. "Where does a parolee come up with ten grand?"

Her cheeks reddened. "My father gave it to me."

"Your father?" His eyebrows arched skeptically. "I find that hard to believe. He didn't seem to be Grant's biggest fan."

Sophie chuckled. "He's not, but he's, um, he's coming around." Her voice dropped as she confessed, "My dad doesn't exactly know what I'm doing with this money."

This kind, beautiful woman made Joe's heart swell with pride. "Thank you, Sophie," he said. "But I can handle the fees. I'm sure they won't be too bad. How about you pay off your student loans?"

She looked surprised, and Joe continued. "Grant told me about those. He was hoping the loans might convince you to move in with him someday—you know, to save money."

A faint smile brushed her lips. "Are you sure you have enough money to cover it?"

"No worries. I have a rainy day fund."

"But it's not raining."

Joe grinned. "Even better." He glanced out at the calm river, feeling the ship rock gently beneath them, and his grin faded. "It may not be raining now, but it sure hasn't been smooth sailing for you or Grant. You've both survived quite a storm."

Sophie knew she and Grant still had a long way to go to recover from all they'd endured, but she had a sense that together they could do it. *Bonnie-and-Clyde style,* she told herself, smiling happily.

Grant brought the boy over and stood behind him, resting his hands on the teen's shoulders. "Sophie, I want you to meet my nephew, Ben."

So, here was Logan's son. She gazed into yet another set of arresting eyes. What was it with the men in this family and their gorgeous baby blues? Logan's voice floated into her mind: *I spent the day with my son. He just turned fourteen in July.*

"Hello, Ben." Sophie smiled, suppressing her sadness.

"Hey," he murmured, looking embarrassed. Glancing at his uncle nervously, he nodded toward her sling. "Uh, Carlo … um, he did that to you?"

"Yes. But I'm going to be fine."

Biting his lip, Ben sniffed. "That's, um, good."

Grant squeezed his shoulders and advised, "You better get back to work."

Ben sighed. "This sucks."

"Yep," Grant nodded, "Being the chief toilet cleaner does have its drawbacks. But maybe if you work hard, you can get promoted like I did."

Ben shuffled off dejectedly, and Grant called after him, "See you tomorrow!" Then he grabbed Sophie's hand. "Let's get out of here. Rog said I could take the day off, and I want to leave before he changes his mind."

"Oh!" Sophie cried. Sage-colored sheets awaited them both. She asked Joe, "Will I see you again?"

"After I book my flight home, I'll stop by to get my stuff," he promised. Reading the eagerness in their flushed complexions, he added, "I'll, uh, knock first."

Sophie's cheeks bloomed crimson, and Grant laughed. "Good idea." Clasping her hand tightly in his, he told her in his silky voice, "Come on, Bonnie. Let's go home."

41. Con-habitation

Jerry Stone drummed his fingertips impatiently on his government-issued metal desk, feeling more and more irritated by the second. It was three minutes past nine o'clock. Taylor was late.

He growled as he surveyed the office. The drab cornflower-blue paint peeled from the walls, the grimy blinds were swathed in a thick layer of dust, and the linoleum floor was cracked and warped. He hoped Marilyn Fox would never see this shithole. He'd have to keep her away from his office—either that or redecorate.

Muttering under his breath about the nonstop drama surrounding the first two parolees scheduled for this morning, he opened the door, letting himself out into the hallway. Greeting him was the typical bustle of the DOC on a Wednesday morning—parolees filing into various offices or shuffling down the corridor to get drug tested, uniformed officers discussing the latest Cubs game over a cup of coffee, administrative assistants typing away—but still no sign of his particular parolee. Was somebody returning to prison today?

Finally he noticed a slender pair dash around the corner and head in his direction. They were moving quickly, though it seemed Madsen wouldn't let Taylor break into a run and thus jar her injured elbow. He regulated their pace with a protective hand on her uninjured right arm.

At last they stood in front of their PO—panting, biting their bottom lips, fidgeting, and averting their eyes from his hostile glare.

His arms folded, Jerry glanced at his watch and growled, "Nine-oh-five, Taylor."

She swallowed hard and slowly raised her eyes to meet his.

"It's my fault, sir," Grant said. "If anyone has to get in trouble for Sophie being late, it should be me. It's my fault."

"No, it's not!" Sophie protested.

"Whose fault was it then?" Jerry asked her. "Why were you late?"

"Um, it took…" Sophie's voice faded, and Jerry watched with fascination as her exquisite porcelain skin flushed with color. He was also intrigued by Madsen squirming next to her. "It took, um, longer than we thought—than *I* thought it would take, um, to get dressed."

Jerry narrowed his eyes, trying to sniff out what was going on between the two.

Sophie felt her pulse race even faster as she recalled their morning…

After an evening of passionate lovemaking, they'd fallen into a deep slumber. Only Grant's alarm clock had prevented them from oversleeping.

To keep her bandaged wound dry and stationary, Grant had helped her shower. He'd attempted to be focused and gentlemanly about lathering her body, but he'd been completely turned on by her, glistening in the pounding stream of water. Somehow he'd managed to wash her hair and help her step out of the shower, but by the time he'd toweled her off and stood before her in the bedroom, clutching her lacy bra and underwear in preparation to dress her, he'd lost all resolve.

She looked into his blazing blue eyes, and there was a suspended hush in the air. Apparently their prior coupling had not quenched their thirst for each other; on the contrary, their scorching sex-fest had left their throats dry and parched.

They needed to get to their PO, lest they return to lockup, but both felt a hot craving to lock onto each other instead, never letting go. Their brains acknowledged a pressing need to hustle to the courthouse, but their hearts desired to press their bodies together even more urgently.

Emotion trumping logic, Grant caressed the back of her neck and drew her face to his, their lips crashing together with a palpable, bruising force. Tongue on tongue, three hands groped for each other's skin. The only piece of clothing between them was Grant's boxers, which he'd slid on after the shower. Their deep kisses made their desire an insatiable compulsion.

Sophie took blind steps back to the bed, drawing him with her by the suction of her lips, and somehow they managed to fall onto the sheets without jolting her arm. He helped her scoot back toward the pillows, resting his weight on his elbows while hovering over her. Their long, bare legs became entangled and a fine sheen of moisture from the shower coated their skin. Grinning against his probing mouth she reached into his boxers and took him in her hand, causing him to halt his flurry of kisses and inhale deeply, staring down at her with longing, half-lidded eyes…

"…is no excuse." A gruff voice drew her out of her enthralling memory, and she found herself staring not into her lover's cool gemstone eyes, but her parole officer's heated brown ones.

"What?" she asked, turning to see if Grant could catch her up on the conversation. His shoulders were back, spine stiff, and his face bore the anxious expression of a man getting chewed out by a superior.

"I *said*," Jerry repeated, "your injury is no excuse for being late. Don't think just because you've been shot I won't shoot your ass straight back to prison."

Grant tensed, and Sophie gulped. "I'm sorry, Jerry. I won't be late again." But her response did not break the PO's stern stare.

Sophie decided to try a different tactic. "I apologize for being late, but I hope you won't hold it against me since you were late once too."

Jerry's bushy eyebrows arched as his glare intensified. "What the hell are you talking about, Taylor?"

"You were late for our meeting once last month," she said. "You were, uh, coming from the hospital." She noticed a shadow of grief cross Jerry's face. "I'm sorry to bring that up, sir, but I'm sure you wouldn't hold me to a higher standard than yourself?"

Grant tried to get Sophie's attention, pleading silently for her to shut the hell up before their PO arrested both of them, but miraculously Jerry's upper lip began to twitch toward a smile.

"Whenever I was late for psychotherapy clients, I figured I couldn't be upset if *they* were late." Sophie shrugged, wincing from the movement to her left arm. "The golden rule—that's all I was thinking."

Jerry shook his head. "Damn shrink parolee." He opened his office door and ordered, "Both of you get inside, now."

Grant looked startled. "You want me in there too, sir?"

"Yeah, I'll see you two together. That way your tardiness won't make me fall behind in my schedule. And I won't have to listen to your bullshit twice, either."

Grinning, Sophie allowed Grant to guide her into the office by the elbow. She still wasn't sure what she thought about his chivalrous behavior. It felt reassuring to be ensconced in his protective shell, but she was *not* a delicate flower.

And now that they were finally together, it certainly was not okay for him to take the blame for her mistakes—especially if that meant he might land himself back in prison. She couldn't bear to be separated from him again.

Once the three were seated, Jerry pulled out their files and made a few notations.

"So," he boomed. "Anything new to report? Well, besides one of you getting shot, the other killing a man in self-defense and getting arrested, and both of you being exonerated of murder?" He smirked.

"Uh, at least we're not boring," Sophie said.

"Hardly," Jerry agreed.

Tapping her index finger on her chin, Sophie piped up, "Oh! I do need to tell you my new address, I guess."

"Holland's place spooks you now, huh? That's okay. I already got your father's address in your file." Jerry nodded smugly.

"Um, Jerry? I'm not living with my dad."

He tilted his head to one side and caught Sophie slyly glancing at Grant. It took him a second to understand their delight. "I see," he said, holding up Grant's file. "I can put the same address down for both of you now?"

Sophie nodded shyly, and Jerry rolled his eyes. So, the cons were *con*-habitating. The parolee dating service had produced a perfect *con*-nection indeed.

Grant felt a pleased grin on his face. His Bonnie was no longer over the ocean or over the sea. He had brought her back, he mused, *and now she's living with me.* She would live with him! She would share his bed. Reliving their most recent experience in that very bed, he closed his eyes dreamily...

Hovering over her, stomach to stomach, he rested on his forearms, careful not to press against her injured elbow. One hand cradled the side of her face and the other smoothed her thick hair, fanning out the strawberry strands on the pillow. Her hand was doing amazing things to him down below. He had shimmied out of his boxers and there was nothing left between them. Truly.

"We don't have... time," he panted, kissing the tip of her nose.

"We'll be quick," she responded breathlessly, feeling the hard length of him brush her thigh. Stroking him, she remembered their encounter after the baseball game. "I'm just warming up the hot dog first."

Grant shook his head. "Hon, my sausage has been cooked from the second I touched you in the shower."

"Is that so?" she asked. "Well, my buns are toasted and ready."

They burst out laughing, and in the midst of their good cheer, Grant slid on a condom. The hilarity passed the moment he held himself just above her, grazing her skin and teasing her quivering center. He gazed at her lustfully while her eyes reciprocated pleading desire.

Feeling simultaneously aroused, astounded, and amused by the beautiful woman in his arms, Grant murmured, "I love you, Sophie."

"Christ, maybe I should just *combine* your files," Jerry griped, bringing Grant back to the present. "You parolees used to work together and now you're living together?"

"I think you should keep separate files because there *are* some differences between us," Sophie said. "Like how many months of parole we have left, for example." She batted her eyelashes, adding, "I'm not sure, but I think one of us will be done with parole long before the other."

Jerry just sat back and watched.

Grant narrowed his eyes. "Yeah, and another difference is that I've had two drug tests already and Sophie's had none." He turned to Jerry, "Are you going to let that go, sir?"

"Hmm, I agree. That's not right," Jerry said. "You both will go get a drug test when we're done here."

Sensing that his retaliatory plan had backfired, Grant slumped in his chair. But Sophie sat up and protested. "I was taking pain medication in the hospital!"

"Make sure to give them your doctor's name, then, and they'll check it out," Jerry advised, inwardly chuckling as Sophie glared at Grant.

"Hmph," she retorted, slouching. Suddenly she sat up again. "What about therapy?" she demanded. "You made me go to counseling, but not Grant. Why is that? Do you think I'm a total nut job or something?"

Grant stared at her. What the hell was she doing?

Jerry smirked, watching them throw each other under the bus. They were surely making his job easier. "Not a *total* nut job," he told Sophie. "But you *have* benefited from the counseling, haven't you?"

Reluctantly she yielded. "Yes, sir."

"Then perhaps Madsen could benefit as well. Once-a-week therapy, Madsen. It's a condition of your parole."

Fear gripped Grant. "What? You can't do that!"

Jerry wondered why he hadn't previously mandated therapy for Grant. Although the parolee surely had no desire to delve into his destructive family dynamics, they were precisely why he needed counseling. Arching one eyebrow,

Jerry stood up and moved swiftly around his desk. "You're telling me what to do now, Madsen?"

Sophie cowered as the PO sat on the edge of his desk, leaning forward to challenge Grant.

Glancing at the handcuffs swaying from the officer's belt, Grant sat up a little taller and cleared his throat. "No, sir. I'm not trying to tell you what to do. I—I—I'll go to therapy, sir." But he couldn't stop himself from adding, "This sucks." He sounded just like sixteen-year-old Ben.

"Maybe you can see the same shrink Taylor goes to," Jerry offered. "If he'll have her back." He frowned at Sophie. "Dr. Hayes left a message yesterday that you didn't show up for your session."

She gasped. "My therapy appointment! I forgot all about it!" Looking first at Grant, who appeared panicked, and then at the officer, she begged, "Please, Jerry, don't send me back. I didn't miss it on purpose. It's just with everything going on—"

"Relax, Taylor." This was exactly the response Jerry was looking for. She still took the threat of returning to prison seriously. He didn't want these parolees to think they could manipulate him just because he had a soft spot for them. "I'm not sending you back inside for that slip-up. I know you were in the hospital yesterday, and therapy was probably the last thing on your mind. But don't let it happen again, or I won't be so nice."

"Yes, sir." Sophie nodded, and Grant exhaled with relief. She had hated it when her clients didn't show up. She'd have to call Hunter immediately to apologize.

"At least you'll have Madsen to help you get to your next appointment," Jerry said, thinking for a moment. "Maybe you can schedule back-to-back sessions to make sure you both get there. Hell, maybe you two should do couples therapy instead—kill two birds with one stone." *Or monitor two parolees with one Jerry Stone.*

Both Sophie and Grant looked at him with startled expressions.

"Yeah," Jerry mused, liking the idea more and more. "Couples therapy. If you're going to try to cohabitate, you're really going to need it."

"B-b-but I—I—"

"Don't even try to argue with me, Taylor," Jerry ordered. "Weekly couples counseling for as long as you need it."

"And how long will that be, sir?" Grant looked pained.

"Knowing you two, I think you can count on being in counseling for the length of your parole." Grant's subsequent look of misery made Jerry's day.

Rising from his desk, Jerry suggested, "Let's see if you both can stay in the forty percent who don't return to prison, okay? I really don't want to complete all that paperwork. Now, any questions?"

A stunned silence enveloped them.

"Well, off to your whiz quiz then, both of you."

Grant waited for Sophie to rise before he stood. Although still miffed about his impending therapy, Grant felt a world of gratitude toward his PO. Jerry was largely responsible for him not being behind bars at the moment, and he wondered if he might also have had something to do with him and Sophie having a chance together. Their relationship had blossomed despite all the obstacles in the way.

Fidgeting, Grant said nervously, "We'll see you next week, sir."

"Don't be late."

As Grant led Sophie of the office, she paused and looked back at Jerry. "Thank you for not giving up on us, sir."

With that farewell, Bonnie and Clyde exited. Jerry wondered if Taylor would heal from her physical wound, if Madsen would heal from his emotional scars, and if they would make it as a couple. There were many uncertainties, but one thing he knew: The drama was not over with this couple.

Standing outside on the courthouse steps about twenty minutes later, Sophie breathed in the fresh summer air. The sunlight buoyed her spirits, and finally she spoke to Grant—her first words since leaving Jerry's office.

"Do you know how *completely* embarrassing it was not only to pee in a cup, but to have to ask a police officer to help pull my pants down to do so?"

Grant tried not to smile. "Yeah?" His eyes twinkled. "Well, that was a one-time deal, Bonnie, unlike the weekly torture you just subjected me to." He imagined therapy would be like a metaphorical pulling down of his pants, leaving him utterly exposed.

He joked, but she could read the real dread in his eyes. How could a man who so bravely protected them from Carlo feel such intense fear about just *talking*? She would have to show him the way.

Placing a slender hand on his arm, she confided, "I know you're not looking forward to counseling, Grant. But let's face it, we need it. Both our mothers have died, and our relationships with our fathers are hardly healthy." She gazed at him earnestly, anxiously. "As devoted as we are to each other, there's a lot that could come between us if we let it." She didn't have to mention Logan for both to sense his presence.

Grant sighed loudly and nodded, which encouraged Sophie to continue.

"Besides, I always told myself I was going to have a better marriage than my parents did. To achieve that, I knew I would probably need couples counseling with the man I wanted to marry."

His eyes lit up, and without a second thought, Grant grabbed her and drew her to him. Their eyes locked for one intense moment before he leaned in to unite his perfect, full lips with hers. Her mind and body raced with exquisite pleasure, and once again, time stood still on the busy city street.

Grant could not get enough of her soft, inviting mouth, and he could focus on only one singular thought: a promise for the future. *She said she wanted to marry him!*

From *Bad Behavior*, the forthcoming sequel to With *Good Behavior*, by Jennifer Lane

Angelo took a seat outside the cage as he awaited the prisoner's arrival. Feeling rather tense, he sucked in some deep breaths, which led to a coughing fit.

Angelo was still coughing when two COs led his brother, Enzo Barberi, into the cage, the chains of his Y-cuff rattling as he shuffled forward. Small patches of gray colored Angelo's temples, but Enzo's hair had gone completely white. Yet they were both still the same height—a little over six feet—with the same black eyes, eyes that bored into each other.

After plopping their chained prisoner on the wooden bench, the COs backed out of the cage. "Have a nice visit, Barberi," one scoffed.

Angelo was shocked not to hear an immediate "Fuck you" from his brother's mouth. Instead, Enzo ignored the comment and studied his brother. "You look like shit" were his first words.

"I was just about to say the same," Angelo responded, noticing that the color of his brother's hair seemed to leach into his ashen complexion. "How long you been out of the hole?"

"Just got out this morning," Enzo replied, exhaling a loud sigh. "Fucking warden. Figures that the CO I punched was his motherfucking private pet. Twenty-two years … I've been on the inside for twenty-two years, and that's the first time I've been in the hole. And it better be the fucking last time too."

Angelo winced.

"Maybe you should up the ante with the guards," Enzo added. "I'm not getting the treatment I'm used to."

"Uh, Enzo, business ain't so great lately. Not sure if we can swing it. We're already forking over five hundred a month to each of those assholes."

Enzo narrowed his eyes. "What do you mean 'business ain't so great'?"

Clearing his throat, Angelo admitted, "We're having a few, uh, *personnel* problems."

Enzo clenched his fists as he fought to control his reaction. Leaning forward, he seethed, "You find Logan's killer, Ange. Find him and …" His teeth clenched. "Find him, cut off his dick, and shove it down his fucking throat."

With no idea how to respond to this instruction, Angelo sat frozen. His brother continued speaking, his voice low and tight.

"Do you know how fucking miserable it is to be locked up in this shit-dump while my son's murderer goes free? To be stuck in here while some cocky son of a bitch struts around town thinking he can pull one over on *me*?"

Angelo slowly raised his eyes to meet his brother's belligerent gaze. He gulped, then confessed, "Logan's murderer didn't go free."

Enzo lunged forward then sprung back, restrained by his chains. "You caught him? You got Logan's killer?"

Angelo averted his gaze, sickened to be the one to deliver the news. But with palpable waves of fury and anticipation coming through the metal grating, Angelo could wait no longer. "It was Carlo."

A stunned silence blanketed the brothers. When Enzo finally spoke, his voice was carefully controlled. "Your son … killed my son? Carlo killed my boy?"

Angelo nodded, still not meeting Enzo's eyes.

"Look at me, you fuck."

Angelo obeyed, finding Enzo seething now, the control in his voice long gone.

"Your son Carlo—the reason I've been locked in this shithole for twenty-two years—he m-m-murdered my son?"

"Yes."

"Why?"

The one-word question was so vehement, so forceful that Angelo flinched.

"I—I—I'm not sure. He was always jealous of Logan—you know that." Angelo sighed loudly, defeated. "There was something wrong with Carlo from the start. I …" His voice dropped off. "I didn't raise him so good."

Enzo shook his head disgustedly. "You think just because I saved Carlo once I won't retaliate this time? This is my son's *life* we're talking about, Ange. You better fucking hope you can protect that little sniveling bastard—"

"He's already dead," Angelo interrupted, earning him a surprised look from his brother.

"Carlo's dead?" When Angelo nodded, Enzo quietly asked, "Did you kill him?"

Angelo's eyes widened. He could never kill his own son! His cheeks flushed with embarrassment as he remembered how he'd detested the reminders of all of Carlo's screw-ups, how many times he'd wished his son was gone. Now Carlo *was* gone, and Angelo felt no relief. All he had was remorse.

Finally he answered. "It wasn't me who killed him. It was … Grant."

Enzo's mouth dropped open and the blood drained from his face. He remembered Grant on his first day at Gurnee, his defiant bravado completely failing to hide his trembling fear. Then he flashed to those big, sky-blue eyes framed by a chubby little face that looked up at him through glassy tears. Enzo had towered drunkenly over the boy with a folded belt in his hand. He remembered Grant's pleas, his small, strained voice. *Please, Dad. Please no more. I'll be good. I promise.* Enzo shuddered.

"Do the cops know?" When Angelo nodded, Enzo asked, "Why isn't Grant back inside then?"

"It was self-defense. Carlo came after a couple of girls, and Grant intervened. They, uh, apparently wrestled for the gun and it went off—Carlo got shot in the chest."

This didn't sound like his younger son at all, Enzo thought. This didn't sound like behavior that fucking pansy Joe Madsen would approve of. "Did Grant … did he know Carlo killed Logan?"

Angelo nodded guiltily. Enzo felt pride bloom in his chest. His son, formerly useless in helping the family, had exacted revenge for Logan's death. Grant had taken care of business more expertly than Enzo's own men—swiftly seeking justice while neatly keeping himself out of prison. Enzo was impressed.

"You give Grant a message for me," Enzo ordered, and Angelo listened intently. "You tell him I want to see him. I need to talk to him. And if you so much as *touch* him for what he did to Carlo…"

"I already told Joe Madsen I wouldn't retaliate."

Enzo's face flushed crimson red. "Who the fuck cares about Joe Madsen? You promise *me* you won't touch my son, and that's all that matters."

"It's done," Angelo replied succinctly, abruptly looking sad. "Carlo deserved what he got."

ACKNOWLEDGEMENTS

Thank you to …
The team at Omnific Publishing, particularly Jessica Royer Ocken
Aunt Nancy for reading the original manuscript, giving some editing tips,
encouraging my writing skills and me as a person
Mom and Dad for being such avid readers and for fostering creativity
My sisters Laurie and Susan for introducing me to the great city of Chicago
My nephews Nick, Dylan, and Henry for teaching me the depth
of Joe's love for Grant
Pamela for helping me with the plot, namely suggesting that
Uncle Joe live on a naval base
Lorne Griffin for making the banner and tolerating the Muffin torture
Ina for a fellow shrink's perspective and ardent support
Amy Watson for her ongoing encouragement
Nora for editing the synopsis and medical expertise
Marilyn for her hilarious and thoughtful reviews
Riem Harper for the McSailor marquee, poem, and awesome support
Jaquita Chaquita for her incredible sense of humor
Leah for her listening and editing help
Nix for her legal insights and encouragement
Online friends: Elke, Deb, Danni, Karina, Spunky Ashley, Adriana,
Thania, Sim, Lily, Ginger

ABOUT THE AUTHOR

Jennifer Lane has found that writing fiction is much more fun than writing a psychology dissertation! While she writes under the name Jennifer Lane, she practices as a psychologist in Ohio. The tales of healing and resilience from her profession have inspired her to write her own stories, planting the seeds for her first novel, *With Good Behavior*, as well as its forthcoming sequel, *Bad Behavior*. She loves stories that make her laugh *and* cry. In her spare time Jen enjoys competitive swimming, attending book club, and hanging out with her sisters and their families in Chicago.